PRAISE FOR *DAU*
THE NIGHT

"Fans of *The Nightingale* will be transfixed by this thrillingly original portrait of wartime valor."

—Jennifer Robson, internationally bestselling author of *Somewhere in France* and *Goodnight from London*

"*Daughters of the Night Sky* was everything I love about historical fiction. Runyan crafts the perfect balance between plot, characters, and setting, all while educating the reader in an unknown part of women's history. At once compelling, tragic, and uplifting, this is one that I will not soon forget."

—Camille Di Maio, author of *The Memory of Us* and *Before the Rain Falls*

"Aimie K. Runyan breathes life into the gripping tale of the Night Witches—Russian female combat pilots in World War II. A page-turner!"

—James D. Shipman, author of *A Bitter Rain* and *It Is Well*

"Aimie K. Runyan has combined my three favorite literary topics: historical fiction, World War II, and courageous and strong women. She is an incredible historical fiction writer."

—Cathy Lamb, author of *No Place I'd Rather Be*

"A lively and stirring tale of the brave vanguard of female pilots fighting for Russia and, as often, for respect from their male counterparts. As enthralled as I was by this dive into social and military history, it was the humanity of *Daughters of the Night Sky* that won me over: comrades, lovers, and families swept up and torn apart by war. Runyan delivers a well-paced and heartfelt story that fans of World War II novels should not miss."

—Sonja Yoerg, author of *All the Best People*

"*Daughters of the Night Sky* is a compelling World War II story of bravery, determination, and love set within the Forty-Sixth Taman Guards—Russia's all-female pilot regiment. Author Aimie K. Runyan brings four unique women vividly to life: Katya, a superb navigator; Taisiya, her pilot and best friend; Oksana, who risks all for love of her country; and Sofia, the major who leads the women to triumph. Highly recommended."

—M.K. Tod, author of *Time and Regret*

DAUGHTERS OF THE NIGHT SKY

DAUGHTERS OF THE NIGHT SKY

AIMIE K. RUNYAN

This is a work of fiction. Names, characters, organizations, places, events, and incidents are either products of the author's imagination or are used fictitiously.

Published by Lake Union Publishing, Seattle

www.apub.com

Amazon, the Amazon logo, and Lake Union Publishing are trademarks of Amazon.com, Inc., or its affiliates.

ISBN-13: 9781503946774 (hardcover)
ISBN-10: 1503946770 (hardcover)

ISBN-13: 9781542045865 (paperback)
ISBN-10: 154204586X (paperback)

Cover design by Laura Klynstra

Printed in the United States of America

First edition

For Jamie.
Honored to be your copilot in this crazy business.
Proud to have you as mine.

CHAPTER 1

1931, Miass, Chelyabinsk Oblast, the Gateway to Siberia

I stared as the rainbow-hued blooms danced in the breeze, imagining them ballerinas on the Moscow stage. The expansive steel-blue mountains, always capped with a hood of ice, were so different from the narrow streets and towering buildings of the city where I had spent my earliest years. My memories of the capital were garish with color. On bleak days, I could see in my mind Saint Basil's with its earthy, sienna-colored body and onion-shaped spires swathed in rich tones of emerald, ruby, sapphire, and topaz, always set against a flurry of snow. The white swirl of frost made the colors reverberate even more, the memory refusing to be erased from the brilliant palette of my youth. The people—happy or cross, handsome or plain—were more colorful, too. Miass was gray, and the people with it. They mined in the hills, tended their shops, managed their farms. Mama worked in the laundry, day after day in a fog of gray.

But for two weeks in July, the muddy hills along the riverbank outside Miass were a riot of color. The summer of my tenth year was a particularly magnificent display. The splashes of lavender, crimson, and indigo against the sea of grass were the closest thing I could imagine to heaven. It was as though the Ural Mountains had been given an annual allotment of color by the new regime and they had chosen to use it up during those two glorious weeks.

I should have been at home in the cabin, doing the mending or preparing supper for Mama. She would be too tired to attend to these things when she came home, but to waste any of that color seemed inexcusable. So I left the chores undone, reveling in the light of summer.

When the hulking, olive-green airplane scarred the sky with its white trail, I thought perhaps my mother's worst fears had been realized, that my imagination had run wild and I had finally gone mad. She would be so disappointed, but there was always a satisfaction in being proved right, I supposed.

But then I saw the neighbor, a squat old farmer with a face like a weathered beet, emerge from his cabin and follow the winding white exhaust from the sputtering engines with his dull, black eyes until the green speck was low on the horizon. It was real, and it was landing in the field outside the town square.

I knew I was running the risk of making Mama angry. I had no school that day, or marketing, or any other errand that would call me into town. She didn't want me there more than I had to be, but she could hardly blame me for my curiosity. Papa used to talk about the airplanes he had flown in the European War—the war that had made him a hero—and Mama had to know the lure of seeing an aircraft for myself would be too great to resist.

I ran the two kilometers into Miass, and by the time I reached it, the townspeople had abandoned their work and gathered in the field to the east of town to see the remarkable machine and its pilot. He was a tall man with dark hair and a bristling black mustache that gleamed in the afternoon sun. He spoke to the crowd with a strong voice, and they stood captivated, as though Stalin himself had come to speak. I had seen Stalin once when he addressed the people of Moscow, and was far more impressed with this new visitor with the leather helmet and goggles atop his head.

Mama, who had been straining to take a peek, spotted me as I approached the crowd, and wove her way through the throng to my side, clasping my hand when I was within reach. Her power for worry was a formidable monster, and I had learned it was easier to placate it than to fight it.

"I thought this would bring you in, Katya. I wish you'd stayed home." Annoyance or sheer exhaustion lined her face. "I can't afford to leave early to see you home."

"I made it here, Mama. I can make it home," I answered, careful to keep any hint of cheek from my tone.

"Very well," she said. "But I won't tolerate this again."

I laced my fingers in hers and kissed the back of her hand, hoping to soften her mood. I wouldn't enjoy this if she were angry with me. "What has he told everyone, Mama?"

"He's flying across the whole country," she said, absently stroking my hair with her free hand. "He says there is a problem with his engine and he had to land for repairs."

She strained her neck and stood on the tips of her toes to get a better view of the aircraft, but it was useless for me. I was a tall girl but still could not hope to see over the heads of the swarm that encircled the astounding contraption. I broke free from Mama's grip and squeezed myself through the cracks until I was standing only a few centimeters from the metal casing. It was not smooth, as it appeared from a distance, but dimpled by the rivets that attached the sheets of metal to the frame beneath.

The pilot answered the townspeople's questions with patience.

"How does it stay up?" one of the town's mechanics called out.

"Aren't you afraid to crash?" a young woman with a squawking toddler asked.

They didn't seem like interesting questions to me, but all the same he didn't answer the mechanic with a sarcastic "Fairy dust" or the young mother with a "No, I wouldn't feel a thing if I did," as others might have done. He gave a very simple explanation and spoke as if each question was the most important matter in his world. No one chattered when he offered his explanations; no one muttered about men forgetting that their place was on the ground.

Emboldened, I placed my hand on the metal of the plane's body, warmed by the summer sun, but not too hot to touch for a few seconds. I removed my hand before the pilot could chastise me. Though I longed to run my hands along the wings that spread outward forever, I wouldn't have the stolen caress ruined by a reprimand. Papa's descriptions had not come close to doing the machine justice. My mind could only begin to understand the freedom this aircraft gave its pilot. He could go anywhere he pleased: If he could fly from the western border of Russia to the farthest reaches of Siberia, there was nothing stopping him from continuing on to see the wonders of China. Better still, he could go back west to see Geneva, Madrid, Florence, and all the cities Mama had dreamed of seeing but no longer spoke of.

I knew that if I had one of these machines for myself, I would never settle in one place for the rest of my days. I would hop from the pyramids of Egypt to the Amazon to the streets of New York and wherever else my fancy flew me. I looked at the pilot and tried not to let my jealousy consume me. He had *earned* his wings, his freedom. Someday I could earn mine, too. I would take Mama on my adventures, and she could leave the laundry behind her. She'd never do so much as rinse a blouse out in a sink ever again. She would smile again. Sing again. We would eat like queens and hire people to see to the less pleasant tasks of daily life. I would never speak that aloud in front of my teacher, Comrade Dokorov. He'd chastise me for setting a bad example of capitalist greed.

In an unprecedented gesture of generosity, Mama's boss allowed her to come home early that day without docking her pay, owing to my presence in town. The plane must have bewitched him as it had me. The entire way home and all throughout preparations of dinner, I spoke of nothing but the pilot and his airplane. Mama listened patiently, but her cornflower eyes began to grow hazy.

"I'm sorry, Mama. I'm boring you," I said, adding the potatoes to the stewpot.

"No, darling. I'm simply tired, as usual." She wiped her brow with the back of her hand as she stirred.

"I'm going to learn how to fly a plane of my own someday, Mama. I'm going to get us out of here." I looked down at the simmering stew and added a pinch of salt. It was not a hearty stew, or a very flavorful one. I wanted to do more for Mama.

"I don't think they license many lady pilots," she said, taking a seat at the wobbly kitchen table as we waited for the flavors of the stew to meld together as the chunks of tough meat—not more than a fistful—softened with the potatoes and vegetables. "You ought to consider becoming a schoolteacher. It's regular work and decent pay."

I blanched at the thought. Helping the village children learn to read and add their sums seemed as interesting as watching the paint dry on the neighbor's barn. "I don't want to teach, Mama. You said they don't license 'many' lady pilots, Mama. Many doesn't mean none. I can be one of the few." I tried to summon the confidence of the visiting pilot. I placed her bowl in front of her and tore off a large chunk of the black bread I had made that morning and placed it by her spoon.

Mama looked up from the stew, the dark creases under her eyes so deep I was sure she'd never be completely rid of them if she slept twelve hours a day for the rest of her life. "You're right, Katinka. If you want to fly, go earn your wings. Just don't let them stop you. And make no mistake, they will try."

I blinked in surprise, expecting Mama would continue to dissuade me. "I won't give them the choice, Mama. I'll be so good they won't be able to turn me away."

She smiled weakly at me and sighed as her eyes scanned, taking stock of our small cabin. It had belonged to my babushka Olga, and when she passed away it came to Mama. Which was fortunate for us, because we had no means to stay on in Moscow, which I think broke Mama's heart almost as badly as losing Papa. Mama had told me Miass had been a nice enough place to grow up, but that she had yearned for life in the city when she was a girl. She studied dance and became skilled enough to garner the attention of the right people.

She earned her ticket to the capital when she was eighteen and then danced on the great stages of Moscow until Papa, a well-respected professor of history, coaxed her down from the limelight and into domestic life. They had lived happily together for nine years before Papa was taken by a stray bullet during one of the little uprisings against the new regime. Papa, who had done nothing to anger either side, was simply collateral damage to them. A tragic but ultimately inevitable loss in troubled times.

If Mama missed dancing, she'd never once said. The city? Yes. Papa? Like she would miss one of her lungs. Dancing, though, she rarely mentioned.

"You'll have to work twice as hard as the boys, Katinka," she mused as I ladled stew from the steaming pot into her bowl. She lifted her spoon and blew gently on the steaming broth. "And avoid distractions, no matter how pleasant they might be."

I nodded solemnly, knowing that she spoke from her own experience. She had danced for five years, which was a long run according to Mama. The girls got distracted by boys, city life, or other mischief. And they were in a career deemed suitable for women. I would not have that advantage.

"If this is what you want, you will need excellent marks. Especially in science and mathematics." Mama's tired eyes appeared to look past me and out the window over my left shoulder as she tore the black bread into tiny morsels and popped them into her mouth.

"I don't think Comrade Dokorov much cares for teaching the girls," I said quietly into my bowl. "Especially 'serious' subjects like mathematics and philosophy."

"And I don't give one whit about what he 'cares for.' He's paid the same to teach you as he is the boys." Mama's eyes flashed from cornflower to cobalt, as they tended to do when she was truly angry. It was beautiful to see when her fury wasn't directed at me. "The party wants to see you educated. But we'll see how serious you are in time, Katinka. There are many years yet."

Mama, I was sure, had no particular affection for Stalin, speaking of him with more reluctance and fear than admiration, but she found no fault with his stance on women's rights. More than once, she predicted he would declare us equal citizens to men. *"Then you will see change, Katinka. Then things will start to set themselves right."*

"Talk to him, Mama. I'm sure Comrade Dokorov will listen to you," I said, wishing the words would make it so. If Papa were alive, the grimy old man that ran the schoolhouse would have to listen. Here no one cared that she had been the wife of a celebrated professor; they only knew her as a simple laundress with an extra mouth to feed. As though the life we'd had in Moscow never existed. The voice of a washerwoman carried little weight. I could see that burden, among others, in the dark circles under her weary eyes. I cleared the table and handed her a teapot brimming with boiling water.

"Play for me, Katinka," Mama said, adding tea leaves to the pot from her little tin. "It's been too long."

I went to my little room and fetched Papa's violin, which I kept propped on the table next to my bed. It was no grand instrument. Old when it had come to him, its russet varnish was fading to a tawny yellow at the edges and the middle, and the strings were well beyond the need for replacement. I handled the instrument as though it were made of paper-thin glass and played just as gently. If a string broke, it would remain so.

I scurried back to the table and pulled my chair out to the center of the room. I placed the violin under my chin and touched the bow to the strings. I played one of the folk tunes Papa had loved. Sweet, but with a hint of melancholy, like the violin itself. Like much of our folk music.

Papa was barely proficient as a musician, but Mama and I loved to listen to him play simple tunes after dinner. He had begun to teach me before he was killed, and Mama had taught me to read music. I had no real talent, either, but my playing made Mama smile when little else did.

I used to tell Papa that Russia was too cold for too much of the year for anyone to be truly happy. *"There is truth to that, my Katinka. And music, if nothing else, must be true if it is to be beautiful."*

I plagued Mama all summer until courses resumed, and in an act of utter capitulation, she spoke to Oleg Dokorov. The schoolteacher was a tall man, with a long, pointed nose. His greasy black hair and yellowed teeth repulsed me, but Mama insisted that I always treat him with the respect his position commanded. Mama addressed him firmly, but respectfully, in front of the entire class before lessons began on the first day of school. I stood a pace behind her, my clasped hands shaking behind my back. If he refused her, I would never fly. Most of my classmates were boys, as many families in the area still chose to teach their daughters at home. This largely meant the girls were taught enough reading and arithmetic to do the marketing and keep the family accounts in order, and little else. In Moscow, girls had to go to school along with the boys, but no one paid attention to us here. The presence of a handful of girls was accepted because people assumed our mothers needed a place for us to stay while they worked. It wasn't entirely untrue.

"Comrade Dokorov, I insist you provide my daughter with the same lessons as you give the boys," Mama said, placing my primer from the previous year with a thud on his polished desk. "I have no wish for my daughter to be reading these fairy stories when she should be learning geometry and physics." She stood tall and wore her best dress, which was no high compliment to the worn frock.

"Comrade Ivanova," he replied, "you have not had training in education. *I* must insist that you leave the classroom and let me begin the school year without further disruption." He stood to his full height, as though to intimidate Mama into hasty retreat to the laundry. He clearly had never had extensive dealings with my mother.

"I'm afraid you misunderstand me. This was not a request. I may not be a trained teacher, but I am an educated woman. My husband, a loyal and true patriot of this country and decorated hero of the European War, was an honored professor. I will not see his daughter given a second-rate education by the likes of you. You will teach my daughter, and the rest of the girls, the same material as the boys, or I will speak to the party officials. Do I make myself plain?"

"I hardly think it's appropriate—"

"But Comrade Stalin does, Comrade Dokorov. Your quarrel is with him, not with me. Nor is it with my daughter or any other member of this class. Know that I am a woman who makes good on her promises. Good day."

My mother turned heel and exited the classroom without a word to me. I was grateful, at least, that she hadn't given me a parting kiss or any sort of endearment. I would never have lived down the shame. It wasn't her usual practice, anyway.

"Well, Ekaterina Timofeyevna. It seems your mother wants you educated like the boys. Is that right?" His lips curled into a sneer around his putrid, yellow teeth as he addressed me with mock formality. I wasn't aware he'd even known my father's name to address me by my patronymic.

"Yes, Comrade Dokorov. I wish to be a pilot. For this, Mama says I will need a proper education." I tried to summon my mother's moxie and succeeded in not running from the room in tears. It was victory enough.

"She is not wrong about that. But it is hardly a profession for a woman. Russia needs women to build families. Aviation is a man's field." He spoke as though he made the final pronouncement on my career path. The matter dismissed in his mind, he placed my antiquated primer back on my desk and returned to the blackboard.

"I disagree." My tone was hardly louder than a whisper, but the boys on either side of me sucked in their breath. This would mean the strap, if I were lucky.

"What was that, Ekaterina?" The teacher turned around, slowly, giving me time to retract my words.

"I disagree, Comrade Dokorov. With respect." I had found my voice—a reedier version of my father's baritone—and it did not waver. I stood straighter and jutted my chin in his direction.

He walked back to my desk, took the primer, and fixed me with his black eyes. "Very well, young lady. But if you waste my time on a whim, I will be sorely disappointed." He took the book, placed it on a shelf with dozens of other dusty volumes, and began his lesson.

I pulled my notebook and my father's favorite fountain pen—simple and sturdy, like him—from the worn leather bag he had used for carrying students' papers to and from the university each day. The pen was handcrafted from wood—rosewood, he had guessed. It was a gift from one of his professor friends, and a token he was quite fond of. I loved using it and had even had one of the craftsmen in town teach me how to fashion new nibs from steel scraps in exchange for running a few errands.

I sat ramrod straight in my chair and used my father's pen to write down every word pertinent to the lesson. When it came time for mathematics, the other girls and I were allowed to participate with the boys. The figures confused me at first, as I had little instruction beyond basic arithmetic, but I took copious notes. If the teacher would not help me with my questions after class, I would ask Mama. If Mama couldn't help me, I would find someone who could. There were always floors to scrub or marketing to be done in exchange for knowledge.

Deep within me I knew my work had to begin that very moment if I was to have wings of my own.

CHAPTER 2

April 1941, Chelyabinsk Military Aviation School of Fast Bombardiers

The sun beat down on me in the rear cockpit of the small training craft, and my stomach lurched as Tokarev dove the trainer in the final approach toward the painted patch of grass that was our target. I leaned over the edge of the cockpit to get a glance of the terrain below. Until Tokarev banked, the only things I could see were the back of his head and the terrain past either side of the wing. Nothing ahead or directly below. I verified we were on course for the coordinates the instructor had given me and checked my chronometer.

"Five seconds to target," I said, speaking clearly into the radio so my pilot could hear each syllable. I opened the top of the metal flare. "Three seconds. *Mark!*" I tossed the flare over the edge to illuminate the target for him.

When he circled back around to drop his dummy bomb, Tokarev hesitated just a few moments too long before he released. As he banked right to set course for the airstrip, I saw he'd missed the bright painted X by a wide margin. If we'd been aiming for a military outpost, we'd have hit the school next door.

My hands shook as Tokarev landed the plane on the edge of the academy's airstrip, and it was just as well. If they had been steady, I might have throttled the clumsy dolt. He had completed the passes with adequate technique but still managed to miss two of the seven practice targets.

My job was to get us to the target and mark it so the pilot could focus on keeping the plane aloft. I was armed with nothing other than coordinates, a chronometer, and compass, flares, and my own eyes. I hadn't missed a single mark that run, nor had I missed more than I could count on my fingers since Captain Karlov had reluctantly let me in the rear cockpit to begin practical training as a navigator toward the end of my first year. I could see Karlov's distaste for women in uniform every time I came into his view, but my performance record gave him no choice but to advance me through the three-year program. Women were beginning to make names for themselves in aviation, setting records and joining flight schools and civil aviation clubs in droves, but it had taken the looming jackal at our western gates to encourage our leaders to take women's emancipation to heart.

Honestly, I hadn't wanted to fly for the military, but the cauldron of war that boiled on every Russian border had afforded me the opportunity to earn my wings. I hadn't particularly wanted to serve as a navigator, either. I wanted training as a pilot, but the rear cockpit was the place I was given. It was better than staying on the ground, at least.

"A decent run, Tokarev," Karlov said when we rejoined our classmates at the edge of the airfield, "but Cadet Ivanova could have left you a wider margin for error with your targets."

"Thank you, Captain," Tokarev replied to the lukewarm praise.

This was nonsense, but I remained silent, as I did so often in Karlov's presence. Opening my mouth was rarely worth the resultant flare of temper. When Karlov looked away, Tokarev shrugged and turned a *Golly gee, that stinks for you* smirk my way.

"He should have been able to hit those targets, Captain," another third-year spoke up. Ivan Solonev had transferred into our division a few weeks prior. Karlov had been thrilled, as Solonev was a military legacy of sorts. His father was a hero of the European War and a brilliant strategist. My father had been decorated in the war as well, but Papa wasn't a local man, so his reputation wasn't known here like Solonev's father's, and I didn't crow about it to ensure it was.

Karlov had whirled his way. "What was that, Cadet?" he asked, the ends of his walrus-bristled mustache twitching in annoyance. Almost anyone else questioning his appraisal would have been launched halfway back to the barracks by now from the sheer volume of his tirade. A bead of sweat trickled down the nape of my neck as I wondered what Solonev would say and how Karlov would blame me for it.

"With all due respect, Captain, when Tokarev is at the front, he'll be flying in every sort of condition. If he can't hit a perfectly marked target in clear weather and with no enemy fire to contend with, he has no hope of making his mark in battle."

Karlov nodded and turned his attention to the pilot and navigator then taking their turn at the run. I watched with interest, noting the idiosyncrasies of the pilot and the technique of the navigator. There was almost as much to learn on the ground as there was in the cockpit.

I looked over at Solonev, with his chiseled features that looked so much like the ones that graced the propaganda posters the party was so fond of. I had hoped when he arrived he'd be all flash and no substance, but he was, much to my annoyance, as skilled a pilot as had ever crossed the academy's threshold. A tad arrogant and none too fond of authority, but no one begrudged him his pride after they saw him in the air.

Should I thank him? Scold him for butting in? I couldn't decide which. Aside from Taisiya Pashkova, my dearest friend at the academy—perhaps the dearest friend I'd ever had—he was the only person who had championed me in the three years since I'd entered the academy. I was more than capable of championing myself, but it was exhausting work at times.

I wanted to shove my elbow into Tokarev's ribs and hiss, "At least someone here knows the truth," but a little prat like Tokarev would certainly whine about it to anyone who would listen.

Only a few more months. This will all be over in June.

When Karlov dismissed us from our practicals and we dispersed for the evening meal, I caught Solonev's eye and mouthed, *Thank you.* He shot me a quick nod with a somber expression. He didn't like Karlov's behavior any better than I did. As much as I hated that he had felt the need to stand up for me, I hadn't so many allies that I could afford to be less than grateful to any of them.

"Germany has invaded Yugoslavia and Greece," Taisiya said by way of greeting as I perched on the end of my bunk to remove the heavy combat boots that still pinched and rubbed my feet raw after three years.

The women's bunkroom was little more than a large, repurposed supply room lined with nine bunks and a small space heater keeping us from freezing in winter. As in so many areas of military life, our group's presence forced improvisation.

"Hello to you, too," I said with a roll of my eyes, massaging my feet. "It's so wonderful to have a friend who always greets you with such cheerful news." Though the fact was I appreciated her keeping me informed—better to get news from her than read about all the warmongering for myself. There was nothing good coming from the papers these days.

She peeked over her gray newspaper curtain and stuck her tongue out at me. "Katya, the Germans are moving forward every day. It's nothing to take lightly."

"The nonaggression pact will hold," I said dismissively. She was right, of course, but it was too much reality to take on after a full day of classes and practicals.

"We can hope, but Hitler's reach keeps growing. All this land grabbing frightens me," Taisiya said with a heavy sigh.

I grunted my reluctant agreement. The more I learned of Hitler, the warier I was of him. Then I thought of our own Stalin, who preached equality and the rise of the proletariat while extending his own grasp farther and farther west. I hoped Stalin wasn't simply Hitler in a different uniform but dared not voice my concern.

"How were your practicals?" I asked to divert the subject.

"Fine. Made every mark. Yudin of course said nothing." She placed her newspaper down and stretched her arms over her head to loosen the knots in her back. "The usual."

"Better than me. I made every mark, but Tokarev still missed two. Karlov blamed me." I pulled on my cotton uniform slacks, wishing they issued us something in between the thick wool of our winter uniforms and the thin cotton for summer. The women's barracks were cold and drafty, but the mess hall was always stifling.

"Sounds like Karlov. What an ass." Taisiya stood up and followed my lead, changing into her uniform for the evening meal. "Three months left," she said. "We can endure these idiots for three more months."

There were only the two of us in the third year, the others having joined the academy after us. The younger girls were just as ambitious, though not quite as serious yet. The second-year girls, Iskra in particular, were fairly driven. Marta and Klavdiya, our first-years, fell far short of their standard. They performed at the middle of the pack, neither brilliantly nor poorly, and never strove to break into the upper echelon. Just as Taisiya and I did, they idolized women like Sofia Orlova, who had shattered world records and been named Hero of the Soviet Union, but they were still learning the amount of work it took to achieve such lofty goals.

I was grateful to have Taisiya. School had been a lonely slog, and she was one of the first people who truly understood how deeply the desire to fly had sunk into my bones.

Taisiya gave herself a quick glance in the mirror and gave an impassive nod, which meant her uniform looked tidy and she was pleased enough with her appearance to go up. On the rare occasion she had to wear a dress, the effect was charming. She looked like a young matron who ought to be chasing a ball with her three sturdy sons. When she was in uniform, her middling height, brown hair, and even features simply blended into the academy walls. It was possibly her greatest asset in her advancement so far. My towering height and auburn hair attracted much more attention than I would have liked, but I refused to slouch. Nor would I cover my red tresses with dye to make myself invisible.

We joined the rest of the cadets in the mess hall to endure a supper that grew more and more inferior as war drew nearer to our doors. In a room buzzing with over two hundred cadets, the nine women of the academy sat together at a long table in the back of the hall. As was our custom, we pulled out our training manuals, textbooks, and notes during the meal and saved our chatter for the hour just before bed, when we were too tired to get much good out of studying.

"If you ladies are nervous," a jeering voice called out from the next table, "why don't you do something else? Sew uniforms, perhaps? Or go west and dig trenches when the time comes?" The comedian was a first-year student with rust-colored hair and crooked teeth, surrounded by mates shaking with laughter.

"Shut your insolent mouth, boy," I snapped. "And learn some humility in front of your superiors before you open it again, if you have brains under that godforsaken orange mop you've got."

The cadet and his entire table went quiet and returned to their meal while the women all looked over to me with silent approval. We studied constantly because we didn't have the luxury for error, and I refused to accept cheek from underclassmen for it. I had to be even-tempered with the instructors, but junior cadets were welcome to the full brunt of my anger when they deserved it.

"Jackass," Taisiya hissed under her breath. "He doesn't know which side of the plane to keep upright."

If that were true, he'd have a hard time earning promotion from theoretical studies to practical runs toward the end of his first year. If he wasn't promoted soon, he would be either transferred to a nonflight field—learning to run the wireless, most likely—or shown the door. I'd gone through the very same thing, despite stellar theoretical skills. It took my registering a formal complaint with the academy's commanding officer to get in the air.

It was always a battle, and some days I worried I'd be tired of fighting before I even got to the front.

I retreated to the dank and chilly confines of the bunkroom after supper. Most of us reviewed notes or perused our books for another couple of hours, but uniforms were shed. I gratefully traded my coarse uniform for my quilted flannel pajamas and dressing gown. Mama had been careful to send drab greens and blues my first year, thinking it would be best in my military setting. When my second year came around, I begged her for periwinkle, pink, lilac—anything feminine—much to my mother's astonishment. She rose magnificently to the occasion, sending me thick quilted pajamas of the softest pink flannel adorned with tiny rosebuds along with a matching pink dressing gown. I knew it had to have cost her dearly, but as my burden on her finances was so light now, I didn't begrudge her the little indulgence.

Taisiya had a letter from Matvei, her beau, who had taken over the running of his family's farm near the little village of Serbishino. Matvei's letters were one of Taisiya's few sources of unmitigated joy, but her face turned ashen as she read his words.

"He's been called up." She looked down at the paper, incredulous.

"It sounds like things are worse in Poland," I said, not knowing what reassurances might help. "But it may all come to nothing. They need troops at the ready in case the worst happens, but there's no reason to believe he'll see action. And if he does, at least he's enlisted and training now."

"He's a farmer, Katya. He's not built for this. He hasn't been trained like you and I have." She set the letter aside and buried her face in her hands.

I sat next to her on the thin mattress of her bunk and wrapped my arm around her shoulders. "They'll train him, Taisiya. It makes no sense for them not to."

"Logic has never been the strong suit of the Red Army," Taisiya snapped, picking up the letter and placing it in her bedside table with the rest of his correspondence. "Stalin needs warm bodies, and I don't think he cares how long they stay that way."

The other women had taken notice but said nothing. Their sympathy was evident, but their words remained lodged in their throats as they thought of their own sweethearts, brothers, and fathers. I didn't blame them. I held Taisiya close but offered her no hollow words. Either Matvei would survive the war, or he wouldn't, but Taisiya would suffer until the last bullet flew.

Hours later, when the lights were out and the soft breathing of the other cadets wafted through the chill night air, I could hear Taisiya's ragged breathing and sniffles, despite her efforts to muffle the sounds of her sobs with her pillow. I slipped out from my bunk and knelt next to hers, placing my hand on her back.

"Taisiya," I whispered, "what can I do?"

She wiped away a few of the tears and rolled toward me. "Be a lamb and keep Hitler in his own damn country? Could you manage that?"

"Would that I could, Taisiyushka," I said, adopting her pet name as I climbed into her bed and cradled her close to my chest, tucking her head under my chin. "I'd keep Matvei from the front for your sake if nothing else."

"I know you would, Katinka. But it doesn't change anything." She embraced me closer and forced herself to take even breaths to quell the raking sobs. "I don't know what I'd do without him. He was the only one who didn't think me half-cracked for wanting a life that didn't revolve around farming and babies. He was always so understanding." Her body began to shake with sobs once more, and I felt the tears spill over onto my chest.

"Taisiyushka. Enough with the past tense." She was the last woman I expected to let her life revolve around a man. I knew she loved Matvei dearly, but I had expected a well-reasoned anger or worry—not this despair. "And even if . . . the worst should happen, you won't be lost. You have me," I said, tightening my embrace. "Don't cry. Matvei wouldn't want it."

"I have you until the war claims you or you run off with a husband and have a gaggle of babies. Who else would want to marry a woman like me? Men don't want to marry pilots."

"Well then, there's no worry about me running off with a husband to make babies. I'm a pilot, too, in case that slipped your notice."

A quiet laugh shattered Taisiya's gloom, just for a moment. "I don't know how women have done this since the dawn of time. Waiting for men to come home from war. He hasn't even gone yet, and it's killing me."

"Just be grateful. You'll be able to help him more than most girlfriends would be able to. And not just by knitting socks. It will be different for us."

"God, I hope you're right, Katinka. I hope you're right."

CHAPTER 3

"Where is Tokarev, Ivanova?" Karlov barked as he noticed the cadet's absence.

"I wouldn't know, Captain," I answered, staring straight ahead into the airfield rather than making eye contact. Unless Tokarev was at death's door, he would face weeks on the ground for missing his training. "He was in class this morning and in the mess hall at lunch. I can't say what happened to him in the quarter hour since."

"A good navigator keeps tabs on his pilot, Ivanova. And vice versa," Karlov pontificated for the assembled cadets as we awaited our rotation. "There is no excuse for your carelessness."

"Only lack of access to the men's barracks, Captain." I wanted to regret saying those words, but they tasted sweeter on my tongue than raspberry jam.

"He twisted his ankle, Captain," Solonev called from the back of the crowd, clearly having jogged to join the group. "I helped him to the infirmary just now."

Karlov rolled his eyes but nodded at Solonev. "Very well," he said, looking over his roster. "Ivanova can observe this afternoon."

"Begging your pardon, Captain," Solonev said. "I can make a second run. Ivanova could use the hours, and so can I."

The group of pilots and navigators turned their eyes to Solonev, then back to Karlov.

"Very well, Solonev," Karlov said after a pause. He had sought an excuse and found none. He ordered us to go first in rotation. Presumably he didn't want me to have the advantage of watching any of the others fly the pattern first, and he wanted my nerves raw. He assumed I would be rattled at the prospect of going up with a new pilot on a moment's notice. He wasn't as misguided in this as I would have hoped, but I was happy to get up in the air and have my turn rather than stand about and stew over it.

We trained on Yak UT-2 trainers. A low-winged, open-cockpit aircraft with basic controls and a low cruising speed. Designed so that even rookies like Tokarev could learn on them without disaster, though he had tried often enough to test that. Though modern, it was simple and small compared to the monsters needed for the long-distance, record-setting missions Stalin loved so much.

Solonev took his place first, stepping onto a reinforced section of wing and swinging himself into the front cockpit. I followed into the rear. When given the signal, Solonev fired up the engine and ascended as high as he dared, not descending until we were within a few hundred meters of the target. This would keep us out of sight of ground troops for as long as possible, giving us a few seconds' advantage. It was all we would need.

He had to bank fairly hard to the right or left to be able to see the target below, so we had to circle our target like a vulture long enough for me to mark the target with a flare and for Solonev to make a direct pass to drop his dummy bomb.

"Five seconds to target," I called over the radio as the hand ticked away on my chronometer.

"Banking," he replied, tipping the plane hard left so I could get a clear view of the painted grass below.

"Steady," I replied. I opened the flare and aimed. The flare was outfitted with a small white parachute that, when winds were calm, helped it to stay the course as it fell. It would be invaluable in a combat situation where he had to distinguish a strategic building from an unimportant one. When I released this one, it fell true, landing right in the center of the target, leaving a bright-red flame for Solonev. *"Marked!"*

Without a twitch, he dropped the dummy bomb right on top of my flare.

"Well done," he acknowledged over the radio.

Two simple words that I'd yet to hear from a pilot or instructor.

Solonev signaled from the front cockpit to acknowledge we'd completed the pass to his satisfaction and were heading back to base. A flawless run with a more-than-capable pilot. I felt tingling in my fingertips and the bottoms of my heels, as though they were preparing to fly of their own accord. Too long since I had felt the joy of being in the cockpit. Karlov waved off another crew as we disembarked our plane. He was never one to waste daylight.

"Excellent, Solonev," Karlov said with a nod as we rejoined our classmates. It might as well have been an ode in Solonev's honor, stingy as the captain was with his praise.

"Thank you, Captain. You have a very skilled student in Cadet Ivanova. As talented a navigator as ever I've flown with." My lips turned up in an involuntary smile.

Karlov emitted a grunt, and his eyes returned to the mild-blue April sky to observe the crew taking the same pass we had just completed. The flying was competent, but the navigator missed his mark three times and they kept circling back around. It's a wonder they didn't get airsick from the failed attempts. Not a word of censure was uttered on landing. I watched as the men flew their patterns one by one, each receiving praise or criticism. Every student was worthy of an assessment except me. Not for the first time did I have to fight the urge to throttle Karlov with my own bare hands. I watched each flight, paying the utmost attention to every skillful maneuver and every gaffe. I stood with my hands behind my back, my left hand gripping my right wrist so tightly that a painful rush of blood back to my fingers when I loosened my hold reminded me to cool my temper.

We had one hour of rest between practical training and the evening meal, but I had no desire to face the rest of the academy. I unzipped the front of my flight suit to let the sun soak through the thin material of my uniform blouse and tramped off through the fields in my heavy boots.

In less than ten years, Chelyabinsk had become a major center for industry, particularly for the military. It made good sense. It was far from Moscow to the west and a world away from anything that mattered in the east. Defensible. But with growth came a price. I could not go for a ramble off in the hills, see if the wildflowers were emerging, leave behind the bustle of the academy even for one hour. I would have to make do with the expanse of open fields beyond the runways that was the closest thing to nature I could get to without a few hours' leave.

I lay down in the grass, perpetually dewy until the last weeks of July and into August, but paid no mind to the dampening of my suit. It would dry by the following afternoon, if in fact I had call to wear it again. If Tokarev's ankle were badly sprained, Karlov would have an excuse for keeping Solonev or any other pilot from flying with me.

For a few minutes, I wasn't sure how many, I simply took in the crisp air, still tinged with the acrid smell of fuel and oil, and watched the clouds as they floated lazily across the blue canopy over my head. I thought of Mama, still toiling in the laundry day in and day out, now without me to help with meals and tending the cabin. At least now she had laid aside enough money for an old truck that would save her the walk into town every day. Were I the praying sort, I would have included the truck in my nightly vigil. It was perhaps the oldest motor vehicle in all of Chelyabinsk Oblast, and she didn't have the means to replace it if it broke down beyond repair. If it survived another winter, it would be nothing short of a miracle.

I could go home. With my skills, I could find a job here in town to ease Mama's burden. No one here would care if I left. I would at least be of use to her.

"He's just a bitter old man, Ivanova. Ignore him." Solonev's voice floated to my ears, so supple I wondered if I had dreamed it.

"It's Katya, and you're a mind reader as well as a splendid pilot, Cadet Solonev," I said, resting up on my elbows and cocking my brow at him as he came to sit beside me. "No wonder you do so well here. How did you know to look for me here?"

"Vanya, if you don't mind. I've seen you wander out here almost every day in fine weather for the past year. And I'm not a mind reader. No one could be around the cold-shoulder treatment he gives you and not be affected. I'm surprised you've lasted this long."

"Thank you," I said sourly, clutching my knees to my chest. *You think I'm weak, too, yet you notice my wanderings.*

"That's not what I meant. He's unbearable to you. Few of the other women have it as bad."

I thought he inched closer but convinced myself I had imagined it.

"Or the men," I agreed. "He's taken a special liking to me; that much is certain."

"Because you're the only woman in his class," he explained, lighting a cigarette. Not long ago I calculated the cost of each of the half-smoked cigarettes he and the rest of the male cadets left strewn about outside and in the ashtrays near the campus doors. I could easily buy Mama a year's worth of groceries with what they wasted in a month.

"Is that supposed to be comforting?" I picked at the dewy grass rather than look at him.

"I don't know, but you shouldn't take it personally. I meant what I said. You're a damned fine navigator." He nudged me companionably with his elbow. I looked up from the blade of grass I twirled between my thumb and forefinger and locked eyes with him for just a moment before fixing my gaze on the tip of my boot.

"I know I am. It would just be nice to be acknowledged." I chucked the blade of grass back out into the field.

"Are you here to fly to get noticed?"

Fair point, but it's easy for you to say when your flying is complimented at every turn. "To fly. It's always been about the flying. I want to pilot my own plane."

"And you will." His black eyes shifted from flippant to serious. "A navigator's skills are even more valuable than a pilot's. I'm grateful for every minute I sat in the navigator's seat. It's made me a far better pilot. Forget the rest. You won't be grounded again. From what I saw, Tokarev's ankle isn't twisted—it's broken—and he'll have to take the rest of the year off and finish in the fall. I'll insist that you fly as my navigator. You'll get the hours you need to graduate and do whatever it is you want."

"So I have to rely on your kindness to get my wings," I said. "I thought Stalin had emancipated us, but I feel just as dependent as ever." I exhaled and stared out into the vastness of the field. Shouting about the injustice was a waste of precious energy.

"Changes like these can't happen overnight. Not while stubborn old men like Karlov are in charge. They see women as the bearers of children, the providers of meals, and the scrubbers of floors. Or decoration. But change *is* happening."

"You're a philosopher as well as a pilot," I observed. "I suppose you're right, but it never happens fast enough. If he can't see the need to train anyone with the drive and the brains to fly a plane, he's no business being an instructor."

"Well, Moscow agrees with you, Katya, and that's really all that matters."

~

Taisiya grabbed my arm and pulled me into a shadowed corner.

"I heard Cadet Solonev sweet-talked Karlov into letting you fly. How did it go?" The whole academy would know about the flight before I made it back to the barracks. That's how things worked in any school as small as this.

"I made every mark. What would you expect?"

"Well done, but don't be glib. It's already going around the academy that Solonev was sitting with you in the field." Her brown eyes probed my blue ones, looking for the truth as she might hunt for a blemish.

"And since when is it bad form for a pilot and his navigator to discuss their run after they've landed?" I answered, exasperated.

Her grip loosened on my bicep, and she took a deep breath. "As long as that's all it was. You can't afford gossip. You're too close to graduation to risk everything."

"I know the 'rules,' Taisiya," I said, rubbing my eyes. "It's nothing."

Taisiya seemed satisfied and let me pass into the barracks with a quick squeeze to the elbow. As much as I hated to admit it, she wasn't wrong to warn me of the gossip. It would affect all the women if one of us stepped out of line and got sent home. The instructors would treat all of us badly, as though we had all colluded in her downfall.

Of course, the moment Vanya and I were seen alone together, onlookers' thoughts immediately turned to the romantic or the inappropriate. The idea that a man and a woman could not share company with a motive such as friendship or business, or in my case with Vanya, simple camaraderie between cadets, caused blood to rush in my ears.

But in the next few weeks, there was no avoiding him, as he used his influence to ensure I would fly as his navigator so I could complete the program.

"You're lucky to have Solonev in your corner," Karlov announced in front of the entire class before we went up on our run.

"Indeed I am, Captain. Just as he is lucky to have me as his navigator."

Vanya winked at me, stifling a chuckle as he hoisted himself onto the wing. "Let's show him what we can do, eh?" He lowered himself into the front cockpit and signaled to the ground crew once I'd taken my place.

This time he was fearless, flying as though legions of enemy aircraft were on our tail. I would have two seconds to mark my targets, not five, and I felt my fingers shaking with anticipation as I readied my flares. Tokarev had never flown so fast or so daringly in the two years I'd navigated for him. I should have been terrified, sick, or both. But all I felt was my heart pumping and every nerve ending dancing as he glided through the skies, diving and weaving like a magnificent bird of prey. We bandied about the phrase "to have our wings," but this was the first time I truly felt like I had them. Despite the adrenaline that coursed through my veins, time seemed to slow down to the point where I could almost see the tick marks from the maps I studied in the classroom traced out on the ground.

"Two . . . one . . . *marked!*"

Vanya released his dummy bomb the precise moment the flare made contact with the ground. Direct hit. Followed by five more.

When we landed on the airstrip, I felt my legs go heavy, as if caked in wet concrete, as I tried to stand. I hated to return to firm ground, like a bird was loath to return to her cage. I would have been happy to fly on to the endless horizon. I wanted to keep going to the far reaches of the globe.

We rejoined our class, exchanging brief smiles. The run was flawless.

"Excellent flying, Solonev. Well done, Ivanova." Karlov offered my praise almost under his breath, but he couldn't deny we'd had the best run of the year. For the first time in memory, the class gave a decorous round of applause before the next team took off.

I took a wide stance next to Vanya and watched intently as the others made their runs. The pilots went faster, though fewer of them made their marks.

"Showboating," he muttered, crossing his arms over his chest and shaking his head.

"Don't think you're not responsible," I whispered, casting him a wink when Karlov wasn't looking.

He wasn't able to conceal his grin. "There's a difference between testing your limits and being foolish," he said. "And they'll gain no points with Karlov for this, either."

Proving Vanya's case, Karlov rattled off blistering insults to the pilots as they landed, occasionally giving navigators grudging praise for doing well despite their overeager pilots. He dismissed us, and for once I was one of the few in the assembly who hadn't been dressed down or ignored. I wanted to bound off to the dormitories to tell Taisiya, but Vanya pulled me aside.

"I'm proud of you, Katya. I knew you could do it," he said quietly so the passing ears couldn't hear him. "Karlov must not know what to think." Vanya's lips were only a few centimeters from my ear, which garnered more attention than his words would have done, so I kept walking, making Vanya change his position.

"He probably thinks that you've been slipping me pointers and that I'd not do nearly as well with another pilot," I countered. And it was partially true. His confidence in the pilot's seat made my job much easier. I softened my tone. "Thank you for a wonderful run."

"It was my pleasure. It's a joy flying with a skilled navigator for once." I cast my eyes downward at his praise and forced myself to look back at him as he went on. "Just do me a favor and venture over to the men's tables in the mess hall, would you? It's important for a pilot to know his navigator."

Tokarev had shown no interest whatsoever in getting to know me, but Poda, Taisiya's pilot, had made similar invitations for her to join the men's tables. When she ventured over, it was always a lonely meal for me at the women's table, but Poda's request was a logical one.

"Sure," I agreed. "It makes sense. I'll join you for breakfast tomorrow?"

"I'll look forward to it, so long as you leave your books in your bag." He flashed a roguish grin, and I couldn't help but return the smile.

"I can manage for one breakfast, but do your best to be more interesting than a flight manual."

Back in the women's barracks, the news of our flight had already made the rounds, and I was greeted with a round of squeals and hugs from each of my bunkmates. It wasn't just for the flawless run, but because Karlov had, for once in his career, acknowledged a woman as an aviator. It wasn't just a victory for me; it was a victory for us all.

CHAPTER 4

May 1941

"You know the theory better than I do, Katya—better than half the instructors. Why do you pore over your books at every chance?" Vanya chided as he playfully collided into me in the hallway.

"I can't control how many hours I get to fly, but I can control how well I know the techniques."

I rolled my eyes at his shrug. It all came easily to him, or so he made it seem. Vanya's assessment of Tokarev's ankle had been correct—badly broken and torn tendons to boot. One act of clumsiness—falling out of his bunk—and he was grounded for the rest of the year and would finish his training after he healed. It would keep him from conscription off to Poland or the Baltic for several months, at least. Apparently he bore that news with a measure of good cheer, and I couldn't say I blamed him.

"All you girls are the same," Vanya said. "You might make better friends with the male pilots if you spoke to us every once in a while."

"We're not here to make friends; we're here to fly," I countered, turning his earlier rebuke on him. *And we have to be better and faster than you to have the chance to be taken seriously.*

"You need an afternoon away from your books," he announced. "We have nothing scheduled, miraculous as that sounds. Drop off your bag in your barracks, and change into civilian clothes. Something nice, but sturdy shoes."

"I need to study," I said, not bothering to soften my tone.

"I've told you, part of what makes a good navigator is knowing her pilot as well as she knows herself. Consider this a valuable part of your training."

I wanted to argue, but he was right. And the prospect of an afternoon away from the steel and concrete was deliciously enticing.

"Fine," I said. "But tell me where we're going."

"To enjoy the outdoors. That's all I'll say. Meet me here in fifteen minutes." He tempered his words with a wink, and I cursed myself for not coming back with an appropriately biting reply.

Every female cadet in the academy was sprawled on her bunk, manuals and notebooks strewn before her. Taisiya sat perched over hers, her pen scribbling furiously with her right hand while she clutched her text with the left.

"Quiz me," she said, not looking up from her book.

"I can't," I said, flipping open the lid of my footlocker and unbuttoning my uniform jacket.

Taisiya cast her eyes over the top of her manual, wordlessly awaiting explanation.

"Vanya asked me to spend the afternoon with him," I said in low tones, but not a whisper. There was no sense in hiding the truth. The academy was too small for secrets. If I tried to hide it, it would cause more talk and lead to even more trouble.

"Don't let him become a distraction," she warned, and cast her eyes back to the text.

Perhaps I need one. It's been a long three years.

"Hardly. But he's asked me to spend the afternoon out, and he's saved my rear with Karlov. I can't tell him no. He's my pilot, and we need to know one another better than we do."

"Be careful, Katya," she cautioned.

"Don't be that way, Taisiya," I said, pawing through my meager pile of clothes. "You defect over to the men's tables to eat with Poda from time to time."

"I have Matvei, and he knows it. We keep our discussions to aircraft, navigation, and the weather. The latter only when it affects the former," she said, her notebook now discarded onto the bed instead of perched on her knee.

"And it's the same for Vanya and me," I said, unable to keep all the annoyance from escaping the footlocker, where my head was buried. "None of this is against regulation."

"Yet," Taisiya pointed out. "We haven't been allowed here long enough for them to write it down yet."

There was something to be said for the simplicity of my wardrobe. I owned exactly one summer dress worth looking at, a simple thing that had been Mama's. It was a lovely shade of turquoise blue that complemented my eyes, and it was in good repair, being too light to wear for more than two or three months out of the year. Taisiya looked as though she wanted to comment on my choice of dress. She knew it was the best I had, but to her credit she knew she'd already spoken her piece.

I threw on the dress, loosened my hair from its bun, and ran a comb through it to force the auburn waves to frame my face, hoping the countless hours trapped in pins didn't give my hair the appearance of a dented tin can. All the while, as I exchanged my uniform for everyday wear—my finest at that—I could feel the eyes of my sisters in arms on my every movement. I could all but hear their thoughts: *She's fallen for him, and it's going to cost her wings.*

"I'm just sick of itchy uniforms," I mumbled lamely. *And tired of dressing like a man all the time.*

Taisiya nodded; I knew everyone in the room had to understand. As much as we wanted to fly, denying our own womanhood most every hour of the day was exhausting. On a lark I grabbed the battered case with my papa's old violin along with my thinnest wrap. As I exited the barracks to the world beyond, part of me felt compelled to turn around and spend the afternoon quizzing Taisiya and studying with the others, but I couldn't bring myself to turn back.

Vanya greeted me at the exit to the barracks with a massive case in his left hand. He'd exchanged his uniform for a smart-looking suit of civilian clothes in a deep navy blue that complemented his complexion far better than the dismal greens and browns of military uniforms.

"Dear Lord, how long do you plan on keeping me out?" I said, pointing to the case. "I was expecting an afternoon off campus, not a two-week pleasure cruise."

"You clearly aren't entirely opposed to the idea. You brought a case of your own."

"My papa's violin. I haven't played in ages, and since you told me we'd be going outside, I thought I'd bring it. The great outdoors is my favorite concert hall."

"Perfect," he said, offering me his arm and escorting me out into the vibrant late spring sun. I liked the feel of my arm in his but reminded myself it was no more of a gesture than he would offer his maiden aunt. "An exchange of talents it is."

We walked for a half hour until we breached the perimeter of Chelyabinsk and found ourselves in a meadow surrounded by evergreens. Vanya placed the case on the damp grass and knelt before it. He removed a large woolen blanket crafted from soft ivory yarn, probably hand knit by his mother to while away some of the long winter hours in years past. With a flourish he spread the blanket out as a barrier against the soggy ground. He gave no thought to how the pale fibers would come clean; it would never have occurred to him.

"Sit," he ordered. "Make yourself comfortable."

He took off his suit jacket, placed it on the blanket opposite me, and turned his attentions to his case a few feet away from where I sat in the center of the meadow. He removed a wooden frame that he quickly unfolded and assembled into an easel, and placed a blank canvas on its waiting ledge. "The light is spectacular," he explained as he mixed colors from tubes on his palette. "I've always wanted to paint here."

"But why bring me?" I asked. "I'd much rather see the finished product than watch you paint. The trees are beautiful, though. It'll be a gorgeous picture, I'm sure."

"I didn't come to paint the trees, goose. Now angle your head slightly to the left," he said, gesturing with his brush. "Just like that. Try to stay as still as you can."

"Me?" I squeaked. Iron-coated butterflies buzzed around my stomach. I suddenly felt as though my dress were too sheer, as though too many eyes lingered on me, though it was only Vanya. I crossed my arms over my chest and tried not to look in his direction.

"Yes, you, Katya. Consider this an exercise in trusting your pilot. Please put your arms back down the way they were, and look at me. I'll endeavor to do you justice."

I forced my breath to slow and placed my arms back by my sides. I cast my eyes to him, and did my best to relax as he painted. He wanted me to know him, and this was his way of baring his soul. I fought the urge to wrap the blanket around me, to protect myself from the intimacy of his gaze.

If I could place my life in his hands every afternoon, this ought to be simple enough. The longer he worked, the more I felt myself at ease. His brow did not furrow with concentration as he painted, as it did when he prepared for takeoff. His shoulders were low, his breathing even, as his brush—an extension of his arm—swept over the canvas with measured strokes. Never before had I seen an artist at work, but I had not expected it to appear so graceful. He looked more like a dancer than a painter. I found the sight of him entranced by his palette and canvas both mesmerizing and soothing.

Vanya worked in silence for over an hour, but I was so transfixed and he worked so intently that the time swept past.

"You can move now," he said at length. "I still have some shading to do, the landscape to fill in, but you can get up."

I stood, stiff from the long sitting, and circled around to see what he had produced.

"That's not me," I said as he played with the texture of the grass on the edges of the portrait. The woman had a proud chin, her expression defiant. She was beautiful.

"You offend me," he said without looking up. "You don't think I have the skill to capture your likeness?"

"It's a lovely painting," I said. It was true. The color was remarkable, the texture so vivid I longed to touch it. "I just don't think you painted me."

"It's very much you. You just can't see yourself the way I do." He glanced over at me and back to the canvas, his brow furrowed.

"I had no idea you were so talented," I said, keeping my blush at bay, though only just. "You ought to be studying painting instead of how to fly a plane."

"The son of Antonin Solonev does not study art. He studies war," Vanya said in a voice that was not his own, obviously quoting his father.

"I thought you weren't one for tradition," I said, placing my hand on his shoulder. Was it too bold? "Following your papa's orders certainly qualifies as that."

"He's a hard man to ignore." His strokes grew short and furious, the bristles scratching against the canvas like dry pine needles as he added one last flourish of pale yellow to highlight where the sunlight bounced off the red of my hair. "But to own the truth, I'm glad he pushed me. The war is coming, and I'll be better off in the air than in a trench."

"Let's hope the peace treaty stands and we avoid the worst of it." I clung to that piece of paper like a life preserver, but each time I said it, it sounded more and more feeble.

"I'm not used to such optimism from you," he chuckled, at last taking his eyes off the canvas. "And I'm afraid it's wishful thinking."

"And far too nice a day to worry about such things when we don't have to."

"True, and now you owe me a display of your talents. Take out your violin and play for me, Katyushka."

I blushed at the endearment and thought of Mama, her eyes weary after a day at the laundry, sitting back in her chair. *"Play for me, Katinka,"* she would urge me. It gave Mama a few moments of pleasure, and I found there was no better motivation to practice.

I obliged him, pulling Papa's violin from its case, grateful I'd been able to scrape together the funds for new strings. Usually I favored Papa's mournful folk tunes, but today wasn't a day for tears. Nor did I feel equal to a giddy tune for dancing. My repertoire wasn't vast, but I opted for a short ballad that was wistful, bittersweet, but one that always filled me with hope.

"You have skill," Vanya said as I lowered my bow.

"Not as much as I would like, but I don't have much time for practicing."

"I understand that." He cast a glance at his painting, his brow furrowing yet again. A wayward brushstroke? A poorly chosen shade? He was a pilot; that he was a perfectionist was no shock to me.

"The best light is nearly shot," he said, gazing into the sky. "I can steal odd moments in the dormitory to finish it up. Perhaps your mother would enjoy it when it's finished? I can't very well hang it next to my bunk. Half the time I just paint over my old canvases, but I'm partial to this one."

"God, no," I muttered, imagining the reaction to the display of my portrait in the men's barracks. "Your bunkmates can't see it. I'd never hear the end of it."

"I'll be careful, I promise." His hand took mine for a moment, then dropped it just as quickly. "So should I send it to your mother?"

"I'm sure Mama would love to have it." The painting would stand out in our shabby old cabin like a ruby necklace on a coal miner, but I would not embarrass him or my mother by saying so. It was a beautiful thing, and my mother could do with more beauty in her life.

"Excellent," he said, and packed away his easel. He protected the wet canvas by attaching it to another with little hand screws. Like so much in Vanya's life, it was all so well ordered and meticulously planned. I envied this, for so much of my life had been determined by circumstance rather than choice.

"Thank you, by the way," he said once his equipment was sorted. He took a seat next to me on the blanket, watching as the sun dipped behind the trees.

"Whatever for?"

"For letting me paint you. I've been wanting to for some time. The first time I saw you was after one of your practice runs. The sunset caught the glint of your auburn hair. I knew I had to capture it on canvas." He tucked a finger under my chin, drawing my lips to his.

Mama's cautionary tales, Taisiya's warnings—all drowned by a single kiss.

I leaned in, allowing him to wrap his strong arms around me and drink more deeply from my lips. When he pulled away, I could see his dark eyes scan my face, assessing my reaction.

"I've been wanting to do that from just about the same time," he admitted, leaning his forehead against mine. His embrace was like a down comforter on a winter morning, and for once I wanted to ignore chores, lessons, and duty and have a morning to luxuriate in it.

"I've tried not to think of you that way," I said, finally pulling away to see his face. "I couldn't afford the distraction." I winced as the word tumbled from my lips.

"'My distraction.' That will never be my favorite endearment, but I've been called worse," he said through a chuckle. He stood, offering me his hand. "I've had enough of the mess hall. Perhaps for a lifetime. Let's have supper in town, shall we?"

"And who knows how long we'll be confined to army rations after this?" I said, lacing my fingers in his and pulling my wrap closer against the rapidly cooling night air.

"Too right, but no more of the world tonight, Katyushka."

We detoured to the barracks to stow the art supplies and violin, thankfully going unnoticed as everyone was eating in the mess hall, and continued hand in hand into town. The sun wouldn't set fully for hours yet, we being so far to the north, but the evening light was reedy and feeble, somehow not quite sincere about illuminating our path.

I had never ventured inside an establishment more refined than one of the public houses near the academy that served a respectable *ukha*, where I went when I was homesick for my mother's good fish soup. Vanya didn't have his eyes on one of the loud taverns full of factory workers but rather directed us toward one of the smart restaurants that had sprung up to attend to the heads of industry, visiting officials, and important guests. The décor looked lavish to my untrained eyes. Dark wood and pristine white tablecloths. Low candles encased the room in a soft glow. I didn't need to look at the menu to know I couldn't hope to afford a meal here.

"I'm not terribly hungry," I said. "Maybe we could go to a little pub instead?" He would insist upon paying, and I didn't want to be indebted to him any more than I was.

"Nonsense," Vanya replied, placing a bill in the hand of the maître d' as he showed us to our table. A crisply dressed waiter scuttled over, looking as though nothing were more important in his world than Vanya's next command.

"We'll have the lamb pelmeni, roasted potatoes, and two lagers," he said to the waiter. Lamb dumplings and crisp beer. Rich and savory, but nothing too exotic. "My treat," he said softly as the waiter scurried off to the kitchen.

"I can't let you," I said, gripping my handbag in my lap, wondering if I would be able to scrape together my half of the meal's cost from its contents.

"Please don't think about it. Nothing gives me more pleasure than spending Father's money on little luxuries he doesn't approve of. A canvas, paints, and now a good meal with a lovely woman, all in the space of one afternoon. Father would be properly fuming. Let's drink to him."

His eyes met mine as he lifted his glass. *"Za tvojo zdorovie."*

"Za tvojo zdorovie," I toasted to his health in turn, then brought the foamy brew to my lips, savoring the cool trickle down the back of my throat after hours in the sun.

"I have wanted to thank you," I finally said as I pushed a piece of potato about the edge of my plate. "I know Captain Karlov would have been perfectly happy to see me grounded and miss graduation since Tokarev can't fly." *And why* did *you help me?*

"It's high time those bastards practice what they preach. If they're going to admit women to the academies, they'd better damn well train them; else they're just wasting Russia's resources and everyone's time. And Karlov is a special case, for sure."

My shoulders tensed at the thought of Karlov's onion-perfumed grimace on his walrus-whiskered face. "That's the truth."

"I'm shocked the headmaster dared assign any woman to him. I'd take it as a compliment if I were you. He must have thought you were either tough enough to survive him or worth the trouble of getting rid of. Either way, you made an impression."

"Well, that's something, I suppose." I laughed, not knowing which option I hoped was true. I sipped through the foam on my lager, wondering how much would be prudent to drink. No more than half, though it seemed a waste.

"You know what you're doing, not that you need me to tell you that. Insecure little prigs like Karlov will spend their whole lives trying to convince you otherwise, but you don't have to let them." He rearranged his roasted potatoes into a pattern as he spoke, unable to fully leave his art behind him.

"I do try. It's not always easy, though." I wished I were the sort of woman who could easily ignore Karlov's rebukes and oversights, but I was an academic's daughter and couldn't entirely ignore the opinions of my instructors—founded or unjust.

"I can only imagine. Just do me one favor to repay me for getting you back in the cockpit."

I set my fork aside my plate. "What exactly is that?"

"Remember how much fun this afternoon has been. Look up from your books every once in a while, and enjoy yourself. And enjoy what you can before graduation . . . no matter what else happens."

"I will try," I said, "but I have a favor to ask of you as well." I felt my hands shaking as I sought the words I needed. "Today *was* wonderful, but I don't think we should do this again."

"Katya, we're two grown people enjoying an afternoon off. No one could have a thing to say about it." He reached into his pocket for his cigarettes. I'd made him nervous.

"Vanya, you don't know how it is for us. You can't possibly. We're held to different standards." I folded my hands on the table in front of me, resolute. "Women like me have to choose between career and romance. I can't let myself get distracted. If it's any consolation, this is the first time I regret that."

"'Distraction.' That charming word of yours again. Very well, then." He lit his cigarette, his eyes drifting off to inspect something on the wall behind me for several moments. "If this *is* a date, and it is to be our last, then indulge me and let me drag it on a bit. Let's have dessert and coffee, unless you worry for your reputation too much."

"Of course."

We dropped the subject and talked of painting and music, then lingered over the subject of our parents. His father sounded like a brute, and his mother too docile to temper him and protect her son. I spoke of Mama with concern and Papa with reverence—his sweet temper, quick wit, and brilliant mind. The courses he taught and how widely respected he was. Even the mention of him twelve years after his death caused the air to catch in my chest and form a dull ache that rivaled the swell of pride I felt telling Vanya of his accomplishments.

"I envy you your happy memories of your father. He must have been a wonderful man." He exhaled cigarette smoke from his nostrils. He resembled an irritated dragon for a moment; then his shoulders drooped again. What was he remembering? More aptly, what was he forcing himself to forget?

"He was," I agreed. "And brilliant. I'd give my wings to speak with him again."

"He'd be furious with you for making such a sacrifice," Vanya said, extinguishing his cigarette in the chipped glass ashtray. "Let's get back before we're missed."

I felt my heart sink at his pronouncement but knew he was right. It was several hours until curfew, but the earlier we returned, the less chance there would be of rumors spreading.

Though it was the middle of May, the night air was still cool, and I wrapped my shawl tightly around my shoulders. Vanya slipped his arm around me, and I wanted to tell him to take it back, but the words wouldn't come. His warmth across my back and waist was too inviting, his musky scent too enticing. Taisiya had been right: he would be a distraction if I let him.

"You're right about something," he said as we walked down the main road in town. "I *don't* know how hard it is for you and the other girls to make your way in the academy. I can try to understand, though." Regret lined his face, but so did sincerity. That he had the largeness of mind to think about a woman's ambitions beyond marriage, babies, and housekeeping lifted him a wide cut above most men.

"Thank you for saying that. Some days it's murder just to show up to class, knowing how Karlov will latch on to the tiniest flaw in my performance, or invent one when he can't. I know that's exactly what he wants. You having to intervene for me just to get my rightful place in the cockpit infuriates me. That's part of the reason I haven't gone out of my way to be friendly."

"You have every right to be furious with him, but I'm glad you seem to have forgiven my interference." He placed a gentle kiss on my forehead, and I found myself snuggling in closer to his side, his arm taking up the slack. "And since we're making confessions, I admit, I did want this to be a date. I noticed you from our first day at the academy, and not just because you're beautiful. You're smart, talented, and strong. I was thrilled to transfer to your class, even though we're almost finished. It would give me a good reason to talk to you."

"I wish things could be different," I said, leaning my head against his chest. I could feel the thrumming of his heart beneath the soft fabric of his shirt. We stopped our slow stroll back to campus altogether and tucked out of the way by a grocer's that had closed for the day.

"So do I, Katyushka." His fingers brushed against the hair on the side of my head, as comforting and warm as the endearment he fashioned for me. "Russia will enter the war; there's no chance we won't. When we're drawn in, I'll be called up just as soon. But after—"

"It seems like a bad idea to make plans," I interjected. "Tempting fate, and all that."

"I need a reason to come home, Katya." His voice was barely above a whisper.

I looked up into his dark eyes, wondering if I had imagined the words—if years of self-denial had finally caught up with me and I was imagining the sort of future I didn't think I'd be able to have for many years, if ever. As he held me in his arms, nothing seemed more real than the curve of his chin, the perfume of his breath, and the truth in the depth of his words.

"Vanya, if we both emerge from this war in one piece, you can expect me by your side within the hour of the cease-fire." As I spoke the words, I thought I felt his heartbeat just a bit stronger and faster, or at least I imagined it did—in time with my own. The promise seemed so weak compared to what I wanted to offer him, but it was all I had to give. "I understand if you don't want to make promises. It may be a long war."

"It likely will be, so you must allow me one liberty," he breathed. He pulled back a half step, cupped my face in his hands, and again pressed his lips to mine. Slow and gentle at first, then more insistent. It was wonderful, but it could go no further. A hole had formed in my heart. I'd done everything I was supposed to do for so long, deprived myself of so many pleasures—but in denying myself Vanya I didn't feel like the decadently plump woman refusing a second slice of raspberry tart. I was the woman in the Sahara declining a canteen of water.

"I *do* want to make you one promise, Katyushka," Vanya whispered in my ear. "One I am certain to keep."

"Go ahead, then," I said, looking up into the dark pools of his eyes.

"I won't do anything to keep you from getting your wings," he said, planting a kiss on the tender skin just below my earlobe. "Just the opposite. I'll do everything I can to make sure you're in the cockpit at every opportunity."

I put my hands on either side of his face and pulled it down to mine, my lips eager for his as I wound my fingers through his hair.

"Vanyusha," I whispered after I found my breath some moments later. "My Vanyusha."

"Really?" he asked, a slight tremor of disbelief crossing his face. "Do you mean it?"

I nodded, feeling not a trace of regret. "We all need something to fight for, don't we? Mama was a good reason, but so is this." I took his hand in mine. "The chance to find out if we can make a life together."

"The best reason I can think of," he said, taking our entwined hands and kissing the back of mine.

"I'm not ready to go back," I admitted. "I want more time like this. No uniforms. No books. No commanders. Just us."

Vanya paused, pensive a few moments. "The hotel?" he suggested, studying my face for a reaction. "I can't think of any other place to be properly alone—if that's what you wish."

Mama had explained to me the nature of things between men and women and warned me that men could not always be trusted. But this was Vanya. I trusted him with my life each time we went up in the air. To withhold my trust with this seemed ridiculous. All the same, I had no experience with such things and felt as green as I had on my first day at the academy.

"Let's go," I whispered, feeling my color rise.

"We'll take things slowly, my darling Katyushka," he said, taking my hand and leading us back to the center of town.

I stood back in the lobby, pretending to admire a painting as Vanya went to the desk and requested a room. He came to me, key in hand, and offered me his arm.

"Shall we, Comrade Soloneva?" He winked at me as I took his arm.

"That does sound lovely," I said, caressing his arm. I wondered if the war, by some miracle, didn't separate us, what it would be like to settle into a domestic life with him. Most women my age thought of keeping a house and enjoying the early months of marriage before children came. Such dreams would be a long way off for us.

Vanya opened the door to a lovely room, decorated in deep reds and golds. Plush, warm, and inviting as his embrace.

"We'll go slowly, my darling," he repeated. He wrapped his arms around me and pulled me to his hard chest. I felt my pulse quicken in response to his touch. "We don't have to do anything you don't want to do."

"I want to do this with you, Vanyusha. Show me . . . how." I'd rebuffed every boy who'd expressed any interest in me for so long, I wasn't sure how to say yes. I wrapped my arms around his neck, taking all the kisses I'd denied myself for years.

"As my lady wishes," he agreed, holding me tight in his arms and burying his face in my hair. His hands found the zipper at the back of my dress and lowered it into a pool of turquoise at my waist. With delicate movements of his fingertips, he caressed my arms, my back, and eventually the tops of my breasts, his eyes once again studying mine for any sign of hesitation. The more he touched me, the more I knew I could not refuse myself the pleasure of his embrace.

He freed my breasts from the brassiere I wore several sizes too small to minimize their appearance in my uniform. He took them in his hands, massaging them until I felt myself going limp with pleasure against him. I removed his shirt, longing to feel the warm skin of his muscled chest against my own.

Excited by my boldness, he lowered my dress completely and removed my garter belt and stockings—slowly, as though he were unwrapping a much-anticipated gift on New Year's Morning. I tried not to tremble as his fingers tucked into the front of my undergarments—my last vestige of modesty—and lowered them to the floor. His eyes scanned every centimeter of me, but I didn't feel the color of shame rise in me.

"I take it you're pleased?" I whispered.

"So beautiful," he whispered, his breathing ragged. "I only wish I had my canvas and paints."

"You'd rather paint?" I asked, finding some bravado in his reaction to my nudity.

"Excellent point," he chuckled, his hands lowering, gripping my buttocks with his strong fingers, his mouth on mine.

"Vanya," I said, forcing myself to step back one pace. "We . . . there can't be a child."

"No, not with things as they are," he said, reaching into his pants pocket and retrieving a small tin with three rolled-up bits of rubber bound in the middle by strips of white paper. "Condoms. They will protect us from a baby."

I nodded, not fully understanding how they worked, but trusting him to do what was right. He took me in his arms again, and I lost myself in his kisses. He was chiseled and strong, though not hulking with muscle as Stalin's posters showed the ideal Soviet soldier. He was real, and he was mine. My initial nerves had worn off, and I wondered why I wasn't shaking, why I didn't feel the urge to cover myself. Wasn't that how it was supposed to be the first time? Instead it felt as natural as breathing.

We lay on the bed, kissing and caressing for some minutes before his embraces grew less tender and more insistent. I felt him slip the condom over his length before he dipped his fingers into the soft flesh between my legs.

"Please," I breathed into his chest. "Please."

He climbed atop me, his kisses never ceasing, and eased himself inside me. I felt an uncomfortable pinching sensation, then relief and pleasure as he filled me. I pulled him closer.

"My God, how I've wanted you, Katya," he said into my hair as he moved gently above me.

"And I you, my Vanya," I mumbled, memorizing the wonder of him commanding all my senses.

He paused and pulled me on top of him so I could ride him astride. "I want to see you, my love," he explained, cupping my breasts in his hands and then pulling me closer so he could take my nipple in his mouth. I still felt a tinge of discomfort, yet I shuddered with pleasure as I moved, timid at first, but growing bolder until I felt my muscles tighten around him and spasms of bliss lapping over my body from within.

He groaned beneath me, and I collapsed on his broad chest when I knew he'd taken his pleasure. For a long while I just lay in his arms listening to the cadence of his heartbeat, breathing in the minted perfume of his warm breath, and enjoying the soft glow of his gleaming skin in the dim light.

"Whatever happens, I'm so happy to have this memory to take with me," he finally whispered.

"As am I," I said, lifting my head and kissing the soft skin of his cheek. "I don't want it to end."

"Nor do I, Katyushka." He caressed my damp skin with the tips of his fingers, and I melted against him.

"I-I had never . . ." I felt the heat in my skin as I stammered out my confession of innocence.

"I know. You have given me a precious gift. I am sorry I can't say you were my first, but you will always be my most dear."

I felt jealousy seize my stomach like a vise for a moment, but it passed just as quickly. It was best that one of us knew what we were doing. I had no desire to know of his past conquests but felt the sincerity of his words. I'd been his navigator long enough to know if he were telling an untruth.

"What now?" The question fell from my lips with an almost-audible thud to the carpeted floor.

"We go to war when we're called. It doesn't seem wise to make plans beyond that."

"Perhaps it doesn't," I admitted. "But we *will* get through this. We won't be digging trenches on the front lines. And when this whole mess is over, I'll take a job teaching at a flight school and you can spend your days painting." I caressed his cheek with my fingertips.

"You have a promise, my love," he said, pulling me close and brushing his lips gently against mine. "My God, I don't want to go."

I wasn't sure if he meant back to our solitary bunks in the barracks or off to war, but I agreed on either count.

For an hour or two, we curled up in each other's arms, occasionally sleeping, mostly engrossed in exhausted, dreamlike chatter about our future. A home in Moscow, a tribe of children, a workshop for Vanya's painting. Making plans for a future we couldn't begin to envision, too shadowed by the looming threat of war.

We scurried back to the barracks moments before curfew. If Taisiya noticed anything amiss, she said nothing, and I loved her for it. It had been hasty and foolish to stay with Vanya, but I wanted no reprimand from her to mar the tender young memory that was forming in my heart.

CHAPTER 5

June 1941

The mess hall silenced as the metallic hum of the intercom system buzzed to life over our heads. "All cadets will report to the auditorium immediately following luncheon."

Eyebrows arched and questions buzzed about the room as cadets hurried through the last bites of their meals.

"Likely another lecture," Vanya hypothesized, opening the auditorium door for me, his hand lingering on the small of my back as he ushered me in. "Some of the third-years are being nothing short of reckless on their runs these past few weeks."

"They're all wanting to impress the officers," I said, taking my seat next to him on the bleachers. "The war has them all imagining themselves as future aces, heroes of the cause, and all that."

"If they want to impress the officers, if they want to be aces, they need to follow the goddamned rules," he said, leaning back against the bleacher behind him with a grunt of annoyance. There was little that irritated Vanya more than a careless pilot. He'd taken to lecturing the more egregious offenders, always within earshot of the first- and second-year recruits. Most listened, but some found his interference presumptuous. He wasn't a commander, so it wasn't really his place, but my loyalty was with Vanya. If he was willing to share his knowledge, his classmates ought to be grateful and listen.

I looked away from his profile, silhouetted in the afternoon sun that streamed in from the high windows, and saw Taisiya breaking ranks, leaving the rest of our female contingent to sit next to us in the cavernous auditorium. I patted her knee as welcome, glad that for once I didn't have to choose between Vanya and my sisters in arms.

"Cadets, we have a special treat for you today," the headmaster himself said, standing on the enormous podium that was generally only wheeled out for ceremonies of special importance. "Major Sofia Orlova, Hero of the Soviet Union, is here to address you all. I trust you will give her your undivided attention."

The headmaster's admonition was unnecessary. Every cadet in the room sat straighter as the petite blonde stepped to the microphone. Her name was known to all of us. She had shattered so many records in aviation that Stalin himself had presented her with the highest military honor, Hero of the Soviet Union. We'd all grown up hearing about the exploits of these famous pilots, mostly men, who gained notoriety for flying from one end of Russia to the other, or setting records for speed. They were the heroes who had inspired us to earn our own wings, in many cases. This was the first time I'd been in the same room as one of these famous aviators, and I felt my childlike giddiness rush to the surface, coated in the honey-and-spice scent of my nostalgia.

"Comrades. My fellow pilots," a confident, remarkably deep voice emanated from the woman who looked to be several centimeters shorter than I, and much smaller in frame. "I come to thank you for your efforts in your studies. What you do here is one of the most important endeavors our great nation is undertaking. We are moving into a new age, and

Russia must be at the forefront of technology and training if we are to take our rightful place in this new world. Our great leader, Comrade Stalin, has wisely invested many resources in your training, and I know you are all working tirelessly to make the most of this opportunity to serve your country.

"The time may soon come when your lessons and training will be put to real, practical use. Comrade Stalin and Hitler have an uneasy peace for now, but we cannot count on a greedy foreigner to keep his word. I want you all to be ready to answer Mother Russia's call if she has need of you. Even if we are not called into the war in Europe, even if the troubles in Asia quell themselves, the situation in the Baltic will demand many of us to serve. Men, if you are needed, I hope your sense of duty will call you to the front before you are called by conscription. I know you will serve with honor. Ladies, the choice is yours, and I understand it is likely to remain so. Know that Comrade Stalin sees you all as equal to your brothers in arms, and just as capable in combat.

"We were all born in a country where women were considered lesser. Second to their brothers, husbands, and fathers. We know this is not so, and you, my sisters, have already benefited from the laws enacted by Comrade Stalin. We are not chained to our stoves any longer. Fight for the liberties we have been given. If you are in this room, you are worthy of service, and I am confident Mother Russia will be proud of the men and women who will defend her in her hour of need."

The speech was met with thunderous applause as the other cadets and I rose to our feet. Orlova posed with the headmaster and some of the instructors for a photo; then the rest of the cadets were allowed to approach the podium to shake her hand.

Vanya stayed back, but Taisiya and I rushed to the front of the crowd along with the rest of the women. We were of course the most anxious to meet her, but most of the men seemed just as thrilled to meet such an accomplished aviator.

"Thank you" was all I could say as I took her hand in mine. Her grip was firm, but her hand was soft.

"I know," she said with a smile, knowing the words that I could not express. "It's not always easy, but it *is* worth it. I promise you. Will you serve if you are needed, Cadet . . . ?"

"Ivanova. You have my word," I said, feeling a broad smile stretch across my face.

"Good woman, Ivanova. I'll be proud to fly with you, sister."

Sister. I caught Taisiya's eye, and she returned a grin as ridiculous as my own. Orlova knew the struggle, just like the rest of us.

Vanya waited for me at the door to the auditorium, his face not reflecting the patriotic glow on our classmates' faces. "Practicals are canceled this afternoon," he said with no sign of his usual sly smile or roguish wink.

"Probably wise," I said. "No one will be able to concentrate after that."

"I'm sure that's what Stalin is hoping for," Vanya said, his lips set in a grim line. "Let's get out of here, shall we?"

I followed him out of the cement corridors into the weak spring sun that still wrestled for victory against winter. He took my hand for anyone at the academy to see, but I didn't care. They could talk all they liked. Vanya and I walked for perhaps a quarter of an hour before he finally dropped my hand and turned to me. He cupped my face and kissed me slowly, reverent as a penitent man saying his prayers. We hadn't shared an embrace in the weeks since our date, too busy with the demands of our exams to steal time for one another away from the airfield. Was the sacrifice of that time with Vanya worth the reward?

"Katyushka, can you promise me something?" he whispered in my ear, kissing the soft skin of my jaw, earlobe, and neck in succession.

"What do you need, my Vanya?" I returned the favor by lacing my fingers in his hair and pulling his lips back to mine.

"Could you stay home?" His voice was still hushed, but I heard a note of panic I'd not heard from him before.

"What do you mean?" My brain whirled with excitement at having him near me again, but I felt myself slipping back into reality.

"They wouldn't have Orlova come if war wasn't around the corner. They're trying to get us inspired to fight. The generals don't trust Hitler to stay put, even if Stalin is too foolish to see his true colors. They'll be loading the men on the train as soon as they hand us our diplomas. You have the choice, though. You heard what she said. I'm begging you to stay so I can fight knowing you're safe."

"You promised you'd not keep me from getting my wings," I reminded him.

"And I won't, but that doesn't mean I can't urge you to find another use for them."

What he asked was as simple as breathing: the day after graduation, I could return to Miass and to Mama. I could find work and ease her burden. Perhaps even manage a way to help the war efforts from the safety of our isolated mountain town. War was the province of men, and no one would give my absence from it another thought. It was simple, but impossible. "Am I to let you go and spend my days mad with worry? Do nothing with all the training I've had?"

His hands slid down to my hips and pulled me so close I could feel his chest rise and fall with each breath. He lowered his lips to mine once more and drank slowly from them before finally pulling back. "Damn you and your good conscience," he muttered, tucking my head under his chin.

"Would you want me if I were otherwise? A biddable waif who'd be happy to wait at home and darn your socks?"

"Maybe not, but I'd be a damn sight happier if you could be one until the war is over. You can go back to being a shrew after we've won."

"If only it worked that way," I said, and exhaled slowly. "But we shrews can no more hide our shrewishness than a tiger can hide her stripes."

"It's all part of your charm. But if you can't promise to stay home and be safe for me, promise you'll fly smart. The stories my father has from the last war would tear you apart, and we're headed for more of the same. To think of you anywhere near there kills me. My father is a ghost of a man. Mama says you used to never see him without a smile or a song. I wish I had known my father before the war took that from him. Don't let me see that light in your eyes grow dim."

He caressed the side of my face with his finger, his coal eyes intense with concentration, as I had only ever seen them before he went up on a challenging pattern. I thought of my own mother. I remembered the days when her heart was light. The war hadn't silenced my papa's song, and it wasn't a war that had stifled Mama's. I opened my mouth to protest, but he claimed my mouth with his, lingering until I could feel my knees dissolve into gelatin. I clung to his broad shoulders as I regained my breath. I had spent so many weeks stifling any feelings for him; my confusion was as dizzying as his kisses.

I wish I could say my determination to fly never faltered, but in that moment I wished I had the resolve to hang up my flight suit and keep a little house in the hills of Miass and wait like a dutiful bride for him to return. But the waiting—the interminable waiting—and the brutal uncertainty of praying to whomever would listen that the uniformed man with the telegram wouldn't turn down the lane. Facing the Germans would be a far lesser torture.

For the first time the volume in the women's bunkroom outstripped the commotion in the men's.

"She was so beautiful," Marta breathed. "How on earth does she manage that while setting world records?"

"Likely a combination of good genetics and not giving a damn," I said. "The better question is how she maintained the discipline to set those records and how she got Stalin's support to attempt it in the first place."

"Sheer talent, from what I understand," Taisiya added. "Which makes me hate her just a little."

The rest of us laughed.

"She wouldn't have come if war wasn't on the horizon," I said, repeating Vanya's prophecy. "And not just the mess in the Baltic. She's here to drum up patriotic fervor."

"Well, Hitler is on the move, isn't he?" Taisiya replied. "Stalin seems to trust him like a brother, but the generals may not be so convinced. It only makes sense to get troops at the ready." It seemed a few weeks was enough time to give Taisiya a bit of perspective about Matvei's conscription. A letter in the interim, describing his training regimen, had certainly helped that along.

"Oh, do we have to drag the war into this?" Klavdiya moaned from her bunk. "It's the only thing people talk about these days."

"Klavdiya, if you think there is anything more important to discuss right now, you're sorely mistaken."

My tone was harsher than it should have been, but girls like Marta and Klavdiya made my blood boil. They came to the academy with romantic ideas about flying, and when they found out the work involved, they neither buckled down to do it nor went home and ceded their place to someone more eager. I had little use for girls who had their heads turned by the likes of Sofia Orlova but weren't willing to make the same sacrifices to achieve their goals.

"Well said," Iskra piped up from her bunk. "This school likely wouldn't be here if it weren't for the goings on to the west . . . and the east. I'm no more keen to go to war than the rest of you, but I'm willing to do my part for the education I've been given."

"Then you're silly," Marta replied. "Orlova herself said we would have the choice. Why fly into harm's way when we don't have to?"

"It's called honor, duty, and pride, Marta," I seethed. "And I suggest you acquire some in the coming months. You may find yourself in need of them."

CHAPTER 6

The last two weeks at the academy were intense. When we weren't in the air, we were in our books until we passed out in our musty bunks from sheer exhaustion. None of the men teased us for having our noses in books anymore. Not even Vanya. Our exams started in two days, and the instructors and students both seemed determined to cram a review of three years of instruction into our last week. A headache had settled behind my eyes, and I was ready to burn every beloved text in my battered footlocker.

We had just completed an extended theoretical session, and the mess hall beckoned with a subpar dinner, after which I would crawl into bed until Taisiya dragged me from it by my toes, when Vanya came up beside me and took me by the elbow.

"Headmaster Rushkov has an errand for us in town," he said. "Let's get moving so we don't miss dinner." The head of the academy frequently called on students to run his errands, but I'd never been called on to so much as post a letter.

"Let me stash my books," I said, veering toward the barracks.

"No time. We're taking one of the academy's trucks. You can stow them in there."

I nodded and followed him to the parking lot where the dingy green trucks stood, parked in a row with rigid precision. I wanted to ask what Rushkov needed that required my assistance—if there were supplies to fetch, surely he would have sent a man—but then decided I didn't care. As Vanya drove the rumbling pickup off campus to the city that lay beyond, he reached over and held my hand, but we didn't speak as the truck rattled over the uneven streets, neither wanting to break the comfortable silence.

We didn't park in front of the post office, nor any other of the locations I thought likely for the errand. Instead he parked in front of the small Chelyabinsk city administration building.

"Rushkov needs documents of some sort?" I asked. It was a logical errand but didn't require two cadets, days away from their final exams, to complete it.

"Rushkov owed me a favor," Vanya said quietly, turning off the ignition. His hands remained on the wheel of the truck. "I asked for a night off base for both of us, the use of this truck, and no questions."

"How nice." I pulled the back of his hand to my mouth and pressed my lips against it. The exams still loomed in the back of my brain, however, and I was losing the fight to keep them there. As much as I wanted to be alone with him, was this not precisely the sort of distraction that could cost me on my exams?

No, I decided. Might not a good meal and good company do as much for my exam results as yet more hours poring over my texts? In any event, I was determined to find out.

"I'd dearly love to know why Rushkov owes you a favor."

"To tell you would violate the agreement he and I made, but it's safe to say that Comrade Rushkova would not be pleased with her husband's behavior if I made her aware of it."

I rolled my eyes. The usual tale, I was sure. A young woman—a maid, a shopgirl, or even one of the cadets from my very own bunkroom. Well, it wasn't my scandal, and if Vanya used Rushkov's indiscretion to our advantage, I would enjoy it for tonight.

"A date isn't precisely what I had in mind, my Katyushka," he whispered, scooting closer to me on the bench seat of the truck and wrapping his arm around my shoulders. "I have something important to ask of you."

He's going to ask me to stay home, isn't he? Will I be able to refuse him again? I tried to relax into his embrace but found I couldn't. "What is it, Vanyusha?"

"If you won't stay home from the front, there is one other thing you can do to send me off to war with some peace of mind."

I gave in then, melding closer to him on the seat, oblivious to the people who walked on the sidewalk in front of us, peering through the windshield. "I'll do it if I can, sweet Vanya."

"Marry me, Katyushka."

My heart strained painfully against my ribs for a moment before I reminded myself to draw breath. I'd known Vanya for less than three months. Did I know him well enough to spend the rest of my life tied to him? I looked into the serious black eyes as he studied my face, awaiting my decision. I willed an answer to come but found nothing but a cold ball of fear in my gut.

I thought of Mama, who would be denied the chance to see her only child married. I thought of his mother, who might resent me for stealing her son from her without so much as a word of warning. Of his father, who could hardly be expected to approve of his son marrying a laundress's daughter, no matter who my father had been. And I thought of Papa, who would not be there to give us his consent and good wishes. To offer his blessing and dance with me at our wedding. At least in the last case, there was nothing I could do to rectify it.

But did they matter? They would not be the ones going to war. Could they deny us our happiness when the jackal was scratching at our door?

I realized then that I trusted Vanya with my life each day that he took us up for practicals, and he took that duty as seriously as any pilot I'd ever seen. I knew he would take the same care with my happiness when we were on the ground. And anyway, to assume that "the rest of our lives" would stretch decades and decades into the future seemed an arrogant presumption.

"Yes, Vanya. I will."

He leaned down to kiss me, blinking furiously, then pulled away and murmured, "We need to hurry, my love. The office closes in a half hour."

He descended from the truck. Rather than waiting for him to open my door, I followed him out the driver's side and laced my fingers in his.

"Everything is hurried these days," I said. "Why should this be different?"

"I am sorry we haven't time to change—"

"Soldiers marry in uniform, Vanyusha. It's better than a silk gown. And better my dress uniform than my flight suit."

Vanya's tension eased into a weak chuckle as he leaned over to kiss my temple. It took ten minutes for us to show our identification, fill out the forms, and speak our vows. He placed on my ring finger the small signet ring with a bold *S* that he wore on his little finger, and we were man and wife. We sealed our union with a kiss, though the clerk hadn't included it in our vows.

"Well now, sweet husband, I don't think we can rush back to the barracks and announce our marriage, can we? What shall we do with our evening? I can't imagine you haven't concocted a plan."

"I'm afraid I can't give you a proper honeymoon, dearest Katyushka, but we can have tonight. I told Rushkov we needed leave until morning." My stomach lurched as I realized the brass would find out, sooner or later, that we'd married. Would that disqualify me from finishing my program? I didn't want to find out, but we would only have to keep the secret for a few weeks.

"You whisked me off my feet so quickly, I hadn't time to expect a honeymoon, let alone be disappointed by not having one." I reached up to kiss his cheek, thrilled that now not a soul alive could object to me showing my affection for him.

"So much the better. But you shall have one someday. Cannes, Florence, the Greek isles. Weeks and weeks in the land of endless sunshine."

"I can't imagine heaven itself could be more pleasant," I said. "But what about tonight?"

"A wedding feast," he said, ushering me past the army truck and continuing on the sidewalk past the registry office onto the block in Chelyabinsk that housed the few nice restaurants and the hotel where we'd spent our one evening together.

I let him take my hand and escort me to the hotel's posh restaurant. As the maître d' took us to our table, I scanned the small dinner crowd. There were several men in uniform, but the women were all dressed impeccably in fine dresses and furs. I was glad my uniform was crisp and neat, at least, as I took in their finery. *They aren't serving their country. I may not be as elegant as they, but I am useful.*

"I wish you could have worn a lace gown to our wedding, soldier or not," he whispered. "But you're the loveliest woman here."

"Tonight I feel it," I whispered in return.

Vanya ordered a whole host of dishes, this time straying from the familiar rustic fare and venturing into the world of caviar, fine wine, smoked herring mousse, and other foods I'd only heard of. The waiters served small portions of what seemed like dozens of dishes, each providing a few bites before we moved on to the next delicacy. In some cases I was glad to move on, but most of the courses placed before us were beyond what I had imagined food could taste like. The idea of eating fish eggs had repulsed me, despite my mother's assurances that caviar was quite good. The explosion of flavor—a burst of seawater and the most delicate fish—was an experience unto itself. I knew the meal had to cost a small fortune, and I offered silent thanks to Antonin Solonev and his deep pockets.

"I hope you don't mind me throwing this together without telling you first," he said after the waiter cleared away the poached salmon.

"I'll forgive you on one condition," I said. "You will not spend one minute of this evening discussing war or trying to persuade me not to do my part. Let me enjoy one night in peace as your beloved wife."

"How delicious that sounds," he said, unable to keep the smile from his face. "But, agreed. Tonight isn't meant to be spent on such matters. God, I wish we'd had more time, though."

"I know, but we can't speculate on the 'woulds' and 'shoulds' these days. We should be grateful for the time we have."

~

I woke up nestled in Vanya's arms in the moments before dawn. I could have luxuriated in his caresses for a lifetime, but we had to face the morning. Rushkov's goodwill would only last until the morning bell signaled the beginning of classes.

"I wish you'd weaseled a full week out of him," I moaned into his chest.

"Unfortunately for us, I did not catch Rushkov in the act of murdering a party official, so one night was the best I could do. Comrade Soloneva, let your husband admire you one last time before you dress," he purred from the comfort of his down pillows and thick bedding.

I obliged, standing in the brisk morning air, opening a curtain to let the light shine on my pale skin.

"I love to see you when you're thinking like an artist," I mused, unabashed by his gaze on my bare flesh.

He gave a slight start. "How can you tell that's what I was thinking?"

"You expect your wife to betray all her secrets on the first day of wedded bliss? I don't think so."

He pounced atop me, tickling me with fingertips and tender kisses until I begged for mercy.

"It's your expression," I confessed, breathless from his playful assault. "You look both focused and relaxed. Except the time I saw you painting, you've only managed one of those expressions at a time."

"I will spend a lifetime painting you, my love," he said as his eyes and hands roved over every slope and curve of my body. "Thin and agile as you are now, round with my child, wrinkled with old age and contentment. You will be my greatest study."

"And I your loving subject," I said, leaning in to drink in a few more kisses. "But dress, my love. My Vanyusha. I won't have our wedding night marred by a lecture."

With a reluctant sigh he released me, and we checked out of the hotel. We didn't speak as the truck rattled along, but he drove with my hand in his until we crossed onto the campus grounds.

Rather than the usual order and precision we were used to, there was a nervous energy, a thinly controlled chaos, as we entered the mess hall.

"Where have you been?" Taisiya demanded as I took my place next to her.

"I had some leave. I'll explain later." I couldn't risk the entire mess hall overhearing about our elopement. "What is going on here?" Though everyone seemed to be speaking, the volume in the mess hall was about only half the usual buzz, and the tone at every table was strained.

"Katya, Germany invaded yesterday. They've taken Kiev already and are getting closer and closer to Moscow as we speak."

I felt my eyes widen, looking for some sign on Taisiya's face that it was some cruel joke, but there was no trace of irony on her face.

"What's being done?" I asked. "Are we called up?"

"No one knows yet. It sounds like Stalin refuses to believe it's possible. We're all on alert. Graduation and exams are canceled. Every candidate who was passing their courses and who has their hours will get their certificate. The first- and second-years will be promoted tomorrow and continue their training. No summer leave." At least my marriage wouldn't have to remain a secret long. The commanders had far more pressing matters to deal with now.

"So we have our wings," I said numbly.

"Not quite the fanfare we hoped for, is it?" she said, shaking her head.

"It never is, Taisiyushka."

It's not often in the weeks following an invasion that a sentimental wish comes true, but so far mine had. Vanya wasn't called up immediately, leaving us with a few weeks to enjoy our married life. They needed troops quickly, so they called first upon the men at hand in the western cities. We spent two days near Korkino with Vanya's parents, who made their distaste for their new daughter-in-law, so plainly from the working class, quite clear. The Solonev family had amassed a small fortune in coal mining, and while they played by the party's rules, they were allowed to retain much of the wealth they had passed from generation to generation so long as they didn't live lavishly or try to broker power. The trip ended with Vanya storming out of the house with me in tow, and I wasn't sorry to end our visit.

We then took a short trip to Miass, where Mama had the chance to meet Vanya and give us her blessing. He offered her the painting he'd made in the meadow as a token of his filial love and appreciation. My mother was simultaneously overjoyed to have us home for a few days and embarrassed that she had no better home in which to welcome her new son-in-law. She knew what kind of people the Solonevs were. She'd lived among their sort in Moscow and would no longer be truly welcomed among them, save for those who remembered my father. Vanya, however, made not the slightest hint that our humble home was in any way less welcoming than the old Romanov palaces. I loved him for it. He'd immediately set about making himself useful, and was chopping wood for the kitchen fire while Mama and I busied ourselves in the house. He wasn't used to these sorts of chores, but he performed them with enthusiasm, if not skill.

"Put the mending aside, Katinka," Mama said, having set her own hemming aside after ten minutes of staring out the tiny, cloudy window rather than sewing. "Indulge your mama, and let me wash your hair."

A smile tugged at my lips as I followed her to the kitchen sink, placed the back of my chair from the table against it, and tucked in my collar as Mama heated water on the stove. No matter how tired she was, how hard she worked, she always had time to wash my hair on Wednesdays and Saturdays—and long after I was old enough to do it for myself. She made a ritual of it, chatting and taking the time to massage my scalp and scrub gently. She scrimped to buy the good soap for the occasion. I always thought it was her way of apologizing for not being able to do the little motherly things she used to do before Papa was killed. But in those evenings, those long, soapy chats with Mama's strong fingers relieving all my childish worries were worth more than all the homemade cookies and embroidered dresses that she could never provide.

"Do you mind at all, Mama?"

It was usually she who opened these conversations with a query about school or the goings-on with my friends. Given that I had stolen her chance of seeing my wedding, I figured opening the chat was my duty this time.

"Mind that you married an intelligent, handsome, talented young man of good family and solid prospects who also happens to worship the ground at your feet? Not in the least. That I wasn't there to see it? Perhaps a little. That your father wasn't there to give you a proper wedding breaks my heart."

"So you approve of Vanya?" I asked, closing my eyes as she tilted my head and poured the warm water over my red tresses.

"My dear, who could not approve of such a young man for her daughter? And your father would have, too, which is the greatest compliment I can offer."

"Thank you, Mama."

"I must confess, I worried you'd never marry or have a life outside your studies. It seemed you'd spend your life shifting from having your nose in a book to having your head in the clouds—quite literally."

"You always warned me that boys were the fastest course to a derailed dream. You saw it so many times on the stage in Moscow with the other dancers."

"I worried I drove that message to heart a little too well at times," Mama said with a chuckle, her long fingers easing months' worth of tension from my scalp. "Your father cut short my dancing career by a few years—probably not even that much—but I never regretted it. A career, no matter how noble it is, can't be the whole of your life, Katya. You need to have something to work *for*."

"Vanya understands my need to fly," I said, breathing in the deep notes of honey and herbs wafting from the soap. "I don't think I would have been able to marry him if he didn't. Not with the war on, especially."

"He's a remarkable young man, and I am so happy you found him. You deserve some happiness after your hard work in school. I'm just sorry this infernal war will cut it short."

A pall had been cast over Mama's voice. I could offer her platitudes. Tell her that we'd repel the Germans back to their borders by the new year, but I couldn't lie to my mother. That hadn't been the case in the last European War, and it wouldn't be the case this time.

"There were times I wondered where you learned your tenacity," she said. "You must have inherited it from your father. I wanted to be a good role model for you, but I didn't know if a laundress could raise a pilot for a daughter. I'm glad you got that gift from him." I heard a sniff and felt a hand disentangle itself from my mane to wipe away a tear.

"Mama, how can you say that? A less tenacious woman would never have been able to keep food on this table for the past ten years."

"Thank you for saying so, Katinka. I just wanted to give you the best life I could. I couldn't bear to see you at the washing tub next to mine."

"I'm none too proud for that, Mama. But I am glad you urged me to further my studies. Do you remember coming to school to tell Comrade Dokorov I would be studying math and science with the boys?"

"Such a sniveling rat of a man. I heard the party finally gave him a talking-to about how he separated the girls from the boys in the 'serious' subjects. I expect he's changed his curriculum—the party won't 'talk' to him a second time."

"You went in a laundress," I said. "He saw your clothes and your red hands and dismissed you like a scullery maid in a great house. Then you opened your mouth and he saw you were no mere washerwoman. You spoke with eloquence and poise he hadn't expected, and you demanded my education. You were a dragon. If I learned anything about tenacity, it was from you."

Mama wrapped my hair in a towel and motioned for me to sit up. She wrapped her arms around me and kissed my cheeks. With her arms encircling me, I didn't think of all the embraces I'd missed as a child, but of how grateful I was for this one.

A vision of children—little boys with dark hair and little red-haired girls—playing in front of a warm fire flashed in front of me. I had never planned for children, but now they seemed as inevitable a part of my future as taking my next lungful of oxygen. I hoped the war's tide would quickly turn, and I could make sure my children lived in a world where their mother wasn't too broken by work and grief to love her children the way she longed to.

CHAPTER 7

October 1941, Moscow, Russia

"If I never see a train again . . . ," Taisiya muttered after a clanking sound from the next compartment stirred her from a shallow slumber.

"It can't be far now," I consoled her, stowing my novel in defeat. *Moscow.* As the train propelled itself toward the capital, I felt my head throbbing in time with the incessant rattle of the wheels against the rails. Neither reading nor conversation was tolerable, so we both settled in to rest as best we could.

The journey should have only taken two days, perhaps three with bad timing, but we were now on our fifth day. I had always valued Taisiya's friendship in our three years together, but I'd never been more grateful for her presence in my life as on the trek to the capital. At almost every stop anyone who was not an enlisted soldier heading to the front was displaced to the next train. Four nights trying to sleep in drafty train stations, hoping our cadets' uniforms would ward away anyone who might see two women traveling alone as targets.

Since our would-have-been graduation, Taisiya and I had spent two hours each day writing letters to anyone who we thought might listen, begging for our chance to go to the front. There were women at academies and flight clubs all over Russia doing the same. I had hoped our numbers would spark a change, and it seemed that they had. More likely the German troops that had all but waltzed through the western part of the country before arriving just outside the capital had scared Stalin and his men into accepting that they needed us not just in the kitchens, the bedrooms, and the factories, but also behind the wheels of ambulances, in the trenches, and in the air. There is nothing like coming within a hairsbreadth of losing the capital to inspire our leaders to espouse their own ideals of equality.

The letters from the army recruiters finally came in October, and we had to get ourselves to Moscow for interviews to be considered for placement in one of the three airborne female regiments. While they were taking any man or boy able to stand, we had to prove our worth for a few hundred coveted spots. I couldn't think about the odds as the train lurched on, creaking ever forward on the rusty tracks. I couldn't even think about the fact that I was finally returning to Moscow. It had given Mama a smile to think I would be returning home, even if it meant war—or rejection. I wasn't sure which fate she dreaded more for me.

I had thought I might enjoy the three months with my mother between graduation and my deployment, but her eyes looked haunted every time she saw me. And though he was still in training, my worry for Vanya overshadowed everything. I wanted to go to the front and do my part to end the war.

"You're so much like your father," she would say, her dusty blond curls shaking as she chopped the potatoes for the evening soup. *"Bound by duty and honor. You will do your country proud, Katinka."*

Behind her pride, there was unvoiced fear: *Don't let your fate be the same as his.*

She sent me off to the train station with a hug as warm as she'd ever given me. She'd had so little warmth to spare since Papa died, and I thought I had done well enough with the love she'd had to give. As I took my place on the train and felt the engine groan to life, propelling us to Moscow, I felt an emptiness settle into me. What would it have been like to spend my youth with a mother who sang and smiled? What if I had known the strength of my father's embrace, and not just from faded memories? The images of a childhood—brighter, purer—stole the oxygen from my lungs. One question loomed larger over all the others: Would I be on this train, prepared to fly, to fight, to be a warrior, if a stray bullet hadn't claimed my father's life decades too soon?

By the second day on the rattling train, I had become acutely aware that the answer didn't matter. My course was set, and I knew it was the one I needed to take.

When we arrived in Moscow, the interviewers organized us into groups, then had us wait in hard seats until they called us one by one to answer their volley of questions. They didn't bother holding the interviews in heated buildings, but rather drafty tents that gave us little protection against the October chill. It was no accident. If any woman complained about the cold in a tent midday in the autumn, there was no way the army would accept her for flying missions in an exposed aircraft midwinter. I gave wordless praise for the woolen uniform and thick socks, and waited my turn while Taisiya buried herself in the newspaper. She left her manuals and texts in her valise so the others didn't think she needed to cram for her interview. I leafed through one of my advanced flight-training manuals but found the words just swirled on the page.

A guard escorted me to the interviewing area. I avoided eye contact with any of the other recruits who had finished their questioning as they exited to the mess hall or the barracks. I didn't want to read too much into their expressions. Was the major cruel, or was the pilot merely unused to his brusque military manner? I had no way of knowing, and it didn't matter. When the alternative was spending my waking hours in a factory building tanks, or worse, cooped up in Miass knitting socks for the men at the front, to fail this interview would be a disaster.

A young lieutenant, only a few years older than I, took notes as Sofia Orlova herself presided over the interview. The young man had hair somewhere between brown and blond, watery blue eyes, and the weakest chin I had ever seen. He breathed with an irritating wheeze. The perfect sort of man to keep holed up in an office. Major Orlova looked mildly annoyed at his presence but ignored him with her quiet civility as he scratched out my responses to her questions on his notepad.

"Name?"

"Age?"

"Place of birth?"

The litany of questions progressed through all manner of expected topics relating to health, mental stability, and fortitude, but it wasn't until they turned to technical experience with aircraft that I felt the muscles in my shoulders loosen, though I hadn't realized how tense they had become. There was nothing in his dossier that would stump me. If she did not select me, it would not be for my deficiency, but for an overabundance of qualified pilots. That risk seemed remote.

Major Orlova shifted her gaze and attention from the papers before her to my face. She was scrutinizing not only my words, but also everything about my reaction to her final question.

"What calls you to serve Mother Russia as an aviator, Comrade Soloneva?"

The new surname still startled me, but I kept my expression impassive. I sat straighter in my chair and looked into her assessing eyes. "Major, because I was given a gift. I am an excellent navigator, and it is only thanks to the education I have received through the generosity of Mother Russia that I have been able to develop my skills. How could I, in good conscience, not use that gift to come to her aid in her hour of need?"

"Well said, Comrade Soloneva."

I saluted the major and in the coming days, as I waited for her answer, was left with little occupation other than vision and medical screenings. Those of us who completed our interviews early had a few days of relative freedom while Major Orlova personally saw to the rest of the candidates. She insisted on selecting us herself. There were more than two hundred of us, after all, and choosing the best of us was not the task of a single morning. They did their best to keep tabs on our comings and goings, but I had to escape to Moscow on my own, if only for a few hours, to explore the city of my birth and early childhood.

Taisiya, as was her custom, was making friends with all the other women, learning who were the viable contenders and who was likely to be sent home. I had done my share of small talk, though, and sought the freedom of the streets, subdued by the great crowds of gathering troops. It wasn't the safest decision I'd made, but who knew when I would have the chance to see the city again or what would be left of it when I did? Taisiya agreed to explain my absence as an urgent errand in the unlikely event my departure was noticed.

I grabbed Papa's violin and wandered the streets of Moscow until I found the university. It had been more than a decade since I had seen the crumbling brick buildings that my father had so loved. They were full of his history—that which he lived, and that which he taught—and I wanted to be near them, just for a few hours before I left for training or returned to Miass. I removed the instrument, the finish faded so that only hints of the lovely russet color remained. I sat on the steps in front of the building where I was reasonably certain Papa had done the bulk of his teaching, and played his favorite tunes.

I paid no heed to the cold stone steps that chilled my spine, and very little to the scant crowd that buzzed about the campus that seemed unnaturally, uncomfortably quiet. I remembered the buildings humming with life and passion from both instructors and pupils. The war had claimed most of the youth and some of the staff; most of the rest had been evacuated to continue their studies in Turkmenistan. The grounds had taken on an abandoned feel—just as I imagined the old mining towns in the north looked like when the supply of ore was depleted. The conditions weren't much different. The university had been stripped of its most precious commodity and was now left a haunted ruin.

A few passersby stopped to listen, some offering polite applause between songs. I smiled for them on occasion but mostly lost myself in Papa's music. I'm not sure how long I played; it could have been an hour or three. By the time I placed the instrument back in its case, my fingers were numb from the exertion. But for a short time I felt just a little closer to my father and the life that should have been.

It was three days later that the rosters for the female regiments were posted in our makeshift barracks. Against all odds, Taisiya and I were both assigned to the 122nd Aviation Group, where we would presumably serve out the duration of the war.

"I knew they'd keep us," Taisiya said, gripping me in a hug after we cleared the throng of pilots straining to see if they had been assigned.

"Easy to say so now that we have our answer," I said, returning the hug, relief pulling the corners of my lips upward. "But we seemed to have more training than most. I'm hoping that means I'll get a plane of my own."

Taisiya narrowed her eyes for a moment. "Not just training—military training. That's worth months, if not years, of civil experience," she said, her face rapidly turning somber. She'd spent the past three days performing her own interviews on any recruit who would speak with her. She knew the rest of our division as well as Major Orlova by now. "But I'm glad it's worked out for both of us. Serving without you, or being sent home while you got to serve, would have been awful."

The thought of being stationed away from her caused my breathing to grow shallow. I'd considered being sent back while Taisiya got selected—she had more hours as a pilot than I did—but never the possibility that I would be placed in a regiment without her.

We reported to the lieutenant, the wheezy one who had assisted Orlova in interviews, for a short briefing, which concluded with instructions to relocate to the regular barracks on the other end of the grounds. By the time he dismissed us, the women who hadn't been chosen for duty were already gone.

"Orlova made good choices with the recruits," Taisiya said, stowing her things in her duffel as we prepared to move to the training barracks. There wasn't a trace of self-satisfaction in her voice. "A few times I think she favored experience over temperament more than I might have done, but there were a lot of evenly matched candidates. She had to make more than a few tough calls."

"That's good," I said. Taisiya wouldn't have offered her praise lightly. "Do you like them?"

Taisiya looked up from her bag with knitted brows. "I suppose they all seem nice enough. Some had heads a few sizes too big for their helmets; some weren't particularly anxious to chat. Why does it matter?"

"We'll be living and fighting with these women for no one knows how long. It would be nice to get along," I said, folding my uniform blouse around the tiny frame that encased the one photo of Vanya I brought with me. That there was a picture of Matvei in the depths of practical Taisiya's duffel was a marvel to me at times. I pictured her weighing the cost of the extra few grams of the picture in her pack against the benefit of keeping his likeness close. I was glad, for once, to see sentiment win.

"Well, camaraderie is always important," Taisiya conceded, zipping her bag with one fluid movement.

"I wish we could have had the chance to wish the others well." I hoisted my duffel on my shoulder, thinking of the women who had suffered bitter disappointment that afternoon. Some would stay and find ways to make themselves useful on the ground—digging trenches, sewing uniforms, building tanks and ammunition—but many would be returning home on the next trains out of the city.

"I'm not sure how much they'd appreciate it, coming from us," Taisiya said. "I hope they know we *do* wish them well, though."

I remembered the metallic taste of burning jealousy in my mouth every time I was passed over for a less deserving male classmate at the academy. Our silence and good wishes were the greatest kindnesses we could offer.

The regular barracks were not unlike those at the academy, though not as new and sleek. It would be cold in the winter and stifling in the summer, but none of us had any delusions of luxury, or even comfort, as we enlisted. There was an air of giddiness in the room that night, relief at being selected to serve, but no burden of duty yet placed on our shoulders.

"Tomorrow we train; tonight we celebrate. *Une petite gorgée de champagne, mes chères amies?*" A little brown pixie of a woman named Irina floated about the bunkroom serving us cheap sparkling wine in tin cups she'd commandeered from the mess hall when the cook and his staff were occupied with cards.

"Bien sûr," I answered, accepting a cup of the bubbling wine. It smelled sour compared to the wine I'd shared with Vanya, with its clean notes of citrus and perfectly toasted bread that had heightened our palates to a new plane of existence for a few fleeting moments. The best I could say for Irina's offering was that the effervescence was festive and fitting for the general mood in the barracks.

"To my father," said Irina, wearing a smug smile and raising her glass high, "who said Comrade Stalin would never allow women to fly for his country." We lifted ours in answer and let the bubbles trickle down our throats.

A tall blonde named Lada raised her glass, the defiance plain on her angular face. "To my mother, who said I'd never pass muster at the aviation club and told me to look for a nice boy instead."

"To my brothers," Svetlana, a mechanic from Stavropol offered, "who never told on me for borrowing their old trousers so I could play with them like the other boys."

"To my mother, who never told me I couldn't do this or anything else," I said, holding my glass high, not bothering to hide the glistening tears that menaced in the corners of my eyes. "And my husband, who didn't stop me from trying even though he would have traded his own teeth for me to stay home."

"Hear, hear," a few of them said, drinking deeply.

The stories continued for over an hour. We all had someone to thank—either for their support or for exasperating us into success with their doubts. We settled onto bunks, sitting cross-legged, three to a bed on top of the covers. Irina was from Stalingrad. Lada from Minsk. We came from every corner of the country, our families from every kind of circumstance.

"You all ought to get some sleep," a waif of a woman, Oksana, bade us all. She had sharp features and a perpetually unhappy look about her. "Never forget there are several hundred women who would be happy to take our places."

"No need to be a spoilsport," Irina chastised. "We're entitled to a little fun before training, aren't we?"

"Do you think this is cause to celebrate?" Oksana asked. "Any of this? The women who were denied their place? The men at the front dying in droves for a few meters of land?"

"We worked hard to get here," Irina insisted. "I don't see what the harm is."

"And I don't see what the cause is for cheer," Oksana countered.

"I think you've made your point," I said, stepping between them. I stood a full head taller than either woman. My eyes met Oksana's icy-blue stare, and she turned on the ball of her foot, stalking back to her bunk.

"Well, isn't she a box of kittens," Irina muttered as she downed the remains of her champagne and began collecting the tin cups on the ill-gotten tray from the mess hall.

"She's one of the best pilots to come out of Kiev in the past five years," Taisiya said in a quiet voice. "And Orlova knows it. I'd stay on her good side if I were you."

Irina bit back a reply, expelling a resigned sigh. Though Oksana had effectively ended the party, she hadn't quashed the buoyant atmosphere in the barracks. Whispers continued long into the night. Most of us were still in the shallowest stages of sleep when distant blasts sounded and the screech of sirens pierced the night air.

"Get up, ladies!" a commanding bark came from the door. Major Orlova stood at the entryway to the barracks. "Get dressed, grab your duffels, and leave by the east door. Do not run, or I will send you home myself."

Silent panic painted the faces of my new comrades in arms, and I was sure it was mirrored on my own. I threw my coat over my pajamas—army-issued long underwear now, having forsaken the soft flannel back in Miass—and donned my clumsy boots, cursing each second it took to lace them. I tossed my duffel over one shoulder and gripped Papa's violin in the other hand. I now questioned how wise it had been to bring the instrument with me, but I couldn't bring myself to part with it when I left home. I exited the barracks to find panicked-looking officers lamely watching the legions of German aircraft approaching from the west, illumined by searchlights that scanned the sky over the city.

We stood, just as dumbstruck as they for a moment, as the reality washed over us like the frigid waters of high tide.

The Germans had reached the capital. We were going to lose Moscow.

The horizon glowed orange with artillery fire. *How close were the ground troops?* The metallic tang in my mouth let me know I didn't want to know the answer. The usually unflappable Taisiya's eyes were wide as we surveyed the scene before us. Half the base was ablaze, and everyone was looking for orders where there were none to give. Before now war had been but an idea. Now it was a very real thing that had come to our doorstep.

"To the mess hall!" Orlova barked, and we lurched into motion. There was a cavernous basement below it that was the closest thing we had to a proper bomb shelter. It wasn't blast-proof but would withstand a lot more than our exposed barracks. I didn't want to hide below-ground like a coward, but we had no training together as a unit. We would be worse than useless.

An unearthly screech streaked over my head, and I fought against the urge to cower. We had to keep moving. The bomb made contact with the squat gray training building to our south, shaking the ground beneath our feet so violently my teeth cracked together. Taisiya stumbled over a stray hunk of brick that landed in our path, and I grabbed her hand before she fell to the asphalt.

"My God," she rasped. I could feel her body trembling as I gripped her elbow and waist to steady her. The German planes were swooping down like falcons over our airfield, leaving our aircraft and equipment in a wake of fire.

"Keep moving," I urged her, scanning the scattered lines of recruits that stretched in front of and behind me. No one had fallen back, no injuries serious enough to slow their progress. *Keep moving, all of you. Anyone who stops is a much better target.*

Two men in uniform emerged from their blasted building. One limped so badly his ankle had to be broken; the other looked to be nursing severe burns on his arms. Both had lacerations and scrapes on their hands and faces. The burned man looked at us, his wild eyes desperately hunting for a helpful face. I longed from the center of my gut to reach out to him. To help him to safety, to put salve on and bandage his wounds, but I marched on. I was no medic, and we didn't dare break ranks now. He could follow us if he was able.

We marched forward, though we wanted to run to safety. Another bomb whizzed overhead, landing on what had been our barracks five minutes before, but we did not run. I forced in a smoky breath that singed the hairs of my nose and gnawed at the tender flesh in my throat and pressed on.

We reached the relative safety of the basement below the mess hall. The walls trembled as bombs dropped, raining down furiously at first, and slowing as the night continued. None of us attempted to sleep on the damp floor amid the rumbling and crashing above us, but as I looked at the faces of my new comrades in arms, I noticed concern, but no fear or dread. No tears.

This was only the first taste of what we would see in battle, and it was clear Orlova had chosen women made of ice and steel.

CHAPTER 8

Muscovites fled from the city like grains of sand spilling from a shattered hourglass. The Germans had made it to the heart of our country, and there was nothing for the residents of the capital to do but seek the safety of the countryside. I hoped safety was somewhere to be found for them.

There were three hundred pilots who needed new training grounds, and all of us looked to Major Orlova for guidance. Three days after the attack, she had ushered us to these mercifully (if ineffectively) heated freight cars, clearly designed for equipment and supplies instead of passengers. Now we sat on their floors, letting ourselves sway back and forth in time with the discordant rocking of the train. I had fashioned my duffel into a cushion and propped it against the wall of our car, finding a small measure of comfort in the padding against my aching shoulders.

"Do you know where we're going?" Irina whispered after several hours of rattling.

After years of seeing the military machine in action, Taisiya and I knew we'd have the answer when they were prepared to give it. That wasn't the answer the other girls wanted to hear.

"Southeast is all I can tell," Taisiya replied. "Like everyone else who isn't going to the front. They're likely hunting for new training quarters for us and want us farther from the front."

"I wish they'd tell us how much longer we have in this wretched box," Lada muttered, her face a shade of frog green violent enough to be visible even in the dim light from the cracks in the doors of the freight car.

"A pilot who gets trainsick?" Irina chided. "Fine picture that paints."

"Go play on the track, will you?" Lada growled.

"Play nice, girls," I chastised with a wink. "They'll tell us when they have news, I'm sure. We just have to pass the time."

"Matvei is well," Taisiya said, poring with a tiny flashlight over one of the letters that had been forwarded to Moscow, her head bobbling along with the rattle of the train. "The food is dreadful, and he misses his mother's *kotleti* and potatoes, but he likes his comrades well enough. It doesn't sound like he's at the front."

"I'm glad," I said, patting her knee. She hadn't been able to read the letter, with the chaos of the last few days, but seeing his handwriting on a piece of paper no more than two weeks old had caused her shoulders to drop a few centimeters and her breathing to deepen, visibly. "I haven't heard from Vanya since we arrived in Moscow."

"I'm sure he's fine," she said, taking my hand for a moment. "He's one of the best pilots Chelyabinsk has seen."

"He didn't seem particularly distressed in his last postcard," I admitted—not right at the front, no imminent danger, from what I could read. The situation may have changed in the passing weeks, but I knew deep in my gut that he was still alive. Not happy. Not well. But at least alive.

"Your Matvei would do well to be grateful instead of bemoaning the loss of his mother's cooking," Oksana said, looking up from her book, the title of which I couldn't make out because her hands obscured it. She'd made her nest across from us, and I'd hoped we'd be able to use some of the interminable journey to become better acquainted. She showed no interest. "Compared to the villagers that surround him, he's eating like a king."

"So that he has the strength to defend them," Taisiya countered, folding the letter and stuffing it carefully, though forcefully, back in its envelope.

"It does no good to defend a people who have starved to death," Oksana said, returning to her book.

A rush of blood warmed my cheeks. "You know we're going to be defending those same people, right? And will be fed the same soldiers' rations?" At least, I assumed that was going to be the case. If they gave us men's clothes, they ought to feed us like men as well.

"Yes, but I won't complain about the food I don't have while I *have* something to eat and others don't." Her blue eyes blazed hot over her tattered pages.

Taisiya made to stand, but I gripped her hand to stop her. No good would come of whatever she had planned.

"Matvei is making a remembrance of home," I said, my voice clear enough to bounce off the walls of the clattering metal tube. "He's honoring who he's fighting for and the life he wants to go back to. He'll be a better soldier for it."

Major Orlova moved over to our portion of the car just in time to hear my pronouncement. "Hear, hear, Katya," she said, taking the spot on the floor next to Oksana. "The best soldier is a homesick one. They know what they're fighting for."

"I agree," Taisiya said, flashing a superior glance at Oksana and beaming a smile at Major Orlova.

"Are you ladies faring well enough?" Orlova asked.

"As well as can be expected, Major," I replied. "I've had all I'll ever need of never-ending train rides, though."

"Too right. It looks like it will be more like a few more days," Orlova said, her expression showing no stoicism at the prospect. "For a trip of nine hundred kilometers. We'd practically do as well to walk, but we have supplies to take with us. And when we're not in training, call me Sofia, please."

The three of us looked at our commander without blinking for a moment. That was not the behavior of a major in the Red Army, but it was not for us to question her.

"Do they know where they're sending us, then?" Irina asked, wrapping an arm around Lada, who had slipped further into her misery.

"Not precisely," she answered. "They're looking at a few options. Military schools the chief among them, given that we'll be in training."

"Will we be in training long?" I asked, sitting up straighter. "When do they expect to send us to the front?" Surely our three years of training should be sufficient.

"I like your enthusiasm," Orlova said, smiling. She recalled all our names without hesitation, though she'd only known us for a few days. "But I don't think there are any expectations yet. We have a wide range of experience in this group, and we need to see where each of you belongs. The commanders in place will call us up when we're ready."

"Or whenever they have need of us, whichever happens first," Oksana said humorlessly.

"There is truth in that," Orlova agreed. "But there are more trained pilots than there are aircraft for us to fly. We're going to have to prove we're ready before we're deployed. It took all my influence with Comrade Stalin to get this operation off the ground. But I promise you the training will be nothing like what you've been used to."

~

The train deposited us near the base in Engels, and we arrived well past dark, and under blackout conditions. We walked carefully to avoid stumbling on the path that was lit only by the glow of the waxing moon. Our airfield was perched on the edge of a sprawling plain, unprotected from the howling winds that ripped through the expanse like razor blades. Fog pierced our thick woolen uniforms as though they were thin muslin frocks. From what I could see, the training grounds were bleak and industrial, like most every single structure that had been built in Chelyabinsk in the past ten years. The party had no time for grace in architecture anymore. Vibrant colors and elegant lines fell victim to efficiency and function.

Those of us with training fell in line first just behind Orlova, everyone else clamoring for a place in the rear. I had never thought I'd see the value in learning to march. The guards on duty scrambled at the sight of three hundred women approaching the gates of the air base.

"W-we were told to expect one hundred, possibly one hundred and twenty recruits, Major," a sergeant stammered, looking out over our shivering forms as he swung open the chain-link wide enough to admit us.

"You were misinformed," Orlova replied, tugging her woolen uniform jacket tighter about her chest against the bone-penetrating fog. "And no one was told to show us the way from the train station?"

"I'm sorry, Major. All I can tell you is that I wasn't given the order to do it." The young man had the good sense to look ashamed at the breach of conduct.

"Nor was anyone else. No matter now. Do the best you can for tonight, and we'll sort things out in the morning. My recruits need sleep."

"Very well, Major," the sergeant said, visibly relieved to be able to pass the task of finding us proper accommodations along to someone else. "Please follow me."

He led us to a massive gymnasium with thick concrete walls and a wooden floor that amplified sound. I could only imagine what the snores of three hundred exhausted recruits would sound like in fifteen minutes' time. There were dozens of bunks matched up in precise rows, lining the walls and in two long rows in the middle. Gray, fraying mattresses offered next to no protection from the metal supports, and we'd have nothing but our bedrolls for linens. The room hovered somewhere just above freezing and smelled distinctly of unwashed latrine.

Welcome to the military life, ladies. Taisiya and I exchanged a quick glance, wondering who would be the first to grouse and how quickly Major Orlova would find her a place on a train heading eastward. Had they shown us this space as part of our admissions questionnaire and warned us it would be the best lodgings we could expect for the duration of the war, our responses would have given Sofia and the rest of the brass a very accurate picture of which of us were capable of service.

"Make yourselves as comfortable as you can, ladies," Major Orlova said, likely calculating the number of needed bunks.

"So long as we aren't on a moving train, I won't complain," I said, throwing my bedroll on an open spot on the floor, away from the chill that wafted off the concrete walls like frozen fog. *Let the unseasoned girls have the beds.*

"Your bedroom is this way, Major." The sergeant motioned for her to follow him through the doorway that led to an adjoining hallway.

"What do you mean, Sergeant?" Orlova said, tossing her duffel on a nearby bunk.

"The commanders thought you'd appreciate your own accommodations," he explained, blanching a little as she stood, arms akimbo, willing him into oblivion.

"This I have to see," she announced, walking toward the hallway, the sergeant scrambling to match her pace.

In little more than a minute she returned, the sergeant noticeably absent.

"Absolutely incredible," Orlova growled, rolling out her bedroll on the rank mattress. "A private room with a rug? Flowers? What am I doing here—training pilots, or debutantes?"

"I'll be happy to cede my place on the floor if you really want to show them how angry you are," I called from my nest, the unyielding cement beneath me causing my hips to ache.

"It's a good thing I like you, Soloneva." Orlova crawled into her bed with an audible grunt. Chuckles bounced off the walls as the major's disdain dissipated.

I rolled to my side, the floor cruelly reminding me of its presence with every movement. I tugged my bedroll tighter, though I knew it wasn't equal to the cold that enveloped the room. Taisiya's breathing had already given in to soft snores as she lay curled up on the patch of floor next to mine, and again I envied her gift of falling asleep almost instantly.

I listened to the breathing go shallow all around me. Was Vanya any more comfortable than I was? Was he reasonably warm? Well fed? Unlikely.

I thought of Mama in her cabin. Comfortable and warm most of the time, no real want of food—but isolated. Unprotected.

It didn't soften the unforgiving floor but made me far more tolerant of it.

We were called to assembly to begin our training just after dawn the morning after we arrived. The icy hangar where we gathered did little more than shield us from the bitterly cold wind.

When we returned, we found our scant belongings waiting on the feet of our new bunks, our uniforms folded in piles so neat they appeared to have been placed on the thin mattresses by machine. I discarded my flight-school uniform and took the drab-green jacket and trousers from the pile, lamenting that I could never replicate the precise folds.

The jacket fit well enough, though somewhat tight across the bust and hips, but loose at the waist. The trousers were a disaster; they were so large at the waist that I had to cinch my belt to the smallest notch to keep them from falling in a green woolen puddle around my ankles. Only the thinnest women with few curves were able to wear the uniforms properly. Oksana's and Polina's uniforms fit passably well, but neither fit as well as Major Orlova's, who clearly had a uniform that was made to her size.

"Who tailored these things?" I wondered aloud, looking down at my figure in disgust.

"Men," Taisiya said without humor. Her uniform was as ill fitting as mine, and she looked just as happy about it. She held up a pair of standard-issue underpants with the telltale flap in front. "Tailored by men, and for men to do a man's job."

"They know how to make us feel wanted, don't they?" My underpants were just the same, and my boots a size 42—so large they rattled loose on my feet like those on a boy sporting his father's shoes.

"Let's go see the quartermaster," Taisiya suggested, tossing her uniform aside and changing back into her cadet garb.

"Do you want to come with us, Oksana?" I asked, thinking as I donned proper-fitting clothes that to include her would be a kind gesture.

"To what end?" she asked, cinching her belt tighter around her waist.

"New uniforms?"

"Good luck with that," Oksana said, bitterness dripping from her every syllable.

Taisiya and I rolled our eyes in unison as we turned away and started off. Oksana's skills had to be enviable if she'd advanced this far with such a foul attitude.

The quartermaster sat in a massive room next to the hangars, where endless racks housed everything from helmets and ammunition to canned food and boots. When we knocked at the door, he did not bother looking up from the smudgy-gray pages of his ledger.

"What is it?" he croaked, taking a drag off a stubby cigarette.

"Our uniforms," Taisiya said, her voice lowering an octave as she spoke to the wizened old man. "It seems you sent men's uniforms to the women's regiment."

"What did you expect?" He finally looked up from his tattered volume. "The army doesn't make women's uniforms."

"What are we to do about it?" I asked, my tone sharper than I intended. "They don't fit properly, and we've got to stand for inspection this evening. The boots are all enormous."

With a dramatic sigh, he pushed back his chair and rose, hobbling over to a large cabinet with a stiff gait that betrayed the fact that he probably hadn't risen to his feet in hours. He returned to his desk with four spools of green thread, the same dismal shade of green as our uniforms, and two packets of needles.

"If you want uniforms that fit, I suggest you ladies call upon your proper skills and get to work."

I bit back an insult and could tell Taisiya was swallowing her words as well. I wanted to hurl the spools back at his shriveled face and tell him to do the sewing himself and let us pilots do our jobs, but quartermasters were always senior officers. Anything remotely that insulting would have seen me on the next train back to the Urals and stripped of my wings.

As we returned to the barracks, armed with our thread and needles, I silently thanked my mother for the late-night sewing lessons she forced on me. By the time we started our lessons, after the dinner plates were cleared away, she was so tired she would fall asleep when I was midseam, and I would have to wake her to get her instructions on how to continue. I loathed disturbing her, but now I was glad she insisted.

Back in the barracks Taisiya flung herself on her bunk and held up the underpants once again. "Well, at least we have a place to keep our lipstick," she said, sticking her fingers through the flap.

I laughed despite the absurd task before me and smiled appreciatively at Taisiya.

"They didn't completely forget that we're women," Renata lamented, strapping herself in the shining, white, army-issue brassiere. It held her breasts in like a girdle, making her wince uncomfortably as she hooked it closed. "Damned torture device."

"A joy," I agreed. I'd been wearing a similar brassiere since I started at the academy. Anything to make my femininity less apparent.

Two hours later I'd done a passable job of taking in the waist on the trousers and had basted in the waist of the jacket well enough to stand inspection. I would have to find a larger block of free time to let out the bust of the jacket and alter the silhouette properly.

Sofia came in to find us with our uniforms in pieces and questioned what we were doing.

"There must be a mistake," Sofia said when Taisiya explained the problems with the uniforms. "Perhaps the quartermaster was sent the wrong uniforms."

"No, Major. We asked, and there was no mistake. Since the uniforms aren't suitable as they are, we're doing our best to make them fit," I said, gesturing to the green mass on my bed.

"I'm not sure why I expected differently." For a moment Sofia's bravado vanished. Her lips formed a grim line. "It will be the first of many times we're called to alter things to suit, ladies. Carry on."

CHAPTER 9

"Lieutenant Soloneva, may I speak with you? And Lieutenant Pashkova?" Sofia called to us between training runs as we stretched our legs, cramped by hours in the tiny cockpit. Oksana was at her flank, but her expression didn't betray any distress.

"Of course," I said, falling into pace with her, Taisiya joining behind us.

"Ladies, you have an advantage that many of these women don't—military training. Discipline," she said, turning to face us when we were several yards away from the nearest pair of ears.

"These women are some of the most dedicated pilots I've encountered," I said, remembering the antics of some of the cadets at the academy who had the full benefit of "military discipline."

"I don't mean to imply otherwise," she replied without malice. "I wouldn't have picked them if they weren't. But they're new to our way of life all the same. I'm looking to you to set a good example."

"I hope we've done so thus far," Taisiya said, the color in her face draining a few shades.

"Without question," Orlova replied. "Your calm during the evacuation, your cool heads were admirable. I need you to know that I'm relying on you to be the model for this continued exemplary behavior. Especially when resolve is tested—which it will be."

We nodded our assent, not that we had much option to do otherwise.

We assembled an hour later for our evening briefing. She offered her praise for the day's performance and a few notes of censure and advice.

"The last act of the day, ladies, is to report to the post barber." Fretful whispers broke what had until then been a respectful silence. The blue of Orlova's eyes looked bright as she scanned the crowd. More than a few women patted their manes, most of which dipped well past their shoulders. Orlova's blond locks were already cut to just below her ears in a bob, giving her a tidy appearance that Stalin himself would have applauded in one of his warriors.

We walked with all the cheer of pallbearers in a funeral procession to the building that housed the post barber. Two or three women cried openly at the sight of the team of barbers waiting grim faced for the first of us to claim the six open seats. We all hung back as though the seats were torture devices. Sofia waited with another officer in the corner, their eyes scanning the throng of nervous pilots.

This is simply the first test. The first of the sacrifices we will be asked to make.

Military discipline. This is what she'd meant. I took a step forward, inhaled deeply, and took my place with the sternest looking of the men. I freed my wavy auburn hair from its chignon and closed my eyes. I tried not to think of the stolen hours with Vanya as he ran his fingers through the long tresses. Fiery, he'd called them.

I fought to keep from cringing as I heard the slow metallic scrape of the scissor blades as the barber severed the locks from my head. I opened my eyes and focused on the women who looked at me. They dreaded having to follow my lead, but it was the price of service.

Snip. Snip. Scrape.

I could not look at the pool of red at my feet as the barber snipped, but I would not let my anguish travel from my heart to my eyes. Taisiya took the seat next to mine and released her hair from her pins with a curt order to the gangly young barber she'd selected to get on with his business. My eyes flitted over to her seat, where she kept her own grimace at bay. *Well done, Taisiyushka. We'll be ugly together.*

The barber made short work of my mane, and I escaped the chair the moment he tapped my shoulder to signal that he'd finished with me. Sofia shot me a shallow smile, appreciative I'd been the first to fall in line. Once free of the barbers' quarters, I sought out my bunk, glad at least that the sting of tears didn't threaten.

I groaned as I heard Oksana's footsteps echo through the otherwise empty barracks. Her hair was already cropped fairly short, but she had allowed the barber to shape her bob to a crisp angle that set off the severe lines in her high cheeks and long, shapely nose. Her hair wasn't the lustrous golden blond that Sofia had been graced with, but a shade or two closer to silver or platinum. A bit more down to earth. I might have found her less intimidating than Sofia if every word from her lips, every movement she made, wasn't calculated to keep the world at a distance.

"It will grow back," she said, opening her duffel to recover a book.

"I'm not that worried about it," I said, realizing it was true. I could have my length back in a few years. It wasn't as though there would be anyone at the front lines with the time to worry about our haircuts. "I came in here because I just wanted some peace while the others got their cuts."

The post was always a hive, so silence was a rare commodity. She reclined on her bunk with her novel, happy to oblige my need for quiet.

After perhaps a quarter of an hour, I summoned the courage to take my small hand mirror from my trunk to assess the barber's handiwork. He was not deft with his scissors, but it wasn't a ruthless hack job, either. The short cut threw every line and angle of my face into sharp relief, though my face would never have the chiseled quality that Oksana's did. I did look harsh, though, the softness in my face all but gone.

I wondered if I could ever reclaim it again.

~

If we lamented our haircuts, the saving grace was that we weren't given much time to fret. Sofia coordinated all the training, and we were in the classroom or in a plane for almost eighteen hours every day. As thorough as our training in our academies and flight schools had been, the intensity was now doubled. The women who'd been trained in little flight clubs were getting three years of military curriculum in a few months, and the rest of the trained recruits wouldn't exactly be on holiday. I'd been selected for navigator training, which meant an extra hour of studying Morse code in the morning, before the pilots and crews woke.

Even Taisiya, as stoic and calm as she was, had become more withdrawn and had lost a few kilos.

"Eat," I chided her at lunch one afternoon. "It may not be appetizing, but it's worlds better than what we'll have at the front."

"I'm not hungry," she muttered, poring over a text Sofia had specifically recommended to her, chewing the end of her pencil as she read. But to silence me she picked at the mashed potatoes and gray hunk of meat the mess sergeant had slopped onto the metal tray. It was just as well she wouldn't abandon her text for the meal; the best way to eat military rations was quickly and while looking at the food as little as possible.

Lada, sitting several places down at the long table, shrieked. A tendril of her thick, blonde hair had fallen into her hand.

"For God's sake, stop twirling it," I snapped. "Cropped hair is bad enough—do you want to be bald?"

"I'm not doing it on purpose," she protested.

"Well, you'd better learn to control yourself," Oksana cut in. "The doctors will ground you if they think you've got the mange."

She chuckled softly, and everyone stared in response, unsure how to take her uncharacteristically flippant remark.

"It was meant to be a joke," she said, tossing her fork on her empty tray, depositing it in the washing bin, and stalking out to the airfield.

"I'll never understand that girl," Lada said, shaking her head.

"We don't need to understand her; we just need to work with her," I said, scraping up the last mouthful of tasteless potatoes so as to avoid censure from the cook. "Coming, Taisiya?"

"Mmm-ummm," she murmured, still not looking up from her book.

"Suit yourself," I said, following Oksana's trajectory out of the mess hall.

I fetched my violin from the barracks and found a seat in the little makeshift recreation center that was usually empty save for the hour or two just after dinner and before we dragged our weary bodies to bed. Music seemed a better outlet for nerves than ruining my hair or straining my eyes over books I'd already memorized.

The violin cupped to my chin, familiar as an old friend, as I let the bow glide over the strings. I refused to play the laments Papa had favored. There was not room in my soul for more sadness and worry. Sweet waltzes and simple tunes took me away from the steel and concrete ugliness for a few stolen moments, rendering the endless sea of grays, browns, and dirty greens almost endurable.

"You play well, Soloneva."

The male voice called me back to the present in the midst of a song. I stifled a sigh of disappointment as I saw an instructor, Captain Fyodorov, stride in to take a seat near mine. He lit a cigarette and reclined in his chair. He seemed generally the good sort—more amused than annoyed by our presence. I'd navigated for him on a number of runs, and he was a more-than-capable pilot, though he lacked Vanya's grace and Taisiya's instinctive tactical skills.

"Thank you," I said. "I find that playing at lunchtime refreshes me for the afternoon classes."

"They have you girls on a tough schedule, that's for sure," he said with a dismissive wave of the hand that gripped the cigarette. Some ash flitted over in my direction, and I had to brush the hot ember from my instrument before the finish was marked by it. Were he not a superior officer, I would have berated him for the careless gesture.

"Military school at top speed," I agreed. "But it's good to know who can handle it and who can't." I remembered the cadets at the academy—male and female—who bent under the strain of rigorous training even outside the immediate threat of war.

"The brass wanted to be sure you girls could handle combat so we don't waste aircraft. I think the whole exercise is ridiculous," he said, taking a long drag off his cigarette. "A few of you with military training can handle it. Most will be begging to go home in three weeks, mark my words."

"I won't contradict you, Captain. I can only do my part to prove you wrong." I placed my violin and bow back in their case, snapping the latch harder than I should have done. Now that my peace was shattered, there was no sense in trying to piece it back together.

"Now, now. Don't get in a huff," he said. "I rather enjoy my post, if I'm telling the truth. Far from the front and all that. And you girls make for much nicer scenery than the trenches."

I rolled my eyes and stood to leave. I might get a reprimand for disrespecting a senior officer, but I would ask for forgiveness later.

"You're angry with me." He stood and placed his nose even with mine. It wasn't a question.

"You're observant," I said, gripping my case until I could feel the skin straining painfully over my white knuckles.

"Of course you are. You're out of your proper element. Anyone would be out of sorts to be so out of place."

"In fact, I am 'out of place,' Captain. I'm expected in class in just a few moments, and unless I want to explain why I've arrived with my violin in tow, I need to be on my way." I turned to the door but felt his hand grip my elbow.

"Don't be churlish," he said, mirth and malice seeping from his words. "That's not what I meant."

"I know what you meant, but I haven't any desire to spend time in the brig for telling you what I think. Let me go." I motioned to leave, but he refused to loosen his grip.

"You do know where a woman's proper place is, don't you? I can see it in your eyes. You like men, don't you?"

"My husband in particular," I said, yanking my elbow free.

"You know he's probably got a flatback in every town he's been to, right? They're all like that. Why not have some fun yourself?"

He grabbed my arm again, this time pulling me to his chest. He gripped my hair with his other hand and forced my lips to his. His tongue invaded my mouth, probing, claiming. He moved his hand from my elbow to clutch my backside, squeezing painfully. I tried to push him back, but his bravado was matched by his bulk.

Clamping the handle of the violin case as tightly as my fingers would allow, I drew the case out wide, then drove its narrow end with all my might into the side of his head. He released me at once, staggering backward, and I stormed from the recreation center before he could retaliate.

Thankfully the barracks were empty. I would not need to face my sisters in arms or my instructors with the hot tears of anger tracing the contours of my face. Had I less respect for one of the few mementos I had of my father, I would have thrown the violin in my trunk with enough force to send it through the reinforced wood at the bottom and ten centimeters deep into the concrete. As it was, I worried the captain's thick skull might have damaged the scroll or the fragile pegs when I sent the case crashing into it.

I sat at the edge of my bunk, put my face in my hands, and focused on quelling my rage. I had to show mastery of myself, for there was no doubt I'd be called in for what I'd done. Well, at least Mama and Vanya would have their way. I'd be sent home. But with a black mark on my record that would keep me from teaching anywhere but a tiny flight club in some far-flung eastern village.

"Lieutenant Soloneva." Sofia's voice pierced the silence of the empty barracks. "You're wanted in the officers' quarters. There seems to be some concern as to why Captain Fyodorov may be suffering from a concussion."

I took three more steadying breaths before looking up at her in the doorway. I couldn't appear weak—not even to her. "I was trying to get him to stop," I said, keeping my tone even.

As her blue eyes scanned my face, I saw comprehension wash over them. *What had she endured? What did she know of men like him? Can any woman like us be completely sheltered from this?*

"I believe you, Katya," she said, stepping fully into the room and taking a seat next to me. "But it's not me you'll have to convince."

"They're going to send me home, aren't they?"

"Not if they listen to me. Fyodorov won't fare well if I have my way." She did an admirable job of keeping the rancor from her voice, but the anger was there.

"Will they listen?"

"It's not their strong suit, Katya. But you have me on your side. It will count for more than nothing."

"The fact remains that she assaulted her superior officer," the colonel, a gangly man by the name of Krupin, growled from his seat. "Do you think we can tolerate such behavior from a junior lieutenant?"

Sofia and I stood at attention. I could tell from the tone of her voice to this point that she was rankled that she had not yet been ordered to stand at ease, much less sit, in his presence. He was two ranks above her, but such formality was rarely exercised with the other commanders.

"I would usually agree with you, but this is an unusual case, Colonel Krupin."

"Because Junior Lieutenant Soloneva is female, I suppose?" He blew a huge cloud of gray smoke from his wheezing lungs and extinguished the butt of his cigarette in an overflowing ashtray.

"Not precisely. Because Captain Fyodorov is male and was trying to make unwanted advances on one of his students." The muscles in my neck ached to turn and see the expression on her face, but I didn't dare.

The old man, who greatly resembled a goat in a drab-green uniform, grumbled but said nothing.

"Don't you agree that's the offense we need to be addressing here, Colonel?" Sofia pressed on. "With all the dangers our soldiers face, they should not expect to be on guard against their own commanders and instructors. I needn't tell you what these pilots will be up against. What they are sacrificing. Will you allow one of your own junior commanders to make light of their dedication, Colonel?"

His watery gaze shifted to me. "Why were you not with the rest of your regiment, Soloneva?"

"We have a short break between lunch and the afternoon tactical sessions, Colonel. I was using the time to practice the violin. It soothes me." I felt my hands shake behind my back and hoped the rest of my body appeared still.

"You find the classes that taxing, do you?"

Sofia stepped in. "Most soldiers find intense training on five hours of sleep to be taxing, Colonel."

"Careful, Orlova. My patience has its limits, no matter how much I like you. Soloneva, do you think it was wise for you to be alone?"

"I hadn't thought to consider my fellow commanders a threat to my safety, Colonel. I have never been given cause to think so in my three years in a military academy or at one moment before now since I enlisted."

"Well said, Soloneva," Sofia said.

"And you take her word as truth, without reservation, Major?" the colonel asked.

"Unreservedly," she replied. "I chose these recruits carefully, and I assure you I had more talented applicants than we could find planes and uniforms for, Colonel. She has a spotless record and is one of the finest navigators who applied for service."

"Very well," Krupin said, sitting back in his chair. "Soloneva will have no formal consequences for these unfortunate events. Though I suggest you have a good talk with her about appropriate conduct, Orlova."

"It will be a short conversation, Colonel, as Soloneva has never shown any tendency toward *inappropriate* conduct. What of Fyodorov, Colonel? What will be done about him?"

"That's of no concern to you, Orlova," he said, lighting a fresh cigarette.

"You're much mistaken. He took advantage of his position with a junior officer. He compromised the safety of one of *my* navigators. You cannot think I can allow that to go unpunished."

"That's not for you to decide."

"It's for you to decide his punishment, Colonel, but I will know he has been dealt with satisfactorily, or I will take it above your head." She relaxed her stance without invitation and took a step closer to his desk.

Krupin had the good sense to blush at Sofia's words. He was not a fool, and he knew exactly how high her influence reached.

"I'll give him a stern talking-to," he said after a pause.

"That's not sufficient. He must be disciplined proportionately with his offense. If you caught him assaulting a civilian woman, what would be done? Soloneva has every right to the same consideration."

"Very well . . . I'll have him transferred. They'll have need of him at the front soon anyway."

"That's better. And I suggest you tell the rest of your men why the transfer is happening. If I catch another of your commanders so much as taking an unwanted second look at a woman under my command, a transfer will be the least of his worries. I'll personally strap him to a bomb and drop his carcass from my very own aircraft over the nearest German outpost. Is that clear enough for you, Comrade?"

"Inescapably, Major." He shook his head darkly. "You know, this entire program of yours is causing me more headaches than it can possibly be worth. Wives of my officers writing to complain about women serving alongside their husbands. Knowing what mischief they might get up to as night falls."

"I thought you above housewives' petty gossip, Colonel. I'm sorry to find out I was mistaken."

We saluted and left his quarters at a brisk pace. I felt my shoulders tense and my breathing become shallow as we put distance between Krupin and ourselves, as though he might change his mind and send me back to Miass anyway, despite Sofia's threats.

"Thank you," I managed to say as we approached the training area. "I owe you my wings."

"Don't thank me. You did nothing wrong. Never forget that. If you want to thank me for your wings, then get back to your training and use them."

CHAPTER 10

January 1942

The bleary faces of the other recruits blurred together as we stumbled back to the barracks. The training continued from before dawn to long past dark. Every night we dragged ourselves to our bunks as quickly as our feet would carry us. Every moment of sleep was precious.

"Soloneva, Pashkova. A word, please." Sofia's brisk footsteps echoed behind us against the concrete walls.

She's inhuman. How can she have so much energy?

"Yes, Major?" I replied, turning to face her.

I wasn't proud of the perverse pleasure I took in seeing the dark circles under her eyes, but they were the only sign the hours were taxing even her seemingly indefatigable reserve of energy.

"Come with me."

She ushered us to the closet-sized room she'd commandeered as an office. Room just enough for her desk and three chairs. Tidy stacks of papers lined her desk at perfect right angles. No photographs or anything that betrayed this as a personal space.

"Ladies, I know you're anxious to sleep, so I'll get to it. I'll be dividing us up into three regiments tomorrow. We're to have a fighter regiment and two bomber regiments—one a regular bomber regiment, and the other to fly harassment missions at night."

"I'd prefer to fly with the fighters, of course," Taisiya interjected. "If you brought us in to ask our assignment preferences."

"I already knew the answer to that question, Taisiya. It's the assignment you all want. Unfortunately I don't have the planes to make that happen for all of you. I need you two with the night bombers. Your primary mission will be to keep the Germans awake and destroy as much of their camps as you can."

"That seems like a poor use of our training." The fatigue was too great for me to use any sort of filter, even with Sofia. "This seems like a job for newer pilots. It won't take much tactical finesse."

"First, don't assume that. Second, winning this war will have a lot less to do with tactical finesse and a lot more to do with leadership. Good pilots are much easier to come across than good leaders."

"If this has already been decided, then why are you talking to us, if I may speak candidly? You simply could've posted our assignments along with everyone else's." Taisiya's tone wasn't impertinent—she was looking for the logic in the decision-making, as she always did.

"Behind closed doors, I hope you will always speak freely," Sofia said, rubbing her bloodshot eyes and abruptly busying her hands with a pen, perhaps to avoid making the gesture again. "I wanted you to know the assignment has nothing to do with your abilities as pilots. Quite the contrary. If we staffed the night bombers with only our least experienced recruits, we would be putting them at a perilous disadvantage. They need our strongest pilots and navigators to show them how it's done. I'm asking you to do this for me."

"Are you giving us a command, Major?" Taisiya asked. I tried not to look boggle-eyed at the prospect. I expected to fly in combat, not to lead a regiment.

"So important is this regiment, that I'll be forgoing my place at the head of the 586th and will command the night-bomber regiment myself, despite risking Comrade Stalin's displeasure. I've asked Lieutenant Tymoshenko—Captain now—to serve as my deputy commander. She's got a few years more experience than you have and has earned the attention of the good colonel. It took some persuasion, but she's agreed to accept the post."

"Begging your pardon, but Oksana isn't exactly the sort to inspire camaraderie. She's brusque, to put things kindly."

"I'm well aware. And you two have no such deficiency. I expect you to help her where you can. I've made her aware of my expectations on that front, so don't feel like you can't approach her—in private—to make suggestions. But two officers aren't enough to lead a regiment. We'll need you."

"Much appreciated," Taisiya said. "Though if we're not to have places with the fighter regiment, I have a request."

"Name it, but I can't make promises."

"Of course. I want Katya as my navigator—with her assent, of course." Taisiya didn't look directly at me. By making this request, she was denying me a plane of my own. I was a trained navigator, but with far more experience than many of the other recruits, I thought I stood a chance at the assignment. I gritted my teeth but didn't contradict her. Sofia looked to me, and I gave a curt nod. Taisiya had her reasons, and I wouldn't call her out in front of a superior officer.

"Those decisions are yet to be made," Sofia said, "but I have noted your request and will do my best to honor it."

"If I might risk impertinence," I said, "wouldn't you rather be with the fighter pilots, since the choice is yours? And the preference of Comrade Stalin, too?" The question was audacious, but the words burned on my tongue.

"The first rule of military leadership, Katya, is to go where I will do the most good without reference to my own preferences. And to trust my own instincts above those of others who do not know my division as well as I. It's a lesson you'll learn in time."

Sofia dismissed us to the barracks, but I pulled Taisiya aside into a vacant corridor.

"Do you think it might have been prudent—or at least kind—to ask *me* what assignment I might have liked before putting me on the spot?"

"The opportunity was there," Taisiya reasoned. "We had the best position for bargaining."

"All the same, it wasn't your right to ask."

"Sofia would assign you as a navigator anyway if she has brains at all—which she clearly does. But she might use your expertise as a reason to place you with a less experienced pilot, and I don't want you with someone who might choke under pressure. You're not the only one who made a promise to Vanya before we left."

At the mention of my husband's name, I felt my heart make an uncomfortable thunk against my ribs. "What did he tell you?" I whispered.

"He asked me, given any opportunity, to do anything in my power to keep you safe. That's what I just did."

~

"Ladies, welcome to the 588th Regiment," Sofia said, pacing before us as we stood in assembly. "Over the next few months, we will be honing our skills in order to join the others at the front. The most important task we have is to learn how to fly as a team. These, for the duration of the war, will be our aircraft."

Sofia gestured to a long row of small biplanes, rudimentary machines at best, that looked as aerodynamic as writing desks. They had wooden frames with a few aluminum braces, covered with taut linen, each painted a drab green to match our uniforms. The only ornamentation was a crest with the requisite red star to show our allegiance to Mother Russia. They resembled massive children's toys rather than proper military aircraft and looked just as durable. They would ignite like candles with the slightest flame and didn't look as though they could survive too many bullet holes before they fell from the sky. The engines looked as sophisticated as sewing machines.

It was going to be like battling German panzers while driving my mother's truck.

"It looks like my father's crop duster," Lada muttered. "This is just for our training exercises, Major, am I right?"

"If it looks like your father's crop duster, that's because it's no more sophisticated. The Polikarpov U-2 is easy to fly, maneuverable, and will allow us to fly lower and slower than the enemy aircraft, which is ideal for the needs of this regiment. They're quick to repair. Most of you learned how to fly on this plane or one much like it, so you'll be able to fly them as naturally as breathing. This will be our regiment's greatest asset."

I had a decent view into the cockpit and noticed one startling omission.

"Where are the radios, Major?" I asked.

"There are none," Sofia answered, blanching slightly.

"Surely they will get us equipped before we move to the front?" Taisiya interjected. Everything was in low supply, but certainly a few dozen radios could be found.

"I don't expect so," Sofia replied. "You'll at least have your interphones."

I glanced back into the cockpit. The interphone was about as useful as two tin cans and a string, but it was something. We'd be able to talk to one another, but there would be no communication with our ground crews.

Never had I thought flying at low altitudes and slow speeds to be of any sort of advantage in any military strategy, but it made sense. The low cruising speed of the Polikarpov and its ability to fly so close to the ground would make us incredibly hard to catch. They couldn't tail us or give proper chase because they'd stall their engines. The best they could do was fly past us and hope to hit, but we were far more maneuverable than they were—especially flying at five hundred meters. But it was clear our superiors entrusted the expensive equipment and the important tactical missions to the male regiments. I wanted to be philosophical about it all, to say that there had never been a regiment of female aviators before and we had to prove ourselves to get the same consideration, but the male regiments were largely no more experienced than we were. What was worse was that they had the equipment and support to succeed. As I looked at the long row of small biplanes better suited to searching for missing cattle than for fighting in a war, I had my doubts that we had been given the same opportunity.

"We will be working in teams of five," Sofia went on. "Each team will consist of a pilot, navigator, armorer, and mechanic. This way each pilot and navigator will learn how to work seamlessly as a unit, using your strengths and weaknesses to your advantage. Each armorer and mechanic will learn the nuances of their aircraft and how to anticipate the needs of their particular flight team. The fifth member is always your aircraft. I expect you all to care for them as such."

Sofia announced the teams, stopping in front of Taisiya first. "Lieutenant Taisiya Pashkova, pilot. Lieutenant Ekaterina Soloneva, navigator. Sergeant Polina Vasilyeva, mechanic. Sergeant Renata Kareva, armorer."

Just as Taisiya had requested. Taisiya squeezed my elbow in a quick gesture of solidarity. She knew it wasn't what I wanted but knew better than to say anything, and I was grateful.

"We'll be looking after you." Our new armorer, Renata, greeted us with hearty handshakes. The mechanic, Polina, followed suit, but with a measure less buoyancy.

"I'm glad to have you," Taisiya said, assessing our crew, looking satisfied.

"Yes, we look forward to working with you," I interjected.

Taisiya cast me a sidelong glance, and I bit my tongue. Up in the air, we would be partners, but our crew needed a leader. Sofia had chosen her for the task, not me.

We were dismissed to the barracks to get outfitted by the quartermaster and settle in.

"The Polikarpov is a good plane," Polina said as we left the quartermaster's with our supplies in tow. "She may not be fancy, but she's sturdy and hard to break."

"You know them well?" I asked.

"My papa had a similar plane he used for crop dusting, as well as for training my brothers and me."

"You didn't take your pilot's license?" Taisiya interjected, matching our pace. "You seem rather keen on aircraft to not have an interest."

"Oh, I wanted to," she assured us. "But aviation clubs cost money we didn't have."

"I know how that is," I said, patting her shoulder. "Had it not been for my scholarship to the academy I'd never have been able to afford it."

"Or me," Taisiya admitted. "My father is a farmer, too."

Polina smiled at us, looking wistful for a moment as she glanced up at the winter clouds whirling in the sky. Had she been closer to a military academy her chances might have been better.

"My mother refused to let me," Renata piped up, holding the door to the barracks open for us. "She doesn't like that I've enlisted at all. She only allowed me to come because I wouldn't stop haranguing her about it and she was convinced they'd send me home."

"It's a mother's job to worry. You'll make her proud," I said, eyeing my assigned bunk longingly. We would sleep and eat together as a unit, per Sofia's orders. As before, Sofia had rejected the option to sleep in private officers' quarters, choosing bunks close to ours for herself and her crew. We changed into our long undergarments—the closest thing we had to pajamas—and crawled into our new bunks.

"Thank you," Taisiya whispered as the rest of the room drifted off to sleep. "You could have objected, and Sofia probably would have listened to you. I'll rest easier knowing it's you up there with me."

"We've got a fine team," I agreed. "And I trust you to lead it."

CHAPTER 11

March 1942

Moscow winters, as I learned as a girl, can in the course of a few minutes go from merely unpleasant to the sort of cold that tears at your flesh. When I was a young girl, maybe seven years old, I got locked out of our apartment one afternoon in January. Mama thought I was with Papa; Papa thought I was with her. I'd actually gone to the bakery to buy *pryanik*, sweet gingerbread baked into small cakes and stamped with pretty designs or cut into shapes. I had collected coins from Mama for doing little tasks for her and finally had enough for the massive *pryanik* shaped like a matryoshka doll. I had no idea when I might be able to persuade my parents to let me buy the coveted treat, so I let each believe I was with the other and ate the honey-and-spice confection in clandestine solitude. The kindly shop owner, Comrade Brusilov, even gave me a cup of strong tea that smelled of musky spices and campfire smoke to accompany my cake, knowing my little savings wouldn't stretch to include it.

I savored every bite of the gingerbread and every sip of the tea, oblivious to the trouble I would be in when my parents discovered my deceit. When at last I could find no reason to delay my return, I walked slowly back to our building only to realize I had no way in. I waited for one of them to come home, but it was at least two hours before either had need to return. Mercifully Papa arrived home before the frostbite set in, but I didn't miss it by much. With a vow never to pull a similar stunt again, I asked for an emergency key that night and never again left without it tied to a ribbon around my neck.

I thought of that key as a talisman against the vicious bite of winter, but now, as I craned my neck around the small windshield to get a clearer view of our target, the wind ripped like claws at the unshielded skin on my face. The snowflakes matted my lashes, making it next to impossible to see the target I was to mark with my flare.

I removed my gloves, pinning them tight between my knees—there was no replacing them—and prepared to lob the metal flare over the edge of the plane onto the target. The frozen metal stuck to my hands, warmed by the wool-lined gloves, but there was no way to remove the flare's cap while my fingers were covered.

"Taisiya!" I yelled into the archaic interphone, longing for a modern radio and decent instrumentation. The trainers from Engels were infinitely more sophisticated than this. I looked down at my chronometer as we neared the coordinates. "Five . . ." I opened the flare. ". . . three . . . *marked!*"

She swooped back around, releasing the dummy bomb on the next pass. We both peered over to see the bomb fall to the earth about a hundred meters from the target.

"Dammit," she growled a moment later, loud enough for me to hear.

Even with a map, I wasn't sure how well I would have been able to mark the target. A smooth flight in a modern trainer plane in broad daylight was a different proposition altogether from a training flight in pitch dark in the middle of March.

As we taxied our plane to the hangar, Polina and Renata rushed out to prepare the plane for the next run. We had three more runs to make before dinner, after a grueling morning of tactical training. The rigors of our last months at the academy were nothing compared to this, and I found myself cursing Karlov for every run he'd held me behind. Each one of those hours would have made me more valuable to the war effort. I didn't have experience navigating for anyone other than Vanya and Tokarev, while Taisiya had flown with a half dozen other navigators.

I would have to learn Taisiya's style, but it took only minutes in the air to see she was nothing short of exceptional. She didn't have Vanya's swagger, but she had all of his confidence. It made concentrating on maps and targets much easier when I didn't have to worry about the competence of the pilot. I thought of poor Tokarev from the academy and felt pity for whoever was navigating for him now.

"Come sit and rest where it's warm while they get the plane ready," Taisiya prodded me when my eyes remained locked on the gray sky, watching the flimsy wood and canvas contraptions putter about the horizon. That sleek metal fighters could take flight was a marvel; that these dilapidated machines managed it was a miracle.

"I'm going to watch the next run," I said. "You go."

"You have to learn to conserve your strength, Katya," Taisiya chastised. "I need you on form."

"I'm fine. You can bring me some water when you come back."

Taisiya shook her head and walked back to the mess hall, but my eyes never diverted. From the deft handling, I could tell the pilot was Sofia. I could see Oksana hurl the flare overboard and Sofia make her mark without a single meter of error. I wished I could sit behind Sofia and watch the movements of her hands, to get a sense of how she melded with her machine, but that was Oksana's place. I could learn much from watching Taisiya as well, but nothing would serve as well as hours in the front cockpit.

Sofia landed the plane, the wheels touching the ground as lightly as a robin on a spindly branch.

Both pilot and navigator seemed surprised to see me watching when we weren't next in the rotation.

"Just trying to learn what I can," I explained. "Your run was right out of a textbook."

"You're a fine navigator, Soloneva," Oksana said, reprising my surname, as was Sofia's custom when we were in training. Sofia patted my arm in approval before walking over to the crews waiting for instructions.

"I want to be a fine pilot," I countered. I hadn't voiced my disappointment to her about being named navigator, but I'd felt it all the same.

"You'll have your chance, I'm certain of it," Oksana said, looking over at Taisiya, who reemerged from the mess hall. "But as a fellow navigator, I'll be content to stay in my current role for the duration of the war, as I hope you do."

I blinked a few times. Oksana was a mystery, but there was always an ambition she couldn't quite conceal. "Really?" I finally sputtered.

"It shouldn't surprise you. So long as you're a navigator, it means your pilot is still alive."

As March progressed, the temperatures rose slightly, but the snows gave way to bone-chilling rains. If they were confident it was warm enough that we weren't at risk of the rain turning into ice at altitude, we flew. There was no suit in existence that could keep the rain from soaking through to our skin, but we went up anyway. Such conditions would have canceled practicals at the academy, but the commanders looked at this foul weather as the best sort of opportunity for us.

Battles were not delayed on account of rain.

Renata had refitted the plane with the dummy bomb, and Polina had done her customary system check. Now they sat near the heater with Taisiya and some of the other pilots. I decided that with the miserable drizzle I would do just as well to absorb the heat and rest with the others until it was our turn to go up.

"The rain was bad enough you had to give up sentry duty?" Taisiya chided. I rarely took the time to regroup after runs anymore, watching the others, hoping to learn some maneuver or trick by observation.

I nodded, accepting a cup of coffee from Renata. "You should rest in between runs," she admonished. "You need to save your strength instead of watching all the time."

Lifting bombs, some as heavy as fifty kilos, into position on the aircraft was physically strenuous, but as it wasn't particularly complicated work, Renata had taken it upon herself to look after Taisiya and me, fetching food and drink at every turn. Taisiya and I had both tried to disabuse her of the notion that she was any less valued than we were, but she insisted on tending to us like a doting grandmother.

Polina craned her neck to get a view of the swirly gray quagmire of the spring skies and shook her head. "It's days like this I'm glad to be a mechanic," she said. "My hands are chapped enough as it is. I don't know how you all stand it."

Polina may not have trained at a military academy like ours, but I'd never met the match of her for technical knowledge of aircraft, with the possible exception of Taisiya. Renata and most of the armorers were strong farm girls. They needed both strength and incredible stamina, and our Renata was indefatigable. I never saw her sitting entirely idle. Even now she sat embroidering flowers on the cloths we used in place of socks we'd been given with our uniforms. They stuck out of our boots by a solid five centimeters, but they were the only thing that helped keep the massive boots in place on our feet. Polina had started the trend of making elaborate patterns in the cuffs of her makeshift stockings with blue thread she harvested from her long underwear.

The post came as we sat near the heater, Sofia following the young lieutenant who dispersed it. Six of us had letters from husbands or beaux; Taisiya and I were among the lucky.

"Matvei is sick," Taisiya said, her brow knitted. As much as I valued the post, I silently cursed our courier. We had at least two more runs to make, and I did not need Taisiya distracted when she was flying in good weather, let alone the mess we would be flying into that afternoon. "He's been moved from the front. It sounds like pneumonia, from what I can make out."

"Well, he's better off at a military hospital," I said. At least he'd have access to antibiotics. I didn't say what was really on my mind at that moment—a death from pneumonia would be a blessing in comparison to what might await him at the hands of the Germans.

Taisiya said nothing but tucked the letter in her breast pocket and turned her attention back to her coffee.

Vanya's letter, the familiar script scrawled on the envelope, weighed heavy in my hands. I wanted to read it as much as I craved my bed after one of our endless days, but stowed it away unopened in my own pocket as Taisiya had done with hers. The letter might be filled with triumph or regret, or worse, injury and despair, but his words would have to wait until I found the comfort of my bunk that night. In the meantime they would stay warm next to the beating of my heart.

Sofia saw what I had done and nodded her approval. She was a married woman herself. Her husband was a major in another division farther north. She mentioned him only rarely and was never seen poring over letters as some of us did. That she loved her husband, I had no doubt, but she forced herself to be present with us until she could claim an hour as her own.

A commotion among those in the flight yard demanded our attention, and we all wordlessly rushed to see what had caused it. A pillar of smoke off in the distance confirmed our worst fears.

Another crew landed a hundred yards from us and jumped from the cockpits, running to join our growing crowd.

"Irina and Lada," the pilot, a spindly girl called Darya, sputtered as she regained her breath. "I couldn't see what happened, but they were too low. I'm guessing the dive was too steep and Irina couldn't recover in time. I circled overhead to get a look but couldn't get close enough to see anything other than flames."

Sofia ordered three medics to go out with her to the crash site to assess the situation. The rest of us were left to wait. Darya and her navigator, Eva, watched with tears streaming down their red, wind-chilled faces. My lungs were incapable of taking in their full capacity, and I knew it had nothing to do with the frigid air or the stinging pelts of the frigid raindrops that assaulted us. Darya and Eva had seen the crash, and their faces betrayed the fate of our sisters.

~

The reconnaissance crew managed to extinguish the fire in short order with help from the damp conditions. They claimed the bodies from the wreckage, which we hoped would give Irina's and Lada's families some solace. When we joined the fighting, any of us who were lost would be irretrievable. Our families would have to make do with form letters and telegrams if there was time to notify them at all.

Sofia's face looked taut with restraint as she descended from the ambulance, and she did not make eye contact with anyone as she went off to the officers' quarters to do her duty by Irina and Lada. No orders were given to the thirty-eight of us who remained, nor were any of us brave enough to ask for them.

"Let's go back to the barracks," Taisiya offered up. "We're doing no one any good freezing in the hangar."

Thinking of nothing better to do, we complied, our steps dragging as we went. I sat up on my thin mattress, wrapped my woolen blanket around my shoulders, but I still shivered, for the chill of the day seemed to have entered my marrow.

"It's just awful," Darya said after a time as she busied her hands embroidering her own socks. "It's one thing to die in battle, but this seems like a waste."

I took a deep breath and swallowed a rebuke. Darya's need to break any uncomfortable silence was often ingratiating in good times. At the current moment it was maddening. *She saw it happen with her own eyes,* I reminded myself. *Be kind.* "She died in service to her country," I replied, keeping the sheath on my razor tongue at some cost. "It's as good a death as any of us can hope for."

"Hear, hear," Taisiya shot from her bunk. For once the tome in her hand wasn't a technical manual, but a tattered copy of *Anna Karenina* that she'd had since girlhood.

"They ought to have us up flying," Oksana interjected. She had a pen and notebook in her hands. Whether she kept a journal, wrote poetry, or was sketching figures, I knew not. My heart strained against my ribs as I thought of Vanya shivering in his barracks at the front, or more likely sleeping in the mud, sketching his comrades to distract himself from the misery.

"You are so unfeeling," Darya said, not looking up from the tangle of blue threads that were slowly becoming a field of spring flowers. "If you can't mourn for our sisters, stay silent."

"Watch yourself," I urged quietly. Oksana had assumed her place as second in command of the regiment when we deployed to the front. Angering her now could mean unpleasantness in the months to come.

Oksana rounded on her. "Do you think you'll get an afternoon off if we lose a crew in battle?" There was no countering this logic. "If Eva is shot out from behind you on a sortie, you will come back to base, land your plane, and be given another navigator before you miss a spot on the rotation. You'd all better get used to flying with heavy hearts."

"Thank you for the vote of confidence," Eva shot from her bunk, her wry tone cutting the ice in the air. Even Oksana chuckled.

The silence settled over our heads once more, but this time it was Oksana who broke it.

"They're lucky," she breathed quietly.

"How dare you?" Darya spat, casting her stockings aside. I saw the flash of temper in her eyes and let my blanket fall to my sides. The last thing we needed on top of two fallen sisters was two more in the brig for fighting. "We all know you have no feeling heart in you, but how can you say such a thing about our own sisters in arms?"

"You're from the east, aren't you, Darya?" Oksana asked, the usual rancor missing from her voice.

"What does that have to do with anything?" she replied, shaking her head.

"You didn't see the massacres in Kiev. The Germans slaughtered men, women, and children by the hundreds. Anyone with the least trace of Jewish blood. Anyone who got in their way. When they died, there wasn't a roomful of women sitting about mourning their loss. There was no one to remember them. Lada and Irina at least have us."

Oksana's blue eyes shone with a haunted light I hadn't noticed before.

"I would hardly call them lucky all the same," I said, and cast a glance over to Darya—a warning for her not to press further.

Sofia padded into the barracks, her expression stony as she scanned our faces, several of them tear stained.

"To the mess hall, ladies. Katya, bring your violin." I raised my brows at the order but voiced no surprise.

Sofia took her place at the tinny piano that usually sat ignored in the corner of the hall and lifted her voice, clear and true, to the exposed metal beams in the ceiling. I removed my violin from its case and followed along with the familiar folk tune. A few of the women chimed in; some had sweet, lilting voices, others richer altos. Though none of us would find careers on the great stages of Moscow, Paris, or New York, we were worth listening to.

Sofia chose familiar tunes, none too gay nor too morose. She wasn't of the traditional Russian stock, who liked to bathe in her grief like one might luxuriate in perfumed bathwater, and I felt grateful for it. Darya hung to the back of the group and did not sing, arms crossed over her chest. Perhaps she thought the attempt to liven our spirits was disloyal, but I remembered Lada and Irina too well to believe they would think so. Irina had been quick to laugh, and Lada had a biting wit. Neither would have wanted us to stew in our sadness.

They were also soldiers in the Red Army, and staunchly pragmatic women. They knew we would have to press on.

While we sang, the cook had brewed a huge pot of tea and put together sandwiches and little spice cakes as fine as we'd seen before the war broke out.

"We'll be light on flour rations for a few days, but I thought we needed an extravagance," Sofia declared.

We appreciated the bounty, though none of us ate with much enthusiasm.

"Irina loved to bake," Darya reminisced as she took a bite of her dessert.

"And Lada was fond of eating," Sofia remembered, "though she said she was no great hand in the kitchen." We shared the few memories we had of these women who had been in our lives for such a short while. They were sweet girls, and it seemed fitting to take an hour to honor their memory. I stood to the back of the crowd, not wanting them to see the tears that threatened at the corners of my eyes. We would never have the chance to honor our fallen sisters in such a fashion again. Oksana was right. To know that my own death could be passed over with nothing more than a letter to my mother and Vanya—perhaps months after the fact—chilled me worse than flying into the miserable deluge.

I didn't allow myself to brood in my tea. I plastered a smile on my lips and pretended to enjoy the gathering. I used my violin like a shield and hid behind it until Sofia sent us to our bunks.

"Thank you," Sofia said as we retired. She patted the case of Papa's violin as we walked. "We needed music tonight."

"My papa always said that music is a balm for a weary soul. He said the same of food, so I think you did as much for us as you could."

"Thank you for saying so, Katya. I confess sometimes I worry that when things really matter most, I won't have the answer for you ladies."

"Your doubt makes you human, Sofia," I said. "And it's your humanity that we respond to."

Sofia turned and embraced me, so quickly I might have thought I imagined it had it not been for the warmth her arms had left behind.

CHAPTER 12

May 23, 1942

As the ground crews readied our aircraft, the pilots and their navigators from the 588th Regiment looked on. The bulk of the equipment we would need at the front, along with our support crews, had been sent forward on trucks and Jeeps the Americans had donated by the shipload. There was nothing left to take with us but the twenty-five aircraft and their crews. We would be in Morozovskaya the following morning, where we would join our brothers in arms and enter combat.

This was what we had trained endless hours every day for.

This was what we had studied endlessly for the past four years for.

This was what Sofia had envisioned when she petitioned to establish our division.

The energy in the hangar was electric. Though we stood at attention, we struggled to remain perfectly still. I felt the tingle of anticipation in my calves, and longed to dash to my airplane rather than wait dutifully for instruction.

We would now have the chance to prove to Stalin, Mother Russia, and the world that we were capable in the cockpit and deserving of the country's resources.

Sofia paced as she addressed our assembly for the last time before accepting active duty. "Ladies, remember to keep your eyes open. You will be flying very near active combat when we arrive at the front, and there is no way for us to know how far the enemy has advanced. You are not equipped with weapons, so you'll be flying low, light, and as fast as the aircraft can go." Sofia's last words were met with a few derisive titters. We joked daily that the planes were about as aerodynamic as our grandfathers' rusty old tractors and just as swift. "Since you're flying unarmed, you'll have to do your best to evade enemy aircraft, if you encounter any. I know you can."

As we walked to our aircraft, I offered Sofia a salute. She returned hers with her usual crisp efficiency. She paired it with a covert wink. *I'm counting on you.*

When given the order, Taisiya brought our plane into formation, and we soared off with the other aircraft to the southwest. Our destination was only six hundred kilometers off, but as that would test the range of our planes, the officers had decided to break the journey into two parts—a decision we welcomed, after four hours subjected to the pervasive hum and drone of the planes' small engines.

We stopped overnight at an intermediary air base between Engels and the front to refuel and to sleep. A base filled with men was a foreign sight after months training in our almost exclusively female division. From the looks we got—ranging from sidelong glances to contemptuous glares—they weren't any better used to the sight of a woman in uniform.

At once I was taken back to my early days at the academy. In my head every male cadet had looked at me to size me up. *Can she fly a plane? Isn't she too pretty to be a pilot? Does she think she's too plain for marriage and children?* I was only about three-quarters right, I decided;

the rest were too busy worrying about their own capabilities. The boys with their appraising glares made their opinions known and seemed confident I would be eager to hear their assessments. The men on this base were no exception. A dozen of us were walking from the mess to the barracks they'd partitioned off for us when we caught the attention of a line of young officers enjoying their after-dinner cigarettes.

"Darling, why would a pretty thing like you go off to the war?" a leering lieutenant said to me between puffs on his cigarette. Being the tallest, I was always apt to be the one to attract attention first. "You ought to be back home, where it's safe."

"My husband is at the front, and I thought it right to do my part," I hissed between clenched teeth. "I'm sorry your sweetheart thinks herself above doing hers. And if you think any place in reach of the Germans is safe, then you're as big a fool as you look."

He looked blankly, blinking a few times before turning on the ball of his foot to return to his comrades.

The rest of the women maintained their composure on the short walk to the barracks but erupted in peals of laughter once the door fell shut behind us.

"What has my ladies in such a state of merriment?" Sofia asked. She'd been detained on business by one of the senior officers during dinner, as was so often the case.

"Our Katya was just giving a lieutenant a lesson in manners," Taisiya said, wiping tears of mirth from the corners of her eyes.

"They need it," Sofia said with a wary nod. "Their mothers would be horrified by their behavior, but then they would make their beds and brew them tea. It waters the message down a bit." This earned a laugh from some of the others, but I was thinking of the captain back in Engels who'd been sent to the front for his "lack of manners." Now there would be no place worse to send them. A cold chill washed over me. We would have to be vigilant. Aside from Sofia, only Taisiya knew of the incident at the training camp, and possibly Oksana. The others would have to know. My fists tightened at the idea that I would have to expose the events in Engels to the whole regiment, but if it kept them safe I would sacrifice my pride for their well-being.

That night I offered them my story as a cautionary tale—all of them horrified that such a thing was possible. But they seemed convinced of the need to remain guarded around the male servicemen, which made the uncomfortable revelation worthwhile. We left shortly after dawn, none too sorry to leave the base behind us. It would be another three hours to the front, and apprehension was giving way to excitement.

There was precious little for me to do on the flight except check the compass from time to time to ensure we were on course, but with twenty-four other planes flying in formation, the task was next to unnecessary.

I wondered if Vanya's letters would find me at the front as regularly as they had found me in Engels. He said all the right things in them—that he was well, as safe as he could hope to be, and that he had confidence in the skills of his regiment—but there was a melancholy he could not, for all his talent with words, erase from the text.

I struggled to keep my mind on the flight and felt a gnawing guilt in the pit of my stomach that Taisiya was left with all the work while I was free to daydream. My reverie came to an abrupt halt when the planes around us began scattering out of formation. Sofia and Oksana had broken away and begun evasive maneuvers. A fighter plane followed them into the dive, and several others emerged from the fluffy summer clouds.

The breath caught in my throat. We were thrown into battle fifteen minutes before reaching base. Unarmed.

"Dive!" I screamed to Taisiya over the tinny interphone. If we managed to take the dive steep, slow, and low, they would stall out long before we lost control of our craft. She had already begun her descent before I shouted the command, and flew to Sofia's flank, taking her place back in formation.

Instead of using our training, trying to shake the nimble fighters with our evasive maneuvers, most of the pilots panicked. I couldn't decipher what was going on with the enemy aircraft. They were in perfect attack formation, but I didn't hear the telltale rattling of the guns. If they meant to take us down, they were missing their opportunity. They flew off into the distance, leaving us for some other, more important target. At least Taisiya hadn't overreacted, and I was heartened by it.

The landing strip came into view, and we circled, desperately waiting for our turn to land. There were officers and pilots looking at us from the ground, but there wasn't the bustle of activity we expected with enemy aircraft so close. How could they not have seen the flock of fighters that had just encircled us?

By the time we landed, several of our regiment had rushed over to tell the commanding officer of the nearby threat. As Taisiya and I joined the throng, we overheard General Chernov, an imposing man with a red face and deep lines of experience, expel a formidable guffaw.

"You dolts. That was your escort. Can't you tell the difference between a swastika and a star?"

"Two more weeks of training. It's insulting," Taisiya growled as she tossed her duffel on the lumpy mattress in her corner of the tiny bedroom.

We had been expecting a rudimentary version of the barracks and mess hall that we'd known in Engels and Moscow but were instead quartered in the village in the homes of the residents—whether they wished for it or not. Taisiya and I were the "guests" of the Utkin family and would be staying in the back bedroom, just large enough for two mattresses to lie side by side, with a couple of meters of room at the feet for us to stow our belongings, which were mercifully scant. I had little more than two books, one spare uniform, and Papa's violin.

"If the training can teach us something that will save our lives," I countered, "I'll gladly wait another two weeks for combat. I'm in no rush to be a martyr." I spoke like a peacemaker, but in truth I was just as irked at General Chernov's edict as she and the rest of the regiment were.

Taisiya was having none of it. "If a new regiment of male pilots had been joining them, the general would never have allowed such antics. His pilots swarm around like unsupervised schoolboys, yet *we're* being humiliated for it."

"I can't argue with that." I sighed, stretching out on the mattress, hoping the lumps would conform to my back over time. They seemed stubborn in their lumpiness, though. The room was drafty, and the entire house was even shoddier than our little cabin in Miass. It would be fine in the summer, but it was a miracle the family hadn't frozen to death winters ago. But if the front hadn't moved by winter, we would have problems far worse than drafty bedrooms to contend with.

"In the general's defense," I said, "he seemed more disappointed in our aircraft than the women crewing them."

"Well, it's certainly not our choice to be going up against proper fighters in dinky trainers." Taisiya had pulled out her notepad and pencil. I couldn't imagine anything about the room or our situation worth committing to paper, but scratching away seemed to soothe her. She hadn't spent much time on the hobby in Chelyabinsk, being too devoted to her studies, but she'd taken it back up again in Engels. It calmed her more than reading or writing letters to Matvei, so I encouraged it. Though watching her fill the blank pages—she sometimes shared her sketches, little poems, and anecdotes, both tender and bitter—I felt my heart ache for the dewy afternoon in the meadow with Vanya, when he made his poetry with paints and canvas.

A knock sounded at the door, and Taisiya opened it to find the mistress of the house on the other side.

"Girls, will you come join us for tea and *medovik*?" Our host, Lina Utkina, was as sweet a woman as Russian soil ever saw and seemed genuinely pleased to have us with her. She could be no older than forty-five, but work and worry had aged her far past her years.

"You don't need to go to the trouble, Comrade Utkina," I said, sitting up and pulling my jacket straight. "We'll be having dinner with our regiment before much longer." Our mess hall was a row of tables set up under some trees, and we were just as happy for the meals in the great outdoors as we would have been for a proper refectory.

"It's no trouble, my dears. And please, call me Lina." She turned her back to us, leaving the door open. There was no polite refusal, though we hated for her to use her rations on us. We'd have to find a way to sneak her back some flour and eggs at the next opportunity.

"Come sit, ladies." Pytor Utkin motioned to two empty seats at the scarred kitchen table. "We hope you will join us for our afternoon tea when you can. It's a pleasure for us to have company since our Lev went off to fight."

"Do you hear from him often?" Taisiya asked, smiling at Lina, who placed a massive portion of honeyed layer cake before her. Apparently she thought to feed us like the adolescent boy she pined for.

"Not often, no," Lina admitted, placing a similarly gargantuan piece before me. "He was never fond of writing, though."

"Do you know where he is, more or less?"

"They took him to Leningrad when the fighting broke out, and I expect that's where he'll stay until they break through the blockade," Pytor said. "They'll get through one way or another, mark my words." He stared into his cup of tea for a moment, his face grim.

"Those poor people," Lina clucked. "Prisoners in their own city."

Taisiya and I exchanged glances. We hadn't heard any real news from Leningrad in months. The propaganda posters reminded us that the blood of our brethren entombed in that city had to be avenged, but we didn't know for certain what was left.

The cake before me looked as beautiful as any I'd seen before the war. The thin layers of cake and honeyed cream smelled as decadent as a perfumed bath. I took a bite, and while the cream and honey tasted sweet and smelled inviting, the cake itself was tough and ashy.

"The flour isn't what it used to be," Lina said, bowing her head briefly.

Color rose to my cheeks, and I was ashamed I hadn't been able to conceal my distaste. "There are shortages of almost everything. We all have to sacrifice."

"The tea is wonderful," Taisiya added. She'd been more successful in hiding her disgust at the cake, always better at adopting a neutral expression than I was.

"It's our pleasure to have anything to share with brave girls like you."

"You're kind to have us stay with you." I stumbled on the words, knowing the choice wasn't truly theirs.

"It's a lovely turn of events," Lina said. "The men fighting for us are brave and noble, but it's much easier to house the two of you."

"And you're a far sight prettier to look at than the poor foot soldiers at the front," Pytor said with a chuckle. "It's not a usual path for a woman, though, is it?"

"We're all called to help Mother Russia in whatever capacity we can," Taisiya said, placing her cup back on the ridged wooden planks of the kitchen table.

"And we're grateful to you," Lina said quickly, fearing her husband's flippant comment had caused offense.

"Yes, yes," Pytor added. "I'd be in the fracas myself if they wanted me, but with a bad knee I'm not of much use."

"You do a great deal for the war effort by housing us here so comfortably," I said, forcing myself to eat more of the unfortunate cake.

"Will you do me one service, my dears?" Lina asked, her eyes welling with tears. "Ask after our boy. Lev is all we have. He was proud to go and fight. Signed up before he had to. He's a good boy, but I want—"

"You want him home," I said, finishing the sentence for her as her tears choked back the words too painful to speak. "We can't make any promises that it will do any good, but we can try."

"Thank you, girls," Pytor said, his voice gruff with his own unshed tears.

I felt a deep ache in my heart, knowing that they were only two of millions of parents living for the next postcard from the front.

CHAPTER 13

June 1942, the Southern Front, Sorties: 0

We stood at attention, waiting for the general to give his instructions. We'd completed the extra training he'd insisted upon. Sofia promised that he would have no choice but to send us out on missions, as his excuses were growing feebler and the need for our skills more undeniable by the day. As we waited our faces were somber. No glint of pride or enthusiasm shone in our eyes to betray our solemnity, as it might have done even months before.

"You will be flying your first sortie tonight," Chernov said without preamble.

One sortie? A mission comprised multiple flights—sorties. What was this?

A look at Sofia's face answered the question. It was not a resolute mask of determination and duty. Her brow was furrowed, and her jaw was set. She was displeased and only just keeping control of her tongue.

We would only be allowed to fly one sortie, as a test of our battle readiness.

"Three teams will fly out at 2100 hours," the general went on. His usually ruddy skin was now tinged a sickly shade of orange, likely caused by poor health and stress—by-products of the war in which we would now take our place. "Those teams are charged with destroying a stockpile of German munitions. If the mission is a success, the rest of you will go out the following evening. Your missions will be tactical in nature. Bombing supply lines and bridges, a few strategic buildings. You'll be flying over German territory, so above all we want you keeping the damned Huns awake as much as you can. If there is anything your crop dusters are good for, it's making a racket. We want to use that to our advantage."

He nodded to Sofia, who had gained some composure. "Comrade Chernov is correct in this," she said to us. "A tired Nazi is a poor soldier, and we will use this to regain a foothold in the area. We will have the element of surprise on our side, for a time, and I cannot emphasize how important these missions will be for the success of our ground units.

"I will be flying with Captain Tymoshenko, as I would not send any of you up when I would not go myself. Junior Lieutenants Kozlova and Andreyeva—will you fly with us?"

The pilot, Darya, and her navigator, Eva, stepped forward and replied "Yes, Major" in unison, then stepped back into formation.

"Excellent. Junior Lieutenants Pashkova and Soloneva, will you fly with us?"

I felt my stomach rise to my throat. We'd wanted this since Sofia first came to Chelyabinsk. Since we had learned of the war's spread over the Russian border. Now that it was upon me, the reality of flying over German territory terrified me. My feet felt encased in cement and steel, as though I had become one of our efficient new buildings. I heard the clack of Taisiya's boots as she stepped forward. She was no coward, and I could not afford to hesitate. I stepped forward, a split second after her, and slipped her the briefest of sidelong glances. We had to be in this together.

"Yes, Major," we answered in one voice.

"I expected nothing less of any of you," Sofia said, a grim smile finally pulling at her lips. "I'm dismissing you for the rest of the day to get as much sleep as you can. Navigators will be provided with flares and grenades. You will carry nothing else except your service pistols."

"And parachutes, of course?" I asked.

"No," Sofia said, blanching a few shades. "We need every available gram of load on these small craft to carry bombs large enough to inflict damage."

There were no murmurs of dissent. Only stunned silence.

"One last directive. If we encounter enemy fire while out on a sortie, we have been given permission to return fire. That is a standing order. Everyone, flying or not, will report back at 2000 hours."

A cold comfort—all we had were our sidearms and a few grenades against German machine guns.

Taisiya and I walked in silence back to the Utkin farm, surprising the kindly couple with our midday return.

The sun shone mercilessly down on the hut, flooding our room in an unwelcome pool of light. We did our best to block the offending rays with our winter coats, but this only caused us to bake in our beds as we choked out the little circulating air from the tiny windows. We shucked our uniforms and wore our thinnest shirts and undergarments in search of sleep. Our lives depended on it.

Just as I thought I might be able to achieve something like a shallow sleep, a timid knocking came at the door.

"I'm so sorry, Lieutenant Soloneva. There is a letter for you."

Vanya.

When I opened the door, Comrade Utkina placed the letter in my hands and pulled the door closed in one fluid motion. She knew we would not be home sleeping at midday if the need weren't dire, but neither would my mail be delivered to her home if it weren't urgent.

My hands shook as I turned the envelope over, then trembled with relief as I saw my mother's tidy script. It wouldn't contain the news that Vanya was well and safe, but it wouldn't contain the worst, either. I opened it gingerly, as though her words might escape if I weren't careful to keep them captive.

> *My dearest Katinka,*
> *I hope you are well, my sweet girl. As well as any of us can be in this dreadful time. All is well here in old Miass, though your mama is lonely with you so far from home. The only way I am able to keep from running mad with worry is to keep myself busy. Thankfully that is not a challenge. I have taken a job in an ammunition factory in Chelyabinsk. While it's not exciting work, it's useful. And not nearly as backbreaking as laundry. I've managed to save up for a new (still old, but slightly less ancient) truck, so getting to and from the city isn't the worry it once was.*
>
> *While Miass is as quiet as it ever was, Chelyabinsk is becoming an industrial hub—tanks rolling out of the city each day as you can't imagine. I can only hope these horrible machines will serve to keep you safe. Please write to your mama, and let her know that you are safe, and any news you might have from your Vanya, too.*
>
> *Be well, my darling girl.*
>
> *-Mama*

I exhaled a breath I didn't know I was holding, relieved by the anticlimax of the letter.

"I hope your letter has good news?" Taisiya asked. I smiled at her optimism but didn't chide her. *Good news* was a relative term these days.

"You're not able to sleep, either?" I said, lamely stating the obvious.

"No, for the same reason you aren't," she said, rolling to her side.

"It's Mama. Just letting me know she's well." I didn't give any details. If Mama was working in a factory, she'd be getting a worker's ration and faring better than Taisiya's farmer parents, who were forced to hand over the lion's share of their crops to the troops. Her father had written that he was happy to make the sacrifice to the cause, but it left him with precious little to feed his family and nothing with which to trade or barter for other goods. Their situation was far more dire than Mama's—and even they were better off than the Utkins.

"I suppose they wanted to get us our mail in case—" Taisiya mused.

"Don't say it."

"I know."

I lay back on my cot and searched my brain for a topic of conversation, but it all came back to the mission before us. What could I ask? *Are you afraid?* Of course she was. She was no fool, and she knew the value of fear. As long as Taisiya had a healthy respect for our mortality but did not allow her fear to choke her, it would be our greatest ally in the air.

"Have you heard from Matvei?" I asked after a while. None of the women spoke of the letters from husbands and beaux at the front anymore. It was cruel to those who hadn't received word. Some of us never would, and that unspoken truth made each letter that we were lucky enough to receive as precious as treasure.

But with Taisiya I could inquire. I could share her joys and tragedies, as I would my own sister's, had I been lucky enough to have one.

"Two weeks ago. Fully recovered. It wasn't pneumonia, as they feared. He's going back to the front and sounds anxious to do his part." I could hear the smile in her voice as she spoke of sweet, gentle Matvei. I tried to reconcile the peaceable young son of a farmer who had sounded no better suited for war than a kitten with the reality that he was now a grown man and a decorated soldier.

"War has a way of surprising us. It makes heroes out of the unlikeliest of men, and villains of the ones you usually expect, as my father used to say." I wondered what sort of man Taisiya's Matvei would be when we all returned home. Would she know him? Would he be a broken man like Vanya's father, or simply a wiser version of himself, as my father had become?

"That it does. How is your Vanya?"

"Just about the same. Captain now. I don't see the pride in his words, just fatigue."

"He's earned his fatigue, Katya. You can be proud of him. And he of you."

"I hope you're right," I said, looking at the patterns in the wooden planks on the ceiling. "I wanted this. So did you. And now that we're facing it, I wonder if we weren't fools to do this."

"We didn't want *this*," Taisiya corrected. "Only madmen and sadists want war. We wanted to fly, and when the war came, we wanted to do our duty. It's not foolish. It's brave."

I nodded quietly as the sweltering heat of late June stilled the air. Taisiya was as smart a woman as I'd ever met, and pragmatic, too. But I didn't find myself reassured by her words. They could be either the truth that she believed to the core of her being, or the words she knew her navigator needed to hear. As I willed sleep to come, I made the compromise with myself that, like so much in times of war, it was neither one nor the other, but both.

"I need you to promise me something, Taisiya," I said, keeping my words barely above a whisper. As though to project them into the world would make them somehow more tangible.

"No. I'm not making you any promises." She sat up straight in her bed, glaring down at me. "I won't listen to this kind of talk."

"I'm not going to ask you to take care of Mama for the rest of her days or anything. I just want her and Vanya to be told properly—if the worst should happen."

Taisiya tossed her pillow so it whacked me smartly across the face. "No."

I sat up in turn and lobbed the lumpy mass back at her. "You can be rather heartless, you know."

"Pragmatic. It's a stupid request."

"How can you say such a thing?" I asked, wishing I had something harder within arm's reach to pitch at her. "Do you want your parents or Matvei to go months without hearing the news?"

"Of course I don't, Katya. I'm not the one who can make you these promises. If you go down, I'm going with you. And I wouldn't have it any other way."

Shaking, I pulled my own notebook and Papa's fountain pen from my knapsack. I wrote words of love to Mama and Vanya. I had to believe they wouldn't be my last but wrote as though they would be. With each carefully scripted letter, my trepidation seeped out onto the page with the bright-blue ink so I would not carry it with me.

The crews that were flying assembled around a blackboard, papered with a large map of the front and reconnaissance photos of the German munitions we were charged with destroying. Sofia indicated our heading and the calculations that determined how long it would take us to reach the target based on the Polikarpov's cruising speed. I'd have to keep one eye on my compass to make sure we stayed on the right heading and the other on my chronometer to let Taisiya know when we were approaching. The weather report looked favorable as well—no crosswinds expected that might blow us off course or make flight impossible altogether.

Renata and Polina had our craft's systems checked three times, bombs loaded, and every centimeter of the dilapidated crop duster freshly painted and in perfect working order. Like mothers loading down their children with baked goods and lovingly knitted blankets as they headed off to university, they buried their worry for us with constant activity. The plane looked better than the day it came off the assembly line, and I smiled broadly to see my name painted below the rear cockpit.

I embraced Renata, Polina having absented herself from the emotion of our departure. If I knew her, she'd be watching from the sidelines, near enough to be present when needed, but removed enough that she would not have to show her tears to her comrades. "She looks beautiful," I said, patting the side of the aircraft, not embarrassing Renata by embroidering the compliment. "Thank you."

"It was our pleasure," Renata said, holding her chin high and smiling bright. I loved that about her. The pride she took in her work, the joy she still showed despite the inferno to the west.

"You have your orders," I told her. "You won't need them, but it makes me feel better knowing that you have them all the same." I fixed my gaze on her brown eyes, and she patted the three letters she'd tucked into her breast pocket that I'd scrawled out when we were supposed to be sleeping. Even a missive for the Solonevs. They might not love me, but they had given me my husband and deserved the attention. I gripped Renata's hands for a moment and gave her a hard smile. *I'm glad you're here for me.*

"Clear skies, ladies," Sofia said, shaking our hands before climbing into her cockpit, and giving the signal that she was ready to depart. The second crew would depart six minutes after they were up in the air, and we would follow six minutes after them.

My hands were stock still as I took my place in the rear cockpit, but as the engine roared to life I felt deafened, though I'd heard the drone hour after hour for the past few months. I deepened my shallow breaths and kept my eyes on the back of Taisiya's helmet to calm my nerves. She seemed so steady. I didn't know if I ought to find comfort in her resolve or berate myself for my lack of it. I chose the former. She waved to the ground crew to signal our readiness and turned her head forward.

Up in the air, we flew in tight formation. Our bombs would be more effective if dropped in rapid succession. It was twenty minutes before the target came into view, owing to our slow aircraft. The German camp was orderly. Proper barracks, a large mess hall fashioned from canvas. They didn't improvise like we did, with bunks in tents, trenches, and obliging villagers' homes. It appeared they didn't have to. The munitions store came into view, obvious by virtue of looking so unremarkable. We cut our engines and swooped low, banking to the left so hard, I gripped one of the metal support beams until I could feel my fingers cramping in my leather gloves.

The plane emitted an unearthly whistle as we glided down, unaided by our engines and only minimally controlled by Taisiya's gliding skills.

While daylight would have given the Germans a clear target, sound is more fickle. All they heard was an eerie squeal as we whooshed toward our targets. While it was logical for them to assume the enemy would come from the east—they knew where we were encamped, in the broad sense, if not precisely—they couldn't pinpoint the exact direction from which we approached. The wind carried our sound where it willed, and by the time the Germans realized that the humming sound was not coming from three sewing machines that inexplicably found themselves in their camp, we were upon them.

Sofia dropped her bomb first. Then Darya.

I removed my right glove to pry open the cap, then pitched the flare over the edge, illuminating the path for Taisiya to loose the bomb.

Before the bombs made contact, Taisiya fired the engine back to life and made her course back to our airfield. I craned around to see that all three bombs made their target in rapid succession. Seeing the munitions tent send off a series of small explosions, like fireworks, as their precious instruments of death blazed below us, I let out a whoop that was swallowed by the roar of the engine.

The Germans, having at last realized what was happening, opened fire with their pistols and small arms—whatever they had by their bedsides. We were only five hundred meters high, so in the light from the fires, we could see their tiny figures below pouring out of the barracks, aiming their pistols in a futile attempt to ward us off. There was no time for them to launch an effective counterattack, so they fought back with what they had at hand.

In a proper aircraft their bullets would have been about as effective as throwing rocks in the sky—we could have evaded faster and flown higher. As it was, I could hear a few of the bullets make tearing sounds in the canvas that coated our wings. Sofia's plane was up in front and quickly escaping the range of the enemy bullets. Taisiya and I were catching the brunt of the fire, but it was the haunting squeal of metal from Darya and Eva's plane that worried us.

Their engine sputtered. Then stopped.

The Germans saw they had hit their mark and kept firing at the craft. Darya and Eva were in a perilous dive, and flames were shooting from the engine. We could feel the whoosh of air from their rapid descent as we flew over them. There was nothing we could do to save them from going down.

I forced my eyes to stay locked on the back of Taisiya's head. This was no time to think. I called course corrections to Taisiya over the interphone and longed to have a throttle in my own hands, to have some control over whether we lived or died, but I could only grip my hands together and will our plane to safety.

We cleared the German camp, but it seemed like hours before we reached our own. Again and again I glanced behind us, certain I could hear the whirr of German engines, ready to retaliate for their destroyed munitions, but they launched no counterattack. We saw a spire from the church in the nearby town, and I felt myself give in to my trembling.

As I clambered down from the cockpit, the ground seemed too firm, too real. I felt Taisiya's arm around me, and while the onlookers would think it a gesture of consolation or solidarity, it was the only thing propelling me forward.

Sofia was white as bleached cotton when we touched down and staggered back to the throng that awaited us. Renata and Polina looked horrified by the condition of the plane they'd so painstakingly prepared. The wings would need hours of patchwork. It was a miracle we'd been able to return unscathed.

"Darya and Eva?" Sofia asked quietly when no one else could find their voice. She'd been at the head of the formation, unable to see for certain what had happened.

"Gone," I replied. "We saw them going down. If they manage to land, they're only a few meters from the German camp. There is no way they won't be found."

"They did their duty," Chernov said, emerging from the darkness to join us. "And the mission was a success. You'll all be up tomorrow night."

We nodded as the general retreated to his quarters. This was what success would look like. This was why we couldn't contemplate failure.

CHAPTER 14

Early August 1942, Sorties: 27

The evening of our first mission rehashed itself in my mind like a newsreel played too slow on the projector—the first glimpse of the enemy base, watching our bombs turn their munitions into useless piles of rubble, our haphazard escape on shredded wings—forever etched in my brain. It was the sight of Darya and Eva's plane, the engine enshrouded in flames, that was the most prominent memory. I could not look at our campfires or even the flame of a gas stove without remembering the terrifying screech as their plane went down.

Now the missions blurred together. Five to eight sorties in a single evening. Bridges, ammunition, hoards of supplies—all destroyed. Better, we kept the Germans awake, and they had to hate us for it.

"Congratulations, ladies," Sofia said as we sat down to an early supper before dusk gave us the cover our missions required. "According to the latest intel, you're considered a priority target."

"That's a comfort," Taisiya said with a wry smile.

"Isn't it, though? They've given us a charming nickname to go along with it, too."

"Oh, don't keep us in suspense," a pilot named Zoya said with a giggle as she cut into her potatoes.

"Die Nachthexen," Sofia replied with an admirable German accent.

"The Night Witches?" I said, remembering the German vocabulary from my language classes before the academy. I was unable to control my giggles as the peals of laughter from my comrades floated up to the trees. "How fitting. I think it suits us."

Even Oksana, usually so solemn and quiet, smiled with the rest of us. They meant the nickname to be demeaning. They sought to make us sound like something inhuman with their taunt, likely so they would feel less remorse about opening fire on women. We knew the truth, though. If they went to this trouble, we were affecting them. It was exactly what we wanted.

"We also have a new order from Comrade Stalin," Sofia announced. She kept her voice steady as she read the decree:

> *Form within the limits of each army 3 to 5 well-armed defensive squads (up to 200 persons in each), and put them directly behind unstable divisions. Require them, in case of panic and scattered withdrawals of elements of the divisions, to shoot in place panic-mongers and cowards and thus help the honest soldiers of the division execute their duty to the motherland.*

Panic. Cowards. Easy words for advisers to bandy about in boardrooms and safe houses hundreds of kilometers from the rain of mortar shells and bullets from German guns. Harder to stomach when it was you who had to constantly fight against your gut instinct to flee from the inferno of hate that sprawled to the west. That the generals didn't want troops to flee made sense, but to ban retreat was tactically questionable—and to assign troops to shoot anyone who even appeared to withdraw was worse than cruelty. It was madness.

"Can he mean such a thing?" Svetlana, now promoted to navigator, asked after a long moment of stunned silence.

"Comrade Stalin rarely speaks a word he doesn't mean," Sofia answered matter-of-factly. "But don't let the directive make you uneasy. You're all volunteers. There won't be gunmen behind us to keep us in line."

Renata spoke up from the back of the formation, where the armorers stood. "But what about our husbands and brothers on the ground?"

Sofia's serene countenance faltered as she considered the question. It wasn't our own necks we worried about. It was never about that—at least, never entirely.

"We have trained and flown together for months now, ladies. If your men possess a fraction of the bravery you have shown, I wouldn't fear for them." I could see the truth in Sofia's blue eyes. She believed what she said, which counted for something.

We were dismissed, but none of us were quick to scatter back to our huts and farms for a bit of rest. Stalin's words had shaken us too badly for real rest; what we wanted was the camaraderie of our sisters.

It was no afternoon for tunes on my creaky violin or for songs no one wanted to sing. It was no time for poetry or literature, either. I thought of the tools in my arsenal and found the sack where I kept my personal supplies. I removed my comb, pins, and the bright-red pencil that navigators used to mark their maps.

My hair had grown a few centimeters since they cropped it in Engels, and it now fell nearly to my collar, past the awkward length when it grew past the ear but too short to pull back properly.

I poured a cup of water and took small sections of my hair with a wetted comb, pinning them up all over my head.

"What on earth are you doing?" Polina asked.

"What does it look like?" I responded, pinning the last tendril up on top of my head to curl. I looked at my reflection in the mirror and traced the contour of my lips with the red, waxy navigator's pencil, then filled them in with color. I hadn't bothered with lipstick since the war broke out, and not often before, but Mama had always said that bad times were easier to endure with a pretty face and nice clothes. I couldn't do anything about my uniform, but I could do the best with what I had.

"My Vanya will be here to collect me soon," I said. "Your sweethearts, too. I think it's best to look like we expect them home any moment."

~

I did my best to keep up my cheerful facade for the girls. I never appeared outside the barracks without hair curled and color on my face. They began to pay more attention to their appearance as well, no longer bemoaning the loss of their long locks. I don't know if they thought my efforts were sincere or bravado, but I felt it did a fair amount to help morale.

The improved mood made me smile. We took pains to alter our uniforms to fit better, the skilled seamstresses of the group being called upon to help those of us with less ability.

"You have a waist," Taisiya commented as I appeared in my newly tailored uniform jacket. "Much better."

"No woman wants to look like a rectangle," I said, examining myself in the mirror and smoothing the fabric against my silhouette. It was a relief to wear my belt normally and not as a cinch that bound the excess fabric in clumps at my midsection, lest the ridiculous trousers fall in a green puddle at my feet.

"Too right," she agreed, admiring her own form, looking kilos thinner and much more like a proper soldier in a uniform that suited her frame.

Oksana, assuming more duties as Sofia's deputy, inspected our handiwork and nodded with approval. "You didn't suit the uniforms, so you made them suit you." The turn of phrase was telling. The Russian army had one uniform, made like cakes from a mold, each identical to the other. They were meant for one type of soldier—and there was no mistaking that we didn't fit that mold. "Svetlana, what have you done to your collar?"

"I made a new one from some of the fur from my boots, Captain," she answered, petting it absently. "I think it's becoming."

"I won't deny that, but it's not regulation. It's one thing to make your uniforms fit you properly, quite another to alter them from standard issue. You'll fix it at the next opportunity and not pull such a stunt again. Is that clear?"

"Yes, Captain." She unbuttoned her jacket immediately and had her seam-ripper in hand before Oksana exited the barracks. Svetlana muttered under her breath, but I couldn't fault Oksana's reprimand. Those new to military life would not be well served by a gentle hand.

As we took to our planes that night, charged with bombing tanks as they advanced east, the evening air scratched at my throat. The west was on fire. There would be no way to harvest the crops as the Germans advanced, so the farmers and soldiers burned their wheat rather than let it fall into enemy hands.

I felt a wet warmth against my windblown face as we approached our targets. Tears streamed down, and I didn't bother to stem the tide.

Russia was burning.

The acres of wheat lost would mean thousands of my countrymen would starve this winter. It would mean poor crops for years to come. Stalin was willing to send all of us to our deaths to save his country, and in that moment I couldn't help but wonder if there would be anything left to save.

The German tanks below us rolled on over washboard roads toward a defenseless village, moving like a family of uncoordinated, greenish-brown turtles looking for the nearest entry point to their brook. Using the new chalk lines Renata measured out for me on the wings of the plane, I aimed my flare at the hillside next to a tank in the middle of the formation, hoping if Taisiya made her mark it would bring a fair amount of rock down around them. We wouldn't be able to disable a tank, but we could make the roads impassable.

All I could do to support Taisiya was to throw grenades over the side when she released her payload. It wasn't enough to cause damage most of the time, but it added to the chaos, which was the chief point of the exercise.

The whoosh of the descending bomb and the sickening rumble as the bomb made contact were audible even through our muffled ears. Taisiya pulled up as the bomb exploded, narrowly escaping the flying daggers created by the wreckage in the road. The tanks were now stranded in the rubble of the destroyed roadway. Once we were out of range, I took a calming breath and looked back to observe the destruction below. When I turned back around, Taisiya gave me a wave to let me know we were unscathed and that she'd seen our success.

Shards of metal and glass. Nothing more. I couldn't allow myself to think that there were men inside those machines Hitler sent to flatten us. No more, I hoped, than they thought about the women protected by rickety wood and linen frames when they opened fire on us.

Our encampment, now farther west than where we'd trained and taken our first missions, was always buzzing with activity after dark. Summer nights in Russia were short, and we had to make each minute count. We had to coordinate our takeoffs and landings carefully, spacing them out by no more than ten minutes. Barely enough time to maneuver around one another.

As soon as we landed, Renata and Polina rushed to us. Using a code of their own invention, Taisiya updated Polina on the aircraft's status while Polina assessed any damage Taisiya couldn't have seen in flight.

After asking me about the quantity of my flares and grenades, Renata set to work replacing the bombs and ammunition. She lifted hundreds of kilos a night. The largest bombs weighed fifty kilos and required the help of two other armorers to load. In turn she helped load them for the other teams. She never stopped. Strong before the war, hardened by work on her family's farm, now her arms were chiseled like the arms on a statue of a Greek god. I knew she ached—her efforts were inhuman—but I also knew she was proud, so didn't attempt to coddle her.

When Polina gave us the all clear, we took our place in the rotation. It would be our fourth sortie of the night, and we hoped for seven. Oksana insisted that we make scrupulous records of every single sortie. The reporters were watching. The Kremlin was watching. Most importantly the men were watching. We had to show them what dedication looked like.

~

We slept on wooden folding beds in an abandoned school. There was little privacy, no decent shower facilities, and as we had to sleep during the day, no real quiet. We couldn't expect the villagers around us to stop going on with their lives because we needed sleep.

Oksana still kept to herself, but her dour expression had softened somewhat. Either that, or it had simply become the neutral expression we all wore and was therefore just less noticeable. We bunked in our four-woman teams, and Oksana's crew had claimed the four bunks next to ours, which might have given us the chance to become better acquainted if Oksana had been more open to conversation.

Oksana pinned her hair up to curl like the rest of us but was less skilled, perhaps not having the practice the rest of us did.

"Would you like some help?" I asked one morning. The dawn was still weak, and we all rushed to fall asleep before the sun shone in earnest.

"I suppose," she said, tossing the comb at me with a fatigued sigh. "I don't usually fuss about this sort of thing, but it seems smart to follow your lead in this." She gave me a martyred look, but I smiled upon seeing it was mostly insincere.

"It's good for the spirit," I said, taking the comb in my hand and smoothing her thick locks of fine, silver-blond hair. I took a section of hair, just long enough to reach her collar, between my thumb and forefinger, and twisted it up with a pin and affixed it to the top of her head. Her tresses were soft, and I found the monotony of the task soothing.

"You're right," she answered as I worked. "They like to look like women, even if we do a man's job."

"It reminds us of who we were," I said, painfully aware of the past tense. *Would we be those young girls again—perhaps not carefree and giddy, but at least living our lives in relative calm and safety?* The unasked question hung in the air like Polina's overly sweet perfume that she'd refused to leave behind, and of which she seemed to have an inexhaustible supply.

"Maybe," she said noncommittally. "My best friend, Yana, was far more fond of curls, dresses, and shoes than I. I was the tomboy. I let her dress me and do my hair when there was an occasion, but I spent most of my time in boy's trousers and plain shirts with my hair pulled back with a leather string. It horrified my mother and amused my father."

I chuckled at the admission but didn't want to draw too much attention to myself. It was the first time I'd heard her say more than one sentence that had nothing to do with aircraft, orders, or a mission.

"I'm sure Yana enjoyed it," I said after a moment. "No doubt she'll want to dress you like a girl for months after all this time in uniform."

"There will be more important things to do after the war," she said, her voice mirroring her cold tone. "Rebuilding our country, for one."

I thought of the burning fields of wheat. Who knew what damage was done to the soil by the fires, the shrapnel, the land mines? The land might not grow proper crops for years. This was to say nothing of the decimated roads and bombed-out buildings. Even with manpower and supplies in abundance, rebuilding Russia would be the task of generations, and the war showed no signs of slowing.

"But it will be a country free from tyranny," I said, thinking of the rumors of Hitler's cruelty. "Better to rebuild than to have left the motherland intact and hand it over to the likes of Hitler."

"Do you think Stalin is so very different?" Oksana asked quietly.

"How can you ask such a thing?" I whispered.

"Very easily. He claims to be a man of the people but has no problem sending hordes of his people to die for him. That's not the act of a benevolent leader."

I scanned the room for listening ears and hoped the gentle snores I heard on the nearest bunks were genuine. I pinned the last curl atop her head. She turned to look at me.

"Then why do you fight in his army?" I couldn't help but ask. "You're no draftee."

"Just because I fight against Hitler does not mean I fight for Stalin. I fly to protect my people and my country. I fly for Russia as she could be, if given the chance."

In her gray-blue eyes there was a wisdom born of suffering. I didn't know what she'd seen in her twenty-three years, nor could I bring myself to ask.

"I think we all do, Oksana. We fly for the promise of better times."

"Of course," she said in a tone that indicated the conversation had come to its conclusion.

Part of me longed to press her, to learn more about Yana and her past, but I knew her well enough to know I'd only succeed in brokering more silence, or worse, resentment. So I went on about my daily ritual of lying in my bed, closing my eyes against the sun, and willing each muscle to relax. I started from bottom to top, focusing on each minuscule part of me. *Toes, go to sleep. Feet, you're next.* Legs, hips, waist, and so on. I didn't achieve real sleep, but I found the profound state of relaxation was better than tossing in bed counting sheep for hours on end.

Rest was no luxury. We needed to be alert up in the air. The slightest error in judgment cost lives. Try as I did to relax on this morning, my mind wandered back to Oksana. She appeared hostile so often, but today I saw more sadness than anything. I found myself torn between wanting to soothe her and wanting to unearth the mystery behind a demeanor so clearly designed to keep everyone at a distance. But, as my papa often said, it was no use hoping a wall would become a door.

CHAPTER 15

November 7, 1942, North Caucasus Front, Sorties: 164

The short, warm nights of summer had given way to the interminable dark and relentless ice of winter. Where we had been flying anywhere from five or six sorties, now we aimed for eight to ten. The Germans had attempted a few raids on our camps the previous day, trying to torch our planes. Anything to keep us from interrupting their sleep. But the raids were always poorly planned, and the foot soldiers encamped nearby warded them off without too much trouble. But they had succeeded in being as big a nuisance to us as we were to them. I understood why they hated us.

Of the twenty-five crews, Taisiya and I had gained the reputation of being among the most fearless teams in the air—each earning the rank of senior lieutenant for our efforts—and Renata and Polina had grown into the regiment's most respected ground crew, serving as our eyes and ears on the ground, nursing our plane when she suffered broken bones and keeping us supplied with the bombs and ammunition that kept us alive and the enemy at bay. But today was a day of rest, a holiday in honor of the October Revolution.

Our residence was currently a factory that had been abandoned for a safer location to the east—a wise move, given the amount of bomb damage it had sustained. We lay about our makeshift barracks, unable to make friends with the calm. After a year in service, we were too used to constant activity to sit idle. Though our minds yearned for it on the long nights, our bodies betrayed us now that we had the chance for a few hours of rest and leisure. Some of the girls read; others mended uniforms. A few snores sounded from the corner of the room from the lucky few able to sleep.

Sofia's voice called out, echoing off the bare walls: "Ladies, put aside your diversions, and make yourselves presentable. We're having a proper celebration tonight. Katya, you'll want your violin, and Renata, your flute."

The sluggishness of pilots too long denied proper sleep transformed at once into the bustle of schoolgirls moments before a big dance. Overlarge flight suits were discarded in favor of our daily uniforms, thrown on hastily and in no way ready to stand inspection.

Smells of roasting meat wafted from the dank warehouse designated as our mess hall, and our stomachs rumbled in appreciation. So often we ate what we could between sorties—Polina and Renata always ready with a plate of something, anticipating when we would need it. We never had the time to taste our food, let alone enjoy it. There were other times we were simply too tired, too overwhelmed, to eat much at all.

It was clear the cooks had gone to special effort. This was, after all, in honor of the October Revolution, and the commanders would have seen to it that the best food possible was sent to us to mark the occasion. Roasted beef and pork, piles of white potatoes whipped into clouds, green beans, beets, cakes, and pies. On each table was a large flagon of wine, the first any of us had been offered since training. The male regiments had daily rations of vodka and wine, but our commanders had forbidden it for us. None of us complained at the deprivation—we had more to prove—but we didn't refuse alcohol, either. The burgundy liquid, lush and warm like velvet, with the taste of warm earth and blue skies infused in the grapes, brought color to all our cheeks.

"Let us hope this means our advances are getting noticed," Taisiya said, lifting her glass. We raised ours in unison to toast our achievements.

"I assure you, they are, comrades," Sofia chimed in. "Stalin himself has made it known that he's proud to see how well Russian women have risen to the cause, especially our regiment. You're to be congratulated."

Applause sounded and more toasts were made. The wine flowed freely, more than I had seen even in the days before the war. I found myself eating with more vigor than I had felt except perhaps in the hungriest days of my adolescence, when meals never seemed to sate my hunger. I reveled in the rich meats and sweet pies, giggling with my sisters in arms as though we were not in the clutches of war in a world gone mad.

As the meal waned, the conversation grew still livelier. I removed my violin from the case and kept my tunes light and carefree. Renata accompanied on the flute and Svetlana on a discarded balalaika she'd found in the factory. Sofia's voice sounded clear and true, singing words of happy songs that belonged to bygone days:

Under the pine, under the green pine,
Lay me down to sleep.
Little pine, little green one,
Don't rustle above me.

The wine and song gave warmth to the cold cement room with its high ceilings. The world outside was chilled November frost, but we were wrapped in blankets of mirth for one evening.

"I'm proud of all of you," Sofia declared after a song had ended. "The Russian people will recognize what we have done here as extraordinary. The papers will tell your stories, not just to boost morale for the other troops, but because you are fine aviators—fine soldiers—in your own right. In fact, I have some fan mail for all of you."

She read:

> *My dear comrades,*
> *I have been following your progress in the ladies' journals for many months now and wish to offer you my profound thanks for your service to the motherland. You have shown the women of this great country that we are equal to taking up the mantle of equality that Comrade Stalin has granted to our female citizens. Do not listen to the jibes of the forces that have brought evil to our doorstep. You are not witches, casting hexes down upon innocent men. You are heavenly creatures. Daughters of the night sky who are bringing justice to your people and keeping Mother Russia safe for all her children. I would give anything to serve alongside you, but alas, my age dictates I must find a way to do my part closer to home, but please know that my blessings are with you.*
> *Sincerely,*
> *~ Your faithful countrywoman*

As if to highlight her words, the sirens sounded overhead.

Polina, having excused herself from most of the festivities, was the only one in the regiment who had seen the impending invasion. She burst into the hall, face flushed and panting.

"The Germans are maneuvering. If we don't act fast, they'll take out the aerodrome."

The idea of losing our planes sent us all into motion. We raced to throw on our padded flight suits and heavy boots. I was plodding and clumsy, lacing my boots, slowed by so much food and wine. I gritted my teeth and forced my fingers to cooperate. *Are you a soldier, or a fat housewife enjoying a Christmas feast?*

I continued cursing myself as we waded through the muddy field to the aerodrome. No one moved with more grace than I, and I felt compelled to turn back. If I were so clumsy on the ground, I shuddered to think of the mistakes we could make in the air.

"Taisiya, are you all right to fly?" I asked as we hoisted our muddy feet into the cockpit.

"I have to be," she said matter-of-factly.

I nodded. She wasn't one to overindulge in her drink, regardless of the occasion, and I'd had less than most, having taken up my violin while many others kept drinking.

Renata and Polina, along with their teams of mechanics and armorers, had us ready to fly in five minutes. Others still staggered to their planes, giggling as they fell into their cockpits. I didn't blame them for folly; I was just disappointed they couldn't enjoy one well-earned evening of pleasure. Even in the midst of war, we deserved that. I looked at the glassy-eyed pilots and their flushed mechanics. It would be a miracle if our little feast didn't cost lives.

We were the first to take off, though we saw others following close behind. It was difficult to tell, but they seemed to be flying true. I hoped their hands would remain steady. We were perhaps ten minutes from our target, a German airfield that had been positioned far too close to our front line for comfort, when the clouds came rolling in.

"Go lower!" I called to Taisiya through the interphone. "We won't be able to see a thing."

"I'm already flying at five hundred meters. If I go any lower, I won't be able to drop the bombs."

"Then let's retreat," I said. There were no longer planes behind me, the others noticing the clouds had pushed us below safe limits. There was no shame in turning back on a mission when it would put the crew and plane in unnecessary danger. We hadn't enough of either to treat the loss casually.

Taisiya had begun to speak over the interphone, likely to acknowledge that we'd do better to head back to the camp, when a German spotlight plucked us out of the sky.

"Fuck," she muttered. She attempted an evasive maneuver, banking right and swerving lower, but the spotlight operator never lost sight of her. She dove to four hundred and fifty meters—lower, even—and we were meters away from our target.

"We're too low!" I bellowed, unnecessarily loud, given the interphone.

"Mark it anyway!" she called back, matching my volume.

I could see a munitions tent in good range, and given what I could see—not very much—it was the best target we could hope to hit.

"Three . . . two . . . one . . . *mark!*" The cold metal of the flare felt caustic, like acid, against my warm skin as I removed the cap and tossed it over the side of the plane to illuminate the target for Taisiya. I ripped the little white parachute from the flare, caring more about the speed of its descent than pinpoint accuracy.

Taisiya dropped the bomb over the munitions tent, hitting her mark without a centimeter of error. I swallowed my congratulations for the excellent run when the plane bounced upward with the force of the blast. We'd never bombed from such a low elevation, and it seemed like the regulations were in place for a good reason.

"I think we're going to be fine," Taisiya said, anticipating my question. "We're climbing fine, and she seems to be responding as well as she ever does."

"Let's get back as fast as she'll haul us, then," I said, wondering what damage might have been done that we couldn't tell from our rudimentary equipment.

Taisiya gave me a wave. "Have some grenades at the ready in case we get company."

She needn't have reminded me. Retreat was often the most dangerous part of the mission. Most times we arrived unnoticed, and it wasn't until we were on our way back to base that the Germans were in the air and able to return fire. The best they could do until then was shoot at us from the ground, which was plenty dangerous. They would only have a short window to chase us before they got close enough to Russian airspace that their mission would become suicide. The Germans weren't ones for taking needless risks without benefit, and one of our little planes wasn't worth losing one of theirs.

But there *was* a window to attack us, and they were getting better at using it. They knew to blind us with their searchlights. It made them more visible but kept us from being able to aim or escape with accuracy. We had begun to use planes as decoys to divert the Germans' attention while two others swooped in to drop their payloads, but the risk to the decoy plane was enormous.

My hunched shoulders lowered only as the welcome shape of our aerodrome became visible by light of flares waved by the ground crews. This time no enemy craft pursued us, perhaps owing to the proximity of their camp to ours. Unless they launched a large portion of their fleet for a proper counterattack, it would be too risky to fly so close to our base, which they knew was well awake and prepared to shoot down anyone who got too close.

We landed, and a dozen people, Renata and Polina in particular, dashed toward us. My hands, steady in the craft, trembled now that my feet were back on solid earth.

"We thought you'd gone down. The clouds were thick as soup!" Nika, a pilot, cried out. "We all turned back!"

"What kept you?" Sofia asked, silencing the clamor with the ring of authority. "The visibility was too low. You should have turned back."

"By the time we'd reached the abort level, we'd been engaged by an enemy spotlight," Taisiya answered, the relief of being back on solid ground now replaced with sobriety and discipline. Her answers to these questions mattered a great deal, as would mine. "There was no making a stealthy getaway, so I ordered Lieutenant Soloneva to mark the target, and I dropped our payload. She questioned dropping the bomb at such a low altitude, but in the end she followed my orders."

She was taking responsibility for the damage to the plane, as any decent pilot would, but I had to speak in her defense. "Despite the adverse conditions, Lieutenant Pashkova made the target and destroyed a large stockpile of munitions. It had to be a significant blow to that camp's ability to advance on us. She delivered us back safely."

"With a great deal of luck, it would seem," Sofia said. Her eyes weren't on Taisiya or me, but on the aircraft behind us. The canvas on the underbelly was badly scorched and had to have been within seconds of erupting into flames.

A meter or two lower and we wouldn't have survived the blast.

CHAPTER 16

Sorties: 165

An hour after dawn we were all assembled before the general, whose ruddy face was now a terrifying shade of purple as he spoke to the regiment.

"I expected you to be undisciplined. Girls aren't raised to understand the need for rule and order in the same manner that boys are. But I didn't expect you to be stupid and careless. Worse, dishonest." General Chernov paced back and forth in front of us as we stood at attention in precise rows.

Our reckless flight was the tipping point, but there were myriad misdemeanors that had driven the general to take action. The parachutes on the flares, sometimes useful, but dead inconvenient if there was a wind any stronger than a light breeze, were frequently discarded. Not being the wasteful sort, some of the girls who were handy with a needle had taken to fashioning the discarded nylon into proper ladies' undergarments. We used our red navigators' pencils in place of lipstick when there was none to be had. Little things to remind us of who we were. I was guiltier of these petty crimes than most—I'd been the one to turn our navigation pencils to lipstick, after all—but couldn't feel remorse for my misdeeds.

"You misuse army property, you disobey automatic abort levels that are put in place for the safety of valuable aircraft"—I held back a snort at this . . . the fifteen-year-old, ramshackle planes were worth the army's concern, but not our lives?—"you take your one holiday as an excuse to overindulge to the point that you are unfit for service. If it were up to me, I'd send you all home to your mothers this very afternoon. I'd reserve space on much-needed trains and send you as fast as I could arrange for it and get you out of my hair." The general's bald head under the harsh incandescent lights glowed like the moon. More than a few of us had to stifle derisive chuckles. "But it seems that Comrade Stalin cannot be persuaded of your uselessness."

He glared in Sofia's direction, a wordless accusation in his gaze. He blamed Sofia for Stalin's commitment to our regiment, probably for motives that were not entirely innocent. *Of course* no woman could have influence over a man if there wasn't a shared impropriety binding them. I knew Stalin's admiration for Sofia was born solely from her accomplishments in aviation, but that wouldn't stop the other officers from making their own—incorrect—assumptions about how Sofia had gained her influence. I felt the grinding of enamel as my molars grated against each other while he continued his tirade.

"I have court-martialed two of you this morning for the most flagrant displays of misuse of army property. Lieutenants Mateeva and Borzliova have been sentenced to ten years' hard labor in Siberia." I held my tongue, knowing that Chernov would not tolerate an outburst, but there were quiet titters from some without the same military training, for Svetlana and Nika were still with us, though their red eyes and dour expressions revealed their difficult morning. Chernov's eyes narrowed, but he went on.

"But I have decided, in the greater interests of the motherland, to commute their sentences to serving in this regiment for the duration of the war, provided they perform their duties with no further incident. They will serve their sentence once we are victorious. I trust that from this moment forward they will serve as models of good behavior and military discipline for the lot of you. Let this be a warning to you girls. Further antics of this sort will not be tolerated."

Taisiya and I had not been among those questioned earlier that morning when we were meant to be sleeping in preparation for the night's sorties. Either Chernov considered our actions sheer stupidity, which wasn't an offense that merited a court-martial, or Sofia had spoken for us.

Sofia came to the barracks with us and made no attempt to hide her ire. "He's gone mad," she muttered as we all changed into whatever we had that would pass for sleepwear. "Sentenced to hard labor for repurposing a few scraps of nylon."

"Perhaps things are going worse than we know?" I suggested. "If he thinks the Germans have the upper hand, it seems like the sort of irrational behavior we'd see when they know we're backed into a corner."

"I don't think things are any worse than they have been," Sofia answered, her tone earnest. "He is privy to a lot more information than I am, but I haven't seen one thing to think we're in any more risk of being overrun than in the past six months."

"With all due respect," Oksana said, "the punishment was severe, but the misdemeanors needed to be addressed. If we enforce some rules, but not all, when will our crews know which lines they can cross and which we intend to respect? We have no room for error in an aviation unit. I don't think Chernov was out of line."

"Well said, Tymoshenko," Sofia said, her mind clearly still back in the hangar.

"But why all the foaming at the mouth?" Taisiya asked, pacing by her bunk, arms akimbo. "It doesn't seem rational. It's not as if we're performing poorly. In fact, we could hardly be more effective than we've been."

"Precisely what's making him angry," I answered, remembering the biting comments from the schoolmaster, Comrade Dokorov, when I outperformed the boys in mathematics or the indifference from Captain Karlov when I navigated the aircraft without fault. "We're doing well enough that he can't discipline us for genuine infractions, so he's making capital offenses out of the least missteps."

"God, I think you're right, Katya," Sofia chimed in. "I didn't take him for being so petty, but it fits."

"It's nonsense," Taisiya said. "If the men in a regiment took the parachutes off their flares, he would say they're just doing what was necessary to complete the mission. He wouldn't care what they did with the scrap fabric. He wouldn't berate them for drinking on a sanctioned holiday. They get their daily measures of vodka, and we never touch the stuff."

"We have to leave him with no choice," I said. "We have to fly so well, so clean, that no one would hear a word against us."

"How do we do more than what we're doing?" Taisiya asked. "We fly constantly as it is."

"We have to be the best. Not just good," I said, steel filling my bones. "We need to fly more missions than the men. We have to be more efficient than they are. We can't be excellent. We have to be exemplary."

"Katya's right," Sofia said. "Winter is upon us. They expect us to balk at the long nights and the cold weather. We have to show them how wrong they are. I want all of us to think of what we can do to streamline each sortie. I want to turn around planes after their sorties in half the time. I want to send up groups in a tighter formation—each plane with a gap of three minutes, not six. Speak to your teams. Your mechanics know your planes better than you do. I want every maintenance procedure scrutinized."

We summoned Renata and Polina to the conversation, who in turn called over a few other mechanics and armorers who had shown considerable skill. We didn't sleep, relying on coffee to fuel us through the cruel brightness of the winter day. Before the night's missions and between each subsequent sortie, we began looking at the standard procedures for preparing a plane for flight. Polina scribbled furiously in a notebook as she considered each of the tasks she performed on the aircraft as devoutly as prayer each day.

"You only cut the engine once per sortie, right?" Polina asked, looking down at her notebook instead of up at us.

"Yes," Taisiya answered, then, arms crossed over her chest, went on staring at the simple engine as though it contained the answer to a complex riddle. "Once we lose the element of surprise, there's not a lot of use in cutting it again."

"Don't charge the starter in between each sortie," Polina said, scribbling. "You get five starts of each charge. Charge when you have one left. That will shave several minutes off right there."

"Brilliant," Sofia said, clapping Polina on the shoulder. "What else?"

"Well, I understand why they want one mechanic per plane—it allows us to learn the plane and all of its quirks—but it would be faster if we worked in teams. Each of us would still be the chief mechanic for her plane, but the others can help refuel and see to basic maintenance in between sorties instead of waiting for their own planes to come back."

A crowd of mechanics had gathered around, humming in approval as though they'd been thinking this for months and never been bold enough to suggest it.

"That makes good sense," Sofia agreed. "Though I'm afraid you'll exhaust yourselves."

"It's better to exhaust ourselves working than waiting," Polina replied, earning approving cheers from the other mechanics.

While Sofia, Taisiya, and Oksana looked over our aircraft with Renata, discussing the most efficient ways to load the bombs and reload the navigators' sidearms, I pulled Polina aside, forcing her to look up from the leather notebook she gripped like a life preserver. "You're sure you can do this?" I asked, my tone low. I wouldn't have her answer colored by pride. "It'll increase your workload twenty-five times over."

"Anything is better than waiting for you to come back," Polina insisted. "You have no idea what it's like for us wondering which ones might not make it back. If we're busy, it helps us feel like we're doing more to help."

"We couldn't fly without you," I said. "You couldn't possibly be doing anything more, short of flying the planes yourselves. You don't have to work yourselves sick to do your part."

"Don't you worry about us. Just bring your planes back in one piece, and let us do our jobs."

In four hours we'd dissected the procedures for readying the plane and stripped them down to the barest necessities and decided how the mechanics could work together to make the essential tasks happen as quickly as they could manage. For the pilots and navigators, the plan was simple—stay in the plane. Eat in the plane. Sleep in it if needed.

Dusk descended, and it would soon be time to test realigning the maintenance crews and to see how our proposed new techniques worked. The next night we would work on the systems we had in place for loading the bombs and overhaul those. The work was dangerous and backbreaking, but if there was the chance we could shave minutes off the process without harming the armorers or the flight crews, it was worth examining.

Polina, while never officially titled chief mechanic, now held the role without equivocation. The swarm of mechanics strained to hear every syllable from her lips as she tutored them on the new procedures. They knew that one missed step could mean disaster for their flight crew. The Germans offered enough opportunities for that without mechanical failure helping them along.

I stood back with Taisiya and the other pilots and navigators. We felt helpless, but this was not our domain. The mechanics were in their milieu, and any interference from us would be listened to with respectful attention because we were superior officers, but they would resent our interference unless we were specifically asked for input. If one of us saw something catastrophically wrong—doubtful—she would speak up respectfully. If she had a less urgent suggestion, she would offer it to Polina in private with the order to present the idea as her own if Polina wished to implement it.

"Your 'kites' are ready for flight," Polina pronounced at last, hands clasped behind her back, her chest puffed out. "And a full hour faster."

"You just bought us another ten sorties, if not more," Sofia said, her lips a thin line as she patted Polina's shoulder. "Brilliant work, Vasilyeva."

The pilots took to their planes, we navigators behind them. In minutes the first team took off, followed by the rest of us, spaced no more than three minutes apart. Our target tonight was an outpost that had crept too close to a bridge of significant tactical importance. Destroying the bridge had to be the Germans' objective, and they would achieve it with little resistance in the next day if we didn't cripple them while they slept.

The wind that whipped my face was cruel enough in summer but was nearly unendurable now that the November chill had seeped into the air like noxious frozen gas.

"Sleep," Taisiya commanded over the interphone. We were running on no sleep since our last mission—closing in on forty-eight hours with only short bouts of rest. We'd decided I would sleep on the way to the target and she would sleep on the way back to base, with me controlling the plane from the rear. The logic behind her order was unassailable, yet in practice the idea of sleeping in the air seemed preposterous. The frigid temperatures notwithstanding, sitting in a plane awoke in me an alertness I simply didn't have on the ground. I was trained to scan the sky for enemy craft and to check our course at regular intervals. I didn't think my brain would stop whirring or that my muscles would uncoil long enough to catch any real rest, but Taisiya, as usual, was right. I had to try.

What seemed like seconds later, Taisiya's voice crooned over the interphone, her tone calm but insistent. "It's time to wake up, Katya. We're three minutes from target."

The puddle of drool that had dribbled down my chin and into my scarf betrayed my exhaustion and my ability to sleep anywhere, even with the constant drone of the engines and the vicious gnawing of winter at my face.

I grabbed my map and oriented myself, knowing I had only minutes to get my bearings if we were to make our mark. I called a minor course correction to her—she'd done a remarkable job navigating without me—and we dropped the payload on the ranks of trucks they had parked in such neat lines that it seemed impossible they had been driven by human operators. Had the Germans scattered them throughout the camp, they might not have lost the bulk of their convoy. The insistent whirr from behind us told me that Nika and Svetlana were on our heels and ready to finish off the trucks we'd left in working order.

I took the controls and allowed Taisiya to get her twenty minutes of sleep. I hadn't had the chance to fly without another fully conscious person in the plane before, and—no doubt especially because I was operating on so little sleep—the prospect of taking the stick was a heady one. It was just as well that the plane was slow and incapable of any real acrobatics, or I might have been tempted to test her limits just a tad on the way back to base. She was slower than the trainers I'd flown at the academy, but responsive enough that I understood why the army hadn't discounted her usefulness.

When we landed—Taisiya stirring as I made my approach—the mechanics swarmed the plane, doing their safety checks, refueling, and checking the linen for any weakness. The process took a full hour before, including loading the bombs. Now it took fifteen minutes. Polina hoped to get it down to ten or less.

As soon as our plane was cleared, we were signaled to take off again with orders to target another sector of the same camp. We made our mark, returned, and were back in the air yet again fifteen minutes later.

Taisiya and I flew thirteen sorties that night. Our previous best was seven. When Renata brought our supper to our planes after our sixth flight, we didn't even bother loosening our harnesses while we ate. The meat was dry but still warm and filling, and the tea warmed me to my core.

One of the armorers kept meticulous records of each sortie to pass on to our upper echelon. As a regiment we had flown sixty-four more sorties that night than we had on our busiest night before our streamlining.

A week later, emerging from the mess hall in the early afternoon to begin our preparations for the night's mission, we caught sight of General Chernov deep in conversation with Sofia as he appeared to be reading over her shoulder. His flushed brow furrowed as he peered down at the worn brown leather notebook in her hands—Polina's treasured notebook. He stalked off in a huff, but Sofia bore a smile that was victorious and more than a little smug.

"What was the matter with Chernov?" Oksana asked as Sofia approached and the general was safely out of earshot.

"He was aggravated we haven't been flying according to regulations," she said, her smile not wavering from her crimson lips.

"Did we do anything wrong?" I asked, feeling the tension creep into my shoulders. Would Chernov punish us for breaking the rules, despite our results?

"Quite the contrary. Word of our increased productivity has already gone around the brass. Chernov came to see what sorcery we 'night witches' had concocted."

"What did he think of my plans—*our* plans, Major?" Polina asked timidly, emerging from behind our plane.

"He would prefer we flew by the book."

"So we're abandoning the modifications?" Polina asked.

"No, I simply told him 'the book' was fine, but we decided to write a better one. I expect many of your modifications will become regulation soon enough, Junior Lieutenant Vasilyeva."

"I'm a senior sergeant, Major," Polina corrected. Few of the women who served as ground crews had earned the rank of commissioned officer, nor did they expect to.

"Not any longer," Sofia said, extending her hand. "The general passes on his congratulations. Or else he would, if he weren't such a pompous ass."

CHAPTER 17

July 1943, Sorties: 449

Chernov may have wished us to the deepest pit in the middle of Siberia, but he had become a minority. Because we had come to fly so many missions, we had strengthened the Russian foothold in the Crimea. We were no longer the 588th Night Bomber Regiment; we were the Forty-Sixth Guards Night Bomber Aviation Regiment. The title *Guards* was an honor bestowed on few regiments, and ours was the first all-female regiment to earn it. An unfortunate truth is that those who earn these sorts of honors rarely have time to savor them. When they promoted the regiment, we had as nice a dinner as could be mustered on a battlefield and then went back to our aircrafts.

As it was now again summer and there were no better lodgings to be had, we slept in eight-man tents that barely protected us from the constant clouds of mosquitos that followed us like starving dogs. The advantage was sleeping close to the planes and being able to move our camp with a few hours' notice.

Though Polina oversaw the maintenance on our Polikarpov, we took it upon ourselves to give her a good wipe-down and checkup each week. We redrew the chalk lines on the wings we used for targeting. Any holes that needed repatching, any splotches in need of painting, were tended to by our own hands. Polina handed over these duties once a week with good-enough grace, though we knew to leave anything to do with the engine itself to her attention.

"She's like a dutiful old mare," Taisiya announced one day as she applied with delicate strokes a coat of butyrate dope to a patch. She'd already laid the coat of nitrate dope on the patch, and once this second coat dried, it would be ready to accept paint to match the rest of the linen canvas. The stink of the dope was powerful, like concentrated turpentine, so I was careful to stand upwind to avoid the headache that would be the inevitable result from inhaling the fumes.

"More like a sturdy milk cow," I tutted, patting the fuselage as I might the rump of a faithful Guernsey who had just been given a good milking.

"That's it. We're calling her *Daisy*," Taisiya said, her chuckle nostalgic. "We'll call her for Matvei's best dairy cow."

We shook hands on the agreement, even painting chains of daisies around the cockpits with the moniker *Daisy* spelled out in loopy script in addition to our own names under the lip of each cockpit.

After the long winter the short summer nights didn't exactly feel like we were lounging on the beach in Sochi, but it was far less intense most evenings. The breezes were warmer, and we had longer stretches on the ground during the day. We needed pills the doctors gave us to stay awake. We called them "Coca-Cola" as our own little joke—mostly so we didn't think about what the prolonged use of the medication might be doing to our bodies. Nothing good, that was certain.

That afternoon in late July was glorious. One of the days so drenched with sunlight that the world itself seemed to vibrate with joy. It seemed perverse to be fighting a war under the splendor of such a summer sun. I wanted nothing more than to bask under it in one of the two-piece bathing suits the American actresses wore in magazines.

Hand in hand on a white-sand beach with Vanya, sipping a frothy drink made with raspberries or some such thing.

But he was hundreds of kilometers away. I wasn't sure precisely where—his postcards would have been censored if he'd been careless enough to divulge his location—but he seemed no better or worse with each missive than he had for months. He was suffering, I knew. He did not wax on about how he missed me, how he missed home, but that absence itself was telling. I would have given a week's rations to see him, to comfort him, but leave was about as easy to procure as pixie dust and unicorn hair. I would have to tend to mending his spirit once the fighting was over, and I sensed it would be a task as large as the one we now faced in the air.

Sofia briefed us as she did before each night's mission. We would be flying three minutes behind Sofia and Oksana, as we often did. They would bomb the searchlights the Germans had been so fond of using to aid their antiaircraft gunners and blind our pilots, and then Taisiya and I would swoop in, along with Elsa and Mariya and their navigators, and take out a target of our choice, or else drop bombs willy-nilly just to keep the soldiers awake. Those nights were the most fun. Less precision needed, and the knowledge we were being a proper nuisance to a lot of people who definitely deserved the treatment.

We took off toward the end of twilight, which was odd for us. The nights were so short, we couldn't wait to make our first sorties until after full dark, as we usually did. If we'd waited for pitch black, we might only get in five or six runs, which wasn't even close to our standard. It was getting darker, though, and we'd be well enough protected by the shroud of night once we arrived at the German outpost.

We couldn't see the outline of Sofia's plane ahead once we got closer to our target, but we could hear the unmistakable guttural whirr of its propeller.

It was far too quiet at the base. No spotlights to blind us.

I felt a sinking sensation in the pit of my stomach, much like I had when I once sat for a mathematics examination and had forgotten one, rather essential, formula. Something was missing.

I felt the hairs pricking at my neck, the metallic taste of fear heightening my hearing and drawing the shadows of twilight into sharp relief.

Sofia and Oksana's plane coasted in over the site like a ghost, marked the target with a flare, dropped their payload, and roared back to life—but still no antiaircraft shells were fired, though the German gunners would've had time to take aim several times over. Nor was anyone frantically trying to find Taisiya and me—and they had to know another plane would be behind the first.

Either these German troops hadn't been briefed about us, which seemed like the type of oversight the meticulously organized Germans wouldn't make, or something was terribly wrong.

I didn't see the German night flyer until the pilot was practically sitting in my cockpit.

"Go!" I screamed to Taisiya over the interphone. "They're following us!" To see a German plane in the sky with us seemed as unnatural as a green sunrise. They flew during the day and hadn't had enough intel to anticipate our attacks before now.

"I see that. Get out your grenades," she snarled into her mouthpiece, her hands steady on the stick.

My own hands shook as I pulled a pin from the grenade and lobbed it over in the direction of the German aircraft. They maneuvered much faster than we did, and I could barely see the flash of metal as they made another pass, whooshing by and riddling *Daisy* with bullets. The grenade fell uselessly to the earth below with a pathetic pop as it exploded.

I wanted to run. My legs burned for it. My hands ached to grip the stick. But Taisiya was the one selected to fly—it was my duty to fight. I freed a few more grenades from my ammunition pouch and aimed my revolver. I might as well have been throwing rocks for the good my bullets and grenades were doing against the far more advanced airplane, but it gave me an occupation other than shaking in fear.

Taisiya changed course and took the plane to a lower elevation, where she slowed down to below the fighter's stall speed. She weaved away from the German plane with the grace of a dancer, and we were headed east again in moments. I looked up at our top wing and down at the other. There were more holes than I could count, but we were still—miraculously—airborne.

A second plane came from the south, the metallic whirr of its dual propellers bearing down on us, charging like an enraged dog. Taisiya slowed the plane to a crawl, hoping the pilot would be forced to pull up. It looked as though the German craft was going to slam right into the side of us, so Taisiya dove lower still, knowing there was no way the heavier aircraft could hope to match the maneuver without risking a death spiral. They opened up their machine guns, and it became apparent they didn't have to catch us. They simply had to get close enough before we dove out of range. The engine smoked ominously—the plane shuddered, making screeching, metallic hisses as it labored to stay aloft, and Taisiya hadn't corrected for her dive. The Germans would be thrilled to have two bodies to trade in for their Iron Crosses.

"Pull up!" I called to Taisiya. I didn't bother with grenades this time. I gripped the metal bar on either side of me, fighting the urge to grab the stick and scream for Taisiya to turn over the controls.

I could hear her cough over the interphone. She was trying to tell me something but was unable to speak—the smoke from the engine smothering her words, I guessed. Then she slumped forward. I saw the splotch of red on the back of her jacket and watched for a few seconds, paralyzed, as the red pooled larger and larger on her drab-green uniform.

My controls were unresponsive, rendered useless because Taisiya's unconscious form weighed down on the stick. I stood up in my cockpit, leaning over my low windshield, and moved her backward so I could regain control. She was still breathing, shallowly. A German plane flew perilously close, so I didn't bother to sit and maneuver from my own controls. I heard the roar of machine-gun fire but paid no heed to it. I had to choose between lobbing a grenade at it—next to useless, unless my aim was perfect—and keeping the plane from crashing a few meters away from the enemy's base camp.

I flew the plane, leaning over Taisiya's slumped form, painfully aware that I was exposed to any more attacks the Germans might think to throw at us. I opened the throttle as far as I could, muttering a senseless jumble of prayers that I would be able to get the plane back to base.

~

I expected to find the base a flurry of activity, but the planes were grounded and the crews still. All eyes scanned the sky, and it wasn't until I touched down, landing as gently as I could on the bumpy grass we used for a runway, that any movement began. Medics rushed to the plane, but no one was readying more aircraft.

"Taisiya," I gasped as Polina took me in her arms. My body, now that I was aware I was on the ground and aware that there was no German machine gun aimed at me, began shaking as though I had been doused in icy water. "She's been hurt badly. She's not conscious."

Medics unstrapped her from her seat and lifted her from her cockpit as gingerly as they could, laying her on the bare ground to assess her. Her face was white as moonlight and streaked with crimson. I watched for those keen eyes to flicker with life, her chest to rise and fall, but there was nothing but stillness. I released Polina and knelt by Taisiya's side. Taking her hand, I pressed my lips against her too-cold flesh.

Don't leave me. I can't do this without you.

I didn't mutter this aloud, knowing the only ears that mattered wouldn't hear me. I remembered my horror in Moscow when Taisiya made me realize that we could have been separated into different regiments. I'd not contemplated that fate before she mentioned it, nor could I resign myself to this one. How could I fly without my pilot?

"I'm sorry, Lieutenant," a medic said, his fingers on her wrist, seeking a pulse that I already knew wasn't there.

I could hear Polina's muffled sobs behind me. I could comfort her later.

The medic pronounced Taisiya had passed. He gave orders to have her placed on a stretcher and carried off, motioning for me to move aside so they could carry out their duty.

"Wait!" I snapped.

Taisiya's sage brown eyes still looked blankly heavenward, like they sometimes did when she was contemplating a passage in one of her favorite books or a particularly complicated formula. I closed her eyes with a gentle motion of my fingers, softly kissed her forehead, then took her cool hand in mine once more. I pressed my lips to her bloodied knuckles, wishing her lungs would take a breath of their own accord.

"You promised Matvei, Taisiya. You promised him you would stay safe. You can't—" I spoke in a rasp I barely recognized.

Renata and Polina took me in their arms so the medics could take her away.

"You have to let her go," Renata said, rocking me gently.

My eyes followed the medics until I couldn't make out their shapes in the dark any longer. My breath caught in my chest, and I hadn't the first idea how to expel it.

"Oksana told us about the German counterattack," Renata whispered, stroking my hair. "We thought you'd both gone down . . ."

"You were half-right. Oksana and Sofia made it back?"

"Oksana did. She's bad off, but the medics seemed to think she'd be all right. They're sending her to the hospital to be sure. Sofia . . ."

"They shot the pilots," I said, blinking in realization. "They figured it was enough to take down the plane." I felt ice permeate the marrow of my spine. We'd lost our leader. She and Taisiya were two of the most experienced in the regiment. Who would command us now?

"Effective enough," Polina replied humorlessly. "We're still missing Elsa's and Mariya's planes, and I'm not optimistic. Their mechanics have a bad feeling, and that never bodes well."

"Oh God," I said. "Six of us in one night."

"Seven if we don't get you to the hospital unit," a medic said, racing to my side.

"What are you talking about?" I said, brushing his hand aside. I needed to assess morale and see what I could do for the rest of the regiment. With Sofia gone, they would need some direction. Oksana was on her way to a hospital, far from the front. And Taisiya . . .

No. I needed to organize the women to do something useful. They needed some warm tea and an occupation until they were calm enough to get some rest.

"Oh, Katya." Renata looked down at my right side, and my eyes followed. The side of my flight jacket was drenched in warm blood.

"It must be . . . hers," I said, unable to speak her name.

The medic unceremoniously removed my coat and knelt to inspect my flank. I looked down at my blouse, equally soaked in blood, and noticed he fingered a few small holes in the fabric. Two or three large shards of wood had lacerated my side, but I felt nothing but the night air on my skin. Not even the medic's hands registered as he examined me.

"Get some bandages and a stretcher," the medic called to the rest of his staff. "She's been wounded."

"Oh, I have not," I argued, the cold air lapping at my cold flesh, making my entire body shiver painfully.

I pulled up the side of my blouse and saw that my right side looked more like a side of beef in a butcher's window than my own flesh. The medic quickly assessed that it was just two shallow punctures, but I was bleeding profusely.

"Katya, do as he says," Polina ordered.

I nodded, squeezing her hand as I allowed the medics to assist me onto the stretcher.

"Take care of everyone," I commanded her. "They will need someone."

"You have my word," Polina whispered, brushing her lips against the back of my hand.

I patted her cheek and waved encouragingly as they loaded me onto the ambulance. It was only when the doors shut me off from their concerned eyes that I let the darkness have me.

CHAPTER 18

The lights overhead were harsh, and the gray concrete and steel contrasted sharply with the blinding white of the linens. I moved to sit up and take stock of my surroundings, but the sharp pain at my side and a pair of strong hands kept me down.

"Ah, you're coming around. Excellent." A doctor, his long white surgical gown billowing around him like the perfect negative of a nun's black habit, peered down at me with a measuring gaze.

The strong hands belonged to a nurse with tight brown curls and kind eyes. When she sensed I wasn't going to strain, she loosened her hold and brushed a lock of hair off my forehead.

"You need to stay still, my dear. The doctor is a busy man and doesn't need to be stitching you up a second time." She smoothed my sheets as she spoke, her hands being the sort that could never rest idle. She was perhaps a few years older than my mother, but fewer lines of hardship framed her eyes.

"Of course," I acquiesced, not wanting to repeat the process while conscious. I could feel the tape and gauze that protected a large section of my side. More than a few stitches, I could tell without visual confirmation.

She rewarded my compliance with a cool glass of water and an extra pillow so I wasn't lying completely prone. Until the water hit my lips, I had no idea how parched I had been.

The doctor removed the dressing to examine the sutures that ran the length of my right flank, and I found myself averting my eyes. With each stroke of his fingers, I felt each stitch burn into my skin like a hot ember.

"I'm sorry, my dear. We're terribly low on morphine or anything that will do much for the pain. We have to reserve it for the amputees and the like. I'm sure you understand." The doctor spoke so regretfully, I had to stop myself from apologizing for the inconvenience of being injured. "Healing as well as I might hope for. You'll be back in the air before you know it."

"Thank you, Doctor," I said, my voice still raspy despite having drunk half the water.

"They were worried about you," a voice said from the bed to my left. I craned my head slowly, to see Oksana clad in a white gown identical to mine. "It wasn't until yesterday that they began to sound optimistic. You lost a lot of blood."

"I expect I did," I said, remembering the sight beneath my blouse.

"It's been a long three days waiting for you to wake up, lazy-bones." The warmth in Oksana's voice was uncharacteristic. She had her arm in a sling but, from my sidelong view, looked to have decent coloring, considering her ordeal.

"Three days? I can't possibly have been asleep for three days."

"You snore."

"Thanks," I said, wishing I had the strength to throw a pillow at her. "Have you heard anything from the regiment?"

"Not a word," Oksana said. "Information isn't easy to come by here. And since I've not been cleared to fly, they're not too fussed about keeping me well briefed."

"I'm so sorry about Sofia," I said after a few moments. I thought of the solemn faces of the rest of the regiment and wondered how we'd go on without her as our champion.

"She almost got away. We outmaneuvered the first plane, but only just. We never saw the second one coming. By the time we reacted, it was too late."

"It was the same for us. They aimed for Taisiya, hoping to take down the whole plane." My hands gripped the bleached sheet, and my muscles tensed, causing my side to scream.

"So she—"

"She's gone. They were fairly certain the other crews were lost entirely." The truth of it echoed off the concrete walls. "Taisiya died on the flight back. I was too busy keeping the plane from crashing to try to patch her up."

"Stop now, before you head down that path, Katya. I've been down it. There was nothing you could have done to save her."

"I know," I whispered. I was no medic. Even if I were, I couldn't have simultaneously flown the plane and attended to her injuries in time to save her. *If* there had been time. "I hope you haven't been feeling the same about Sofia."

"No, I wasn't talking about Sofia," Oksana said, turning her head to look at the expanse of gray on the opposite wall. "This war started much sooner for some of us."

A commotion from the other end of the hospital drew our attention before I could ask what she meant. The nurses scurried in a dozen directions, and the doctor spoke rapid fire, though far enough away that we couldn't make out the conversation. A stomping of boots on tile floors then approached from my left, and I wished I could sit well enough to get a view.

"It's Chernov," Oksana whispered.

"How wonderful. Here to wish us a speedy recovery, do you think?"

Oksana chuckled under her breath at the very idea of Chernov making any kind of social call. He'd surely been born dispensing orders to his mother, nanny, and wet nurse.

"Captain Tymoshenko, I am pleased to hear from Dr. Vitayev that you're well on the way to recovery," the general said by way of greeting. He plastered a smile on his lips that looked so unnatural for him that it had to be uncomfortable.

"This is true, General," Oksana replied, lifting her plastered arm as proof. "I'm feeling much better. Thank you for your concern." She shot a glance at me, widening her eyes almost imperceptibly. *You were actually right, and somewhere in hell the devil is putting on an overcoat.*

"Excellent news. And when the good doctor clears you for active service, will you return to your post?" the general asked, posing the question so that the desired answer was obvious.

"Yes, General," Oksana replied with admirable conviction. "I'd like to return as soon as may be to resume command, as Major Orlova would have wanted."

"Well done. You're very much needed. Major Orlova always spoke highly of you, and I am pleased her admiration was not misplaced. You'll have a promotion to major for your service."

Oksana sat up straighter at the pronouncement. "I'm not sure exactly what to say, General Chernov, other than to thank you for the honor. I will do my best to honor Major Orlova's memory."

"Just as I expected," General Chernov said with a satisfied nod. "You've always appeared to be one of the most sensible women in your regiment, and I'm glad to know they're in your capable hands."

"I won't clear you to return for at least two more weeks," the doctor supplied. "I might allow you back to organize your troops if it were just your broken wrist, but your concussion can't be trifled with."

"Right," the general said. "It's just as well. We've put your regiment on light duty for the moment, given the circumstances. We have another regiment supporting you, so things are under control for the time being."

"I will act as pilot of my own crew," Oksana said, making a pronouncement rather than a request. "And I will name my own navigator."

"As you wish, Major Tymoshenko. Assignments in the division will be up to you. Goodness knows you understand better than anyone outside your regiment which of your people will work best together."

"Very well." Oksana gestured to me with her good arm. "Senior Lieutenant Soloneva here will be my deputy commander. She's the best we have."

I fought against the urge to sit up but turned myself in the direction of the general and Oksana to acknowledge my entrance into the conversation.

"You're mending well, Lieutenant?"

"Remarkably," the doctor replied for me. "But I would recommend a few weeks' more healing before returning to service. Her wounds need time to knit properly, or she'll risk aggravating them midflight. That might be more than a little inconvenient."

"Understood. You'll accept Major Tymoshenko's assignment when you're cleared, Soloneva?"

Men were sent back into service as soon as a physician would clear them—often before they were fully healed, if the rumors were true—but we could leave at any time. In a week I could be recovering in Mama's cabin in Miass. Oksana looked over at me, and this thought evaporated like late-summer raindrops. Taisiya wouldn't have abandoned the regiment, no matter how badly injured she was. She would be ashamed to think I would do so. Oksana would need me at her side as she learned how to lead.

"I accept, gratefully," I said.

"Excellent. We'll be promoting you to captain for your actions, Soloneva. You saved your aircraft from falling into enemy hands. Now get rested and ready yourselves to get back to service, the pair of you."

The general exited as abruptly as he arrived, the doctor trailing after him.

"Surely the next visitor will be Grandfather Frost," I said, breaking the silence. "I'd have sooner expected *him*."

"It seems vulgar to take Sofia's place," Oksana said, ignoring my jest. "But I think it's what she would have wanted."

"I know it is," I said, rolling slightly onto my left side to better see her.

"Thank you for accepting. I wasn't sure you would."

"What else am I to do? Knit socks?"

"You're married. You have good reason to save your own skin."

"Not while Vanya is risking his," I said. "I'm flattered you chose me."

"I meant what I said. You know your stuff, and I need someone like you to help me lead, if that's to be my lot."

"Someone like me?"

"Someone people like. I know I'm—I'm not the warmest of people. I need you to help me keep up morale. You're better at it than I am. Sofia always told me to look to you and Taisiya if I needed guidance."

"I'll do what I can," I said. "But the girls need more than just some cheering up. Sofia wouldn't have chosen you without reason. That wasn't who she was." The breath caught in my throat as I registered the past tense.

Oksana sat silent for a few moments, and I began to wonder if she'd drifted off to sleep.

"Do you think I can do this on my own, Katya?"

"No," I answered. "No one can. But with a regiment like ours behind you, you stand a chance."

~

Hospital beds were more precious than the fallen tsar's old gems, so after a week, Oksana was transferred back to the front against the doctor's wishes, and I was sent to a convalescent center even farther east from the front lines, on the outskirts of Stalingrad. I had the privacy of my own bedroom, which was the most luxurious sleeping arrangement I'd known since the war broke out. The beds were more comfortable, the food somewhat better, but the medical staff and their supplies were far more scant than in the hospital. But as my side wasn't in need of close medical attention, I gratefully gave my place in the hospital to those more grievously injured.

One night as I slept, I felt a warm body slide behind mine on the mattress and strong arms encircling me, carefully avoiding the injury on my right flank. It was still full dark, and I was too deep in slumber to be alarmed. My subconscious—the only part of me that lingered in wakefulness—knew the person meant me no harm. A person with foul intent wouldn't have taken care to move so gently or to cover my exposed feet with the blanket. I did not scream but struggled to open my eyes to see who had joined me. I could tell it was a man's arm as I became more aware of the waking world.

I summoned the strength to turn over, bracing my stitches as I turned, to see Vanya's long eyelashes already resting heavily on his high cheekbones. He was seconds away from deep sleep, exhausted from the journey that had brought him to my side. I lowered my lips to his, gently, slowly tasting his sweetness. It had to be a dream. I burrowed my body as close to his as I dared and embraced him with all the strength I had left. His form felt too solid for the dreamworld. He did not vanish as I pulled him closer. I choked back a sob of relief as the reality of him in my arms began to register.

"My Vanyusha," I whispered through my tears. "I love you."

"And I love you, my darling Katyushka. Sleep, my lovely." His soft snores filled the silence as soon as the words escaped his lips.

Vanya must have gotten word of my injury and been given leave to come to me. Such a thing wouldn't have been permitted in a proper hospital, so I lay in the warmth of his arms, momentarily able to bear the restlessness I'd been feeling as my health improved and my regiment moved farther west.

I woke up to find myself still ensconced in Vanya's arms and wondered what I could have done to have made me worthy of this comfort again.

"Good morning, darling," he crooned in my ear. "How are you faring?"

"In your arms? As well as I've ever been."

"Don't tease, Katyushka. Tell me honestly."

"I have a dozen stitches or more in my side. No infection. No pain medication, but I'm handling it well enough." I didn't call attention to the wooden shards that had shredded my skin. His face was blanched enough.

Vanya lifted my blouse and saw only a pristine white bandage covering my flank. He traced the edge of it with the tips of his fingers. When I moved to pull the hem down to hide the injury, he grabbed my hand, kissed my palm, and removed the top entirely. I looked to his face and saw circles dark as my night skies beneath them. His skin was tinged an unhealthy shade of gray, and he was far too thin. What troubled me most was the lack of fire in his dark eyes. An exhaustion that went far beyond sleep.

He caressed my breasts with hands roughened by months of incessant work at the front. "You'll stop me if I do anything that hurts you?" he whispered into my neck. "How I've missed my beautiful Katyushka."

I nodded.

His hands explored enthusiastically, as though mine were the first body he'd ever been given leave to claim, but as gently as if I were crafted of porcelain.

I felt his caresses go from feather light to intense in their desperation. I knew I ought to keep him at arm's length for the sake of my recovery, but he'd been too long denied, and I was no less eager, despite the constant ache in my side. He entered me carefully and supported his weight on his forearms so that his torso barely brushed against my own. He moved slowly and deliberately, scanning my face for the first sign of discomfort.

He found his climax quickly, his expression sheepish, but I kissed the worry from his stubbly cheek as he repositioned himself, cradling me to his chest once again.

"I promised myself I wasn't going to do that," he said, his lips brushing against my forehead.

"You should know better than to make promises you don't intend to keep." I nuzzled his sharp collarbone with my nose, trying not to ruin the moment with the worry for his gaunt frame.

"I haven't disturbed your stitches, have I?"

"Not at all, dearest." The throbbing was no more than it usually was after a walk, so I took it as a good sign that all was still mending. "How long are you here?"

"I have a week, more or less," he said, the lightness in his voice disappearing. "I couldn't be spared for any longer."

"I'll take it," I said, kissing his knuckles. "Tell me how you've been, Vanyusha. Really. The postcards, they conceal more than they tell."

"My commander would be happy to hear that, at least. How else can I do? I fly a mission, hope to survive it, and fly another."

"You look so thin." I rubbed his cheek with my thumb, tracing the cheekbones that now protruded painfully due to the regimen of malnutrition and fatigue on which the army managed to survive.

"You're not exactly plump and rosy cheeked, Katyushka." He ran his fingers over my ribs, which were, admittedly, closer to the surface than they'd been when he'd last held me. "God, I can't believe they almost got you."

"Taisiya . . ." I still couldn't say her name any louder than a whisper.

"I know, darling. I was told. I'm so very sorry. I know she was a good friend."

"The oldest one I had," I said. I stopped stroking his cheek, unable to draw a full breath. I'd not formed any lasting friendships in my girlhood. The others could never understand my ambition. Taisiya was the first.

"I've had some goodbyes to make as well," he said, brushing my forehead with kisses. "One was my own navigator. A freak bullet and he was gone. I kept thinking of our days back at the academy, with you in the rear cockpit. Imagining that it had been you. I couldn't sleep for three nights together."

I gripped him tighter, stifling a grimace as my stitches pulled slightly. "I'm not going anywhere," I whispered into his chest.

"Do you mean it?" he asked, brightening.

"Of course I do. I'm going to survive this mess. You are, too. We're going to make a life together. We made a pact, remember?"

"Let's get you up and go for a walk," Vanya said, rubbing the sleep from his eyes.

The grounds near the convalescent center would have been lovely under good care, but as with so many things, war had made pruning and weeding a needless waste of energy, and the once-orderly flower beds had been left to neglect. I couldn't quite make out whether the stately old building was once a hotel or simply a manor house claimed from the old nobility and repurposed, but the hum of soldiers and airmen in various stages of recovery gave it a renewed purpose the walls hadn't seen in years. I could feel the usefulness radiate from the cool bricks and wondered if the old stones were grateful to be more than a stop along the road for weary travelers or a vain tribute to inherited wealth. I liked to think so.

"I wrote to your mother just before I left the front," Vanya said as we meandered about the patchy lawn. I was irritated that I had to use him for support as I walked but was calmed by his solid form at my arm.

"Just as well that she should know, I suppose. I hope you told her not to worry."

"Darling, I told her I was sending you home to her."

I turned to him, too quickly, and took in a ragged breath as my stitches pulled from the sudden movement. I steadied myself by placing my hands against his chest. "Without asking me?"

"Katya, all I had was a two-line telegram telling me you had been injured in the line of duty and so badly hurt they were sending you here instead of back to the front. You realize that they send men who are half-dead back to the front lines?"

"I'm sure they do, but the doctors are more cautious with the aviation regiments—you know this. We can't be so easily replaced."

"True enough, but darling, I had no idea what was going to be left of you. When they gave me leave to come see you . . ." His voice cracked as he sought the words. "I was sure it was to say goodbye. I promised your mother that if I found you in any condition to be moved, I'd see you back on the next train, plane, or automobile headed to Chelyabinsk. The back of a truck, if it's what I could manage."

"It's not all that bad, my love. It hurts when I move, but I imagine I'll be well enough in a few weeks."

"I didn't think I'd ever hold you again."

"You can't get rid of me that easily," I said. "I'm too stubborn."

"Thank God for that," he whispered. "Please promise me you'll go back to your mother? Stay safe? This was too close, darling. Far too close."

"I can't be a coward," I said, my words muffled against his drab-olive shirt. "I've made a promise."

"And you've honored it. You've been so brave—all of you. We hear about your regiment all the time. It's been my solace. To hear how you're performing beyond anyone's expectations, to imagine you working around the clock, flying a dozen missions a night." He held me now at arm's length, his deep coal eyes blazing into mine. "You could leave service now and sleep knowing you've done more for Mother Russia than *millions* of the soldiers who had to be forced into duty."

I felt the truth of his words wrap around me like a shawl—one knitted just for me with the love and patience of a grandmother. Warm. A thin but comforting buffer from the outside world. I could have shuffled them off just as easily as I could my babushka's wrap, but I let myself luxuriate in their woolen softness.

I could have argued that just because I had accomplished a good deal didn't mean I wasn't capable of doing more. That I was *obligated* to do more if I was able.

But I looked into Vanya's eyes. The desperation there wasn't that of a man fighting to keep his wife's safety—he was a man fighting for his own life.

"You've been in service for almost two years," he said. "Go home. Heal properly. Keep up morale at the flight school with tales of your exploits. They'll give you your teaching post. You'd still be doing your part."

"It wouldn't be knitting socks," I allowed. I'd still have to deal with chauvinist prigs like Karlov, but I had battle experience that even he couldn't belittle now. A few letters from the right people and the job would be mine.

Vanya, knowing me as he did, saw my thoughts as clearly as though they were printed on my forehead. "You'd be invaluable to the war effort. We need well-trained, eager young pilots as much as we need food and ammunition. And you've been at the front. You can train them to know what to expect and how to survive better than any of the commanders in Chelyabinsk. Think of that. Saving lives before they're even put at risk."

"I'll consider it," I said at length. "I can't imagine leaving the girls behind. Not now. We just lost our commander and three other pilots and two navigators besides."

"Take your time," he said, kissing the side of my face. "You're not up to travel just yet. I know what your loyalty is. I've made my wishes known, and what I can only expect are your mother's as well. I trust you to make up your own mind."

"Thank you, my love."

"God, what I wouldn't give for a month alone with you. A week isn't enough."

"I'm grateful for it," I said, stroking the stubble of his chin. "It was even worth this to have you close." I pointed to my side with a wink.

"What a world where a wife must take a side full of shrapnel to spend a few measly days with her husband in a crumbling hospital." Vanya shook his head, looking out over the grounds instead of at me.

"It's the world we've got. Don't disparage it." I gestured to the white bricks and once-stately staircase into the main entrance. "And how dare you call our honeymoon castle a 'crumbling hospital'? It's sheer ingratitude."

Vanya chuckled and wrapped his arm around me as we enjoyed our few hours in the early-August sun.

When it was time for dinner, the cooks begrudgingly served a ration to Vanya, though he was clearly well enough to be at the front. As we sat at the long tables, Vanya made conversation with a young lieutenant who had a badly broken leg but who bore his injury with remarkable cheer. As long as his leg was in plaster, he was safely ensconced here with palatable food and kilometers away from artillery fire.

The post came around as we ate. A courier—a young soldier with a missing foot who hobbled admirably on his crutch and took visible pride in his proficiency—placed a telegraph beside my plate. While Vanya was deep in conversation on the Russian progress westward, I opened the folded missive:

Hoping for your quick recovery and return to your post.
Your position as my deputy commander awaits you.
-Major O. Tymoshenko

Oksana had assumed her position and was already going about the business of making the regiment her own. Sofia had groomed her for the job for over a year, and I was confident, from a tactical standpoint, she was the best choice to lead the women into battle. Whether she could bolster their morale in hard times, whether she could light a fire in their souls in the gloom of winter, was less certain in my mind.

I glanced over at my husband, who cast a sideways smile and squeezed my knee as he continued his chatter about Crimea and Poland. The telegraph shook in my hands, the waxy paper rattling, all but screaming its contents to the bustling room. I shoved it hastily in my pocket to silence it. I took Vanya's hand for one second and brushed my lips against the warm skin of the back of his hand.

To wake up in Vanya's arms seemed a luxury that ought to be denied in the midst of a terrible war. My sisters in arms sweltered in their tents and fought clouds of mosquitos, aching for a few precious moments of rest. His perfume, an earnest musk he could never quite scrub off that was tinged with the motor oil of his aircraft, seemed too decadent for a world torn in two.

Lie still and enjoy your husband. Lie still.

The mantra repeated over and over in my head, but the urge to get up and find an occupation of some kind gnawed at me. Oksana's telegram was tucked in my notebook in the nightstand drawer and seemed to taunt me, resentful of being hidden away.

She needs you. They need you. Don't run away, coward.

"You're not resting," Vanya mumbled as he entered consciousness.

"Sorry, my love," I whispered. "It's not exactly my strong suit anymore."

"I know." He heaved a short, weary sigh. "It's not mine, either."

I sat up, vertebra by vertebra, respecting my tender side. Our little stroll was enough to show me how much healing was left to do.

"Tell me about after the war," he whispered, still lying prone and rubbing my back.

I hung my head. Guilt and fear tangled in my gut like serpents in a pit. I took in a breath, hoping to quell the slithering. "We'll find a little house south of Chelyabinsk. Maybe not too far from your parents in Korkino?"

"You would want that? After everything?"

"They gave me you. I want to give them a chance to know me."

"You're a gracious soul, dear wife. Kinder than I am."

"If I lose my kindness, I've lost the war, no matter what the outcome is."

Vanya traced designs on my back with the tips of his fingers, causing the hairs to rise on my flesh. "Tell me more, my love."

"Maybe Mama can move into town. We can have a family dinner once a week. I'll teach young, arrogant pilots some humility while you cover the world in beauty. No children for a couple of years. Just us for a time."

"I thought you might want to live in Moscow. To be in the bustle of the city," he mused as his fingers danced on my skin.

"I might have once, but Moscow will need to be rebuilt. The whole western part of the country. I'll do my part to save Russia from the Germans, but others will have to put her back together."

"More than fair." He slid down and kissed the flesh on my back, just before the swell of my buttocks, then returned to his fingertip-dancing.

My own fingers slid along the chiseled lines of his bicep, delighting in the truth of his form curled around me. "What are you doing, love?" I asked, unable to sense any real pattern in the movement of his fingers.

"I've neither proper canvas, nor brush, nor paint. I am using what I can to create a painting for you on the pristine canvas you've given me."

"What are you painting, then?" I asked, leaning more heavily against him as my side began to ache.

"Your little dacha. Snug with a little fireplace, perfect for cozying up next to in winter. Well built. Wooden with cross timbers like they used to build. A little garden so we can enjoy the summer sunshine. Acres of evergreen trees surrounding it. A small lake that freezes in winter so I can teach the boys to skate."

"The girls, too," I corrected. "I spent more of my winters in skates than shoes when I was a girl."

"You were raised properly, then." His fingers paused in their tracing, my skin longing for him to continue. "You do want children, yes?"

"I do," I said. "But I worry that I won't be able to care for them like a mother should."

"How can you doubt this?" Vanya abandoned his landscape and sat up next to me. "From the moment I met you, I could see that caring for others was the very center of who you are."

"I've always thought myself to be rather selfish," I admitted. "Instead of taking a job and helping Mama at home, I went off to flight school. Every decision since then has been more of the same."

"And your decision to go to flight school was, if I am not mistaken, meant to help give your mother a better life, no?"

"It doesn't help her much now, does it?"

"You're protecting her, just as your father would have done. I can only imagine how proud of you he would be." He kissed my temple and pulled me against his chest. "You will be an amazing mother."

"Can we please . . . not talk about after?" I asked. "It seems wrong—thoughtless—so soon after Taisiya. She and Matvei had their plans, too."

"Of course," he said. "I understand."

As his arms circled me, engulfing me in warmth and love, I felt a rock of ice forming at my core.

"I have to go back to the front, Vanya," I whispered. "They need me."

"No, they don't, Katya. I promise you."

"You don't understand how it is for us. Oksana just took over command. She needs me. She offered me a place as her deputy."

"And she can find someone else."

"Please, don't. She needs me at her side in this," I repeated.

"Bullshit. This is just you wanting to feel like you're indispensable. Wise up. We're *all* replaceable. Our commanders know it. Stalin goddamn well knows it."

"You said you would let me make my own decision." I swiveled in bed, standing faster than I should have, and reached for my blouse and slacks, which had been discarded on a nearby chair. I gritted my teeth at the exertion but would not show him my weakness.

"That was when I thought you would make the right one."

"Vanya, if you were given the chance, would you abandon your brothers at the front? Would you stay behind and let me fight?"

"That's a ridiculous question. I'd never be given the choice."

I turned around to face him, my shaking hands abandoning my buttons. "Because you're a man. But now imagine those rules didn't exist. Imagine you were injured and had the chance to return to Korkino for the rest of the war. Could you do it? Could you stay home and sleep soundly in your own bed? Look yourself in the mirror each morning?"

His face went slack; his shoulders drooped.

"No," he admitted.

"Good. Otherwise you're not the man I married."

CHAPTER 19

August 1943, outside Stalingrad

The grounds surrounding the convalescent hospital weren't as picturesque as the rugged fields outside the academy in Chelyabinsk, but the August light was such that Vanya couldn't help but lose himself in his paints. He had me posed on the lawn behind the crumbling building, lounged on a battered old chaise in such a way that my side wasn't irritated by long sessions lying still. My uniform didn't lend the same grace to the picture as my turquoise dress, but I was happy enough to have it committed to canvas.

"I worried about running out of paints, but canvases have been so few that I needn't have worried," he said, his brow furrowing momentarily, his eyes staring somewhere over my right shoulder. The cast of light perhaps? "I shouldn't have bothered hauling my paint case with me, but it seemed wrong to leave it behind."

"I haul Papa's violin with me everywhere I go," I said. "It gives me comfort to have it near, even if I don't get to play it often. I expect it's the same for your paints."

"Probably," he said, eyes fixed on the canvas. "There hasn't been much worth painting, but it's nice to know I could."

We sat wordlessly for what had to be at least an hour, likely more. I was doing precisely what the doctors would have wanted—lying still without disturbing my injuries—but I found the lack of activity maddening. My mind wandered to the front, and I wondered how Oksana was managing in Sofia's stead. If her brusque nature and biting tone could inspire the same enthusiasm as Sofia's ebullience.

"Well, it's a start," Vanya said at last. "I've managed to capture something of that spark in your eye, at least. It's not the face I painted back at the academy."

"You wound me, husband. Are you saying I've aged?"

"We all have, and quickly, too. Yours is the face of a woman now, not a girl. A lovely woman at that. At least I can keep this with me even if I can't—"

His hands balled into fists, and he hurled his paintbrush off into the patchy lawn.

"Goddammit. What kind of a husband am I if I can't even keep you safe?" He buried his face in his trembling hands. I hobbled to his side and wrapped my arms around his broad shoulders.

"My love" was all I could murmur.

"My life," he replied.

"Let's not waste our last days arguing this again," I beseeched him in a whisper. "I couldn't handle staying home if you were still out there fighting."

He pulled me onto his lap, as gingerly as if I were made of spun glass. He held me, and in that moment nothing existed but the rise and fall of his chest and the warmth of his arms around me. "If I weren't fighting," he said, "would it be different?"

I lifted my head from his shoulder and looked into the depths of his black eyes. "I don't see why we're speaking in hypotheticals, love. They would never let you leave."

"I'm not talking about getting sanctioned leave," Vanya said, barely audible, scanning the yard for listening ears. "Father has connections. I've served long enough and honorably enough he might not object to me using them. Travel papers."

"You said you couldn't let your comrades down, Vanya."

"There are more important things than duty to the motherland, dearest. My duty to you being chief among them."

I clutched him tighter, weaving my hands in his hair. "I don't deserve you."

"We all deserve better than this. Say you'll come with me. We'll make an excuse for me to accompany you back to Miass, and we can go to my father's contacts while we're there. We'd have to get to Turkey first, then anywhere you like that's not bogged down in this mire. Portugal or Spain. Ireland. Switzerland if you want mountains. I'd prefer America or Canada if we can get passage, but that might be a tall order."

"And if they find us out before we reach the border? You'd be shot on sight for desertion. Me, too, most likely."

"I like my odds better with our own men than the Germans," Vanya said. "There is no shame in saving our own skins."

Taisiya's face loomed in my mind . . . She'd never intended to be a martyr for the cause. She'd wanted to fight, save the motherland, and go home to Matvei. But she'd done her duty willingly.

Vanya blanched at my silence. "Come away with me, my darling. Promise me now."

There were seventy women to the west who anticipated my return. Oksana was counting on me to help guide her as she led us into battle. Yet, compared to the pleading in my husband's eyes, my call to duty was suddenly nothing.

"Will there be trouble for Mama?" I asked, resting my head once more on his shoulder. "I won't save my skin to risk hers."

"The party is too preoccupied to worry about a washerwoman in the Urals. Besides, you can resign your post without dishonor. It's my parents who would face any trouble, and I assure you, Father will be fine."

Remembering Antonin Solonev's iron spirit, I did not doubt this, nor that Vanya's mother would be shielded by him.

"Portugal," I said. "I don't know the language, but I can learn."

Vanya drew my face in for a long kiss, then pulled away. "You're saving my life, Katyushka."

"It's the only thing dearer to me than my own."

"I'm going into town to wire Father. See what he advises," Vanya said, standing me carefully back on my feet. "Stay out here and get some rest in the sun. You'll need your strength to travel."

I caressed his cheek, and kissed him in farewell. "Be careful," I urged.

As he bounded off to the telegraph office, I saw a spring in his step that I hadn't seen since he'd arrived.

I did as he bid and curled up on the old chaise, basking in the sun like a spoiled house cat. Safe and protected. I imagined spending many such hours under the Portuguese sun and wondered how many years it would take for me to learn to rest without the looming guilt of one who had abandoned her sisters in arms.

Vanya returned to the hospital with his father's response and the latest newspaper.

Antonin's reply had been almost instantaneous: *Do not come home. Contact will come to you.*

"What did you put in the wire?" I asked. "Nothing too obvious?"

"No. I just asked if a certain 'friend' of his was still near Chelyabinsk. He knows the only reason I would have need of this man—Comrade

Osin—is for papers. Father's message told me what I expected—he's out closer to the west, where he can profit the most. Father will send him word that I need to see him."

"He sounds like a reputable sort," I said with a derisive laugh.

"There's good reason Mother and I were always sent from the room when he came to see Father, of that I'm certain. Anything more, I don't want to know."

"Wise," I said, rubbing my temples against the thrumming behind my eyes.

"Are you all right?" He wrapped an arm around me, looking up from his paper.

"Fine, fine." I nodded at the newspaper. "Tell me what's going on in the world. My head aches too much for me to read for myself."

"You need to tell the medics," he chided.

"So they can do what? It's the medicine that gives me the headaches. Either my side is unbearable, or my head is. They don't have many choices this far from the front," I reminded him. I closed my eyes, continuing to massage my head, taking in steady breaths. "News, please."

"The usual guff. The tide is about to turn. We'll retake Leningrad and push the Germans back to Berlin . . . the same things they've said for the past year, none of it coming to pass."

"Watch yourself," I said, opening one eye. "Ears."

"Right," he said. "God, I hope Osin turns up quickly. If we don't get our papers before my leave is up, it will complicate things."

"How so?"

"They'll have people looking for me. I'd prefer that didn't happen until we're out of the country."

"Even if he manages to get papers for us, how are we going to get out of here?" I asked, tracing the words on Antonin's wire with my index finger.

"I'll buy a truck," he said. "That should get us through to Turkey, and then we'll rest and figure out what comes next. Portugal, if that's what you want."

"And you trust that Osin to help us?"

"He'd sell his own babushka for a price. And he's never refused Father anything."

"I don't like this," I said, keeping my voice even. "So many things could go wrong. And I don't want to put our lives in the hands of a stranger."

Vanya stilled my tracing with his hand. "You don't trust him, but do you trust me?"

"With my life, on many occasions."

"Then trust me with it once more. I will get us out of here."

I nodded and concealed the grimace, laced with fear and uncertainty, that loomed at my lips.

Osin was two days in coming to us—much faster than we expected. I had expected a man with a weaselish face. The sort where his eyes never fully opened, always scheming, and where his nose came to such a sharp end it seemed he was always pointing an accusing finger at you. But as was typical of the world, he wasn't given a face that betrayed his dubious business connections and shady politics. He'd been graced with a strong jaw, flashing blue eyes, and a convivial demeanor that encouraged openness.

"Young Comrade Solonev and his lovely bride," he said, shaking Vanya's hand and kissing my own with a flourish before taking a seat in the courtyard. We'd opted for an outdoor meeting so there would be less chance of us being overheard. "I admit I was surprised to hear from my old friend that his son was in need of my assistance. Of course, I am so happy to be of use to you in these difficult times."

"Quite," Vanya said, his face lined with a scowl. "I worry for my wife's well-being, Comrade Osin. She was injured in service to the country, but I fear the doctors are treating her injuries too lightly."

"You wish for me to procure some medicines, perhaps? An examination with one of Moscow's finest physicians?" he asked, head cocked sideways. His business had a scope I hadn't imagined.

"No, I don't want to be a drain on resources when there are soldiers in need. I am hoping to get her more adequate treatment elsewhere. If one were to venture as far as, say, Turkey, and then on to a friendly country in the west, then she would be able to find better medical help without harming the war effort."

"Spoken like a true patriot."

Vanya narrowed his eyes at the insinuation. "My father always taught me that, especially in a society such as ours, those who come to privilege must do everything in their power to avoid taking from the bounty of others. I am pleased my family is in such a position to make this possible." A reminder: *Father has money.* I squeezed Vanya's knee. The cover was a brilliant one. I doubted Antonin had said any such thing. It was far closer to Vanya's own philosophies than his father's.

"So you wish for me to secure passage to Turkey for your wife, then. That should be easy enough. I'm sure her papers are in order."

"Myself as well. Given the current situation, I cannot allow her to go alone. I'm sure you understand."

"And your regiment has given you leave? That's highly unusual."

Vanya, his hands clasped on the table and gaze fixed on Osin, said nothing.

"Ah. Now my involvement makes more sense. This does complicate things. I am a man of connections, but I have limited influence when it comes to military affairs."

"If you can secure the papers, I'll attend to the rest," Vanya said, taking his packet of cigarettes from his breast pocket and lighting one as it rested between his lips, his fingers tapping against the table once he stowed his lighter.

Don't show your nerves. It will only play to his advantage.

"Very good. The less I know on that end, the better."

"Agreed," Vanya said, offering Osin his packet. Osin waved it away with a flash of remarkably even teeth.

"I'll see what I can manage, my dear boy. It won't be an easy task these days, but Antonin is a dear friend. I'll do my best."

"I'm sure Father admires your conscientiousness and will make his appreciation known."

"I have no doubt. It's been a pleasure. We'll meet again as soon as I can arrange for it."

We sat silently until Osin had disappeared from view. I put my hand on Vanya's free one as he finished his cigarette, his eyes scanning the hedges as though they contained answers to great mysteries.

"I'll owe Father ten years of indentured servitude if Osin comes through," he said without humor. "Thankfully I won't be in the country anytime soon for him to collect on it."

Mama. I was leaving her to her own devices. Though she'd been in that situation for years now, I had always been within reach.

"When do you think we'll be able to return home?" I asked, eyeing his packet of cigarettes, wondering what pleasure he found in them.

"After the war. When things calm down." Vanya took a long drag of his cigarette and caressed my hand. "It may be some time, but so long as you're safe, that's all that matters."

"I feel like a coward."

"It will pass." He kissed the back of my hand where Osin had pressed his lips minutes before, causing me to shudder. "We'll find ways to help from a distance. There is plenty we can do."

I freed my hand from his and took one of the skinny white cylinders from the packet Vanya had left on the courtyard table.

"Since when do you smoke?" he asked.

"Since now."

With an arched brow and flick of his wrist, he lit my cigarette in one deft motion of his lighter. I felt nothing but jitters as the smoke entered my lungs, but it was easier to concentrate on the foreign sensation than the fear that lapped from within.

⸻

"You're a miracle worker, Osin," Vanya said three days later. He examined the travel documents with exacting scrutiny. "I wouldn't have thought to procure official government orders to show at the border."

"And that is why my services come so highly recommended, my boy. One does not gain a reputation such as I have by cutting the proverbial corners."

"I expect not," Vanya said. "An envoy from the Kremlin. Genius."

"No one will question it. Because your father is such an old and dear friend, I have a gift for you and your lovely bride as well." Osin produced a map from his breast pocket. It was a map of the western part of the country and the countries along our borders. My side throbbed as I angled to get a better look at the document. There was one dark-red line that sprawled from Russia into Turkey, circling around the coast of the Black Sea. There were little side routes outlined in a paler shade of red, making the whole map look like a series of blood vessels sprawling out from our present location.

"The main route is faster by days but is the most heavily patrolled. You can use it for a while, but the closer you get to Turkey, take detours onto the back roads. I've also taken the liberty of securing you a truck that is equal to the task. Wear civilian clothes for the journey. Uniforms will just raise more questions. Once you're in Turkey, I would disavow any military involvement if I were you."

"Understood. Comrade Osin, we owe you our lives."

"I wish you both the best, and I hope the next time we meet it will be under pleasanter circumstances."

Vanya extended a hand, and Osin returned to the streets outside the hospital.

"We're to be Nicola and Andrei Lipov while en route. Traveling on a confidential errand from the office of Stalin. We cannot say too much, because we are kept in the dark about the exact nature of our mission until we reach our destination. It's a good cover."

"When do we leave?" I asked, trying to find a more comfortable position in the chair. "And should I wire the regiment to resign before we go?"

"God, no. If word got back to my regiment that you'd been discharged, they'd call me back immediately. We leave at dawn. I'd say tonight, but we'd be pulled over for breaking curfew."

I wanted to question him, to be sure he knew what he was doing, but I succeeded in holding my tongue. "You'll get us through it all right, Comrade Lipov," I said, smiling as I took another cigarette from his packet.

We packed our meager belongings, Vanya covertly transferring them to the cab of the truck so we would make less noise as we departed in the morning. During the preceding days, Vanya had spent his time acquiring rations, blankets, and plain clothing for us, all of which had left us at risk every moment the supplies lingered under my hospital bed.

At the first sign of light, Vanya motioned to wake me, but I had never fully entered sleep. German tanks. Russian guns. None would be our friend now. As we walked over the gravel in the courtyard that had been our sanctuary these past days, I felt each crunch of our feet betray our location and scream our treachery. The truck was a hulking green thing that looked as though it would travel reasonably well through uncertain terrain. It had a canvas top that extended over the bed, which would be our shelter at night. Our home for days until we reached neutral ground.

Vanya had us on the road leading away from the outskirts of Stalingrad. He followed Osin's suggestions, keeping to the main road as often as he could but diverting onto the side roads whenever we encountered large numbers of army vehicles or patrols that might examine our papers too closely or question our orders.

"Are you well?" Vanya asked hourly. The roads were cratered by constant bombardment over the past months. I smiled and assured him all was well, despite every bump and jostle having me clutching the door handle as pain radiated up and down my side like current down a wire.

Every kilometer we traveled was a kilometer away from duty. I pushed down my feelings of guilt and regret with only moderate success.

By the time night fell, the thin civilian blouse Vanya had procured for me was drenched in sweat from my efforts not to cry out as our wheels found every rock and crater on the ruined roadway. We parked off the road, moderately well protected by some obliging bushes and shrubbery. I stepped down out of the truck, grateful to be motionless. I leaned against the side of the vehicle and clutched my side as Vanya set about making the bed of the truck into a nest.

"Come have some dinner," he called. I wiped the perspiration from my forehead with the back of my hand, glancing in one of the mirrors to see if I looked as wan as I felt. Still rosy cheeked. Nothing that would cause him alarm in his distracted state.

"It isn't much; I'm sorry," he said, handing me a chunk of hard bread the size of his fist and some tinned meat on a metal plate along with a cup of water. "I wasn't able to get much from the authorities, even by dropping all the names I had in my possession."

I looked down at the offering, neither offensive nor appetizing under most circumstances, and felt my stomach roll. "It's more than enough for me tonight, dearest," I said, taking a bite and chewing slowly, as I'd learned to do when rations were scarce.

"We'll see if there are any camps along the route tomorrow. I can don my uniform and use my real papers to see what I can get for us." He'd finished his meal, eating slowly, but the hunger hadn't dissipated from his eyes. "This isn't all bleak, though. Close your eyes—I have a treat for us."

"Children, are we? Isn't this when the class bully pelts the smart girl with a mud pie?"

"You sound as though you might have some experience with that. If I ever find the bastards who taunted you, I'll thrash them until their mothers cry. Now close your eyes and open your mouth."

I felt him drop a firm square onto my tongue. I kept my eyes shut as the chocolate dissolved into cream and sugar laced with earthy cocoa on my tongue.

"A lieutenant had a soft spot for an officer escorting his hero wife home," Vanya explained as I emerged from my reverie.

"A blessing on his family," I said.

"A whole host of them. There's nothing that gives me as much pleasure as seeing you happy, my love."

He lounged on the makeshift bed in the back of the truck and motioned for me to lie out beside him. The aching in my side subsided as I lay prostrate, relieving the pressure it had been under all day.

"You're hurting," Vanya said. "I should have had Osin smuggle us some morphine."

"The last thing you need on your hands is me in a drug-addled stupor," I said with more venom than I intended. I didn't mention the thousands of other injured soldiers who needed the medicine more than I. With the thought of my sisters to the southwest, I knew I wasn't deserving of any such escape from my pain.

With no chemical relief available, I did what I could to ease the ache by focusing my eyes on the stars that glinted, constant and true, through the dirt-splattered plastic window in the back of the canvas bedcover, and on the more immediate comfort of the sound of my husband's steady heartbeat below my ear.

The drive from the outskirts of Stalingrad should have taken three days on good roads, but with the cratered roads near the city and the summer rains, Vanya was now counting on seven—three to go. Vanya's leave would expire before we reached the border, but neither of us mentioned the danger that imposed on us. If the officials from the convalescent hospital had reported us missing, he was already in mortal danger.

"I can drive," I offered for what had to have been the fifth time that day.

"I'm fine, Katyushka. Get some rest." His reply was the same each time. He gripped the steering wheel like a life preserver, his eyes roving over the landscape for any sign of danger, leaving me with no occupation but to redouble his efforts as sentry and let my worry run rampant in time with the ineffective whish-whish-whish of the windshield wipers. Our vigilance seemed as pointless as our service revolvers would be in the face of real danger.

Ahead we saw a convoy of trucks, much like our own, headed north, back toward Stalingrad or one of the bases to the west. "Take a detour," I suggested. "Going in the opposite direction will attract their notice."

"Right," Vanya agreed, glancing at the map. He took a hard left onto a road that looked more like a barely widened walking trail.

Vanya's knuckles shone white as we jostled about on the road, mud splattering at the windows as we pitched from side to side. The road was nothing more than a glorified trench, with muddy walls on either side. We reached a section of road that had partially washed out, and Vanya tried to ease the wheels up over the pile of rock and mud on the right side of the path. Once the front wheels found purchase, the back lost contact with the ground and we pitched to the left and flipped all the way over, landing with the wheels up, like a hapless turtle stranded on its shell. We ended up in a jumble on the canvas ceiling of the truck and scrambled to exit before the flimsy metal framing bent under the weight of the vehicle, crushing us in the process.

"Goddammit," Vanya swore, wiping mud off his face. "Are you hurt?"

"Just shaken. Can we right it and go back to the main road?"

"I doubt it," he said, assessing the damage. Vanya smoothed his hair back with both hands, muttering a curse. "Even if we did, I'm not sure I can repair it without tools. We'll have to find shelter and figure out another plan in the morning. Dammit."

I stooped back into the truck, fetching my duffel and his without putting more than my arm in harm's way.

"We'll need these," I said, handing Vanya his pack and gently easing mine over my shoulders. Vanya found the map, still mercifully dry and safe on the ceiling of the truck, before sliding his pack on as well.

The drizzle became more sincere, and I longed for the protection of my thick uniform jacket instead of the flimsy summer garments Vanya had procured for me in town. A thin lavender dress and lightweight jacket were fine for a stroll on the streets in Moscow in August but hardly suited a border crossing. I would have even been glad for the loathsome oversized boots I kept concealed in my pack instead of the low heels that now filled with sludge as we waded along the eroding side trail in the direction of the main road. I tried to ignore the persistent ache at my side, but it was growing more relentless with each step. Vanya would have to find medication when we stopped.

"There's a village six kilometers west," he said, orienting himself on the map, doing his best to protect the precious paper from the rainfall.

"Good," I answered between labored breaths. An hour until I could rest. Anything was endurable for an hour. "Don't slow down."

We were both soaked though and caked in mud by the time the town came into view. Vanya inquired after an inn, and I followed him like a bedraggled dog. *A bed. A hot bath, if there is any kindness left in the world—though how I'll keep my wound dry is a mystery.*

A fat woman with a sour expression showed us to a room the size of a generous broom closet. "The best I've got for the night. Washroom in the hall. The kitchen is open at six for supper—such as it is." She turned her massive frame and wheezed her way back down the stairs.

"Charming old crone," Vanya said, discarding his mud-caked shoes.

"One who didn't ask questions," I said. "We couldn't ask for better."

"I suppose," he muttered, removing his socks and trousers.

I perched on the edge of the bed to remove my own soiled garments but felt my muscles seize in protest after the slog. My hands shook involuntarily, and the room grew fuzzy about the edges like a newsreel.

"Can you move to the side, dearest? I—I need to lie down."

"Of course. You're run ragged. Let me help you with your coat, and you can rest before we find food."

I stood on wobbly legs, allowing him to remove the thin coat. I felt an uncomfortable tearing sensation at my right side as he pulled the garment loose.

"Sweet Jesus, Katya."

I looked down to see the right side of my dress soaked red.

"My—my stitches," I mumbled, and fell into his waiting arms.

"Look at me, my love," I heard his rich baritone croon in soft tones. "Open your eyes."

For the second time in as many months, I peeled open my reluctant eyes to the cruel glare of hospital lights.

"Vanya?"

"Thank God," he breathed, kissing my knuckles. "The accident—you lost a lot of blood. The doctors are convinced you'll make a full recovery."

"Good," I managed to rasp.

"Ah, Captain Soloneva. Good to have you back with us." A buoyant man in a white lab coat appeared by my side. "Too anxious to return to your post, I understand. Well, not to worry. You're patched up and healing fine. You should be back to the front within a few weeks."

I looked over to Vanya, who blanched visibly at the doctor's pronouncement.

"Very good, Doctor," I whispered.

"That's the way. Now get all the rest you can. I'll be back in the morning to check your dressing."

When the doctor's footsteps faded into silence, Vanya reclaimed my hand. "The only place I could get help was a military hospital. They wouldn't treat you if you weren't enlisted. I had to show them your real papers."

The drab-green uniform jacket and slacks he wore said all I needed to hear. There would be no second attempt at an escape. My heart ached for him, but I felt a sort of relief. Now I would go where I was needed. But then in rushed the fear, which was just as quickly overwhelmed by my disgust with myself for aching to flee my duty. Round and round I went, the morphine spinning me into a blur.

Seeing me stare at his uniform, Vanya nodded. "They wouldn't have let me anywhere near here without showing my rank."

"When?"

"In the morning. It was all I could manage—I don't think they fully believed my cover, but they're in no hurry to execute an officer at the moment."

I closed my eyes against the words. How much he'd risked to bring me here.

"I told them I was taking you home," he whispered. He didn't add the words that I knew were waiting so eagerly at his lips: *Make it true. Please go back to Miass as soon as you're able.*

I stroked the too-prominent ridge of his cheekbone. *Thank you for not asking me.*

"I'm so sorry, Katyushka," he whispered in my ear. "All I ever wanted was to keep you safe."

"I know, my love. Perhaps this is all as it should be."

"No, darling. None of it is. But we have to see it out to the end now."

"We will," I said, summoning all the confidence I felt, and more than a little I manufactured. "Fly smart, my love. You once gave me that advice—keep up your end of the bargain."

CHAPTER 20

October 1943, Sorties: 456

Vanya took the news of my return to the front with his usual stoicism. His letter said that he understood my decision, that he was proud of my dedication and of my promotion. Captain Soloneva. I'd been back only a few days, and while my return was greeted with cheer, there was a darkness in the eyes of my sisters in arms that hadn't been there before. They had seen some horrific battles in my absence. I kept my own betrayal to myself. They didn't need the burden of knowing how close I'd come to deserting them.

We stood today as General Chernov awarded our regiment a new honor: we were now the Forty-Sixth Taman Guards for our work protecting the Taman Peninsula. We smiled for the cameras, and a few of us gave words, but the mood was subdued. Sofia and Taisiya's absence, and that of our other fallen comrades, was acutely obvious in everyone's faces.

The women sat and enjoyed their meal, the conversation pleasant but not lively.

"I'm glad you decided to come back," Oksana said to me, pulling me aside. "How's the side?"

"Fair enough," I said. "It aches in the rain, but I expect it always will. Nothing that will cause any real troubles."

"Glad to hear it," she said. "I was worried you'd scurry back to safety once you got a taste of life away from the front."

"I nearly did. My husband asked me to. Invoked my mother's wishes, even."

"Then why did you come back?"

"Your telegram, not to put too fine a point on it," I said, taking a sip of the warm tea as a restorative against the chilly winds of early winter that licked at our cheeks.

"I hope I didn't incite you to do something against your will," she said, her piercing gray-blue eyes probing mine.

"No. I don't think I really could have gone home, no matter how happy it might have made Vanya or Mama. Taisiya and I worked too hard to get here to leave before the end."

"Brava," Oksana said without a trace of irony. "And you accept my offer? You'll serve as my second in command?"

"Yes, though I'm surprised. You have more-experienced navigators, not to mention pilots, at your disposal."

"But they aren't you," she said. "I have all the tactical skills Sofia imparted to me, I can confer with others, but I need you to help me with the women. I can manage battles and strategy, but I can do nothing for morale. Sofia had the gift—she could manage both—but I know I don't have her way with people. Can you help me with that?"

I nodded and lifted my tea, clinking cups with Oksana. "Whatever you need, Major. One condition, though."

"And what might that be?"

"I assume you're flying your own plane. You have to take me on as your navigator."

"I'll give you your own plane," Oksana said without a moment's hesitation. "You've earned it a dozen times over. Though most of the women here have as well."

"No. If I'm to help you out on the ground, we have to learn to work together. I don't think there's any better way for you and me to get to know one another than in the air."

"You're right," she said. "I do better in the air."

"You know, I don't think we're very different. I've always felt better in my own skin up in the air."

"I miss her, Katya," Oksana said, her eyes scanning the room, as though searching for listening ears.

"And I miss Taisiya. I always will. She was my dearest friend."

"Tomorrow night," she said. "We'll head up together. I don't expect that I'll be able to teach you much, and that's a relief." She looked at the women around us, now chewing their celebratory meal in silence, then leaned in close to me. "Now do your job. What can we do to make this seem more like a celebration and less like a funeral? We've had plenty of those."

I handed her my empty cup and took the battered violin case from the corner of the mess hall where I'd stowed it. Though I hadn't played in months, the chin rest molded to my face like a lover's caress, and the bow felt as familiar in my fingers as taking Vanya's hand in mine. After three notes the eyes of the room were all on me. Cheerful, choppy notes made for dancing. A few girls recognized the tune and began to sing. One pulled out a harmonica to accompany me, but there was no piano. No Sofia to play it for us.

The tunes were happy, the party enlivened as Oksana had commanded, but for the voices silenced, our music would never be quite as rich.

Oksana had dubbed our new craft *Snowdrop* for the sweet little white wildflowers with deep-blue stripes in the center. We painted a chain of the flowers about the cockpits just as Taisiya and I had done. We'd added a slogan on each side: *Revenge for Taisiya* on one and *Revenge for*

Sofia on the other. *Daisy* now belonged to someone else, and I thought it was just as well. I didn't want to fly her with another pilot.

The October air had fangs like January as Oksana aimed the plane to the west. Most of my flying hours had been spent in a state of semi-wakefulness, eyes opening and closing like a camera that never quite focused properly. After weeks with better sleep than I had known in two years, I felt as though the scenery soaring past was almost in too-sharp detail.

"Five minutes out," Oksana called over the interphone. I looked around in the weak light to locate a landmark and found my bearings. Oksana deftly maneuvered the plane as though this were her hundredth sortie as pilot and not one of her first.

The first mark that night was a munitions tent, which I spotted with ease, despite the shadow of night. I took my flare in hand.

"You're on course. Five . . . three . . . *marked!*"

Oksana whistled into the German camp on the stalled engine, deployed the bomb squarely on the marked target, and pulled up to a higher elevation as the engine roared back to life and we maneuvered to return. The rat-a-tat of antiaircraft guns sounded seconds after we made our target, the searchlights now running, hunting frantically for the offending invaders.

Oksana circled back over the camp instead of taking an evasive course back to base.

"What are you doing?" I asked over the interphone. I would have called a course correction to her, but she knew she was well off course. There was nothing inadvertent about her actions.

"We have another bomb. I'm going to use it."

"Got it," I said. "There's a convoy of trucks to the north of the camp. Good a target as any."

She headed northwest, narrowly evading the searchlights' blinding ribbons of death. She banked left, dove low, on course to drop her payload on a row of German trucks.

"Pull up," I called over the interphone. "You're at least twenty meters below the threshold."

Ignoring my warning, she deployed the second bomb before she climbed to a safe altitude. I could feel the heat of the blast bounce the plane upward as the bomb made contact with the ground below. The trucks lay in ruins, their fuel tanks making smaller explosions as they ignited. Oksana deftly pulled us up and whipped back onto course for our own camp.

The craft shuddered as we flew, and I scanned all the instruments—such as they were—for any signs of imminent engine failure. I sniffed as intently as a dog waiting for his table scraps, seeking out the first whiff of smoke. Though it would do little good. If the craft was going to catch fire, it would go up quickly and we likely wouldn't have a chance to land before it became engulfed in flames. In the best case we'd be forced to land in German territory. I doubted my little army-issue pistol would do much good against well-armed German sentries and had little desire to test that theory.

I wanted to growl over the interphone at Oksana for her carelessness. That same mistake had nearly cost Taisiya and me our places in the regiment, and for good reason. I stilled my tongue, knowing she'd respond better to cool logic on the ground, but it cost me every ounce of restraint I had not to hurl insults about her stupidity and that of all her relations—living and dead—over the tinny contraption.

We landed forty minutes later, my knees wobbling as I hopped onto the ground from the wing. We didn't usually exit the aircraft between sorties these days, but it was clear we needed a mechanic's assessment. I motioned needlessly to Polina, who was already approaching as I ran my hands over the linen. The scorch marks on the underbelly showed we had possibly been within mere centimeters of disaster, but there didn't seem to be much damage beyond the cosmetic. I pulled Oksana by the crook of her arm away from the bustle of the ground crews.

"What was *that*, Oksana?" I asked in a low growl.

"War, Katya. In case you haven't noticed."

"You completely disregarded the safe limits of our aircraft. Not to mention my own warning."

"I saw an opportunity, Katya, and I took it."

"And you nearly took our plane down," I said, thinking of where I might be if I had accepted Vanya's offer. Someplace safer than the cockpit of a plane with a masochist as pilot. "Do you think a dozen trucks are worth an aircraft and two crew?"

"We need to get back in the air," Oksana said, turning away. "Polina finished her check."

"Do you want me to find another regiment?" I asked. "Because I will tolerate many things, but never recklessness. And I sure as hell won't fly with a pilot who is too stupid to listen to her navigator."

"You *will* fly the rest of our mission tonight." Oksana's tone brokered no refusal. "We can talk more tomorrow."

We flew seven more sorties that night, and, as though sensing the anger shooting from my eyes through the back of her helmet, she didn't deviate from the safe limits prescribed for the aircraft.

On our way back to the barracks by the early-morning light, I pulled her aside once I'd regained enough sensation in my face to be able to speak.

"We have to talk about what happened on that first sortie."

"It's simple, Katya. I had an extra bomb. I wasn't going to waste it."

"So drop it, but not when we're under the safe ceiling. That was nothing short of stupid, Oksana."

"Katya, we have to take risks to end this war."

"A calculated risk is fine. I don't mind aggressive flying, either. What I *do* mind is recklessness. It wasn't even a particularly stellar target. To waste lives and resources like that isn't just reckless; it's dishonorable."

Oksana paused and turned her head to look at the crews who were stumbling into the barracks to catch some sleep. "You were lucky out east," she said. "Kiev was one of the first cities they came to. Do you know what it was like?"

"No."

"They rounded up people—Jews mostly, and handicapped people, and anyone who spoke out against the Reich or fought back. They slaughtered them. By the thousands, Katya. Families. Children. I promise you, no matter how bad things might get in Miass, they will never be like those days when the Germans steamrolled through Kiev unchecked. Stalin did nothing to protect his own people. Probably thought Hitler had done him a favor until the fighting got too close to Red Square. Don't talk to me about recklessness and dishonor. I've seen what they can do, and I make no apologies for what I did."

"You will not settle a vendetta with me as your navigator, Oksana. I won't do it. I am prepared to give my life for my country, but I'm not going to throw it away if I don't have to."

"They would cut every last one of us down, Katya. Don't think they wouldn't."

"I know. But you have to be responsible for this unit. Did Sofia ever pull such tactics?"

"No, but as commander and as pilot, I can do as I please. I don't answer to her anymore. Nor to you."

"You said yourself that you need me. And now, more than ever, I think you do. But if you want to try leading without my help, keep on doing as you are."

Back in the barracks I threw off my flight suit and threw myself under the covers of my bunk in my long undergarments. I knew sleep wouldn't come, and I didn't seek it out. I thought of the best way to return to Chelyabinsk and the flight school. How I could get word to Vanya of where I'd gone and to Mama to know to expect me. I cursed my folly for not taking my leave of service when I'd had the chance.

"I'm sorry," Oksana said by way of greeting at the midday meal.

She sat apart from the others, as was her custom, and had gestured for me to sit across from her. I placed my tray on the table with more force than I intended but joined her all the same. She was my commanding officer, and though I was her second in command—for now—she was still my superior. I wouldn't let my anger give anyone cause to criticize my discipline.

"I'm willing to forgive a moment of foolishness on your first sortie as my pilot," I said. "On one condition."

"What's that?"

"Fly smart," I said, picking at the grayish chicken on my plate and feeling what little appetite I had shrink further still. "It was the only promise I made my husband, and I intend to keep it."

"Do you think the Germans are flying cautiously?" Oksana asked. "That their commanders are letting their pilots avoid risks?"

"No," I said, looking up from the nauseating mess on my plate. "I know this is a war, Oksana. I don't need you to patronize me. But there are lines we don't cross. I won't be a martyr. Don't destroy what Sofia worked so hard to build. If you cared for her, don't treat her memory so lightly."

"I loved her like a sister," Oksana said. "Don't think for a minute that I didn't."

"I want my own plane. Or at least a new pilot, if you want to keep me in my place," I said, knowing my tongue-lashing was enough to see me downgraded to an armorer. I just hoped Oksana was the judicious sort who wanted her second to speak her mind, not simper and follow.

"If that's what you want," she said, standing with her plate. "I need you to come into the village with me today. I have a few errands there, and I'll need an extra pair of hands."

"Very well," I said, biting my tongue against a refusal.

"Meet me in fifteen minutes." She turned on the ball of her foot without another word, passing Renata and Polina as they entered with their meals.

"It's good to have you back," Renata said, placing her tray next to mine. Polina sat across from Renata, eyeing the food with stoic acceptance.

"Thank you," I said, still watching Oksana's form shrink in the distance. I wanted to tell them I was happy to be back among them, but couldn't voice the untruth. "How have you been managing since—"

"As well as we can," Polina said, cutting short any bumbling euphemism I might have manufactured.

"Oksana got everyone up and flying in two days, even though she couldn't go herself," Renata interjected. "I think it was the best thing she could have done. To see another unit come in and support our missions would have been the worst thing for morale."

"Too much time to think," I said. "I had weeks of it in the convalescent hospital."

"Too right," Polina said. "We've been too busy for too long to take kindly to sitting idle."

"We're none of us built for it," I said. "Do you think Oksana is doing well?"

"She's not Sofia," Polina said. "She doesn't have the . . . I don't know what you might call it. The confidence? The way she made us all pay attention without trying?"

"Poise," I supplied. "Self-assurance. Sofia had those in spades."

"That's it," Polina agreed. "I'm not sure Oksana needs it, though. She knows her stuff, and people respect her, even if she isn't friendly."

I drew my lips into a line, wondering if that was for the best. Should they be willing to follow her when she was capable of risking so much for so little?

"She knows her aircraft, and she's a good pilot," Renata said. "She wouldn't put anyone in unnecessary danger. She's worth following. It won't be the same, though."

"No, nothing ever is," I said, wiping the corners of my mouth and standing to make my departure.

With two minutes to spare, I joined Oksana, who was loading a box of supplies into the back of a truck whose paint was so badly singed, it could only have been in too-close proximity to the blast of a German bomb.

I slid into the passenger side, Oksana taking her place behind the wheel. We drove into a village just outside Taman. The few remaining buildings almost seemed to quake in anticipation of the next air raid. The residents wore the gaunt, haunted look of those who had lived too long in fear. Even the lucky ones who had managed to eat well enough still bore the appearance of a people who could never rest in earnest.

Oksana pulled up to one of the largest buildings, a school by the look of it. She looked around cautiously before exiting the truck and motioning for me to join her.

Oksana whistled, and at once several children scampered from the building and threw their arms around her midsection.

A cherubic little boy missing his front teeth grinned up at her. "Have you brought us any sweets?"

"No, my darling boy. You have new teeth coming in. The sugar wouldn't be good for them. How about some good bread and some soup?"

The children nodded enthusiastically, and she pulled the box from the back of the truck. A little girl took my hand as we entered the building that smelled strongly of gunpowder and coal. She had no idea who I was, but the uniform told her all she needed to know—I could be trusted. I was on her side.

Their teacher, a wizened old man who must have been deemed too old for service, smiled at the sight of Oksana and guided us into the school cafeteria.

"We're glad to see you, my dear," he said. "And you brought one of your comrades. How nice to meet you."

"Excuse me. Captain Soloneva, meet Comrade Mishin. He looks after the children here at the school."

"Pleased to meet you," I said, offering the stooped man a smile and sticking out my right hand. He took it in a firm handshake, his chest puffing with pride, as though Oksana were presenting him to Stalin himself.

"Can the regiment spare all this?" he asked, his eyes widening at the box, which contained a large jug of soup and two loaves of black bread along with a handful of bandages and a few odd first-aid supplies. The food looked like just enough to give each child a few mouthfuls, though they all danced in anticipation of their warm meal. "I cannot accept your help if it will land you in trouble, my dear. I couldn't live with myself."

"The cook himself gave me permission to bring this to you and the children, Comrade. It's my honor to do so."

"You're an angel, Major Tymoshenko," he said, breaking the bread into portions for each child as Oksana dished up the soup into the bowls the children produced from the nearby kitchen. I looked around for an occupation and ensured each child had both clean spoons and napkins for their meal.

The children smiled up at me with dirt-streaked faces that all looked far too thin and far too wise for their years. The oldest child was not yet thirteen, the youngest still toddled, clutching the sides of benches as he learned how to navigate the expansive room. He climbed up into the lap of one of the older girls, gumming his bread in between dimpled smiles.

"The wee one looks a bit young for school," I commented to Oksana, who had served Comrade Mishin a larger portion of soup and bread with an admonishment to eat it all so that he would be better able to keep an eye on the children. "Is he tagging along with an older sibling to stay out of his mother's hair?"

"Not exactly," Oksana said, pulling me a bit farther from the table. "He's here with his sister, but their parents were killed in a raid a few months ago. They're all orphans. They'd be fending for themselves if it weren't for Mishin."

"He's a good man," I said, watching the man who tried, and failed, to siphon off some of his soup into the children's bowls without being observed.

"There aren't enough of them," Oksana replied. "And as soon as we move on, he'll be back to scraping together enough food to keep them alive. Most of them won't make it through the winter. Fewer, if Mishin won't eat his portion and keep himself alive, though there's no reasoning with him."

I looked at the faces, alight with happiness at the prospect of bellies that weren't exactly full, but not rumbling for the first time in several days.

The sun began to hang lower in the sky, and we'd be needed in the air in a few hours. We made our farewells and loaded the empty crate back in the truck.

"It's kind of you to help them," I said after a few minutes on the road. "Not many would think to do it."

"I've tried to do what I can whenever we're near a village. They're all the same. The people need help, especially the orphans." It occurred to me then that over the past two years, much of what I'd considered to be her silence might very well have been her absence as she'd quietly tended to those who couldn't tend to themselves. Knowing that her aid was a small mercy that was likely only to delay the inevitable.

"You didn't need to bring me with you," I said. "Are you trying to show me your kind side, then? Trying to get back in my good graces?"

"No. Trying to show you why I did what I did."

"How do the children have anything to do with nearly blowing our plane out of the sky?"

"The only thing that might save those children and millions of others just like them—Russian, German, Polish, French, Dutch, and otherwise—is to finish this damn war. And we have to win it, Katya. You weren't in Kiev. You didn't see what the Germans were capable of. I will do what I can to follow the safety protocols because I want you in my plane, but I have to do what I can to end this war, even if it isn't always safe. I made a mistake. It was a foolish maneuver, and I'm sorry."

"That I can understand," I said after a brief pause. "I'll fly with you."

Oksana took my hand in hers and shook it. "I won't abuse your trust again."

CHAPTER 21

November 1943, the Crimea, Sorties: 478

My dearest Katinka,

This letter brings with it all the love and blessings a mother can bestow upon her daughter. I am pleased to hear your wounds have mended and that your regiment has earned such honors. Pleased and unsurprised. You have always been one to quash a challenge that others would think insurmountable. You have your father's heart.

I have news of my own that I hope will cause you more joy than grief. I have been in the company of a Colonel Grigory Yelchin. He has been overseeing much of the industry in Chelyabinsk Oblast, reporting directly to the highest echelons in Moscow, including the little factory where the ladies and I sew the uniforms for you and the other brave citizens at the front. We formed a friendship some months ago—he and his late wife were quite fond of ballet as well, so we had much to talk about. Just last week he asked me to become his wife. I confess I have spent most of my hours since then wondering how you will react to the news. He is a good and kind man, dearest Katinka, and I know you will love him in time.

I will never forget your papa, Katinka. I can say little else about the world these days with such certainty. You know what love is now, having found your Vanya, and I want to remember what it is to be a beloved wife once more. It won't ever be the marriage your father and I had, but I think he will make me as happy as I can be until you and your husband are nestled safely around my supper table, warm, well fed, and far from harm's way. I fear this letter won't reach you until after the deed is done, so if I cannot ask your opinion on the matter, I will ask you, humbly, for a daughter's blessing.

With all my love,

-Mama

"Lucya Yelchina." I tested the name on my tongue. Beautiful. Unfamiliar, almost foreign.

"Who is that?" Polina asked from her bunk.

"My mother," I said. "She's remarried. That's her new name."

"How lovely," Renata chimed in. "You must be so happy for her."

"Yes," I said, knowing the nobler side of me wished my mother the companionship her marriage would give her. "She's been alone quite some time. It sounds like she's made a good match for herself."

"You don't look convinced of that," Oksana said, peering up from her book.

"Stop being so damned observant," I said, wishing I had something other than my mother's letter to lob at her.

"Too many years as a navigator," she said. "Risk of the job." She closed her book. "Speak. I won't take you up in the air if you're distracted."

"It's just odd to think of her with someone other than Papa, that's all. The way she spoke about him, I thought she'd never love anyone else again. It's disconcerting to find out it isn't true." I folded Mama's letter and placed it back in the envelope and tucked it in with the rest of her letters and those from Vanya.

"That stands to reason," Oksana said. "Our parents are supposed to be monoliths. Unchangeable. Solid. It's unmooring when we discover they're human."

"Mama deserves her happiness," I said, not wanting to imagine what this Grigory Yelchin might be like and how he'd managed to woo my mother after years of solitude.

"Write her to tell her so," Polina said. "It will make you feel better."

She passed me a sheet of her ivory stationery and a matching envelope. I accepted the papers, noticing there was something hard tucked in the envelope. I shook it out into my hand to reveal a small gold pendant encrusted with gleaming gems in pale blue and deep purple. In the center was a large gem—an aquamarine, I guessed—surrounded by a six-pointed star enameled onto fine gold filigree.

The shine caught Polina's eye, and she leapt from her bed to retrieve it. "So sorry, I wondered where that had got to."

"A Star of David?" Oksana asked.

"Yes. Silly to keep it, really. It belonged to my grandmother before she passed away. She wanted me to have it as a little keepsake of her. No one in the family has practiced in ages. Since my family joined the party in the revolution."

"Wise," Oksana said quietly. "It isn't safe these days."

"It isn't safe for anyone to have faith these days," Renata said, producing a cross from around her neck. She'd managed to conceal it for two years without a hint to the rest of us. "My family is Orthodox. Stalin tolerates us because of the war, but we still don't crow in the streets. I'd never have been given a place here if the party knew."

"Well, you needn't worry," Oksana said. "I'm your commander now, and I'm not sending you home. Just keep it from my superiors, and you won't have a problem. Other than the problem we're all facing right now, that is. Let's move out," Oksana said, closing her book.

Polina and Renata headed out for the airfield, Oksana several paces behind them. I tugged on her arm to keep her behind.

"That was kind of you to quell their fears," I said. "Other commanders might not have been so understanding."

"They're excellent at their jobs," Oksana said. "So long as that's the case, the brass won't question anything, and I have no desire to cause trouble for them. We all have our secrets."

I thought about how close I had come to crossing the border—how willing I had been to escape with Vanya to save my own skin—and the truth of her words washed over me. People had lost their lives for less than what Vanya and I had done. I'd spent years becoming the perfect communist and dutiful patriot, but my actions were far more incriminating than those of my comrades, whose very identities could put them at risk.

"I need to chat with you," Oksana greeted me one evening a few months later as I stood by the aerodrome after our last sortie of the night and mused over my coffee as the sun rose over the plains to the east. It was my moment of solitude, now that I hadn't a spare half hour to meddle with my violin. More often than not these days I paired it with a cigarette, forcing myself to ignore the weakness in the little indulgence. It was early in the new year, but I made no plans to cast off this vice.

"What can I do for you, Major?" I answered, extinguishing the cigarette with the toe of my boot.

"Counsel. We've been offered some male support crews. It would save the backs of our armorers and get us a few more sorties per night."

"I'd advise against it," I said, taking a sip of the rapidly cooling brew. "The men won't have the same work ethic, and they'd make the women nervous. We're working as well as we are *because* we haven't had male influence."

"Well, I don't think you'll like the rest of what I have to say. Whether we take the support crews or not, we're going to be stationed alongside another aviation regiment. I don't have all the details yet, but they're coming and we'll be sharing an aerodrome."

"Fantastic," I muttered. The face of the arrogant, young captain—Fyodorov?—that had nearly cost me my career back in training came into my mind. Who would find themselves in such a predicament this time around? "I'd be sure to set down some ground rules with their commander. Let them know that you expect the same impeccable behavior from their men as you do from us."

"A lecture will probably be as useful as a spun-sugar teapot, but I will speak to him," Oksana said, cupping a tin mug full of piping-hot coffee in her hands as I did. "I'll do as you suggest with the male crew—tell our superiors to send them elsewhere."

"Thank you," I said, grateful she'd sought my advice and taken it. "I think introducing men would be a mistake."

"We're the last holdout," Oksana said. "The other two units from the 122nd have already included men in some fashion or another."

"Do you know how they're performing?" I asked, wondering how Major Orlova would have felt about the change.

"Not with any real specificity, but if I am reading into it correctly, they're not outflying us. Not even close."

"Good. So long as we have that in our corner, it's a reason to give the brass to leave us to our own devices."

"They only have so many oars to stick in," Oksana agreed. "They won't interfere with us if we don't give them reason. They've become used to us. And on that score, I get to do something pleasant for once, and you can help me."

Oksana led me to the bunkroom, leaving the others behind to wipe the underbellies of the planes free from oil, to patch holes, and to get the planes ready for the next night. They had at least two hours before they could consider crawling into their bunks.

"The army has sent us a gift, and if I'm not mistaken, we'll all be grateful for it." Oksana opened a crate to reveal the usual drab-green uniform jackets.

"Good, we were due," I said, pointing to a thin patch on the knee of my uniform trousers.

"Hold one up," Oksana said. "Look at it."

I took one of the garments from the pile, and pinched the shoulders between my fingers to examine it. As it tumbled free from its folds, I was surprised to find not a jacket but a simple long-sleeved dress made from the same coarse woolen fabric as our usual uniforms. Tailored with room for breasts and hips. Not fashionable by anyone's standards, but made for an actual woman.

"They're going to go mad," I predicted. "Actually having clothes that fit?"

"And that's not all," Oksana said, moving to another crate. "Look in this one."

Long woolen stockings to wear with the dresses, new brassieres that looked as yielding as iron, and—

"Underpants," I whispered. Undergarments without a flap and a drooping rear end. Simple scraps of nylon that some of our number had even risked hard labor to fashion for themselves.

"Wonderful, isn't it?" Oksana said, her lips upturned in the most genuine smile I'd seen from her.

"Incredible," I agreed. "They're going to be beside themselves."

We spent the next hour distributing the dresses, accessories, and even new boots to each bunk, checking against sizes. This was usually the task of the quartermaster, but I understood why Oksana had claimed it for us.

We stood back as the women stumbled in, bleary-eyed from the night's toil. A few clambered into bed without noticing the pile of new clothes, so exhausted from fifteen hours out on the field. They weren't left to their sleep very long when the squeals erupted from the others.

"You have to be kidding!" Polina screeched. "It's the most beautiful thing I've ever seen. You can keep your embroidered gowns and velvet frocks—it's magnificent!"

"It's like Christmas morning," Renata breathed.

"Grandfather Frost and the Snow Maiden have been kind to us this new year," Oksana said, covering the gaffe. The party had been wise in co-opting some of the religious customs into their secular ones. There was only so much deprivation even a stalwart patriot could endure.

Despite the weariness driven deep into their bones, they tried on the new uniforms, reveling in the garments—particularly the boots—that fit properly.

"Enjoy them, ladies. You've earned this token of appreciation," Oksana announced as the women admired one another. She pulled me off to the side and handed me a carefully wrapped parcel. "This one is yours."

I opened my mouth to question why mine was given such attention, but closed my mouth just as quickly. I opened the package to find the same contents as all the others, but lovingly wrapped with a card on top:

> *Dearest Katinka,*
> *Thank you so much for your letter of congratulations to Grigory and me. It meant the world to us. I think he read your words a dozen times at least. He tells everyone who will listen how proud he is of his new daughter at the front. These new uniforms are not all our doing. I think the high command had these planned for you and were waiting for the materials and funds to make it happen. Grigory did, however, use every favor in his pocket to ensure that the plans to give you proper uniforms did not*

get abandoned on a desk in Moscow. He insisted that we make the uniforms here in Chelyabinsk, which enabled me to sew the enclosed for you with my own two hands. It's not the candy-pink flannel pajamas that I used to send, but I trust it will keep you warm and comfortable as may be.

With all my love, and a kiss from Grigory, too,

~Mama

"Your new stepfather will be named a hero if this regiment has anything to say about it," Oksana said, peering over my shoulder. I cast her a peevish glance at the intrusion. She shrugged. "I had to know why your uniform had been given such treatment. I see now it was a mother's touch. You're a lucky woman, Katya."

"Beyond measure," I agreed. Grigory's labors on our behalf had to have started months before he and my mother married. He cared enough about Mama to see this done for her daughter and her daughter's comrades before he'd even secured her hand. Even if I wanted to resent his encroachment on my family life, it was plain he was doing his part to try to earn welcome.

I discarded my flight suit like the others and tried on the uniform my mother had made. It was loose at the bust and waist but otherwise contoured to my shape like an expertly tailored garment. She'd made it to fit me as I was before the war. Before I was made lean by labor, exhaustion, and rations that were sometimes more sparse than we might have wanted.

"Twirl," Oksana commanded. "Let's see your mother's handiwork."

I obliged with a slow spin, and as the woolen skirt settled around my knees, I imagined the warm fabric was as close to an embrace from my mother as she could send by post.

The men who would come to share our aerodrome arrived three weeks later, bringing with them the worst of the winter snows as well as ice and crosswinds, two of the only conditions that could ground us, so we found ourselves thrown together without the distraction of missions to keep us occupied for close to two weeks before the conditions finally improved. Polina kept the mechanics running, making sure that every blemish on the planes was attended to and every system in perfect order. Renata had the armorers taking stock of our munitions and discussing their strategies for minimizing loading times between sorties.

"We're glad to share the space with you, Major Tymoshenko," the commander of the male regiment said after seeing the regiment in action for a number of days. I attended their meetings as her deputy, while he had two or three underlings scuttling about after him. "We hope our presence will be of some benefit to you. Teach the girls a trick or two, you know."

Oksana said nothing, letting him come to his own conclusion about her assessment of his remarks.

"You run a very efficient outfit, I'll admit," he said, unable to hide his reluctance.

"Were you expecting otherwise from a guards-designated regiment?" Oksana didn't fold her arms imperiously or stare at him with disdain. She merely moved a stack of his papers from the desk in the command area she'd claimed as her own and placed them on the empty table perpendicular to her workspace.

"I meant no offense. It's just that I'm not used to working alongside regiments run by women—you understand, Major."

Oksana sat and cast her eyes down at a document of some kind rather than looking at his face. "Major Grankin, are you used to working alongside regiments run in accordance with the regulations set forth by the Red Army?"

"Naturally."

"Then nothing will come as a shock to you during our time cohabitating this space. That is precisely what we are. If anyone has led you to believe that our regiment operates under any different circumstances than your own, you've been misinformed."

"Very good, Major."

"And one more thing, Major Grankin. I expect exemplary behavior from your men when they are in the company of my regiment. I haven't the time or the patience to discipline your men or see to it that you do so properly. Are we clear?"

"Crystal, Major."

"Good. Now we've finally got good conditions for the night. I would suggest you use this time to observe how my mechanics and armorers prepare. You might find their tactics useful."

He opened his mouth for a moment, then snapped it shut and turned on the ball of his foot and left, presumably to overlook the proceedings at the airfield.

"That was simply beautiful," I said, putting my hand to my heart for dramatic effect.

"Consider it a preemptive strike. He hadn't shown much in the way of the usual swagger you see in officers, but it was only a matter of time. I simply let him know where he stands in the hierarchy here."

That night Oksana and I led the first sortie. A male crew across the field from us would follow three minutes later. We didn't hit targets of any stellar value but did manage to drop our payload practically on top of their barracks. We could see soldiers spilling out of the building like grain from a silo, brandishing their pistols and shooting uselessly at the sky as our engine roared back to life. We held their attention just long enough to let the next crew drop their payload, and were back on course for our own base before the Germans were able to retaliate effectively.

As we landed and approached the staging area, we could see Polina barking orders and weaving her efficiency from the loose threads of chaos she was handed each night. She was always a model of competence and poise, and the presence of our male guests clearly had her running at peak form. I flashed a smile at Oksana once she had killed the plane's engine and turned her head with a grin. She was a fine commander, but I wondered if it wasn't our mechanic who was really running the regiment.

Renata brought us steaming-hot tea before seeing to the outfitting of new bombs, and we remained tethered into our seats as we drank. From what we could see when the first male sortie had been completed, the men exited their cockpits as soon as their wheels hit the frozen turf. They smoked, drank coffee, ate their dinners, and made small talk as each mechanic and each armorer refueled, reloaded, and fixed any damage incurred on the previous sortie. One pilot, one navigator, one armorer, one mechanic—just as we did in the beginning.

By the book.

By the end of the night, we'd pushed every crew to the point of exhaustion but had more than done our part in ruining the evening for the Germans encamped so nearby. The best part was that despite working at our maximum levels, we didn't lose a single crew.

"How many sorties did your men complete this evening, Major?" Oksana asked Grankin by way of greeting after we'd helped Polina and Renata with the nightly maintenance.

"Oh, I don't think we kept an exact tally," Grankin said, airily dismissing the question.

"Really. I would expect a commander in the Red Army to keep exacting records. We endeavor to log every sortie each of our crews takes. Moscow prefers as many details as we can provide. Is the same not true for you, Grankin?"

"Well, I wouldn't say that," he blustered.

"Sixty-eight, sir," a short man with a squeaking voice supplied from behind the major.

"There, you hear? Sixty-eight. What do your meticulous records say you've done tonight?"

"Eighty-four," Oksana said without referencing a ledger of any kind. "Not our best, but not bad."

"Not at all," he said. "Well done. Your crews are remarkably dedicated. How do you do it?"

"Indeed they are dedicated. If you want to emulate their performance, your men will have to get by with a great deal less socializing while planes are being turned. Just as a start."

Grankin stormed out of the tent, his face as dark as thunderclouds. His underlings followed him at a healthy lag.

"I wouldn't want to be part of that regiment just now," I proclaimed as Oksana leaned back in her chair. She gave a full-throated laugh and rested her boots on the edge of the desk, radiating self-satisfaction.

"Nor would I. They seem like nice-enough boys, but they haven't the hunger my ladies do. That can't be taught or disciplined into anyone. It comes from decades of being told we can't do a thing while knowing we can. They'll never have that."

"No, they won't," I agreed. "More's the pity. It'll be just as well when we move on."

"Well, we're going to have to make room for a man in our ranks," Oksana said, her face falling a bit. "We're getting a male radio technician. They only have one who can be transferred to us, so we'll have to make do."

"Well, one man can be henpecked into submission, I suppose."

Oksana chuckled. "I don't know how much of that will be necessary. They forwarded his uniform to me this morning. If he doesn't find the dress becoming, the panties will do the trick."

CHAPTER 22

December 1944, Poland, Sorties: 794

We'd enjoyed a quiet December in Poland and could smell the sweet tang of victory in the air like the seductive scent of fresh bread wafting out the bakery door. I held a parcel in my hands from Vanya. It had been weeks since his last postcard. I couldn't let my thoughts drift over to the dark places and at the same time maintain the courage to fly, so I invented reasons for the lack of communication to distract myself. Lost sacks of mail—plausible. Too much time enjoying the camaraderie of his fellow pilots—somewhat less so. Far too much work and very little leisure—probable. I couldn't contemplate anything more dire.

But here in my hands was an actual parcel from him. The only one I'd received during the war. A small canvas, not larger than a child's school slate, was coiled up and packed carefully in a leather tube that might have been suited for blueprints or important documents. I unfurled it to find a small but intricately rendered portrait of myself. Every line in my face, the curve of my nose, the shade of my hair, all re-created from his perfect memory. He couldn't have devoted many hours to it—I knew what his life was like on the front—but there wasn't a brushstroke out of place. Seeing each of my features assembled on the canvas, this time without any benevolence of young love perfecting the flaws, I felt a moment of breathlessness as my heart strained against my ribs.

"Your husband is quite the artist," Oksana observed, peering over my shoulder.

I cleared my throat, grateful that her intrusion had interrupted the torrent of tears that would have erupted. "Yes," I said once I'd collected myself. "A fine one."

"He managed to capture the shade of your hair. That's quite a feat. It really is lovely." She took one of my tendrils between her thumb and forefinger and dropped it, as though the red locks were as hot as the flames they resembled.

"Thank you," I said, pretending I hadn't noticed her gesture. "I hated it as a girl and was annoyed by it when I was at the academy. I hated anything that called attention to me. I envied Taisiya her mousy hair." The mention of Taisiya still caused my voice to crack slightly. I still started when I saw one of Oksana's blond locks fall loose from her helmet instead of Taisiya's mousy brown when I was in the rear cockpit.

"My friend Yana enjoyed drawing. She never had money for paints. Or lessons. She made do with pencils or charcoals and her own imagination. She hasn't your Vanya's skill, but I think she has talent."

She fished a large volume from her trunk and removed a loose paper. On the front was a skillfully drawn portrait of Oksana. She was in a field of white-and-blue striped snowdrops, just as Oksana had painted around our cockpits months ago. Oksana's face was soft, kinder than I saw it, but then Yana had the privilege of knowing Oksana before the war had claimed her to service. There were no lines of worry around her eyes, and her lips turned upward in a graceful smile.

"She does. She should go to art school after the war. I'm sure there would be a good conservatory for her in Moscow, once things settle down. I have a feeling there will be a great demand for beautiful things to help us all forget the vile ones we've endured." I had created a fantasy life for myself in the past few months: Whisking Vanya away to the cabin in Miass and spending six months cooking all his favorite foods while he sat in the fields and painted. Wildflowers in summer. Leaves in autumn. Even the austere, spindly branches weighted down with snow as winter took hold. I might even allow him to paint me en déshabillé, as he'd mentioned on our wedding night. I could see every wall covered with his landscapes, masking the scarred wood with his beautiful creations. We would take months to heal, to be ensconced in one another, before setting about rebuilding our lives.

"I want to take her to Aix-en-Provence," Oksana said in a low voice. "I have family there, and they sent my father the fare for our train tickets once as a special treat. Three weeks there and I've never been able to tolerate the cold like a proper northerner ever since. The light there is remarkable. Painters flock to it. It would be bliss for her."

"That does sound lovely," I said, studying Oksana's face. She looked far away, wistful. She looked in my direction, but I felt her gaze glance past my face and to the barracks beyond me.

"It's not too far from Aix to the ocean. We stayed a few days at Saint-Cyr-sur-Mer. My aunt said we couldn't come all that way without putting our feet in the Mediterranean." She folded a uniform shirt and placed it in her trunk, smoothing her blanket before sitting and looking at Yana's drawing once again.

"She was right," I said, placing the tube with Vanya's painting in my duffel. "Mama always dreamed of the Riviera. And Italy. Spain. She always wanted to travel, at least before Papa was killed. It's why I decided to fly. I wanted to take her to see all those places since Papa never did."

"How sweet of you," Oksana said. "I've always wanted to go back to Aix. I cried for three weeks when we left. But heaven knows there will be enough work putting the country back together once this is all over. There won't be any time for holidays by the sea for years yet."

It was the first time Oksana had mentioned life after the war, the first glimmer of optimism I'd ever seen from her. I hid my smile, not wanting to stifle the ray of sunshine when they were so rare. The signs of hope were springing up in more than one quarter. The army was even willing to let us carry parachutes, sacrificing a few kilos that could have been used for bombs. They expected some of us would live.

"Take her there," I said. "When the cease-fire sounds, we will have done our part. We can leave the rebuilding up to others. Those with more energy left than us."

Oksana shoved the drawing back in her book and placed it back in her footlocker, forcefully but carefully.

"Dreams are for later, Katya."

~

Taking off with the benefit of a proper runway was a luxury I could well become accustomed to. The wooded terrain in Poland was far easier to maneuver over than the peninsulas and mountains in the south, with their erratic winds, but we'd traded in the hospitality of farmers' homes and makeshift barracks in abandoned schools for tents and trenches. We might have complained about the dismal conditions in Poland, but we barely had time to sleep, let alone consider our discomfort. The canvas of our tents flapped angrily in the winter winds like geese who had waited too long to migrate. The tents did little to shelter us from the cold of the Polish morning, but it was better than the days we had to sleep outdoors.

We hadn't run at our full effort in a few weeks, but we'd been ordered to harass a German camp just to the west of the front. No specific targets in mind—we were just to keep them awake, make a mess of their camp, and encourage them to move westward back toward Germany. We'd made progress over the last few months, and the Germans were getting more and more desperate. We rarely got a close look at the enemy troops, except when they made the occasional raid of our camps, but the faces we saw were getting both older and younger—old men and little boys. Men of proper fighting age were becoming scarce in Germany. When we saw the faces of our own troops, I saw much the same phenomenon, though to a lesser extent. If we had an advantage over them, it was the size of our country and our sheer numbers.

Oksana led *Snowdrop* over the front lines on our first run, dropping the payload square on a convoy of trucks, the loss of which would hurt. We skittered away from the camp before anyone gave chase and before the searchlights blinded Oksana and prevented a stealthy escape. She powered the engine up and took us full throttle back to our makeshift base. Polina and the crew bustled up to us, prepared to refuel the plane and make a quick scan of the wings for any bullet holes that couldn't go without patching. Renata and three other women from our regiment loaded the bombs and gave the all-clear sign when we were fully armed.

"Don't charge the engine," Oksana called to Polina. "We have three starts left. I want to get back there."

Oksana's drive had become intense as she saw our victories mounting. In my heart I could see she'd begun the war thinking that Russia would stand her ground and keep her territory, or most of it, but that Germany would ultimately be victorious. She fought to keep as much of the motherland intact as she could as a bastion against the cruelty of the Nazis. Now a loftier goal was in sight—she could see a future where the forces of Hitler were expelled completely. She was desperate to fly as many sorties as she could so the tide wouldn't risk turning back against us. Every bomb dropped was another step closer to Berlin and victory.

The moment she was given the all clear for takeoff, Oksana soared back to the front. We were only a twenty-minute flight to the camp, so there wasn't much use in resting before we arrived. Just as we came to the edge of the German camp, Oksana cut the engine before we would be heard. We deployed our bombs, one after another, making a mess of their barracks. The searchlights caught us as we dropped the final bomb, and I was ready with the newly equipped machine gun they had mounted to the rear of my cockpit in case any of the Germans gave chase.

Oksana's movements, usually efficient and assured, became agitated, then panicky. "The engine won't start again," she called into the interphone. I felt the metallic taste of fear at the tip of my tongue. "We're out of starts."

"How? We should have two left."

"I have no idea. We must have miscounted."

The searchlights locked in on us, and the antiaircraft guns had no problem finding their mark. The wings were shredded in short order, and we were losing altitude quickly. If the impact didn't kill us, the Germans would do the job. I saw visions of Vanya and Mama, my breath catching with the realization I wasn't going to see them again. I gripped the open edge of the cockpit on either side of me. The ground was spinning closer. There would be no recovering from the dive, though Oksana still wrestled with the throttle.

"We'll have to bail out," I called back to her, grateful for the large pack on my back.

Oksana gave her assent, and we deployed, pulling our chutes almost the instant we were free of *Snowdrop*. Neither of us had practiced jumping with parachutes in years—even in military academies, we'd rarely had the chance. It was too risky for the aircraft. I felt a cold sweat on my brow despite the frigid air. The German searchlights tracked us, and I was jolted in the air as their bullets pierced my chute, my descent accelerating with every new puncture. I gripped my parachute harness until my fingers grew numb, hoping the chute would hold. I felt exposed as a newborn babe, and just as able to defend myself. I wanted to close my eyes so I wouldn't see the bullets that seemed destined to riddle my flesh, but I had to see the ground if I wanted to land without breaking a leg on the forest floor. Or worse.

I had little control over where I landed but tried to urge my course toward a clearing I could just make out by the light of the moon. Getting tangled at the top of a fifteen-meter pine was a complication I didn't need. The drop was short, and despite the Germans aiding the speed of my descent, my landing on the edge of the clearing was only rough enough to twist an ankle. It would ache tomorrow, I was certain, but not so much I wouldn't be able to walk.

But a walk wasn't enough. We needed to run.

More of our planes were overhead, and the constant rat-a-tat of the antiaircraft guns sounded above us. I ducked as though I expected the bullets to fall on our heads like leaden raindrops. I couldn't recognize who flew the plane that hovered over the camp, but I was mesmerized to see it from this perspective. It wasn't fast but looked remarkably graceful as it glided over its target. The eerie silence, followed by the crash of bombs, then the thrumming of the small engine as it roared overhead was enough to unnerve the most battle-hardened pilot. The careening whistle as the plane dove before releasing the bombs was otherworldly. The nickname "Night Witches" made more sense than I cared to admit.

A thud a few meters away told me Oksana had landed much harder than I did. I discarded my harness and dashed as quickly to her side as I could manage. "We have to move. Into the trees," I said, eyeing the swooping biplanes overhead. Our bombs were anything but precise, and we could easily get caught in a blast. The forest wasn't particularly dense, but it should give us the benefit of cover.

Oksana struggled to her feet, looking woozy and disoriented.

"Put your arm around me," I commanded, supporting her as we shuffled to what I hoped was the northeast, away from the German camp. It was impossible to be certain without my compass, which had been lost in the crash.

The barrage of bombs, grenades, and antiaircraft guns caused me to flinch every few steps, and it never seemed to grow quieter. Despite the dark of night, the path was illuminated by the glow of gunfire against the ankle-deep bed of snow, so I clung to the shadows as best I could, supporting Oksana through the drifts and brambles.

"Katya, I need to stop for a bit," Oksana said through gasping breaths.

I hated to stop, imagining somehow that our movement would make us a less likely target. The reality was that whether we moved or kept still, the only thing protecting us from the bombs raining down was luck until we reached our camp. Oksana's face was ashen when I looked over and opened my mouth to persuade her to keep moving. One glance at her gray features and I snapped my mouth shut again. She was wounded, and I had to assess how badly before we made any attempt to return to camp.

My arms trembled around Oksana as I scanned the countryside, looking for a decent place to take cover. As though I'd called it into being, there appeared what proved to be a small opening to a cave ahead to my right. It seemed relatively well secluded and, if of any depth at all, would provide protection from carelessly thrown grenades or stray bullets—even a measure of cover from the small bombs we dropped. I held no illusions about its ability to protect us from the soldiers who were probably already on patrol, looking for the crew of the downed plane, or better still, the mangled bodies that would serve as trophies. We were worth an Iron Cross to them, and we never let that fact slip far from our minds.

"In here," I whispered needlessly as Oksana leaned on me. We stooped to enter the little opening, and I hoped none of the more vicious creatures were sheltering in our sanctuary. What an embarrassment it would be to escape the hands of the Germans only to be maimed or killed by a starving wolf.

"Thank you," Oksana whispered through a grimace as I helped her to sit.

"Where are you hurt?" I asked, wishing I'd had more training as a medic. I'd bring it up the next time the brass was in earshot. I fumbled in my breast pocket for the flashlight that I hadn't dared use before now. Oksana gestured to her side, and my fingers flew to remove her flight suit to assess the damage. Her entire left side was a bloody mess.

"You've been shot," I said, unzipping the top of my suit and unbuttoning my blouse. It wasn't pristine, but it would do for bandages until I could get her back to the base for proper medical attention.

"I already deduced as much," she said in a flat voice.

I began tearing my blouse into strips. "I need to get you patched up and back to base. You need a medic. A surgeon," I corrected as I assessed the damage to her side.

She sat still as I tried to stem the flow of blood. Her breathing was strong, though raspy, as I applied the strips of cloth to the angry red flesh in a makeshift bandage and held my hands over the covered wound, hoping to stem the flow of blood. I didn't seem to be making much progress, so I zipped her suit back up, hoping her blouse and suit would do their part to help the wound clot before it claimed too much of her blood, and I maintained pressure on the injured area. Oksana was a pale woman by nature, but she had gone from alabaster to crystalline in color from the loss of blood.

"Do you think you can walk?" I asked, barely audible, the image of German soldiers looming in the back of my brain. I could accept a death from being shot down. A good, clean death. What we would suffer at their hands would be worse than any fate I could conjure from the deepest crevasses of my brain.

"I'm not sure. I just need to catch my breath," Oksana whispered. She took in a deep, raspy breath. "I'm cold. It's always so damned cold."

I lay beside her and pulled her into my arms, tucking her head under my chin, doing all I could not to upset her injury. I willed every ounce of my warmth into her broken body. I expected her to rebuff my embrace, as self-reliant as she always was, but she turned her face into my chest and took in a deep, ragged breath.

"You always smell like vanilla sugar somehow," she said. "Sweet and wholesome. Like Yana's cookies."

"I'm sure she'll have platters of them waiting when you get home," I said, wondering how soon that day would come for Oksana. Sooner than for me, I wagered. I was certain she'd need time to heal from this injury and hoped the advances westward would have the war tied up before she was fit for service again.

"No, Katya," Oksana said, her whisper even lower. "She's gone."

I gingerly tightened my embrace for a moment. "When did you receive word?"

"She died before the war started. When Stalin had his head up his ass and refused to stop the German army until they practically set up offices at the Kremlin."

"What reason could they have for killing a young girl?" From the few times Oksana had mentioned Yana, I couldn't imagine she was like us. She wasn't the kind to take up arms.

"She was Jewish." Oksana sighed. "They killed her, her parents, her baby brother. Gunned them down like stray dogs."

"My God, Oksana. I had no idea. You always spoke of her as though she lived and breathed still."

"I couldn't bring myself to say otherwise," Oksana said. "You keep alive for your Vanya. Taisiya had her Matvei. I had to have something to cling to."

The meaning of her words seeped into me like the cold, dank air of the cave. She could never have spoken this way before. One word about exactly how dear Yana had been to her could well have resulted in her losing her wings and her place in the regiment.

What words of solace could I offer? This sullen girl now made perfect sense as I held her bleeding in my arms. She wasn't simply angry. She'd been grieving. She used her churlish mask to protect her from the reality of life without Yana. She needed that mask to fight—to exact some revenge from the people who had cut short a life that had been so precious to her.

"Oksana, I wish I'd known. I would have tried to understand . . . tried to help you cope with it all. I would have been a better friend."

"You were *always* a good friend to me, Katya. Even when I didn't deserve it."

"Nonsense," I said, wishing I could think of more instances when I'd reached out to her when we'd first met. Tried to get to know her when she was still reeling from her loss.

"I need you to do something for me," she said.

"Anything," I said, stroking the back of her head, my fingers brushing over her silver-blond tresses.

"Can you take word to my family in Aix? My parents are gone, but my aunt and uncle, my cousin—I want them to remember me. And I don't want them to hear about it in a letter. Take Yana's drawing to them. You can take whatever you want from my effects and give them the rest."

"Don't talk like that, Oksana. We're getting up. We're going now if you're going to try to give in like this." I moved to release her from my arms and stand, but she summoned the strength to clutch my suit and keep me seated.

"It's too late for me, Katya. Too much blood. I feel light. Like floating. Please just promise me." The color in her lips had gone from rosy to blue, and she'd begun to shiver. She spoke the truth, and there was nothing I could do to save her.

I gripped her close to my chest, hoping to spread my warmth to her. "I can't promise," I said, not wanting any of our final words to be half-truths or empty promises. "But if I survive, I will do my best. I'll beg for papers. I'll do what I can."

"That's all I can ask," Oksana said. I felt her muscles relax, as though I'd relieved her of a heavy burden. "Take your Vanya with you. Have a proper honeymoon by the sea."

"Can't you please try?" I pressed my lips to the top of her silvery head, my tears streaming into her hair. "We can try to get you back to the base."

"I'll slow you down too much, Katya. You need to go. Soon. I can't risk your life for the slim chance of saving mine."

"Oksana—"

"That's an order from your superior officer. The others need you, Katya. And I've done my part. I can die knowing that I have."

"I can't lead them the way you and Sofia did," I said, wiping my face free of the tears.

"No, you'll lead them in your own way. Tell the commanders I named you as my preferred replacement, though I'm sure they will know it. Now go, Katya. Stay low. I haven't heard bombs for a while now, so you should be clear from our side."

She trembled in my arms, from cold, pain, and exhaustion, I was sure, no longer from fear. I wanted to argue. I wanted to refuse to leave. I did not want to disturb the peace of her last moments on earth with a dispute, however, and knew she would only repeat her order if I countermanded her.

My shivers equaled hers as I pulled away from our embrace. I lowered my face to hers and kissed her lips. She'd gone so long without tenderness. Her lips were cold as I pressed mine against them, wishing the air from my lungs could breathe life into hers.

She looked up with her gray-blue eyes, her gaze distant as she tried to focus on my face. "Thank you, Katya. Go and be well. Go home to your Vanya, and make some little painters. The world needs more painters."

"And the first girl will be Oksana. For you."

I kissed the top of her head once more and dashed for the mouth of the cave before I lost the resolve to leave.

The camp can't be far. I can make it there in time and round up a search crew. The brass will allow it for the commander of the regiment. They have to.

I wasn't more than ten meters away when I heard the crack of her service pistol. I stopped stock still for a moment and swiveled back to look at the entrance to the cave where Oksana's body now lay.

I could go back and face the scene she tried to spare me from, or I could follow her orders.

I turned in the direction of the sun, whose weak rays had just begun to break over the crests to the east, and placed one foot in front of the other, back to where my duty called me.

CHAPTER 23

Sorties: 795

It was more than twenty-four hours later before I found our camp due to the blanket of snow, the snarls of roots and branches on the forest floor, and my slow progress as I tried to make my passage as silent as possible. My attempts to avoid the attention of any German sentries made for an arduous slog through the Polish wilderness. With each step farther from the German bases, I grew more certain that Oksana could not have survived the journey. Her orders had been just, and they had very likely saved my life.

We'd been written off for dead, as two other teams had seen our crash. They hadn't seen us deploy our chutes, and even if they had, any attempt to recover us on the German side of the front would have been a suicide mission.

"If we'd seen you—" Svetlana began.

"You would have stayed put or risked your life for no purpose," I scolded, sipping from the piping-hot cup of tea that Renata refreshed as soon as it began to empty. Her mother had procured a tin of fine tea leaves from the factory where she worked. A token of appreciation for her daughter's service to be sent to the front. It was as fine a black tea as one might see on the tables of the highest government officials, perfumed with just the right blend of spices. Renata knew me well enough not to ruin the effect by adding any milk or sugar.

"I can't believe you walked all that way," Polina mused for the sixth time, inspecting the damaged skin on my feet. She wrestled with calling a medic to look at them, but I refused to let her, pulling rank despite my own objections to the practice. I'd endured weeks of convalescence after losing Taisiya. I couldn't bear it a second time while mourning for Oksana.

The women should have been in their tents, attempting to eke out a few hours of sleep. If not sleep, at least some rest before another afternoon repairing planes and another night keeping the Germans from their objectives. Their faces were all the same—haunted. They had once been innocent girls, but they had seen too much. Lost too much.

I remembered Sofia's orders to me after we'd lost Darya and Eva in training. We had no piano, but I still crated my violin from camp to camp, finding space in my duffel and ensuring its safe passage on the trucks and Jeeps that carried our supplies while we flew overhead. I retrieved the case from my corner of a tent, not allowing myself to look at Oksana's possessions, which were still as she left them. Tending to them would be a chore for another day, when I had more strength to sort through the treasures she'd found worthy to take with her.

I rejoined my sisters in arms and for the first time in many months put my bow to strings, playing simple tunes that I hoped were a reasonable interpretation of the Ukrainian folk songs Oksana would have learned as a girl in Kiev. The girls who knew them sang along, reluctantly at first, more enthusiastically as I kept playing. We raised cups of Renata's good tea in a toast to Oksana and her service. She may have seemed joyless in life, but I hoped that in some way she could take joy in this celebration as we honored her as best we could.

As the light grew weak, the women migrated toward the aircraft, the armorers fitting the bombs, the mechanics fueling and making a final check to ensure each plane was airworthy. Polina hung back, waiting for me as I stowed my instrument. I arched a brow at her, for usually she was leading the mechanics and overseeing every check.

"I hoped I might have a word with you," she said, casting her eyes down.

"Of course, Polina. What can I do for you?"

"You know I've been with the regiment since the start, yes?"

"Naturally. You're the best mechanic we have, and *my* mechanic on top of it."

"That's just it. I've served as a mechanic for three years now. I want to serve on a flight team. I don't have the hours to be a pilot, but I could be a navigator. No one knows the systems better than I do."

I nodded my agreement. She knew the planes so well there was no way she would be anything less than an exemplary navigator.

"I was hoping I could serve as *your* navigator, Captain. Since we've been working together this whole time. I assumed you'd be given command, and as such, you'd be taking up your own plane. I'd be honored if you'd even consider me."

The reality of her words hit me. I couldn't be certain command would be mine, but that decision would be made soon. A plane would be mine if I wanted it—that much was sure, at least. I finally would have command of my own plane—the thing I'd dreamed of since I was a ten-year-old child in the fields of Miass. Now that it was mine, I wondered if it had been worth all the loss and sacrifice to have my wings. The question seemed too large. And irrelevant. The plane would be mine, and I could either fly it or make a mockery of all that sacrifice.

I looked at Polina's hopeful face and imagined my own in her stead when I'd first shaken Sofia's hand at the academy. I was awestruck by Sofia's bravery then, dying to join her ranks. Polina wanted the same things now as I did then.

She would be more valuable on the ground as our lead mechanic. It would have been prudent to ask her to keep her place, but I couldn't stifle her dream any more than I could have stopped dreaming my own.

"Get a helmet and a flight suit," I said. "I want you ready as soon as we're given orders."

~

Three days later we got word that Oksana's final wish was to be granted: I would be commander of the regiment, and promoted to major for accepting the position. Mama and Vanya would be proud, but the last thing I wanted in recompense for Oksana's loss was a new title.

I had to stop myself from taking my place in the rear cockpit after hoisting myself up onto the wing. I slid into the front, less gracefully than I might have hoped, and strapped myself in. I waited for Polina to slide into place and fasten her own harness before I started the engine. My hands were steady as the plane roared to life, and I ascended into the night sky under my own power.

From the rear cockpit the view was generally of wing, windshield, and the back of the pilot's helmet. In front the view was of propeller and the vast reaches of the sky. It wasn't like a truck, where you could see the road in front of you. If you wanted to see your target, you looked over the side, sometimes banking the plane to get a better view. I couldn't see straight ahead, but my view upward was unobscured and spellbinding. As we soared the thirty kilometers to the German camp, the blue velvet expanse of the night sky stretched before us, encrusted with stars shining like diamonds under candlelight.

There was no light below, making the tapestry above a breathtaking display. My father used to point out the constellations when I was a girl, and I found myself wishing I'd paid more attention. One of the few constellations I still recognized blazed ahead of me—the *Pleyady*—the Seven Sisters. A star for Oksana, Sofia, and Taisiya, who I hoped were somehow looking out for us. And one for Polina, Renata, and me, the six of us bound by our service. The seventh? The Polikarpov that took us on our missions each night and who was, as Sofia had once wisely said, the fifth member of each crew. Separated by life and death, but always united in duty.

I felt no pleasure, no satisfaction, as I dropped my payload on the German camp, but felt secure with Polina in the seat behind me. I knew now how sincere Vanya, Taisiya, and Oksana had been when they said how much easier the task of piloting was with a good navigator in tow. She was my eyes and ears when I needed them. She allowed me to concentrate on the task of maneuvering the craft as we returned through the midnight-blue abyss back to the safety of our camp.

At the end of the night's work, the women turned to me, their faces expectant. *Orders. They're waiting for me to give orders.* I didn't feel a surge of pride, only the weight of the responsibility I bore to keep them safe.

"Renata, lead the crews in regular maintenance. The rest of you, get some sleep." Renata beamed at the unspoken promotion from armorer to mechanic. She'd had a brilliant teacher in Polina and would follow her flawless example.

I could have taken the time to get some rest but found myself seated behind Oksana's desk. My desk. Maps, official orders, and telegrams covered the surface so that the scarred top wasn't visible. I began to wade through the piles of documentation that had accumulated since Oksana's passing, on the desk that had always been so painstakingly organized.

The newest message, now addressed to me, contained orders to move west, yet again. Closer and closer to the German border. No regrouping to the east in months. Onward, ever onward.

My orders were clear. Longer sorties. As many flights as we could manage in a single night, every single night the weather allowed for it. Any time there was a suitable target within range, we were to attack.

I knew it meant only one thing: victory was in our reach, but we could not falter if we were to grasp it.

CHAPTER 24

June 1945, the Battle of Berlin, Sorties: 1,106

The city of Berlin lay in ashes. Empty husks of buildings teetered and collapsed at random, filling the streets with dust and trapping war-weary citizens beneath the rubble. The German people eyed us with distrust and stooped their heads, avoiding eye contact. They cowered in the presence of the massive portrait of Stalin erected just outside the Brandenburg Gate. The city, and indeed all of Europe, was being cleaved in two—all that was Soviet, and all that wasn't. Comrade Stalin had to be pleased with his victory. He'd paid for it with plenty of Soviet blood.

We stood at alert, waiting for an insurgency. The commanders were certain there would be one, but I doubted there would be attacks of any real significance. With Hitler dead in his bunker, the serpent of Germany had been decapitated. There was no one left with the drive to fight. I wondered if, without Stalin at the helm, Russians would have taken to the streets to defend Moscow. It was all too easy to imagine my own countrymen wearing this haunted look of defeat and acquiescence.

Ground troops were charged with keeping the peace, and we were simply there to await the official surrender orders to return home. We found ourselves with almost nothing to occupy our time. Now that we didn't have missions all night long, we all tried to adjust to a normal rest schedule but found the dark of night too unsettling for slumber.

At odds with idleness, we spent our newly acquired free hours wandering into Berlin during the day as sleep eluded us. Never alone, always in groups. We circumnavigated the outskirts of the city, knowing many of the streets were impassable from the mountains of rubble.

"Do you have the time?" Renata asked, rubbing her bare wrist as we walked along.

"No," Polina answered. "Does it matter? No one expects us until tomorrow."

The deciduous forests to the east of Berlin were a change from the lush evergreens of home, but the parts that remained intact were thriving and verdant—indifferent to the hate that engulfed the city to the west. It felt good and natural to have twigs and branches underfoot instead of the blasted remnants of pavement and cobbles. The air was thick with smoke, not the pine-scented purity I associated with a ramble in the woods, but it was one step closer to home.

"I've written to Mama," Renata said, still fidgeting with her wrist. "I've asked her to make her famous potato pancakes and *zharkoye*. And blintzes with black currant preserves. The minute I get home."

"Your mama will have you the size of a house within the first month of your homecoming," Polina chided.

Renata's descriptions of her mother's *zharkoye*—beef stew—were nearly as longing and tender as our comrades' descriptions of their husbands and sweethearts and had been used more than once as a distraction from our poor rations. "All the better," Renata retorted. "I'm entitled to a few months of gluttony after four years of hard work and army rations."

"Absolutely true," I agreed, remembering the massive gingerbread matryoshka doll *pryanik* of my youth. I had army pay now. I'd buy a dozen if the store was still open and operating as soon as I got back to Moscow. I'd eat three for myself before I crossed the threshold back onto the street, and give the other nine to the hungriest-looking children I came across. And then likely return for more when I realized how many more children were in need of some sweetness in their lives. I spared a thought for Comrade Mishin and the children he tended. For Oksana's sake, I hoped they'd managed to survive, though the odds against them had been overwhelming.

Grinning, Polina kept up her teasing of Renata. "So much for finding a handsome hero to make little Soviet babies with."

"Any man who has been to war will be pleased to see a woman with some meat on her bones," Renata said. "They've all seen enough of the contrary."

"I think they'll be glad for the affections of a healthy, happy woman," I said, then allowed my thoughts to wander as I hadn't since before the height of the war. I hadn't heard from Vanya in three months, but few of us had seen letters or postcards since we crossed into Germany. I hoped he wasn't far from here, but we would have to wait for our reunion in Moscow unless we were remarkably lucky.

We heard a muffled scream up ahead, followed by deep-voiced chuckles. Renata and Polina looked over at me, awaiting orders; we'd been part of the military machine for so long, we didn't even consider breaking ranks, even though we were all but discharged from duty. A second scream pierced the air, and I motioned for them to follow me as quietly and quickly as the root-strewn path would allow.

We happened upon two of our soldiers and a German girl of about sixteen.

One knelt between the girl's knees, his trousers dropped. The other had her pinned down to the forest floor with one hand and was groping her breasts through a tear in her blouse with the other.

"Get off of her, you disgusting jackasses," I snarled.

"What do you care what we do with some German bitch?" the man with his pants down said, barely glancing back at us. "We've won the war; we're able to do with them as we please." This soldier, no more than twenty years old, wore the marks of a lieutenant. The other was a sergeant.

"Get off of her," I spat again. The soldiers looked at me in disgust but made no signs of movement. "That's an order."

"Fuck off," the kneeling soldier said.

The poor girl, her blond hair matted with blood and her eyes pressed shut against her nightmare, whimpered softly.

I pulled out my service revolver and pointed it at the soldier's head. "I am your superior officer. I will not repeat my order a third time." I heard Polina and Renata free their pistols behind me as well.

The man must have seen the eyes of his companion facing me widen, because he turned. If he was alarmed by finding three pistol barrels trained upon him, he didn't reveal it. But he did sigh and sit back. "Disloyal whore," he mumbled, pulling up his trousers. The sergeant at least had the good graces to look embarrassed. "I should report you for this."

"How do you think it would go for you? I'm within my rights to shoot you where you stand, you insubordinate prick. Get back to your regiment, and busy yourself cleaning latrines. It's a far better use of your time."

The soldiers skulked off in the direction we came from, leaving the German girl behind without a thought. So very typical. She wiped her eyes and pulled her ruined blouse over her bruised breasts. I offered her a hand to help her stand, but at the movement she cowered as if I'd made to strike her.

"I don't want to hurt you," I said, remembering the German I'd learned before the academy. We'd all made an attempt to learn a little during our scarce free hours once we'd become confident we'd be crossing over the German borders, and I'd been called on to give a few tutorials for our regiment and others.

The girl said nothing, only scooted farther back into the brambles, her green eyes round with fear. She had seen too much to trust anyone with a red star on their uniform, and I cursed the soldiers, and the thousands like them, who had seen her as nothing more than the spoils of war.

I removed my small knapsack and opened it. We'd intended to eat lunch in the quiet splendor of the woods, but my stomach now rolled at the sight of the canned meat and hard bread in my bag. I offered her the modest meal, making sure both my hands were visible.

"Take this, please," I said in my rough German. "You look like you need it more than I do."

The girl looked at me, cocking her head to one side in appraisal, then looked at the food in my extended hands and accepted it, setting about devouring it before I could change my mind.

"I'm Katya. These are my friends, Polina and Renata." I sat next to her on the bed of ground cover and patted the ground next to me, encouraging the girls to follow suit.

"Heide," she mumbled in reply, still eating ravenously.

"You might want to slow down," Polina encouraged in halting German. "You might make yourself ill."

Heide considered the advice and slowed her pace.

Renata, never one to sit idle, gathered the buttons from the dirt and pulled a mending kit from her day bag. She removed her uniform jacket and motioned to exchange it for the girl's spoiled blouse. Timidly she traded the garments, covering herself as best she could with her hands. She'd felt exposed enough for one day. Renata, with the same devotion and attention to detail as she used when servicing an engine, sewed the discarded buttons back in place. She examined the garment and, seeing none of the other damage was significant, handed it back. The buttons would never lie as neatly as when the blouse was new, but the girl could wear it back into town without shame.

With the girl continuing to look at us like a wary dog who expected a kick at any moment, we spoke cheerfully—alternating between our native Russian and broken German—to keep her at ease, but there was no way for us to quell her nerves.

"Would you like us to take you home?" I asked. "We don't want you to come across any more trouble."

She contemplated my offer, clearly understanding that the likelihood of more soldiers on the road was as certain as the impending sunset. But still she hesitated. Had she come across other Russian soldiers who had baited her with kind gestures only to cause her pain, or was it merely that she'd seen so much atrocity in the past five years that she'd learned to fear the red star on our uniforms just as we feared the ugly black spider on theirs?

"Please let us help you," I prodded. "We just want to help you."

"But why? You are Russian. I am your enemy."

"Do you intend to fire a gun at me, my aircraft, or my comrades here?" I asked, my expression flat.

"No," she stuttered, her face draining of color.

"Good. We don't intend to hurt you, either, so we're not enemies. The war is over. You have nothing to fear from us."

She exhaled deeply and looked at each of our faces in turn, then pointed south down the path, in the same direction where the soldiers departed. They might be waiting for all of us behind any bush or tree, despite the fact that Polina, Renata, and I were their countrywomen. We'd insulted their pride, and at least the younger of them seemed the sort to exact revenge on any women who dared commit such a slight.

She led us to a house on the edge of town that would once have been described as quaint. It was fashioned from thin, rough-hewn logs and a few windows that would have let in the dappled forest sunlight had they not been boarded up to protect against stray bomb blasts and the eyes of lusty soldiers. She showed us inside the cottage, where two children with dirty-blond hair were playing on the unswept floor. At the sight of our uniforms, they jumped up and cowered in the far corner of the room. The little boy wrapped his arms around his sister, who wept onto the collar of his shirt. Though he could not have been more than seven years old, his nostrils flared and he looked at us defiantly.

"Your father or one of your brothers is here to keep an eye on things?" I asked, having noticed there was not another house within sight. The children's raspy breathing seemed to calm as they parsed my German.

"No," she said. "They're gone. Drafted. My father died early on in France, and my brother was shot because he refused to—well, you understand."

"I do." More than a few of my own countrymen had met the same end when they refused to answer Stalin's call, and Hitler was surely no more forgiving.

"How do you manage to keep yourselves out of harm's way?" Polina asked.

"I don't," Heide said, her arms crossed and her chin tucked to her chest. "Such a thing is not possible. They come, and I am powerless to stop them from doing as they wish. Taking food, blankets—whatever it is they desire. For the sake of the children, I can only do my best to ensure they don't have reason to kill me."

In the stoop of her shoulders and the waver of her voice was a fatigue that sleep would not cure. The war had taken from her, but the aftermath had broken her.

"How many times has your home been raided?"

"Over and over," she whispered. "I stopped counting."

"Sweet Jesus," Renata murmured, absentmindedly crossing herself, whispering "God bless and protect you" under her breath.

I emptied my bag of the rest of my rations—scanty though they were—onto the scarred wooden table that dominated the room. Polina and Renata followed suit, adding some tinned milk and two apples to my meager contribution to the family larder. The little boy's allegiance was won over in a flash by the paltry offering. He untangled himself from his sister and raced to the table and snatched up an apple before his older sister could enforce rationing. His teeth sunk into the fleshy globe of fruit with an audible crunch. Juice dribbled down his chin from the upturned corners of his mouth.

"Selfish boy," Heide chided. "Share with your little sister." She turned to us. "That scamp is Klaus, and the little one is Veronika."

Klaus nodded and skittered back to the corner, where the delicate girl of five or six years still stood, eyeing us as she would an unreliably trained wolf.

"Please be as careful as you can," I bade Heide. "I'll do what I can to bring back some more provisions for you, but I can't promise anything."

Heide uncurled from herself and grabbed me in an embrace. I returned her squeeze and pulled back. "This is nothing," I said. "I wish I could do more."

"It is everything," she contradicted. "If all the Soviet women are like you, there may be hope for the future. Go home and civilize your men."

Renata and Polina gave her their promises for a speedy return as well, and the children even favored us with their sticky kisses before we departed.

Nearly at once I sought out Polkovnik Ozerov, the commanding officer who was my direct superior. I relayed to him Heide's situation and the danger she and the children faced alone.

"She is one of millions in that situation, Major Soloneva. We cannot protect them all."

"But we can order the men to act like gentlemen, can we not?" I countered, taking a step closer to his desk.

"We can order whatever we like. It doesn't mean we will have any success," he said, heaving a sigh that bordered on the dramatic.

"Are you or are you not their commanding officer?" I spat.

"Watch yourself, Major. This war is not over yet." He sat up straight in his chair, his expression now hard. "These men have been fighting with barely enough food to survive. They have slept in tents and trenches for the better part of four years. Who am I to deny them some comforts?"

"*Comforts?* At what cost? The safety of innocent civilians?"

"Soldiers are never the only ones who suffer in war, and no civilian is eager to have one fought on his front porch. It's a bad business, I'll admit, but there is nothing to be done."

I felt the blood pulsing in my face, the heat emanating from my pores. He suddenly became very concerned with the papers on his desk, but I did not allow him to escape my stare.

"If we cannot protect innocent women and children from our own troops, then what was the war for? Would you be so complacent if it were your wife? Your daughters? Your *sons* being manhandled by the Germans?"

"Complacent, no, Major. I would be enraged. Furious. But know these two things: First, if the Germans had won, make no mistake they would be doing the same to the women and children back at home. Second, I would be just as powerless to prevent it."

"Coward," I seethed, and walked out of the makeshift office and back to the barracks, where Polina and Renata awaited my report.

"Please tell me they're sending the bastards to Siberia," Renata greeted me. "It would be too good for them, but it would be gratifying all the same."

"Nothing," I said, throwing my uniform jacket on my bunk. "They're doing nothing."

"So what do *we* do?" Polina asked. "There must be something."

"We can take them some rations if we can find enough to spare without raising suspicion. Any more than that and it looks like we're aiding the enemy and stealing food from the mouths of Russians."

"So we do nothing?" Polina asked. "Just leave her there for it to happen again?" Her arms were folded tight over her chest, her lips white with anger.

"We can't exactly stand guard outside her house." I flopped on my bunk and cast my eyes up at the barracks ceiling. "I've taken it up the chain of command. They won't be bothered keeping their men in line."

"We can't just leave Heide like that," Renata said. "She needs help."

"So do millions of other women," I said. "It sounds heartless, but if the commanders don't keep the men in line, all we can do is keep the men under our influence in check. I won't be surprised if they send us home in the next few weeks. They don't need pilots for sentry duty."

"If our soldiers are acting like pigs, what was the point of saving the civilized world from Germany?" Renata asked no one in particular.

"We can't go down that road," I said. "We've sacrificed too much to think this was all for nothing. We need to get home and get back to our lives. The sooner we bring our troops home, the sooner this horror will be over."

"Any news of Vanya?" Polina asked after a moment. "I know it's been some time."

"More than three months," I said. "It's been chaos, though. I'm sure the post isn't able to keep up. And Andrei?"

"Fine. It sounds like his division will be sent home soon. They've been in so long," she said, unable to keep the relief from her voice.

"Wonderful news," I said. "Let's hope we beat them home."

They knew I'd spent the last few weeks trying to track down Vanya's regiment and I'd had no success. The battle for Berlin had been so wrought with chaos that I allowed myself to blame the silence on the breakdowns in communication as units were reassigned and others deployed home.

We all craved our missing luxuries more acutely now that the war wasn't there to demand our attentions day and night. Some longed for proper foods. Others, the comfort of their warm beds. I would have traded every jewel in the old tsar's vault for a solitary postcard.

CHAPTER 25

July 1945, Moscow, Russia

The throng of family members and loved ones assembled on the runway made a roar to put our little engines to shame. We exited the planes and dashed to find our husbands, children, parents, and siblings, who all clamored to welcome us home after nearly four years of separation from the families we fought for. I saw Polina kissing a tall man with a bulbous nose—her Andrei. Renata was in the firm embrace of her parents, who seemed set to keep her there for the rest of her days.

Mama rushed to me, eyes streaming, and flung herself into my arms.

"My darling girl!" She sobbed into my neck. "I am so glad you're back with us!"

"Oh, Mama" was all I could say for my ragged breathing. After a long moment I pulled back to take her in. She'd gained a few kilos back and reminded me much more of the mama I remembered from my youth. She wore a dress that was by no means elegant, but made of good fabric and clearly new. The dark circles under her eyes had been replaced by a few graceful lines of experience and worry for her daughter on the front.

"This is Grigory." She gestured to a tall man with a ruddy face and broad chest. His walrus mustache reminded me greatly of Karlov, which did not speak in his favor, but his sky-blue eyes twinkled with joy and kindness. He was exactly what I would have chosen for her.

"It is a pleasure to meet you, my daughter," he said grandly. "I thank you, most humbly, for your courage and your service. Your mama read much of your letters to me, and I like to think the pride I felt for you was on your father's behalf."

I kissed his cheek and patted his shoulder in appreciation. He was a decorated soldier but looked as nervous to be meeting his adult stepdaughter as he would have felt at greeting the business end of a bayonet in the last war.

"Enough of the flattery. I haven't seen my mother this fit in years. You have earned my approval, Comrade Yelchin."

"Grigory, please, my dear. I hope I might presume to call you Ekaterina?"

"Katya," I corrected. "And of course."

"Let's go home," Mama said, smiling broadly at the warmth of our exchange as she proffered me her arm. I felt my stomach drop with disappointment as I realized Vanya's regiment wouldn't be among those arriving back today. It had been a long shot, but I'd still been hopeful. I held Mama close to my side as Grigory wrestled with my duffel. I looked back at Polina and Renata, clutched tight to the bosom of their families, and knew I could not spoil their homecomings with a tearful goodbye. We would still have business together until the regiment was formally disbanded.

Mama and Grigory had relocated to Moscow from Chelyabinsk as the war began to turn in our favor. Grigory had been able to oversee the supplies sent to the western cities that had been leveled during the war instead of spending his time managing the construction of tanks. It was good to think of Mama in a city that was slowly coming back to life, and not alone in her little cabin near the village that would always be sleepy.

Their apartment was the size of a shoebox, but comfortable, given that every essential of survival was scarce as the nation sought to heal its wounds. Even before I'd taken in my surroundings, the smell of tea and freshly baked spice cake assaulted my nostrils and awakened in me a hunger I hadn't known was there. There was good furniture, if a bit careworn, and because of Grigory's position, they did not have to share the minuscule spare bedroom with another family. The windows were open to allow the July breeze to flow through the living room.

I took a step back as I realized my own mother-in-law, Natalia Soloneva, sat on my mother's sofa. Grigory excused himself to the kitchen, as did Mama once she'd placed two cups of tea on the small parlor table. Mother Soloneva patted the cushion next to her, and I took my seat next to her. I felt myself shake, knowing she would not have come all this way merely to take tea with me. She had news of Vanya. I tried to sip Mama's good tea, but my shaking hands made the task impossible.

A delay. Some sort of bureaucratic hassle. Anything but the worst.

"I'm so glad you've returned safely, my dear," she said, her tone flat as she stared past the cups of tea toward some nonexistent fascination on the parlor rug.

"Thank you, Mother Soloneva. And I'm glad to see you're well. I hope Father Solonev is just the same."

"He's as well as one can expect in such hard times."

I nodded in agreement. "Do you have word when Vanya will be released from the front? I wasn't able to find his regiment near Berlin."

"His regiment didn't get quite that far. They ended service farther east."

"Ah," I said, comprehending. "Then I am surprised he didn't make it home before I did. Is he on some sort of patrol assignment?"

"Darling." Her thin resolve cracked, and she dissolved into a pool of tears. "He . . . he was killed in the final push for Seelow Heights."

Air expelled from me in a torrent as I tried to make sense of her words. My brain seemed unwilling to process why this woman was breaking down before me. All I was able to do was hold out my arms to her and allow her grief to escape into great pools on my uniform jacket. I embraced her, still trying to understand that Vanya would never again do this for me. No more midnight embraces. No stolen kisses between practical lessons. No more tender words. Had we escaped, we might be already planning our return home.

"We received word just a few weeks ago," Natalia explained. "We didn't know if it would get to you before you came home. We expected it would be easier for you to hear in person, so we didn't try to get word to you."

Easier. The word thudded around in my brain, but no meaning registered.

He had survived so much of the war, only to be taken in the last weeks.

I had survived, only to be abandoned.

~

Mama served a dinner unlike anything I'd seen since before the war. Roasted-chicken stew with roasted potatoes and a sturdy, dry white wine to pair with it. Restorative, nourishing. A meal a mother would prepare for a child in need of feeding, but nothing to suggest a celebration. It was a meal prepared with grief in mind. I moved to the table with everyone else. They'd had weeks to process their grief, and mine was not yet real. From the outside we might have appeared like a normal family.

"Where is the vodka, Mama?" I asked, taking a small glass from the cupboard.

"I hope you haven't developed *that* habit, Katinka," Mama said.

"It's not for me," I said. Grigory, taking my meaning, fetched a good bottle from his small stash, presenting it to me without ceremony. I poured a small measure into the glass and handed the bottle back to Grigory, then placed the glass by my side at the small table and set a slice of bread on top. The portion for the dead.

Vanya's mother swallowed hard at the gesture and caressed my elbow. "My dear girl, I know we didn't get off to the best of starts. My husband is of the old sort, you understand. He had great plans for Vanya, and he didn't understand that as a father he must put his vision aside and let Vanya make his own life. Antonin loved him very much, though he wasn't much at showing it." Natalia looked as out of place at my mother's kitchen table as a crystal vase in a trench. She held my hand, her body turned completely in my direction.

"I'm not the sort of girl he would have chosen for his son. I understand."

"He knows Vanya loved you—loves you, I like to think. Antonin has said as much. He's embarrassed for the way he acted when we met."

"Why did Comrade Solonev not come with you?" Grigory asked. "It's not a good time for women to travel alone."

I stifled a growl at my new stepfather's assertion that a woman needed caring for. It was merely gallantry, I reminded myself. I would have to adjust to the notion again. What was more, Natalia was the kind of woman who was very much used to male protection.

"He would not want me to say this," Natalia replied, "but he is far too heartbroken by his grief to be seen. I trust you won't speak of such things outside the family, but he blames himself for Vanya enlisting."

"Vanya wanted to fight," I assured her, seething at the idea of Antonin Solonev cheapening my husband's sacrifice by insinuating he had been anything less than willing to do his part. "He was proud to do his duty to his country."

"Of course, my dear. Antonin just feels like his own military service may have compelled Vanya to take more risks than he might otherwise have done."

"I flew as your son's navigator for months. I can assure you there was not a more conscientious pilot in the whole of the Red Army. He had a crew to think about, and he would never have risked their lives, no matter the glory of your husband's reputation." I sat ramrod straight in my chair, picking halfheartedly at the perfectly golden-brown crust on the potatoes. I did not look up, for my mother-in-law had done nothing to deserve the glare I knew would lance her if lifted from the safety of my plate.

"Come home with me, and tell my Antonin this," Natalia implored me. "It would ease his breaking heart to hear these words."

I took a bite of the potato to give myself an excuse not to speak. I immediately regretted it. The food was unpalatable, but I could not insult my mother's good cooking or my upbringing to spit it out. I labored to swallow, my throat as raw as the day when I was six years old and the doctor had pulled my tonsils in his shining white office.

"He asked me to bring you home," she continued. "We have no children of our own now. He would like to do for you what we can no longer do for our Vanya. We would welcome you in our home as our own daughter."

I looked up, my skin tingling at the suggestion. *Shouldn't you already consider me this?*

"She has a family," my mother interjected, viciously piercing a piece of chicken with her fork. Grigory placed a hand on her shoulder, and I could see her breathing even out.

My hand involuntarily lighted over my heart, massaging as though the ache that loomed there were physical. "I appreciate your offer, Natalia. I really do. But I am only just back home."

"Naturally. You need some time with your mother and new step-father." I blanched at the title but forced a tight smile for Grigory. It would take some getting used to. "But know that you will always have a home with us."

"You are unspeakably generous, Natalia. Please pass my thanks on to Father Solonev as well."

"Say nothing of it, my dear. It's our pleasure. I'm only sorry it's under such circumstances. And far too late in coming."

I nodded, pushing my food aside, a momentary pang of guilt piercing my stomach at the sight of the uneaten food, but I could no more bring myself to finish the meal than move the Ural Mountains to the sea.

The apartment was small, and it was clear which room was intended for me. There was a single bed with a starched white sheet and a welcoming quilt. There was little in the way of furnishings, but my mother had done her best to make the room cheerful. Grigory had placed my duffel against the wall, but I didn't want to see any of the clothes I'd been wearing for the past four years. I'd save most of them for the wood stove on the first frosty morning that fall.

I checked in the small bureau and was pleased to find the candy-pink pajamas from my days at the academy. Something from the sunny days of spring that I spent with Vanya and Taisiya. I cocooned myself in the frothy pink flannel and sunk into the feather mattress. I curled up under the warm covers and shut my eyes against the world. I waited for the tears to come, but the sting of my anguish never made it as far as my eyes. I tried to will the tears to fall. I wanted to feel the release I'd felt when I'd cried for Taisiya and Oksana. For all the other fallen sisters.

If I cried, it would mean I wasn't empty.

But that night I found neither the catharsis of tears nor the respite of sleep.

Vanya's face came to me as soon as I fell to the abyss of sleep, and it warned me. It warned me that the war would break me.

~

I stared at the wall. It had to be two or three in the morning. I gripped my quilt like the stick of my plane when I was trying to pull out of a spiraling dive. As though these layers of fabric and ticking could help me regain control of a life that no longer resembled anything I'd ever planned for.

Years of military training and discipline. I was prepared to approach every situation, equipped for various outcomes—both positive and negative. Logically I had known that one of us might not survive the war, but there was nothing almost two decades of schooling and service could have done to prepare me for this.

The specters in my dreams were the only thing crueler than the reality of my waking hours:

"War will break you, Katyushka. Don't make me see the light in your eyes grow dim."

"It won't, my Vanya. I promise."

I felt the warmth of his arms around me, but when I moved to return the embrace he vanished, reappearing just out of my grasp.

"If you love me, you will come with me. You will stay safe with me."

I took a step in his direction. *"Vanya, I can't. I can't leave the girls behind. Could you really have crossed the border into Turkey? Could I have let us?"*

Poof. He was now directly behind me. I spun to see him.

"This is killing me, Katyushka. What is a man if he can't keep the woman he loves from peril?"

"The best kind. It means you trust me to stay alive. I trust you to do the same."

"You're a fool, Katyushka. I didn't think you were. There are no happy endings in war."

The words he never said ripped at me like fangs. I took a step closer to him. Poof.

He didn't reappear.

I fought sleep, resented wakefulness.

I longed for the darkness to carry me to oblivion, until at last the dawn came again.

CHAPTER 26

Natalia left the next morning, not wanting to leave Antonin alone too long with his grief. I hugged her tenderly and promised that if nothing else, I would come visit to pay my respects to my father-in-law. No matter the animosity Vanya had felt toward his father, no matter how badly he had yearned for another life, he had inherited a good measure of his father's pragmatism. Vanya would have loved nothing more than to spend his days studying art and devoting his life to his craft, but we were not born into a time where many people had the luxury of pursuing their passions.

His father had been wise to see his son trained in aviation. It had nearly saved his life.

Vanya could have gone to a conservatory and studied painting under masters. And he would have been plucked from school to die under a pile of rubble during the siege on Stalingrad or Leningrad. His training had given him at least a fighting chance to survive the war. He fell several weeks short of the mark, but Vanya had done more for his country before his death than a poor foot soldier who only survived service for a few weeks.

His death had not been in vain, and it was this thought alone that kept me sane.

On the dark days I remembered the time in the convalescent center with Vanya by my side. Him whispering in my ear. Imploring me to run away. To let him buy the papers that would allow us to escape safely to Sweden, Switzerland, or Portugal—anywhere neutral. If the truck hadn't crashed, had my body not betrayed me, he would still be alive. It was almost two years since he'd implored me to leave. Simultaneously a lifetime and a handful of moments ago. Maybe Vanya could have coaxed me over the border. We would have been well settled somewhere safe, clamoring for news of the war in any newspaper we could scrounge up. Celebrating the end of the war we'd started but hadn't the courage to finish. We would both see guilt glinting in each other's eyes at every mention of the war. With the news of each fallen friend.

But it would have faded in time as we built our lives together. Vanya would have found scraps of time to paint when he wasn't working to support us. I would have taught young pilots or found some other way to stretch my wings.

There might have been a child by now. A scamp of a boy with Vanya's black hair that curled when it was overlong. My blue eyes and porcelain skin. Perhaps a girl with my red hair and her father's mischievous coal-black eyes. Every time I tried to sleep, if it wasn't the vision of Vanya's face swirling in my mind, it was some variation of the child-that-never-was. The child-that-would-never-be. Or Taisiya. Oksana. Sofia. All the others we lost in three years.

That first week I spent most of my days curled up in the comfort of those pink, lavender, and periwinkle flannel pajamas and buried myself under Mama's quilt. I only ate when she forced the issue. I could neither read nor write. My hands didn't seem equal to mending or any menial task. I found myself staring at the patterns on the quilt to the point where the little white flowers began to dance on the inky-blue backdrop.

Oksana's snowdrops.

I clutched the quilt to my chest and found, inexplicably, that I envied her. She was with her Yana now. Matvei had fallen in Stalingrad and had gone off to join his Taisiya. Even if heaven didn't exist, I had to believe they were no longer lonely for one another.

Polina had her Andrei. I wondered if they waited a full hour to find a civil-registry bureau to have their union made official. Renata was young and would find her beau before long.

I was the one torn between the land of the living and the dead.

Mama came in on a balmy afternoon. It was just over a week since I returned home. She placed a tray with a bowl of hearty soup and a chunk of brown bread on my bedside table, sat on the edge of my bed, and brushed the hair from my forehead.

"I like your hair shorter," she said. "It suits you."

I smiled up at her. I knew what she was saying: *I'm worried about you, but I know you need time.*

"It's better now than it was when the butcher of a barber had his way with it. I like it, too."

Thank you for not pushing. I will try to get better.

"Will you please eat?" She took my hand in hers and squeezed gently. *I can't bear to lose you, too.*

I sat up in my bed and accepted the tray from Mama. The soup was thick with savory beef, carrots, potatoes, and peas. The bread was crusty and rich—ambrosia compared to the black rocks they'd been serving us for the past four years. Grigory was doing his duty for Mama, and I was grateful to him for this. The soup tasted as palatable to me as soot, but I at least felt some of my physical discomfort ebb away. The dull ache in my head subsided, and I was able to focus more clearly.

"It's wonderful, Mama. Thank you," I said, placing the tray back on the table when I could no longer tolerate the food.

"You don't need to say such things, my dear. Food tasted like dirt for weeks after your papa died. But thank you for eating all the same. You probably don't remember your babushka feeding me like I am feeding you. I had no idea she was so sick at the time."

I remembered Babushka Olga with fondness, but her death had barely registered with me after the loss of Papa. I'm sure it was the same for Mama, and I imagine there was some guilt in her heart some years later over not grieving as deeply for her mother as she should have done.

"I am also going to do something for you that my mama did for me."

The image of the little cabin in Miass flashed before my eyes, and I felt my breath catch. I could not spend the rest of my life so far from the rest of the world. "Mama, I can't go back there. Not Miass."

"No, darling. I am not kicking you out of your home. And make no mistake, this is your home. I am, however, going to insist that you get up, bathe, get dressed, and fetch some bread from the bakery for supper."

It was a simple request, but it seemed Herculean in scope. "Mama, maybe tomorrow?" The thought of dressing, let alone leaving the apartment, seemed more daunting than flying another mission over Germany.

"No, my darling, today. You need to move. Get some air." Mama gripped my hand and fixed my eyes with hers.

"That won't fix anything." I buried my face in my hands for a moment, rubbing my eyes in defeat.

"No, but it's a start. You must trust your old mama, Katya. I never wanted you to walk in these shoes, but I have worn them for over a decade. I will help where I can, but you have to make the first steps on your own."

The realization that Mama had endured this same pain, and that I could only now understand it, shook me. I wondered now how she had been able to go on with her life as she had done. To give me a normal, if cheerless, childhood. I had met some brave women during the course of the war, but I now felt awed by my own mother's strength.

"How did you manage to do this, Mama? How did you move on?"

"I'm not sure I ever moved on, Katinka. Not really. But I learned to carry my grief for your papa like the medals on your chest. Proof I had loved and been loved. I had no choice but to find a way to carry on. For you, my sweet girl."

I did as Mama commanded. I rose from my bed and scrubbed away a week's worth of grime and sleep. I washed the grit from my hair and let the warm water trickle down my face, where tears refused to flow.

When I returned from the washroom, I found my bed already made up with clean sheets, and a light dress of dark charcoal gray, appropriate for both the summer heat and a widow in mourning, draped like a shroud over the blue-and-white field of snowdrops.

Mama knew I couldn't face the world in a pink frock. She knew exactly what I needed and now had the means to provide for me the way she'd longed to.

I was a woman grown. A widow. I should be beyond my mother's care. I shook my head, remembering the strength she'd shown after Papa's death. I shouldn't be troubling my mother, as needy for her attentions as an infant.

And I would never have the words to tell her how grateful I was for her.

I found the little handbag I used before the war, and placed a few bills and coins inside. Grigory smiled broadly from the kitchen table as he saw me emerge from my bedroom fully dressed and looking equal to facing the world. I let the corners of my lips turn upward. I let him think this was more than a farce I was putting on for my mother's sake. And his.

I descended into the world below. The July sun only made the ice in my veins pulse a few degrees colder. The crowd looked both weary and jubilant, as one would expect of a people worn down by war. Many of the shops were empty, a few buildings still in shambles from raids and stray bombs, yet there was a buzz of excitement in the air that I never remembered of the Moscow of my youth. I was happy for my people. I had fought for this very thing.

It took nearly a half hour to find an open bakery, and the first one I found was the very shop where I had purchased my illicit matryoshka *pryanik* as a girl. The shopkeeper handed over the loaf of bread for our evening meal with a smile. There were no matryoshka cookies in the case that day. In honor of our victory, the cookies were all shaped like stars, helmets, and tanks. In the corner was a pile of the spiced cookies shaped like tiny airplanes.

"A dozen, please," I said, pointing to the case. So many promises I had made since the start of the war, but this was one I would be able to keep.

I did not eat my fill of the still-warm cakes I had sworn to eat in the depth of my hunger at the front. The spices smelled alluring, but even they could not awaken my appetite. Instead I wandered. It was less than a block before I came upon my first hungry child. The little boy's features were coated in a layer of dirt. His teeth seemed shockingly white as he smiled at the gift. Three more children emerged when they saw his prize. Within moments the cookies were consumed, and at least there would be four children not sleeping on empty stomachs that night.

I couldn't help Klaus or Veronika. I couldn't help the children Oksana tried to protect. But I had done something small for these children.

I returned to Mama and Grigory's apartment to give Mama the bread. She would begin cooking soon, and I would offer to help. I entered noiselessly into the apartment, the door and latch too new to have a telltale creak. I was greeted with the sight of my mother and Grigory sitting companionably on the sofa. She was mending a pair of his uniform trousers while he read the newspaper. He leaned over to kiss her temple as he turned the beige-and-black pages. I took a step back, as though I had witnessed them in the deepest throes of lovemaking. I turned my head and placed the loaf on the kitchen table.

I darted to my room, where I found Papa's violin. I grasped the handle and walked through the parlor without looking back at Mama and Grigory.

"Katya?" Mama called. "I didn't hear you come in."

"I'm going out again, Mama. Please don't hold supper. I'm still full."

"Be home before too late, dear," she called after me. "It isn't safe, even now." I wanted to rebuke her but remembered I had neither my service pistol nor my band of sisters in arms at my side.

I found myself on the warm stone steps of the university, which appeared to be slowly coming back to life, though many of its scholars were forever lost in the war. I fussed with the violin case for a moment but then set the instrument beside me, still ensconced in the love-worn leather case.

I could not make my father's music anymore.

I watched the bustle on the streets thin as the light grew weaker, but could not rise to return to the relative safety of the apartment. When I had seen Mama and Grigory together that afternoon, I saw the contentment and tranquility they shared. I was casting a shadow on the sunshine of their newly wedded bliss. They deserved their happiness unmarred by my bereavement.

The prospect of retreating to Miass, living in Babushka's cabin, was enough to cause me to shake, despite the July sun.

Could I live as a bird in a gilded cage in Korkino, doted on by Vanya's family? It wasn't the life he'd wanted for himself, nor could I imagine myself spending my days with such a constant reminder of what I had lost.

I had to find a way out. Today I had ventured as far as the bakery. Tomorrow I had to venture far enough to find a life.

CHAPTER 27

August 20, 1945

The celebration shook Moscow with a jolt nearly the equal of the bombs that had cascaded down on her four years earlier. Ten Polikarpovs—one piloted by Polina and navigated by Renata—flew overhead, overshadowed by the massive bombers and sleek fighters. I'd been asked, as the commanding officer of the regiment, to lead the honor guard, but ceded my place so that Renata and Polina could go up together. Polina never got her chance to pilot her own plane during the war, and though she never complained, I knew she was happy for the chance to take command.

There had been victory parades before now, but more soldiers and pilots were home to be recognized for their service. There wasn't the pomp of the rain-sodden parade several weeks prior, where our soldiers tossed fallen German standards at Comrade Stalin's feet. This was a true celebration of the people and the soldiers who had defended them.

Mama and Grigory joined me in Red Square to take part in the revelry. Both seemed happy to see me out among the living. I was spending less and less time in the apartment, and I let them think it was because I was faring well enough to be out among people. The truth is that I spent most of my time trying to find some escape. I'd taken the initiative to inquire about a university course. I'd spent hours in libraries, even in the neighborhood church, to see if I might find some comfort in Renata's faith. I'd rather have been nearly anywhere else than the pulsing square that crackled with the energy of a people too long denied a reason to celebrate, but I knew Mama, and especially Grigory, were anxious to join in the excitement.

Even after darkness fell, the lights strobed over the square so brightly it might have been day. I trembled, trying not to think of the German searchlights that had so often spelled our doom.

Do not cower. They're fireworks. Amusement fit for children. Do not cower.

"You look pale, Katinka." Concern was etched upon Mama's brow. "Do we need to go home?"

I shook my head and forced my attention to the podium, where party leaders shouted and congratulated themselves on the victory, as though it had been done at their hands alone. As though millions of soldiers hadn't paid their pound of flesh to defeat the German army.

"You need only say the word, my dear, and we can find our way out of this mob." Grigory smiled at me over my mother's head. He was a soldier, too, and knew something of what I was experiencing.

"I'll be fine," I assured them, taking Mama's free hand in my own. Grigory had long since claimed the other.

The red, gold, and green flashes of light scarred the night sky. Today we celebrated our victory with the naive certainty that such horror would never be seen again. We'd thought the same thing a generation before when we closed the chapter on the last atrocity that had ripped the world apart. The war in the Pacific was boiling to its conclusion. The Americans had destroyed two Japanese cities to end it, and I remembered Oksana's similar justification for her tactics: the longer the war dragged on, the longer the innocent would suffer.

We were disbanded officially in October. My commanding officer gathered us all in a great assembly room in the Kremlin to present us with the medals we had earned since the last time they had been able to attend to such matters. A gold star dangling from a red ribbon was attached to my jacket. Hero of the Soviet Union. There were twenty-four of us granted this highest honor. It was conferred upon both Oksana and Taisiya posthumously, and I accepted on their behalf as the commanding officer and their navigator. I would take Taisiya's medals back to her family, perhaps taking the time to honor my promise and see Vanya's parents, and to see Chelyabinsk and the academy one more time. I couldn't imagine there being many more occasions to travel that far east again.

"You will take care of yourselves," I said to Renata and Polina, who wore their medals on chests puffed with well-deserved pride. "It's my last order to you as your commanding officer."

"Of course, Major," Renata said with a crisp salute. "So long as you promise to do the same."

"I'll do my best," I answered softly, not knowing what that might look like after the months of putting their well-being before my own. "And you take care of your Andrei, too, Polina."

"I will," she said with a smile. She was married already, just as I had predicted, but enrolling at the university, too. Andrei had secured a job in Moscow, and they would make their lives there. A life in the capital suited them both.

"The quiet is strange, isn't it?" Renata said. "I didn't expect it."

"Deafening," I agreed. "Unless I'm out on the streets at the busiest time of day, everything seems too quiet. Too slow." No artillery fire. No roar of the Polikarpov. No din of chatter at every meal. I was glad to not be alone with this thought.

"We'll adjust," Polina said in an unusual show of optimism. "It's what we do best."

I embraced these dear women, confident in the knowledge that Polina spoke the truth.

The image of Oksana fading in my arms loomed in my mind, her skin growing ashen and cold. *"Can you take word to my family in Aix? I want them to remember me."*

It was another wartime promise I could keep, though it would be a great deal harder than a train trip east or a dozen small cakes for hungry children. The remainder of her family was in Aix-en-Provence, which might as well be on the other side of the globe. I would need funds and visas that were both hard to obtain as the country rebuilt itself.

I had promised to inform her family. I had promised to give them Yana's drawing and to ask them to remember her. To entrust her personal effects to the post seemed both foolish and cruel to her family.

I would have to find a way to fulfill my promise in person.

~

Vanya's childhood room still smelled of the innocence of youth—the scent of pine from his bureau, pencil shavings, and books. Even a lingering whiff of chalk on the slate from his school days mingled with the dust particles in the air. His paintings and sketches, ranging from the childish to the masterful, still papered the walls. His favorite books lined his shelf, organized by title, diligently as any librarian. On his little desk was a small toy airplane, not unlike my beloved Polikarpov.

Antonin Solonev had the same ruddy face and walrus mustache as when we had met during the first days of the war, but his eyes looked decades older. Decades sadder. In the depth of his dark eyes, so much like his son's, I saw proof of Natalia's words. He had loved his son dearly, and Vanya's death gnawed at him like an unrelenting cancer.

"I am more glad than I can say that you've come to stay with us, my dear," he said as we sat down to the table. It was laden with good food—beef and vegetables far beyond what Mama was able to procure in Moscow. The farms to the east hadn't been destroyed in battle or were not as depleted in the service of the army as the ones in the west.

"I'm honored that you've asked me, Comrade Solonev," I said, unable to forget the cold manner of our last meeting.

"My dear, please call me Antonin. I trust you'll find your room comfortable."

"I'm sure I will."

"It is my hope that your stay will be of some duration," Antonin said, patting my hand. "Natalia enjoys having another chick in her nest."

"I don't know how long I will be able to stay," I admitted. I thought of the specter of Vanya that permeated his room like smoke, and knew it wouldn't be long.

"We know how hard it must be right now. Everything is so unsettled for you," Natalia said. "You can stay here to find your feet. And when the time comes, we can help you find another young man from a good family. Vanya wouldn't want you to be lonely forever."

I flinched, feeling the blood drain from my face.

"Not right away," she pressed.

"The local officials have been speaking of this," Antonin interjected. "Our young women will need to do their part to replace our fallen soldiers. Young men will not be in great supply, and we can help make sure you find a good match."

"I appreciate your concern," I said. "It's a lot to think about."

"Of course," Natalia said. "You're a beautiful young woman. You have time to sort things out. We're in no rush to see you leave."

"You're very kind," I said, pushing the food around on my plate. *Their son is dead only a few months, and they're marrying his widow off. Oh, my Vanya, how could you have come from such people?*

"We want you to feel like the daughter of this house," Antonin urged. "We will provide for you just as Vanya would have us do."

"There is something," I said, setting my fork down and bringing my eyes to his. "I would like to take one of my fallen sisters' medals and personal effects to her family in France. She doesn't have any family left here. Would you be able to help me arrange for the papers?"

"Things are in a bit of disarray, but I'll see what I can do," Antonin said, stabbing a chunk of beef and looking thoughtfully past me, mentally tracing the lines of red tape he would have to maneuver to procure the papers.

"You shouldn't go alone, my dear," Natalia said. "It's so far."

"I think I can manage," I said, failing to keep the disdain from my voice. *It doesn't matter how many medals I have on my chest, how many bombs I dropped on the heads of the German army. Because I am a woman, I must be protected.*

Antonin looked at me indulgently and shot his wife a silencing look. "We'll see what can be done in the next week or so, dear," he said. "It is right for you to pay respect to your comrade's family. And when you return, you can give more thought to your plans."

Plans. Russia needed to be rebuilt, and I needed to find my place in this new world.

After luncheon Natalia showed me the press clippings she'd collected of Vanya's accomplishments in the war. She'd even gathered a few of mine, though each entry for me was put in as *E. Solonev*. The reader would read of what I'd done and imagine an Erik or Eduard Solonev, fighting bravely for the Red Army. Any mention of Ekaterina Soloneva was relegated to the few articles in women's magazines they'd used to drum up patriotic fervor among the idle peasant women in the east. *Surely if this woman can fly a plane, you can work in a factory for the glory of the motherland.*

I never wanted to be a show pony for the army, but it was clear the opposite was the case. I didn't need to see my face in all the papers or my name on every page, but they minimized all we'd done. As I read my mother-in-law's papers, it seemed the contribution of the women in mixed regiments was almost entirely ignored. My own regiment had a few mentions, but nothing like the male regiments, who had achieved half as much. When the women were released from duty, we were expelled from the military altogether in most cases. They wanted to pretend they'd never needed us. How I wished that had been true. Fine thanks for our sacrifice from a grateful nation.

Perhaps Oksana was more noble than I was. She had wanted to do her part to rebuild the country and see it thrive again. I felt no guilt in leaving that task to others who had not already paid the same price we had. It seemed just.

Later I wandered about the house, looking idly at the impressive collection of books, wishing any one of them held the answer to what path I ought to take. I removed a dusty tome from the shelf. An antique atlas. Some of the countries pictured in it no longer existed; others were yet to be formed when the maps were printed. Even now borders were being erased and redrawn. Men like Hitler and Stalin had great plans to conquer the world and divide it up for their own purposes. The rest of us merely longed for our place in it.

CHAPTER 28

May 1946, Aix-en-Provence, France

Over the course of a week, I saw what remained of Europe. Western Russia, Belarus, and Ukraine were starved and gray, but rebuilding. Poland, Germany, and Austria were attempting to emerge from the cinders. When we descended into what had been the "free zone" in France, we seemed to be entering a different world. There were patches of damage from Allied bombs, but the cities remained mostly intact. The vibrant blue of the sky seemed something from an artist's palette instead of something born of nature.

The train rattled into the station in Aix-en-Provence. Before it came to a complete stop, I had gathered my worn suitcase and was standing by the exit, waiting for the conductor to open the door to the platform. Though the chill of spring had yet to give way to summer in Moscow, I was warm as the southern French sun caressed my bare arms. I wore the simple turquoise dress that had belonged to Mama, remembering the day in the lush meadow when Vanya had painted my likeness. The ache in my heart reassured me he was still there.

In addition to travel papers, Antonin had verified the address of Oksana's family and that they had, in fact, survived the war. I would have gone to find them even without the information, but now that the long journey was behind me, I was glad I would not have long days—possibly even weeks—ahead of me to track them down, nor did I have to worry that the trek had been in vain.

I clutched the paper with the directions to their home, a small villa on the outskirts of town. I'd been told I would be able to hire a car to take me as far as their house, but I'd spent too much time cooped up in trains to be able to contemplate entering another vehicle. A few kilometers by foot in shoes that weren't four sizes too large and on a road that wouldn't have me ankle-deep in mud seemed as close to paradise as I could dream.

As I strolled down the streets, some of the shops shuttered and cafés nearly empty, I could still easily imagine the city in its prewar glory. The residents glanced sideways at me with downcast eyes, suspicious of those they didn't know. I considered smiling at them to ease their disquiet but wondered if the gesture might make me seem even more suspicious in their eyes. I decided to let them find their trust in their own time.

It was less than two hours before I found the little villa belonging to Oksana's mother's family, the Lacombes. The sun hung low in the sky and haloed the house in the vivid orange glow that could only come from a late-spring sunset. It was an inviting home, painted a buttery yellow with rust-colored shutters. Two small children played in the garden while a woman in her late forties plucked stray weeds from her impeccable garden. I could see Oksana's high cheekbones and large eyes on the woman's face. It had to be her mother's sister. A man, presumably Oksana's uncle, repaired loose terra-cotta tiles on the roof.

I stood for a moment, not wanting to call attention to myself and shatter this vision of domestic tranquility. It wasn't more than a few seconds before the older child, a boy with thick brown curls who was perhaps five or six years old, noticed me standing at the garden gate.

"Grand-mère! There is a lady!" He pointed his spindly finger in my direction, and she raised her head to assess me.

"Who are you?" she asked, wiping her hands on her apron and approaching the gate but not offering me a hand to shake. Her lips were drawn in a line, and she looked at me as if I were the tenth salesman standing with a long line winding behind me, all ready to peddle our shoddy wares. The man climbed down the ladder and jogged to his wife's side, his expression even less welcoming than hers.

"I was a friend of Oksana Tymoshenko. I believe she was your niece?" I hadn't used my French since before the war but thought I found the words well enough, even if my accent was clumsy.

The woman fumbled to open the gate and escorted me into the house, muttering apologies for the cold greeting and performing hurried introductions. Her name was Eliane; her husband was Marcel. The children, Didier and Violaine, belonged to their son, Philippe—Oksana's only cousin—who spent his days rebuilding the vineyard now that he was returned from the war. Eliane explained in whispered tones that her daughter-in-law had fallen ill after the occupation, and with medical supplies so scarce, she had not recovered. Eliane ran off to brew coffee, ordering her husband to make me feel welcome. Flustered, he offered me a chair at their large kitchen table and commanded the children to play upstairs.

"How do you know our Oksana?" Eliane asked, placing a mug of coffee before me, the steam rising from the cup in thick spires. Before I could answer, Philippe, a towering man with tanned olive skin and black curls, entered the room. He was covered in a good amount of dirt and was clearly surprised to find a guest at the table.

"I was Oksana's navigator in the war," I explained as Eliane placed a mug before her son, kissing his temple before she took her seat.

"Navigator?" Marcel asked. "I'm afraid I don't understand."

"Oksana was a pilot, and the commander of our regiment for many months. I had the honor to serve with her for nearly three years. I was with her when she died." I didn't tell the full truth, that she had ordered me from the cave and had died alone and at her own hand, but they deserved the comfort of knowing she had been with a friend in her final moments. Not for the first time did I wish I'd ignored Oksana's orders and held her hand in her last moments. I would have likely suffered no worse than my day's trek in the woods, and I would have been able to look at her aunt without hating myself for the half-truths I told.

I opened my small suitcase and removed her medals along with the rest of her personal effects. I took her Hero of the Soviet Union medal in both hands and presented the small gold star to her aunt.

"It was her last wish that I give this to you," I said, speaking as though this were an official presentation. It should have been. "She spoke so fondly of her time with you, and I know she wanted you to remember her and know that she died a hero's death in service to her country."

"She was lucky to have a friend willing to travel such a long way for our sake," Philippe said, taking the star from his mother to give it a closer inspection before passing it to his father. "I remember her visit very clearly. Her French was terrible, and she didn't like having her hair pulled. I have a few scars to prove it." He smiled slightly as he recalled the memory, faded at the edges like an old photograph. He had a kind smile the war hadn't been able to erase. Despite his losses, he was a fortunate man to have retained this.

"I couldn't trust the postal service to get them to you in times such as these," I said, fidgeting with the mug handle. "And she was a very dear friend. I know she would have done the same and more for me."

"God bless you, my dear," Eliane said, taking my hand. "It's a joy to know there are still good people in this world."

"She was a far better person than I," I deflected. "She dreamed of coming here and building a life after the war. I'm only sorry that never came to pass."

Eliane unrolled Yana's drawing, which depicted Oksana so lovingly. Seeing it in the flood of evening light that poured in the large windows, I now saw that it didn't depict Oksana as she was, but who she could have been in a kinder world. The world she deserved. Eliane sniffled, batting away tears as she studied the sketch.

"It would mean a great deal to me if you would hang this in your home," I said. "Her friend Yana drew this. Oksana wanted to bring her to the land of Cézanne to perfect her skills. At least now a part of her will always be here."

"You have my word," Philippe said. "I'll frame it myself and hang it over the mantelpiece. It will be a testament to happier times and a tribute to her bravery. Thank you for bringing this to us."

"Thank *you*," I said, reaching over to squeeze his hand, though I hardly knew this man. "Today I feel as though my war has ended."

EPILOGUE

May 9, 1992, Moscow, Russia

"Grand-mère! I can see spires!" my namesake, little Catherine, squeaked at me, grabbing my hand as we crossed Red Square. Saint Basil's loomed before us, its jewel-toned peaks brighter than I remembered. "They do look like giant onions!"

"Be careful with Grand-mère. She can't run as fast as you," chided Roxanne as she struggled to keep baby Michel tucked safely in her arms. For a boy of two, he could discover more trouble in three minutes than most of us did in a lifetime. I did not envy my daughter the task of raising him, but she had far more patience with her little ones than I could have ever mustered.

Philippe quickened his pace and laced his fingers in mine. His grip on my hand had warmed me from within as I'd walked streets that seemed at once familiar and foreign. At times it still seemed strange to rely on another for strength, as I had never been able to do with Vanya. Philippe calmed my fears when my nightmares woke me, even years after the war. He was the only one I ever confessed to about our near escape into Turkey, and tried to assuage the guilt I still felt on occasion.

He endeavored to understand when I wept for Vanya. He had held me tight when the Iron Curtain kept me from my mother's side fifteen years before, when she lost her battle with cancer. Only in his arms was I able to let my tears flow as the last tie I had to my homeland dissolved.

Mama had been heartbroken at my decision to stay in France, and I was equally devastated when my return home became impossible a few short years after Philippe convinced me to stay in Aix. I would likely been branded a traitor, and would never have been allowed to return to France. On the day Mama died, Philippe promised me that he would bring all of us to Moscow one day to pay our respects. On the very day the Soviet Union dissolved, he purchased the tickets for the entire family. He *did* arrange for the trip to take place in warm weather, for despite having the warmest of hearts, his seventy-six-year-old bones were none too fond of winter. I don't think it was a coincidence that he planned the trip to coincide with the annual Victory Day celebrations. It was the sort of thing I would have tried to avoid, and only he would know the seed of regret I would have harbored for having done so. Though I never lost my love of the open sky and taught at an aviation academy for several years, I found that I was a bird who had found her nest and was contented enough to roost there.

I loved Philippe's motherless children as my own. Violaine walked with her husband, Georges, a few paces behind us as we crossed Red Square. Didier chatted companionably with his brother-in-law. I had given Philippe two more daughters: Roxanne, named for Oksana, and Thérèse, named for Taisiya. Philippe had been willing to give them Russian names, but I wanted them to be wholly part of their father's culture.

While Philippe crafted his wines, I built the business that made it a viable enterprise. We rebuilt the Lacombe vineyard into something worthwhile, and Philippe passed it on to his son and sons-in-law two years before with the pride of having created a legacy to pass on to his family. Thérèse, who had inherited my mind for figures and her father's charms, took my place running the business end of things and was already expanding the enterprise far beyond my own considerable ambitions. One day in the coming years, they would also inherit the little yellow villa with the terra-cotta shutters and the sweet drawing of a girl from Kiev over the fireplace, but it would be our home—Philippe's and mine—for as long as we could manage it.

Now, on Red Square, the parade in honor of the anniversary of the end of the war was just beginning, and the children watched the spectacle with glee. Seven grandchildren in all, and another on the way. We watched the colorful display, and I rested my head against Philippe's chest. He bent his head to kiss the top of mine. My red hair had become streaked with white, and the mirror reflected a woman who had seen both hardship and joy in equal measure. I loved each crease, for they had been hard won.

I sighed at the crisp uniforms as the veterans marched by to the lusty cheers of the crowd. It seemed only moments before that I had pulled up the oversized trousers and ridiculous boots, trying to make myself fit for inspection.

The crowd was young, and I wondered how different it would be if the war had been lost. If the war had never been fought. The children who hadn't been born, the children who wouldn't have been if things had gone differently.

I thought of Sofia and her graceful courage.

I thought of Taisiya and her brilliance and dedication.

I thought of Oksana and her tenacity and unwavering composure.

And I thought of my Vanya, who had the eyes of an artist and the heart of a poet.

They should have been with us to celebrate the victory they had willingly given their lives to ensure.

As I scanned the faces of the crowd and my own family, I wondered why I had been so fortunate. Why I had been given the chance at life—albeit one so very different from the one I envisioned—when my dearest friends and my first husband, the love of my girlhood, had not.

"Are you tired?" Philippe whispered in my ear. "We can go back to the hotel and let the others enjoy the festivities on their own."

"No, my darling. I don't want to leave just yet." I squeezed his hand and looked forward onto the square.

As we strolled we came upon a gathering of veterans who had assembled in a nearby park, singing joyful songs of victory or talking quietly among themselves, reminiscing about their near misses and life on the front lines.

I found myself drawn to a chorus of perhaps a dozen female voices in one corner. They sang loudly in voices young and strong, despite the ages of the women who produced them. For the first time in decades, I wished I had my father's violin to accompany them, but knew my feeble hands would botch the job. I gave Philippe's hand a squeeze and left him to walk over to them and join my own wavering voice to their song.

I began exchanging letters with the surviving members of my regiment only in the last few years. After Mama died Philippe encouraged me to reestablish some connection to my motherland. Horrified by the stories coming from the aftermath of Stalin's reign, I ignored every part of my homeland except my mother, and when she died, I let the connection go altogether. With Thérèse's help I found Polina first, who then led me to Renata. They'd led full lives since last we spoke—Polina had been a scientist and Renata a schoolteacher, and both were now firmly entrenched in the business of grandmotherhood—but I still knew them on sight. I could see the girlish dimples still in Renata's cheeks and the keenness in Polina's eyes. They enveloped me in their arms as we sang the last notes of the familiar tune. My family looked baffled to see their usually reserved mother and grandmother make such a spectacle with what, to them, was a group of strangers.

I hoped they would never have to experience what we had. That they would never be called to make the same sacrifices we had. Philippe was the only one who could smile with understanding, knowing what these women meant to me.

My sisters in arms.

My sisters.

AUTHOR'S NOTE

Let me begin by confessing three things. I am no expert on Russia. I am not a pilot. I am no expert on the Second World War beyond a casual interest that many readers share. Despite these challenges, I had to write this story. So often in history, we dismiss women's work as secondary to men's. The Night Witches were a shining example of women who defied expectation and served with immense valor. Once I heard about these remarkable women, I had to make their story my own.

The characters in this novel are of my own invention. Some take some personality traits from the actual crews of the Forty-Sixth Taman Guards—most noticeably, Sofia Orlova mirrors famous Soviet pilot and founder of the 122nd Aviation Group, Marina Raskova. Raskova, however, did not fly with the Forty-Sixth Taman Guards, choosing to lead the fighter regiment. I wanted to keep the founding pilot in the picture a bit longer, so rather than alter the facts, I made my own cast of characters.

On the other hand, every effort was made to respect the dates and positions where the regiment moved throughout the war. Many of the events described—such as the half-drunken scramble to fly after the women's sanctioned celebration of the October Revolution, the furor over flare parachutes being fashioned into ladies' undergarments, and several of the pivotal flight scenes—were adapted from anecdotes from the Night Witches themselves.

The biggest departure I make from history comes at the very end. These pilots were a very patriotic bunch, and I've not found evidence to support that any of them left the USSR after the war. Katya's departure from Russia to build a life in France is her symbolic fulfillment of her promises to Vanya and Oksana to remain safe, and true to herself. She always wanted to see the world outside Russia, and I couldn't end the story before she had her chance.

The purpose of this novel is to depict what I imagine to have been the emotional realities these women faced. There are precious few examples of historical fiction that showcase these women, and I sought to change that. If you seek nonfiction works that shed more light on the history of the time, please visit my website at www.aimiekrunyan.com for a list of further reading.

Writing this book has been one of the greatest challenges—and joys—of my life. I sincerely hope you enjoyed it.

With love and light to all my dear readers. Clear skies.

~Aimie K. Runyan

ACKNOWLEDGMENTS

Writing a book is a solitary endeavor in its infancy but becomes the work of many as it blooms into adulthood. I am so grateful to so many:

- Melissa Jeglinski, my inimitable agent, for encouraging this project from the outset and keeping me grounded. I couldn't have done this without you.
- Miriam Juskowicz, for her unparalleled enthusiasm, and Danielle Marshall, for making it very clear that my book is in excellent hands.
- The entire Lake Union team for all their hard work in making this book a reality. You made my book look beautiful!
- David Downing, for his astute and detailed edits. You, sir, are a joy to work with.
- Danielle Gibeault and Dave Seymour, pilots extraordinaire, as well as the entire staff of the Flying Heritage Collection in Seattle. My profound thanks for your assistance with all things in the realm of aviation. All mistakes are mine, but they would have been far more numerous without your wisdom.
- Abby Polzin, for sharing in the excitement of this project with me and for being a wonderful photographer and Seattle tour guide. Fortuitous wrong turns and all!

- The ladies of the BWW: Jamie Raintree, Kate Moretti, Ella Olsen, Orly Konig, Andrea Catalano, and Theresa Alan. Your support makes this crazy business all worthwhile.
- To Kate Quinn for being my comrade in Russian headaches for the past year and for being a dear friend. And to Libbie Hawker and Kate Quinn (again) for the Facebook comedy of errors that led to this book deal.
- The Tall Poppies: I learn so much from you each and every day. I am honored to be a part of this movement to promote excellence in women's fiction.
- The Ladies of the Lake for welcoming me into the fold. You're all remarkable authors.
- The good people of RMFW and WFWA: You're a wonderful tribe. I love you all.
- My readers everywhere—you're the reason I do this, and I appreciate all of you! Especially all of the active members of my beloved Facebook readers' groups: Bloom, Great Thoughts Great Readers, Readers' Coffeehouse, A Novel Bee, Women Readers Women's Books, and so many more. It is a joy to get to interact with you every day.

And as always, I thank:

- My family, both the Trumbly and Runyan clans, for your unwavering support.
- My darling children, Ciarán and Aria, for reminding me daily about what's important.
- My brilliant, adorable husband, Allan, for standing by me as I navigate the world of make-believe friends. You're truly wonderful, and I appreciate all you do.

AUTHOR BIO

Photo © 2016 Abby Polzin

Aimie K. Runyan is a historian and author who writes to celebrate history's unsung heroines. She is the author of two previous historical novels: *Promised to the Crown* and *Duty to the Crown*. She is active as an educator and a speaker in the writing community and beyond. She lives in Colorado with her wonderful husband and two (usually) adorable children. To learn more about Aimie and her work, please visit www.aimiekrunyan.com.